W9-BHJ-804

ACCLAIM FOR RACHEL HAUCK

THE FIFTH AVENUE STORY SOCIETY

"This captivating story full of heart, soul, and humor kept me turning pages until midnight to finish it. Rachel weaves the perfect amount of tension and opens possibilities to keep the reader pondering long after the story is over. I loved it!"

—FRANCINE RIVERS, *NEW YORK TIMES* BESTSELLING AUTHOR

"Rachel Hauck's flair for inviting prose and well-drawn characters shines in this delightful story about searching for hope and healing within the most unexpected circle of people. Finely tuned themes of love, self-authenticity and discovering the benevolent hand of providence make this one sweet gem of a book."

—SUSAN MEISSNER, BESTSELLING AUTHOR
OF *THE LAST YEAR OF THE WAR*

"You are cordially invited, dear reader, to step through the doors of an enchanting old library and embark on a remarkable journey with the Fifth Avenue Story Society. In this beautifully written novel, Rachel Hauck has created a cast of masterful characters whose stories seem shattered beyond hope. But Rachel doesn't leave them in their brokenness. She sweeps up the pieces and begins sculpting together a new story. A better story for each of them. Their fireside society is a place where miracles still happen. A space full of wonder to savor and dream. If you dare to step inside these pages, into this mysterious story society, you'll be warmly welcomed as a fellow sojourner and friend."

—MELANIE DOBSON, BESTSELLING AUTHOR OF
CATCHING THE WIND AND *MEMORIES OF GLASS*

"I was captivated by this story from the first paragraph, and my heart soon became invested in the lives of the various members of the Fifth Avenue Story Society. It's magical. My favorite Rachel Hauck novel to date!"

—ROBIN LEE HATCHER, CHRISTY AWARD-WINNING
AUTHOR OF *WHO I AM WITH YOU* AND *CROSS MY HEART*

"What a delightful surprise! Five near-strangers discover the story of their lives after meeting under the most unusual of invitations. *The Fifth Avenue Story Society* is both complex and spellbinding, and I found it difficult not to flip to the back in search of the hopeful conclusion. But I'm glad I held out and, without a single doubt, you will be too. *The Fifth Avenue Story Society* allows readers to slip into another world and, in doing so, find the story of their own lives."

—EVA MARIE EVERSON, BESTSELLING AUTHOR AND PRESIDENT OF WORD WEAVERS INTERNATIONAL

"A delightful and insightful story about broken dreams and dreams reborn. A tale of deep emotion and even deeper friendships. I loved this novel and the memorable characters Rachel Hauck has created. Just get ready for your heart to be changed in a beautiful way."

—JAMES L. RUBART, CHRISTY HALL OF FAME AUTHOR

"Rachel Hauck is well-known to her fans as an author of books with compelling characters, heaven invading earth, and a romance that will win your heart. With *The Fifth Avenue Story Society*, Hauck delves into the space of our greatest wounds and how confronting them brings freedom, healing, and hope. She accomplishes that with a story told from five characters' perspectives, each one rich with the possibility of more constrained by the chains of the past. The characters' search for freedom points the reader to healing while delving into the power of each person's fully embraced story. I'm grateful for the time I spent with this group and these pages. Readers who love a story laced with heart and hope will adore this Hauck's latest offering."

—CARA PUTMAN, AWARD-WINNING AND BESTSELLING AUTHOR OF *DELAYED JUSTICE* AND *SHADOWED BY GRACE*

"Rachel Hauck's rich characterization and deft hand with plotting and setting had me enthralled until I turned the last page of this superb novel. *The Fifth Avenue Story Society* is truly a masterpiece—a one-of-a-kind novel that lingers long after the last page is turned. This is one I'll reread often, and it should garner Hauck much well-deserved acclaim. This should be on everyone's shelf."

—COLLEEN COBLE, *USA TODAY* BESTSELLING AUTHOR OF THE LAVENDER TIDES SERIES AND *STRANDS OF TRUTH*

"One of the best signs of an awesome book is when you can't stop thinking about it when you're not reading . . . and when you just. can't. wait. to get back to it! That was absolutely the case with Rachel Hauck's latest, *The Fifth Avenue Story Society*. The set-up—a group of strangers all mysteriously invited to join a story society at a historic library—was both charming and intriguing. All five main characters were well-rounded and relatable with heart-tugging—and in some cases, heartbreaking—backstories. I loved watching them grow as a group and as individuals as they developed deep bonds, found freedom from their pasts, and discovered new hope for their futures. Another winner from one of my author faves!"

—MELISSA TAGG, CAROL AWARD-WINNING AUTHOR OF *NOW & THEN & ALWAYS* AND THE WALKER FAMILY SERIES

THE MEMORY HOUSE

"Rachel Hauck . . . is a terrific storyteller. *The Memory House* is a flash fiction book that spans two different eras. Fifty years separate Beck Holiday and Everleigh Applegate, but through love and faith, the two find healing in a beautiful Victorian house known as The Memory House. You can't go wrong with one of Rachel's books."

—DEBBIE MACOMBER, *NEW YORK TIMES* BESTSELLING AUTHOR

"The novel revisits common themes in Hauck's books: courtship and Christian values. It is well written and covers well-traveled ground, comfortable in its steadfast delivery and message of the acceptance of closures to make way for the promise of openings. It is not focused on individual tragedy and grieving but a universal tale of faith and love."

—HISTORICAL NOVELS SOCIETY

"Combining drama, romance, faith, and sometimes mystery, Hauck continues to delight her fans and attract new readers."

—PATHEOS

"Rachel Hauck is no stranger to me. I treasure her book *The Wedding Dress*, which I have reread and again laughed and cried at the sheer joy of that charmer. *The Memory House* introduces us to many characters that we fall in love with and cheer for."

—FRESH FICTION

"Hauck (*The Writing Desk*) is a master at weaving together plots from multiple time periods. Here the key theme is memory and how the characters react to tragedy . . . Hauck's fans will be keen for another work rich with character development. Readers of Kristy Cambron, Heidi Chiavaroli, and other time-slip novelists will also want to pick up this book."

—*LIBRARY JOURNAL*

"Accomplished Hauck demonstrates genre finesse as she blends inspirational romance with a cinematic style of storytelling, bringing empathetic characters to life as they cope with grief in marriage and faithfulness, parenthood and adoption, death and tragedy. Challenging decisions, the blessing of finding love again, and the solace of a beautiful Victorian home all come together in this spellbinding, lovely novel."

—BOOKLIST

THE LOVE LETTER

"Enjoyable inspirational romance . . . Jesse and Chloe rewrite Hamilton and Esther's history on screen and their relationship strengthens as reenacting the story helps them reconsider their ideas about a perfect ending. Hauck cleverly uses the play to bring historical flourishes to a strong story about overcoming mistakes through faith and commitment."

—PUBLISHERS WEEKLY

"A [Revolutionary] War love letter is the centerpiece of this delightful read by Hauck as forgiveness, dependence upon God, and second chances are intricately woven together . . . A captivating story line, historical research, and God's truth equal a recommended read for all."

—CBA MARKET

"From its epic opening to its unexpected and wholly satisfying conclusion, *The Love Letter* serves up the perfect blend of modern and historical romance infused with exquisite vulnerability. It sweeps readers into the centuries-old drama of South Carolina and the flash of contemporary Hollywood and delightfully explores layers of social and emotional duality."

—BOOKLIST

"Hauck's latest is a gorgeous melding of two timelines into an unforgettable story. She does an incredible job balancing the two, and the pacing works perfectly . . . What makes this story shine is that it isn't what readers will be expecting, but it will be what readers need. Themes of redemption, love, sacrifice, and loyalty resonate throughout."

—RT BOOK REVIEWS, 4 STARS

THE WRITING DESK

"Rachel Hauck enchants us again! Tenley and Birdie are bound together by the understanding that creativity is a guiding force and that their stories must be told. A tale both bittersweet and redemptive, *The Writing Desk* is your must-read."

—PATTI CALLAHAN HENRY, *NEW YORK TIMES* BESTSELLING AUTHOR

THE WEDDING SHOP

"Hauck seamlessly switches back and forth in this redeeming tale of a shop with healing powers for the soul. As Cora and Haley search for solace and love, they find peace in the community of the charming shop. Hauck succeeds at blending similar themes across the time periods, grounding the plot twists in the main characters' search for redemption and a reinvigoration of their wavering faith. In the third of her winsome, wedding-themed, standalone novels, Hauck focuses on the power of community to heal a broken heart."

—PUBLISHERS WEEKLY

"I adored *The Wedding Shop*! Rachel Hauck has created a tender, nostalgic story, weaving together two pairs of star-crossed lovers from the present and the past with the magical space that connects them. So full of heart and heartache and redemption, this book is one you'll read long into the night, until the characters become your friends, and Heart's Bend, Tennessee, your second hometown."

—BEATRIZ WILLIAMS, *NEW YORK TIMES* BESTSELLING AUTHOR

"*The Wedding Shop* is the kind of book I love, complete with flawed yet realistic characters, dual timelines that intersect unexpectedly, a touch of magic, and a large dose of faith. Two breathtaking romances are the perfect bookends for this novel about love, forgiveness, and following your dreams. And a stunning, antique wedding dress with a secret of its own. This is more than just a good read—it's a book to savor."

—KAREN WHITE, *NEW YORK TIMES* BESTSELLING AUTHOR

"In *The Wedding Shop*, the story line alternates between past and present, engrossing the reader in both timelines . . . and the ways that God's provision [are] shown is heartwarming and can even increase the reader's faith. The weaving in of characters and plot points from *The Wedding Dress* and *The Wedding Chapel* adds depth and meaning to the gorgeously rendered tale."

—RT BOOK REVIEWS, 4 STARS

THE WEDDING CHAPEL

"Hauck's engaging novel about love, forgiveness, and new beginnings adeptly ties together multiple oscillating story lines of several generations of families. Interesting plot interweaves romance, real-life issues, and a dash of mystery . . . Recommend for mature fans of well-done historical fiction."

—CBA RETAILERS AND RESOURCES

"Hauck tells another gorgeously rendered story. The raw, hidden emotions of Taylor and Jack are incredibly realistic and will resonate with readers. The way the entire tale comes together with the image of the chapel as holding the heartbeat of God is breathtaking and complements the romance of the story."

—*RT BOOK REVIEWS*, 4$^{1}/_{2}$ STARS AND A TOP PICK!

THE WEDDING DRESS

"Hauck weaves an intricately beautiful story centering around a wedding dress passed down through the years. Taken at face value, the tale is superlative, but considering the spiritual message both on the surface and between the lines, this novel is incredible. Readers will laugh, cry, and treasure this book."

—*RT BOOK REVIEWS*, TOP PICK!

"*The Wedding Dress* is a thought-provoking read and one of the best books I have read. Look forward to more . . ."

—MICHELLE JOHNMAN, GOLD COAST, AUSTRALIA

"I thank God for your talent and that you wrote *The Wedding Dress*. I will definitely come back to this book and read it again. And now I cannot wait to read *Once Upon a Prince*."

—AGATA FROM POLAND

THE ROYAL WEDDING SERIES

"Perfect for Valentine's Day, Hauck's latest inspirational romance offers an uplifting and emotionally rewarding tale that will delight her growing fan base."

—*LIBRARY JOURNAL*, STARRED REVIEW

"Hauck writes a feel-good novel that explores the trauma and love of the human heart . . . an example of patience and sacrifice that readers will adore."

—*ROMANTIC TIMES*, 4 STARS

"A stirring, modern-day fairy tale about the power of true love."

—CINDY KIRK, AUTHOR OF *LOVE AT MISTLETOE INN*

"*How to Catch a Prince* is an enchanting story told with bold flavor and tender insight. Engaging characters come alive as romance blooms between a prince and his one true love. Hauck's own brand of royal-style romance shines in this third installment of the Royal Wedding series."

—DENISE HUNTER, BESTSELLING AUTHOR OF THE CHAPEL SPRINGS ROMANCE AND BLUE RIDGE ROMANCE SERIES

"*How to Catch a Prince* contains all the elements I've come to love in Rachel Hauck's Royal Wedding series: an 'it don't come easy' happily ever after, a contemporary romance woven through with royal history, and a strong spiritual thread with an unexpected touch of the divine. Hauck's smooth writing—and the way she wove life truths throughout the novel—made for a couldn't-put-it-down read."

—BETH K. VOGT, AUTHOR OF *SOMEBODY LIKE YOU*, ONE OF *PUBLISHERS WEEKLY'S* BEST BOOKS OF 2014

"Rachel Hauck's inspiring Royal Wedding series is one for which you should reserve space on your keeper shelf!"

—*USA TODAY*

"Hauck spins a surprisingly believable royal-meets-commoner love story. This is a modern and engaging tale with well-developed secondary characters that are entertaining and add a quirky touch. Hauck fans will find a gem of a tale."

—*PUBLISHERS WEEKLY* STARRED REVIEW OF *ONCE UPON A PRINCE*

ALSO BY RACHEL HAUCK

The Memory House
The Love Letter
The Writing Desk
The Wedding Dress
The Wedding Chapel
The Wedding Shop

STORIES FOUND IN *A YEAR OF WEDDINGS*

A March Bride (e-book only)
A Brush with Love: A January Wedding Story (e-book only)

THE ROYAL WEDDING SERIES

Once Upon a Prince
Princess Ever After
How to Catch a Prince
A Royal Christmas Wedding

LOWCOUNTRY ROMANCE NOVELS

Sweet Caroline
Love Starts with Elle
Dining with Joy

NASHVILLE NOVELS

Nashville Sweetheart
(e-book only)
Nashville Dreams (e-book only)

WITH SARA EVANS

Sweet By and By
Softly and Tenderly
Love Lifted Me

THE
Fifth Avenue
STORY
SOCIETY

A NOVEL

RACHEL HAUCK

THOMAS NELSON
Since 1798

The Fifth Avenue Story Society

© 2020 Rachel Hauck

Published in Nashville, Tennessee, by Thomas Nelson. Thomas Nelson is a registered trademark of HarperCollins Christian Publishing, Inc.

Thomas Nelson titles may be purchased in bulk for educational, business, fund-raising, or sales promotional use. For information, please email SpecialMarkets@ThomasNelson.com.

Publisher's Note: This novel is a work of fiction. Names, characters, places, and incidents are either products of the author's imagination or used fictitiously. All characters are fictional, and any similarity to people living or dead is purely coincidental.

ISBN 978-0-7852-1667-4 (library edition)

Library of Congress Cataloging-in-Publication Data

Names: Hauck, Rachel, 1960- author.
Title: The Fifth Avenue story society : a novel / Rachel Hauck.
Description: Nashville : Thomas Nelson, [2020] | Summary: "From the New York Times bestselling author of The Wedding Dress comes a captivating new novel about the healing power of story, community, and love"-- Provided by publisher.
Identifiers: LCCN 2019035583 (print) | LCCN 2019035584 (ebook) | ISBN 9780310350927 (trade paperback) | ISBN 9780785216674 (hardcover) | ISBN 9780310350934 (epub) | ISBN 9780310350958 (audio download)
Subjects: GSAFD: Christian fiction. | Love stories.
Classification: LCC PS3608.A866 F54 2020 (print) | LCC PS3608.A866 (ebook) | DDC 813/.6--dc23
LC record available at https://lccn.loc.gov/2019035583
LC ebook record available at https://lccn.loc.gov/2019035584

Printed in the United States of America

20 21 22 23 24 LSC 10 9 8 7 6 5 4 3 2 1

Dedicated to Tim and Kelly Franklin. For all the dinners, all the laughs and encouragement. For ten years and counting Friday night prayer and for being giants in the kingdom.

JETT

AUGUST IN MANHATTAN

Well this was a fine mess. Spending the night in Central Booking for instigating a fight at a wedding reception. What was he thinking?

He glanced at his sore hand through the dull light beaming in from the hallway fluorescents and flexed his fingers, wincing at the pain of his bruised flesh.

He hadn't thrown so many punches since he was a boy in Chappaqua wrestling with his brother.

The next time he got an invitation, *especially* a wedding invitation, he'd RSVP with a big fat no.

Though he could hardly blame the invitation. He alone earned this all-expenses-paid night in holding. For defending a bridesmaid from a drunken groomsman.

Yet he was no hero.

Jett Wilder, associate professor of English at the prestigious New York College, lover of words and literature and the occasional ride through class-five rapids, was a criminal.

Perhaps *criminal* was an exaggeration. Nonetheless, he'd been cuffed, read his rights, hauled off in a paddy wagon, and thrown behind bars, where he spent a long, odiferous night with drug dealers, pimps, drunks, petty thieves, and civil violators.

So he, too, was counted among the transgressors.

What happened to him? He deplored violence, prided himself on diplomacy and statesmanship.

Rising from the bench, where he sat next to the big guy who had also jumped into the fight, Jett made his way to the iron bars.

The cell's shadowy confinement robbed his sense of time. Had he been here for one hour or five? The booking officer took every time-keeping device he owned—watch and phone—before leading him away to rot.

However, by the rumble in his belly, the hour was well past breakfast.

He gripped the bars and fought a wave of claustrophobia. He wanted out. But he deserved to be here. In fact, for the rest of his life, *anything* that came his way, he'd deserve.

Divorced? Deserved it. On the rocks with his boss? Deserved it. Tense relationship with his parents? *De*-served.

What was it about being locked up that made a man assess his life? Besides the jailhouse smells and chorus of snores and moans?

"Hello?" Jett pressed against the gray, flaking bars. "Hey, does a guy get a phone call around here?" If he had used his, he'd forgotten.

Last night was not one for the memory books.

"You refused your phone call." The big guy came alongside and threaded his arms through the steel squares. "Nice punch you threw at the Harness-Neville wedding."

"I'd say thanks for giving me a hand, but look where we landed."

Big Guy offered his hand. "Chuck Mays. Uber driver. Civil offender. The dude had it coming."

Jett clapped his palm against Chuck's. "Jett Wilder. Associate professor of English, NYC. Civil offender."

"If I need a witness that you started it, can I count on you?" Chuck's somber request was accented by his swollen and protruding lower lip. "Even though you were pretty lit?"

Jett pressed his fingers to his throbbing temple. "I don't drink much."

"Then why were you knocking them down like water last night?"

"I'm not a fan of weddings."

"Same." Chuck linked his thick fingers together around the bars.

Jett glanced at him. "You a friend of the bride or groom?"

"Groom. Went to high school together in Jersey. You?"

"Bride. She's a colleague."

The men jutted chins toward each other as some sort of grunted acceptance.

"So, if you don't like weddings and you don't drink, what happened last night?" Chuck said.

"Long week. What about you? Why'd you jump in?" Weddings agitated Jett as much as alcohol. The two together? Disaster.

"Longer week."

Jett laughed. "Eight days?"

"Without the Beatles singing background."

"I'm on the same calendar."

"This will cost me." Chuck gripped his hands into fists and the line of his jaw was taut with tension.

"Both of us. I expect a bill from the bride's father."

"That? So what? This will cost me more than . . . Did they read you the charges?"

Jett pointed to his head. "Took me a minute when I woke up to figure out why I was in here."

Chuck relaxed his hands. "Disorderly conduct. Public intoxication. Assault." His composure changed as he rattled off the charges. His voice thick with anger. "Stupid, stupid, stupid—"

Stupid was one word for it. Jett should've stayed home. Apologized to the bride, Jenn, after the fact.

"I wanted to come, but weddings—"

But weddings what? Reminded him of what he'd lost? Awakened the heartache he'd finally put to rest?

Yet he couldn't go through life hiding from the happiness of others. Besides, being on faculty at the illustrious, private, elite New York College came with certain obligations. He'd be considered aloof and unsupportive if he avoided Jenn's nuptials.

And he sort of owed her. She had listened to his sob stories when his wife walked out, and she had rallied the rest of the faculty around him. Attending her wedding was the *least* he could do.

It was any man's guess how much the reception damage would set him back. A lot more than a humble apology.

"That groomsman was a piece of work." Chuck paced in tight circles, muttering to himself. "The bridesmaid told him to leave her alone, what? A dozen times? This will ruin me."

Jett recognized the underlying darkness in Chuck's expression, shadowed even more by his dark, hooded eyes.

"Ruin you?"

"Ruin me." His reply came fast and hot. "She'll find out. She will. I'll lose them."

"Lose who?"

Chuck sat on a bench someone had vacated for the toilet and covered his face with his wide hands.

"Seems ironic, doesn't it?" Jett walked over and patted his stone-hard shoulder. "The two of us behind bars for defending a bridesmaid's honor while the offender walks free. What happened to chivalry?"

The big guy never raised his head.

"You okay?" Jett angled forward to see his face.

"No." Chuck stood, rising to his full height. Hard to believe he folded himself into an Uber job all day. "I've probably ruined my life."

"Come on, can't be as bad as all that, man. A tussle at a wedding reception?" He cheered himself as much as Chuck. "Nothing more than a civil violation." Surely such a petty crime wouldn't ruin anyone's life. "We'll pay a fine and go home."

"You don't understand. I can't afford anything like this." Chuck touched a laceration on his cheek. "You throw a mean punch."

"Sorry, man."

"Don't be. I should've kept my nose out of it." Chuck pointed to his knuckles, then Jett's. "You're pretty banged up. Will this get you in trouble with your college?"

"Not sure." Jett extended his fingers once more against the swelling and aching.

His knuckles were scraped and bruised, and when he ran his hand along his jaw, he grazed one cut, then another. When he touched the area around his eye, he winced.

With that Chuck returned to his hunched position, head in his hands.

What else could he say to the guy?

"Yo, Mr. Police Officer?" Jett peered down the corridor for a sign of deliverance.

A fellow inmate roused with a laugh. "You stuck here until they come for you."

"What happened to swift justice?"

With a sigh, he sat next to Chuck, his ripped tuxedo collar dangling over his shoulder. He noticed two coat buttons were missing. And his shirt was torn and stained red. Wine. Not blood.

He needed to get home, showered, and to work. Put last night behind him. In the annals of yesterday.

He also had two classes this morning, papers to grade, a dissertation to finalize for publication and present to the Roth Foundation Reception in November. His boss, Renée, the literature department chair, had finally put her foot down. Her words, not his.

"The publication of that dissertation means a great deal to the Roth Foundation and the college, Jett."

Showing up on campus meant he'd have to face Renée. Maybe the English department dean. He hadn't read far enough in the faculty handbook to know what happened to delinquent professors. Especially ones who ruined another professor's wedding.

So, this was life at thirty. A divorced man who couldn't quite find his footing, his excuses no longer able to belay him.

Losing his brother, Storm, that day on the Eiger mountain was hard enough. But when the one person who made his very breath worthwhile walked out . . . well, sometimes it was just too much.

Jett sat back against the wall and succumbed to the fatigue of the past two years.

Could he be tired? Just for a moment?

As he exhaled, his eyes drifting closed, a buzzer sounded. A steel door opened and closed.

Jett sat forward, gently rousing Chuck. "Wake up, Sleeping Beauty. I hear footsteps."

"John Wilder and Charles Mays." A uniformed officer swung open the door. "You're free to go. No charges."

Jett shot out with a curt nod. "Thank you, Mr. Jailer."

"You're welcome, Mr. Prisoner."

In the precinct house, another officer walked him out, handed him an envelope containing his things—imagine, his most prized possessions fit in a manila envelope—and he bolted for daylight. For freedom.

"Jett Wilder." Chuck followed him down the courthouse steps, his smile burning away his former despondency. "That was lucky. No charges."

"I'll take it." He offered the big man a hearty handshake. "Until the next wedding."

"May it be a long time away. And about back there, in the holding. I got a bit emotional."

Jett raised his palm. "No need. It was a long day."

Chuck shot him a sideways grin and turned to go. "By the way," he said, coming back around. "Are you any relation to Bear Wilder, the adventure guy?"

"He's my father." Jett walked backward toward the curb.

"Your father. What was that like growing up? And didn't your brother—"

"Chuck." Jett stepped into the street to hail a taxi. If he hurried, he could make his first class. "We spent one night together. Let's make a note in our diaries and in years to come, we'll look back on it fondly."

"Just asking, man." The big guy started off in the opposite direction.

"Sorry, but I'm in a hurry." A cab pulled to the curb. "I have a class in two hours."

"I was going to offer you a ride home. On the house."

"Thanks anyway." Jett slipped into the back of the cab, rattling off his Greenwich Village address.

He dumped the envelope's contents onto the seat, and a thick, cream-colored card dropped out. He ignored it while he checked his phone for messages—there were forty—and fastened on his watch.

After tucking his wallet into his inside jacket pocket, along with his keys, he examined the card, expecting to find an inventory of the envelope's contents.

Instead, he found an invitation.

YOU ARE CORDIALLY INVITED TO THE
FIFTH AVENUE STORY SOCIETY.
THE FIFTH AVENUE LITERARY SOCIETY LIBRARY
THE BOWER ROOM
MONDAY, SEPTEMBER 9 @ 8:00 P.M.

Jett laughed. An invitation? He flipped it over and back. There was no RSVP or return address. This wasn't his.

He'd never even heard of the Fifth Avenue Literary Society Library. And in light of his night in a holding cell, he had no plans to say yes to *any* invitation *any* time soon.

LEXA

Getting ahead required courage. All she had to do was muster some from the recesses of her being, walk into Zane's office, and ask. Or better yet, tell him.

"I'm your CEO."

He'd posted the CEO position nine months ago and had yet to interview anyone.

To be honest, on the org chart Lexa was nothing more than Zane Breas's executive assistant. He'd hired her seven years ago when she moved here as a newlywed.

She was fresh out of Florida State business school. He was fresh out of Nebraska launching ZB Burgers, a fast-growing gourmet hamburger chain.

In those lean, early days, there was no organizational chart. From the get-go, Lexa functioned as the executive of the fast-growing ZB Enterprises, the parent company for Manhattan's hottest new restaurant.

At her desk, she ate her power bar while combing through email. Hers as well as Zane's. The coming fall season brought one of their biggest promotional events, Zaney Days.

ZB Burgers in cities such as Manhattan, Miami, Omaha, Dallas, and Denver sponsored a family day of fun and food at a local park.

Last year, videos and pictures from their big bash in Central Park with celebrities mingling with "ordinary" people went viral.

The idea began three years ago as her brainchild to marry food with community and to expose hamburger connoisseurs in those major markets to the quality and freshness of Zane's family recipes.

And it had been wildly successful.

"Morning." Zane stopped at her desk looking as if he stepped from the pages of *GQ*. A rich cloud of cologne wafted around him, and the *New York Post* was tucked under his arm.

"Morning." Lexa stood, covering her mouth with her hand as she swallowed a bite of power bar. "Your iPad is on your desk. We have a Zaney Days meeting at ten." She removed the pen holding her twist of damp hair on top of her head.

"What would I do without you?"

Was he charming? Yes. But his Nebraska farm boy swagger gave him an edge. An "it" factor lacking in most young, Manhattan entrepreneurs.

Everyone loved Zane. And if they didn't love him, they liked him. Respected him.

Lexa considered herself lucky—no, blessed—to be on his team.

After her divorce, work kept her grounded. Sane. Able to breathe when she felt underwater.

Up at five, she exercised, then readied for work, hopping the short subway from her Greenwich Village apartment to ZB's new Tribeca offices by 6:45.

At her desk by 7:05, 7:10 at the latest, she prepped for the day, cleaned up email, shuffled items from her calendar to Zane's and back again, answered messages from managers at their more than twenty locations, and reviewed reports from every department.

If she was acting like a CEO, then she should *be* the CEO.

Zane arrived after Lexa took a few minutes to flat-iron her hair in the women's lounge.

And her day was off to the races.

"Do you have the tear sheets from the *Forbes* article?" Zane walked toward her while scanning his iPad.

"On your desk."

Zane Breas was the latest entrepreneurial wunderkind, and he liked to collect his media clippings.

Once he opened the Forty-Sixth Street store, the business exploded. Now, scrambling to meet the demands of franchisees and cities wanting a ZB Burgers, Lexa had ideas on how to get ZB to the next level.

Which led her back to asking—*telling*—Zane to make her the CEO.

"How was your weekend?" Zane perched on the side of her desk and handed her his iPad, calendar in view. "I don't see Thursday afternoons blocked off."

Lexa glanced at the screen, then handed back the device. "I did. Last week. You want it blocked off every week?"

"Until further notice, yes." He took a piece of candy from the dish on her desk. "So, good weekend? I don't know how you live in that eight-hundred-square-foot walk-up."

She launched Zane's calendar. "I worked on Saturday. The Zaney Days commercial scripts were all wrong. We're not hiring that marketing group again. Then I slept most of Sunday." *Speaking of working on Saturday, the CEO job would be*—"What's going on Thursday afternoons? Don't tell me you're taking up golf again."

He had tried to golf with a couple of pros last year. Ended up hitting a ball into the course's parking lot and smashing the window of a Lamborghini.

"No. But one of these days, I'm going to master the green." He started for his office and Lexa followed. "Any news on the food cart? I'd love to hit the streets of Manhattan with a portable ZB Burgers stand, see if we can make an alternative style of restaurant for people in big cities."

"One giant to slay at a time, Zane. I moved that project to next year."

He raised a steely gaze to her as he moved behind his desk. "You should ask me before you move things. I am the head of this company."

"And I'm the neck." Her determination locked with his. *Steady. Don't break.* She exhaled when he flashed his charmed grin.

"My neck is a little *stiff* right now." He kicked out his chair and sat, flopping the *Post* open over his laptop and yesterday's coffee cup. Lexa reached for the cup and set it on the corner to take back to the employee kitchen. "I trust you, but let's be sure to address it in January. That cart vendor offered us an amazing deal."

"Did you read the contract? The small print on his maintenance offer was ridiculous." She read every vendor and supplier contract multiple times, on alert for twisted wording and provisional clauses. "By the way, I've made Quent my assistant."

The Harvard MBA grad was a Zane hire. He reasoned the Boston blue blood gave the Nebraska boy some clout, if not a bit of swagger. But so far, he had proved to be as ordinary as they come, if not a bit lazy and entitled.

"Quent? The man with a Harvard degree in marketing and business strategy?"

"Don't be wowed, Zane. Apparently Harvard needs to add a class on how to show up on time and do the work you've been assigned. I've asked him four times for an update on his Zaney Days projects. So far, crickets."

"He's young."

"You were launching a business at his age. No excuses. Anyway, he's my assistant until he grows a better work ethic."

Zane regarded her for a moment, chin raised, quizzing her with his eyes. She braced for a fight.

"Fine, but have him see me when he gets in."

"I'm doing what's best for the company, Zane."

"It just feels like you're cutting me out, Lex."

"I'm doing the CEO job, and I think you should hire—"

"I know, I know. Hire someone for the job. You're right. I need to fill the position. I'm just nervous to rock the balance of our little family company."

"Yes, you do need to hire someone." Lexa pulled a chair forward to sit. "As a matter of fact, I was thinking—"

Zane's cell rang and he answered it with vigor. "Tim, yes, hello." He pressed the phone to his chest. "Lex, can you give me a minute?"

"Yeah, sure."

Back at her desk, her inner voice mocked her. *Coward.*

What was she supposed to do? Blurt out her request? He always said no when asked a question he wasn't prepared to answer.

The timing had to be right. Perfect.

She'd just started her to-do list when Zane appeared again. Grinning. Like a lovesick teen.

"Yes?" Lexa said.

Zane offered his phone. "Sabrina just texted."

Ah, his new love. A Hollywood starlet he met at a charity benefit in London.

"By the size of your Nebraska smile, I take it she said yes to the Gottlieb Gala?"

The Gottlieb Gala for Young Entrepreneurs had named Zane their Young Entrepreneur of the Year and were honoring him next Friday night at a fancy soiree atop the Waldorf Astoria, in the enchanting Starlight Room.

"She's catching the red-eye next Thursday. Can you order flowers for her room?"

"Done. I figured if she didn't come I'd take the room myself for a luxurious weekend of bubble baths and champagne."

"Why don't you move?" Zane huffed and puffed, but he could not change her mind. "A girl needs a bathtub."

"Not if it costs another two hundred a month. Or more."

"Are you hinting for a raise?" Zane pushed up from the desk and started for his office.

"As a matter of fact, Zane, I would like to talk to you about—"

"Oh, what about my speech? For the gala?" He turned back toward her. "Did you get my notes on your draft?"

"I sent the updated version three days ago. Do you ever read your email?"

"That's what you're for." He laughed without conviction as he aimed for his office again. "I'll go find it."

"You do that."

She had refused to write his speeches at first, but he worked her soft side, her team-player heart, and she caved. She should've never told him she'd aced a speech-writing class at Florida State.

Lexa had a love-hate relationship with her "soft side." It was the one she used to make friends every time the family moved. The one that got her into the in-crowd in high school. Yet it was the side that opened her up to wounding and hurt.

"Oh, one more thing? What about the mini ZB Burgers for the gala?"

"Really, Zane, read my emails if you don't read anyone else's. The Forty-Sixth Street store is making them. You know if they're a success we're going to have to add them to the menu."

"That's the idea. See you at ten o'clock." And he disappeared into his office.

With a sigh, Lexa stared at her computer screen. She should just ask him. Right now. Go into his office and ask.

"Will you make me your CEO?"

She'd been noodling on this plan for almost a year. Without an execution plan, it gnawed at her. Rooted deep and kept her awake at night.

She saw herself in the role to an extent she wasn't sure what she'd do if he said no. So she hesitated. Waited. Surely Zane could see for himself she was the woman for the job.

Lexa gazed out over the common work area called the Think Tank. When she started with Zane seven years ago, they were in a crowded Canal Street office working around the clock to open the Forty-Sixth Street store.

With her husband in grad school, she had been the sole bread-winner, and she loved it. Loved doing her part to help him achieve his dream while living out hers.

Working for smart and savvy Zane was fun, if not wild. There were so many eleventh-hour wins in that first year, they created a Wall of Fame.

Most of all she loved being on a team. Moving eight times from first grade to twelfth, she barely had time to fit in before her air force doctor father would be reassigned.

Her parents and little sister, Skipper, were her best friends. Yet, how she longed to be accepted by the cool kids at school.

She glanced at Zane's door. He was a cool kid. And he'd accepted her. *Almost.*

The trouble with longing for acceptance was inequitable conditions. What one considered acceptance, another did not. Lexa learned long ago to see her inclusion into her peer groups for what they offered, not what she expected.

She might see herself as CEO, but Zane might not. Then what? Did she just have to accept it?

"Lex, is Zane in yet?" Fatima from the test kitchen flashed a requisition form. "I need him to sign it unless you can."

Lexa pointed to his office. "He just complained I don't let him know what's going on."

Fatima laughed. "Doesn't he know you're the neck?"

Lexa raised her hands. *I know, right?* Seeing Fatima reminded her to text Quent.

See Zane when you get in.

What's up? Just heading into the shower.

It was a quarter to nine and he was just getting out of bed?

Not sure but try to make it before lunch.

Gathering herself, she worked on the Zaney Days update for the meeting. But her attention landed on a meme she'd printed out a few months ago and taped to the side of her computer: "'Courage!' he said and pointed toward the land. 'This mounting wave will roll us shoreward soon.'"

The Tennyson poem had been a favorite of her dad's every time they moved. Every time Lexa and Skipper started a new school.

"Courage isn't the absence of fear," he would say. *"It's going forward anyway."*

So why the big chicken imitation over asking Zane to make her CEO? It'd be a huge job-title change and enormous raise.

But could she make such a giant leap? A thin fear twisted in her chest.

No wasn't necessarily a rejection, but it always felt that way to her. If he said no would it ruin their relationship? What if she didn't want to be Zane's executive assistant the rest of her life?

Besides her business degree with a focus on corporate governance, she knew ZB Enterprises inside out.

In the last seven years she'd hired and fired more than half the Think Tank, scouted vendors and suppliers, written the employee handbook, set the job titles and salary ranges, and created every job. Met with accountants and outside contractors. Even sat in on board meetings.

So . . . could she *leave*? Put herself out there and find a position as CEO or close to it?

The truth was, she'd envisioned an entirely different life for herself. But it didn't pan out, and now she was twenty-nine. Time to get going. Move on.

Even Dad was encouraging her to raise her wings.

Last Christmas, as the fog of her divorce began to lift, old Dad sidled up to her with a cup of spiked eggnog.

"You can't stop living, Lex. I know this divorce isn't what you wanted, but it's time to get a new plan."

"I have a plan."

"Tell me about it."

"It's a work in progress."

He chuckled and hooked his arm around her shoulders. *"I did you no favors dragging you, your mother, and sister around the world from post to post, but it made you a strong, independent woman."*

"It also made me an insecure woman. Will they love me? Will I fit in?"

"You're a big girl now. Time to command your own life. Don't get stuck, Lex. The time for mourning your marriage is over. Though

I have to say, he surprised me. I thought he'd love you until his last breath."

So did she. He pledged to do so in his vows and repeated it to her often in their first year of marriage, in the afterglow of lovemaking. Or over breakfast, or during a walk in the park.

Lexa handed over her heart the night he proposed and never expected it back. He was a man she could love and trust without fear or regret.

Then they imploded. In the quiet, between awake and asleep, her heart sometimes asked her soul, "What exactly happened?"

A new email dropped into her in-box. The cast of the Broadway hit *Lost in Nashvegas* agreed to appear for Zaney Days.

Outstanding. Zane would go nuts for this. The cast rarely made appearances and had turned down everyone from the governor to late-night talk-show hosts.

Lexa added the news to the Zaney Days robust agenda.

By nine thirty she had the data she needed and sent the agenda to the printer, then searched her desk for a loose dollar bill to feed the drink machine for a sparkling water.

As she rounded the corner for the employee kitchen, Quent zipped toward her in a wrinkled blue button-down splattered with drops from his dark, wet hair.

"I'm here."

Lexa pointed to Zane's office door. "Go on in. When you're done, grab the Zaney Days agenda from the printer and take it to the conference room."

At the drink machine, she fed the slot her dollar bill and selected a cherry-flavored water. Her ex liked cherry-flavored water. And pie. Ice cream. Pretty much anything with a cherry flavoring. Even her cherry lip gloss.

The reminiscing irritated her. She was over him. At least ninety percent. Maybe eighty-five. Eighty. For sure eighty percent.

Yet love was such a powerful potion. It made a girl dream of things she never wanted before. Like being a wife and mom, nesting

in New Rochelle or a Long Island fixer-upper Cape Cod, where she'd
raise three kids and a dog while proofing her husband's manuscripts
and secretly hunting for a vacation house on the beach in Florida
near her folks.

Heading back to her work space, she peered into Zane's office.
He and Quent were sitting under the large picture window that
framed a million-dollar lower-Manhattan scene.

They chatted like a couple of bros. Probably about football
instead of work.

Lexa set her drink on a coaster, took a sticky notepad from the
middle drawer, and wrote *September 30* on the top sheet. Tearing it
off, she stuck it to the bottom of her computer screen.

The date was her deadline to be ZB Enterprises' first CEO.
Or else.

Or else what? She had no idea but left the answer for tomorrow.
For now, back to work. She might as well get the printouts. Quent
would be in there until Zane left for the conference room.

It was then she noticed the plain, cream-colored envelope resting on the edge of her desk.

Bending back the flap, she tugged out a matching invitation.

YOU ARE CORDIALLY INVITED TO THE
FIFTH AVENUE STORY SOCIETY.
THE FIFTH AVENUE LITERARY SOCIETY LIBRARY
THE BOWER ROOM
MONDAY, SEPTEMBER 9 @ 8:00 P.M.

Chapter 3

CHUCK

In the shadows between the street lamps, he watched from the side of the curb, waiting for a glimpse of his kids as they passed by the plate-glass window.

Every now and then the urge to check up on his kids overcame him. So he returned to the old neighborhood, parked five blocks away, and snuck through the night toward the house, risking his rights, his *future*, just for a glimpse.

He'd already spent a few nights in jail because of his ex-wife. Then, more recently, because of a loud, handsy groomsman.

Chuck winced at the memory. He'd never intended to mess up Jack and Jenn's reception, but once the mean and lean, floppy-haired professor set up the confrontation, Chuck got caught up in the action.

Running his hand over his jaw, he still felt the power of the professor's punch.

He'd contacted his lawyer Monday morning to let him know he'd been arrested but not charged. Not that the slick Manhattan lawyer was worth any of the thousands Chuck had already paid him.

Now, five days later, the knot in his middle was finally easing up. He didn't flinch every time his phone rang. Sunday night had no fallout.

Yet here he was again, being stupid, creeping along the edges of his temporary restraining order, the TRO, for a glimpse of Jakey and Riley.

Trudy kept the twins on a strict routine—which her hyper-organized, control-freakish self demanded.

She had them dressed, ready for bed, and sitting on her fancy designer couch for story time every night by seven.

Crouching near the ground away from the spill of the streetlight, Chuck picked at the summer grass beneath his feet.

Last time he snuck over here, about a month ago, he caught sight of Jakey's head. The boy was growing like a weed. Going to be tall like his old man.

Riley remained his petite princess. How he ached to swing her up in a bear hug.

He resisted the stab of tears. Getting emotional changed nothing. In fact, too much emotion was the reason for this mess. The reason he hunkered down five hundred feet—give or take—from his family.

He stretched up, shaking the kinks from his knees, and sensed the tension in his middle. Once he spied Jakey, or the Old Battle-ax, he'd sneak across the street, press against the house's stone exterior, let his adrenaline drain, then rise up to peek inside.

Six months ago he was nearly caught when Trudy's snot-nosed, hedge-fund boyfriend came home just as Chuck was about to tip-toe up.

What a tale his great romance had turned out to be. The beautiful rich girl who fell for the blue-collar boy turned out to be a cheater.

He blamed himself. Did he really think a smoking-hot Princeton grad with a brand new six-figure job on Wall Street would fall for a junior-college dropout who worked long days at Newark Star Steel?

But Trudy Murdock did fall for him. He'd hit the love lotto.

Twelve years ago—was it that long already?—he and his friends threw a Labor Day–weekend End-of-Summer Beach Party Blow-Out.

When Trudy walked in, she electrified the atmosphere, and Chuck was a goner. Handed over his heart without knowing her name.

Headlights flashed down the street. Chuck ducked behind the lamppost. But the car turned into a driveway a few houses down.

Then a shadow crossed the front window of the house, and Chuck arched up to see if it was one of the kids. Shoot. Nothing but the cat jumping onto the table. He smacked his hand to his chest. Dang, he even missed the cat.

Just as he crouched down again, hiding between light and shadow, Trudy walked by in a tight blouse and shorts, scooped up the cat, and waved to someone beyond the square pane.

Jakey's blond head bobbed by. Then Riley's.

Clenching his fists and filling his lungs, Chuck stole toward the house. Sensing the coast was clear, he looked inside before sliding down to hug the brick.

Beautiful. His children sat on either side of their mother, heads pressed against her arms as she read to them.

As much as he deplored his ex, he admired her parental devotion. She didn't allow the twins to go stupid in front of the television at night or zone out with video games.

She surrounded them with books and puzzles, board games and music. He heard from his mom—Trudy allowed her access to the kids—that they were clever and smart, able to hold conversations with adults.

In about two months they'd turn six, and where was he? In their lives? No—ducked down behind the front hedge, risking his future with his kids because he couldn't help himself. Man, if Trudy saw him, she'd call the police.

Running his palm over his knuckles, still a bit blue from Sunday night's brawl, frustration rumbled through him.

She had cheated, then kicked him out. Now he violated the law to see the two people he loved most in the world.

How was that justice?

Yeah, sure, he'd overreacted. A little. Maybe a lot. But big deal. He was human after all.

Then her father, Chuck's boss at the Murdock Family Trucking Company, laid him off. Between his fists-flying outburst, his unemployment, and the Murdock money, Chuck lost before the divorce proceedings began.

Regret was a bitter, bitter pill.

Checking to make sure the coast was clear, he stretched up again to see inside. Jakey looked through the bookshelf for another read while Trudy brushed Riley's hair.

Dang it, tears. Brushing her hair used to be *his* job.

"Mommy hurts my head."

Riley inherited his hair, thick and silky. As Chuck brushed it to a golden sheen, he told her the story of a magic book and how jumping into the pages took a girl on a fairy princess journey.

"What about me, Daddy?" Jakey said.

"The magic book turns you into a knight or a—"

"Football player."

"Yeah, buddy, a football player."

Sometimes he told them how he met Mommy and fell in love.

"Was she a princess?"

"The most beautiful of them all."

Another shadow touched the glass pane and Chuck dropped to the ground, the sharp twigs of the bush scraping his cheek.

Get out of here.

Did he want to lose his kids forever? Provoke her to file for a Final Restraining Order? *Go home, man.*

He waited for the coast to clear. One breath, two, three, four, five. As he turned to go, planning to shoot into the side yard and roll toward the neighbors, a dark Mercedes parked along the curb. Him. The hedgie boyfriend.

He alarmed his car and moved up the walk toward the door, his Bruno Maglis scraping against the concrete.

Yes, Chuck knew about Bruno Magli shoes. Trudy wanted to buy him a pair for his birthday one year. But what was he going to do with a five-hundred-dollar pair of shoes working at a trucking company? What would he tell the guys, who considered five bills a nice bonus?

Hedgie, aka Will, entered the house, *Chuck's* house, to the squeals of *his* kids.

Chuck gripped the nearest twig and snapped it in half.

What he wouldn't give to knock on the door, grab the slick Wall Streeter by the collar, and throw him to the street.

The exact move that got him into this mess.

The voices, muffled against the windowpane, began to fade. Figuring the living room was clear, Chuck dashed toward freedom.

At his car, he fired up the engine, set his Uber status to available, and dropped his forehead against the steering wheel, wishing for the millionth time Trudy would just *talk* to him.

How could he make amends and win back the right to see his kids otherwise?

He raised his head, catching the right part of his face in the rearview mirror. "Dude, you need a change. A life."

What kind of change? What kind of life? He had no idea.

The Uber app tapped him for a ride and he responded. He tossed his phone to the passenger seat, and it landed on a cream-colored card.

What was this?

He read the gold block lettering in the glow of the dash.

YOU ARE CORDIALLY INVITED TO THE
FIFTH AVENUE STORY SOCIETY.
THE FIFTH AVENUE LITERARY SOCIETY LIBRARY
THE BOWER ROOM
MONDAY, SEPTEMBER 9 @ 8:00 P.M.

JETT

He was restless. Moving from the kitchen banquette, where he dropped his backpack and bike helmet, he shed his jacket and dropped it over the back of the living room club chair.

Down the short hall to his bedroom, he flipped on a light, his thoughts on dinner and his dissertation.

Renée wanted to see something by mid-October. The university publishing arm was ready to fast-track a limited first-edition run, with a second printing in the new year.

But he didn't feel like working. He felt like, like . . . He reached for the cardstock invitation on his nightstand.

The Fifth Avenue Story Society.

He wasn't sure why he brought it home. Or set it by his bed. But he'd been looking at it every night for almost a week.

Cordially invited. By whom? As far as he knew, New York College didn't have any sort of faculty initiation, where they'd catch him off guard and demand he quote a line from a classic novel or remember the publication date of a book pulled randomly from a shelf.

Besides, he'd been on staff for almost four years. Not long enough for a promotion or tenure. But too long for an initiation.

Taking his phone from his jeans pocket, he texted Renée.

Did you send me this invitation to the Fifth Avenue Story Society?

While he waited for her response, he collapsed back on the bed, eyes closed as if he never wanted to open them.

The night in Central Booking symbolized the last two years. Trapped. *Arrested.* Helpless. Frustrated. Without justice. He didn't even know what kind of justice to seek. For himself or for his ex-wife? For his brother?

He sat up when his phone pinged.

No. What's going on at the Fifth Avenue library?

Got me. I never heard of it until now.

You should go, check it out. It's a cute little place. Maybe they're doing some sort of literacy push. How'd you get invited?

Not sure. I found it with my things.

No need to say which things. So far, the college seemed ignorant about his minor civil violation.

Because he rode a bike to and from work and had once taken a spill in the street, no one questioned his scraped knuckles or his puffy, bruised eye.

Go. Check out this library. You know with the Roth
Foundation money (hint hint) we will be able to give back
to the community.

Seriously. Even in a text? I get it. Finalize the dissertation.

How is it going?

Jett started to type a reply, then hit the delete key. He didn't want to lie. But he didn't want to tell the truth.

So you've been to this quaint little library?

Yes, and you can't get off that easy. Talk later.

Jett studied the invitation. A night out at a library might do him good. He always felt at home with books. Stories had comforted him when his parents' divorce ripped through his adolescence.

Might as well check it out. He ducked into the shower for a quick rinse. The city was still warm at five o'clock when he rode home. Especially in the summer.

In fresh jeans and shirt, he stowed the invitation in his hip pocket, made a ham and cheese on wheat, poured a glass of milk, and sat at the banquette, skimming his proofed and peer-reviewed dissertation.

He was proud of this particular work. Proud to write about such an ingenious and timeless author. He'd researched Gordon Phipps Roth as a hobby since high school. The man was a natural choice when Jett had to select a dissertation topic for his PhD candidacy.

Over time, he'd gathered more material on the scope and wisdom of GPR's work than he would ever need, collected from biographies, experts in America and Europe, and conversations long into the night with fellow bibliophiles drinking craft beer.

Then came the one haunting question.

"What about the allegations of fraud? Did the great American author have a ghostwriter?"

It was asked by one of his peers, Colin Hein, as they discussed Jett's dissertation. From that moment on, his forward momentum all but ceased. The manuscript was ready for publication. But he couldn't bring himself to answer the recent whisperings that his literary hero just might be a fraud. It seemed ludicrous. But to do his job, he must investigate.

That was for another day.

At 7:20, Jett removed his bike from the hook in the foyer, rode the elevator to the bottom floor, and started the journey to Fifth Avenue.

To his left, the sunset threaded the remaining blue sky with a fireball of red-and-orange hues framed by royal purple and midnight blue. The evening breeze previewed cooler days ahead.

As he pedaled, Jett pondered the invitation, what he might expect when he arrived. He half braced for it all to be some sort of prank, half prepared for a pleasant surprise.

Maybe he'd find his own space-navy sci-fi, *Rites of Mars*, on the shelf.

He had gone to a local bookstore in search of his novel when it came out six months ago. The salesgirl said she'd never heard of it. So his abysmal quarterly royalty reports were no surprise.

He pedaled harder. All the nights devoted to writing and rewriting, again and again, ignoring the rest of the world, including his wife. For what? For a puny advance check and a chance to be his publisher's persona non grata? Even his agent took weeks to return his calls.

At Central Park, he took a right off Sixth onto Fifty-Ninth.

This area of Manhattan had been Gordon Phipps Roth's literary stomping grounds. He wrote more than ten books about the city's Gilded Age before writing about York, England, with expertise and great detail.

So why was Jett still weighing the man's reputation? He could turn the dissertation in by Friday if he set his mind to completing a final read-through.

But. Colin's challenge chased him.

When he arrived at the library, Jett locked his bike in the foyer and removed his helmet, running his fingers through his hair.

He peered past the square entry into the small, quiet space. Bookshelves were anchored to high-ceilinged walls, and fat leather chairs faced the books rather than the room.

At the reference desk, a woman with a sparkling, round face under a Brillo pad of wiry gray hair worked through a stack of returns.

"Excuse me," Jett said, leaning toward her, touching the serene air around her. "Where's the Bower Room?"

She smiled. Almost as if she knew him. Jett stepped back, his pulse a bit revved.

"To your right. Go on in." She pointed to the wall with a mahogany-stained door between two towering stacks.

He started toward the door, then stopped and backtracked. "What exactly is the Bower Room? Why am I here?" He retrieved his invitation. "Have you seen one of these before?"

She leaned to read the invitation without reaching for it. "The Bower Room, as you'll see on the plaque by the entrance, was the private library of millionaire Joseph Winthrop. Most of his books still reside on his handcrafted shelves. The leather chairs and desk were also his. Beyond that door is another world. One captured in time. Where you stand now was the foyer, living room, and dining hall of the great mansion he built in 1888."

"Winthrop. The same Winthrop of Winthrop Industries on the Upper West Side?" The family were college donors. Renée mentioned them from time to time.

"One and the same. Do go on in. Make yourself comfortable. There are many first editions, signed, on Joseph's shelves."

"I don't understand. Why did I get this?" Jett waved the card at her. "Just to view the books?"

She smiled with an expression that calmed Jett in some deep interior place. "Go on in. Discover your story."

She gathered her books and disappeared behind a door marked Private.

Discover your story? What was she talking about? More intrigued than bothered by this mystery, Jett headed for the door marked The Bower. Maybe he'd find some first editions. Or discover an author history had forgotten.

Then he'd head home. Fall asleep on the sofa watching Monday-night football. Since the divorce, he rarely slept in *their* bed. At first it was too painful, then just a reminder of his stupidity.

The Bower was as she said. Another world. Crossing the threshold, Jett entered the nineteenth century.

The ambient glow of wall sconces flickered as if true gas flames. Breathing in, he caught a hint of pipe smoke and brandy. And the ever-pleasing fragrance of bound books.

Stepping farther inside, he could almost hear the echoing voices of the men and women who must've graced this space.

The room wasn't large, more rectangular than square. The western-facing windows brought in the setting sunlight along with the sights and sounds passing along Sixth Avenue.

As in the main library, the walls were constructed of book-laden shelves.

A circle of chairs graced the center. Five in all. Jett dropped his backpack into the nearest armchair and moved to the plaque on the wall by the window.

The library is all that remains of Joseph Winthrop's Gilded Age mansion. Walls were removed between the formal living and dining room to create the main library. The restrooms are in the same location as the original water closets. You are standing in Joseph's personal library, the Bower Room, where he shelved first editions and held literary, political, and religious discussions on a weekly basis.

Teddy Roosevelt, Franklin and Eleanor Roosevelt, Calvin Coolidge, and the prince of Wales were among his guests. But his favorites were the authors of his day. Mark Twain, Virginia Woolf, C. S. Lewis, and Gordon Phipps Roth.

GPR? Jett swung around almost expecting to see the tall, lean, bearded man awaiting him in a shadowy corner. He imagined what kind of debate he'd start.

"Who was greater, Twain or Tolstoy?"

He moved toward the bookshelves and read the spines. Dickens, Whitman, Muir, Yeats, and Woolf. Gold-leaf first editions.

"I've gone to heaven."

Behind him, on the front wall, was a writing desk next to a white stone fireplace, where a small wood fire burned. A bit warm for a fire tonight, but Jett liked the ambience it created.

Opposite the desk stood an upright cabinet containing china and several old pictures.

Easing down in his chair, Jett grinned. Heaven. At least his version of it. He just wanted to sit and take it all in as the weariness of the arrest, the pressures of his job, the failure of his novel faded away.

The room enchanted and inspired him. Eyes closed, Jett listened again for the voices of the past. Perhaps Gordon would speak.

"Absurd! I'd never use a ghostwriter. I am who I am."

Jett sat forward, eyes opened. Of course he never used a ghostwriter. Such a ruse would ruin his reputation, his name, his work.

Gordon had lectured all over the world. His stories had inspired millions for more than a hundred years.

Jett slapped his palm against the leather arm. This room could be his new haunt. He'd stop by on his way home from the college, rest among his "peers" before heading home. Maybe he'd work on his manuscript about Gordon in this very room. He had time Thursday afternoon.

"Excuse me. Is this the story society?"

Jett launched to his feet as an exquisite woman with bone-china features and blonde waves twisting over her shoulders stepped inside.

"Um, yes." *Move, man. Don't just stare.* "I'm Jett Wilder." He offered his hand.

"Coral Winthrop." Her velvety-smooth hand shook his. "What's this all about?"

She tossed her hair over her shoulders as she dropped her bag into one of the chairs. It was probably Jett's imagination, but it seemed the flames in the fireplace kicked a bit higher for a better look of this beauty.

This weird story society was looking more and more intriguing.

"You tell me." He pointed to the wall mount, gathering his wherewithal to act like a normal, decent man. He'd seen beautiful women before. Married one in fact. "Winthrop? Same as on the plaque? On buildings and billboards?"

"Joseph was my great-great-grandfather. I assume you sent the invitation. I don't really know why I'm here. I just, I don't know . . ." She gave the bookshelves her attention.

"Actually no. I received an invitation as well." Now she looked at him.

"I asked my father if he knew what was going on, but he didn't have a clue. I haven't been in here since I was a girl." She smiled for the first time and tucked her hands into the pockets of her flowing slacks.

"This is my first time. I may never leave. What do you know about your grandfather's collection of—"

"Story society? Sorry I'm late." An older gentleman with deep-set blue eyes and a thick shock of salt-and-pepper hair entered, carrying a bulky black case and holding up a cream-colored invitation. "Got waylaid at work. I'm the superintendent for my co-op and—" He glanced at Coral, then Jett. "Guess you don't care to hear about my job. Do I take any chair?" He cut through the ring and chose a seat opposite Jett.

"Jett Wilder." He extended his hand. "This is Coral Winthrop. Her ancestors built this place."

"Nice to meet you." He shook Jett's hand and nodded at Coral before sitting with the box on his lap. "Ed Marshall. Who's in charge?"

"We have no idea."

The old man made a face. "Look, I got a story to write and when I got this here invitation I wondered if all the saints and angels were telling me to get moving. But if this is just a waste of time—"

"What kind of story are you writing?" Jett said, feeling his way, using his expertise in the world of words and story to engage the man. He was sweet. Almost innocent.

"Did you send the invitation?" Ed snapped open his case to reveal a circa 1920s Underwood typewriter.

"No, I'm as flummoxed as you, Ed." Jett leaned to see the ancient machine. "You know they make electronic typewriters now. Call them computers or laptops."

Coral snickered behind her hand. Ed scowled as he set the case on the floor next to his chair.

"I see we have a class clown. I have a computer. I just prefer this ol' girl for writing."

"What are you writing?"

"My love story with my dear Esmerelda. Love of my life." He kissed his fingers and sent his affection upward. "I miss her every day."

"Is that what we're doing here?" Jett glanced back at Coral. "Are you a writer?"

"Does ex-blogger count?"

"What'd you blog about?"

"Beauty products. I own CCW Cosmetics."

CCW. He knew the brand from his bathroom shelf. "My ex-wife used your products."

Her nod was courteous. "Most women twenty-five to sixty-five use our products." Despite her air of confidence, Jett detected a hitch in her voice. "What do you do, Jett?"

"I'm a professor of literature at New York College."

"Well then, professor, you're in charge. Let's get to work." Ed rolled a piece of paper into his typewriter. "I'd like to know how to get started. Do I start in the beginning or somewhere in the middle? Or a favorite memory?"

"Look, Ed, I'm glad to give some suggestions, but I'm not in charge here. I'm not the one who sent the invitations. I certainly don't have time to run a writing clinic. However, there are writing groups all over the city. I'm sure—"

"Is this the story society? Jett?"

On his feet, Jett faced the big guy, Chuck, from Central Booking. Never thought he'd see the man again, but in the moment, he was kind of glad. They clapped hands.

"What are you doing here?"

Chuck held up an invitation. "I have no idea. I found this in my car and thought, shoot, why not? What else am I going to do on Monday night? Been driving all weekend for a limo service." He circled the room, whistling at the books. "Look at this. Giving me a panic attack. Like I'm back in school only without football and cute girls." He spun around to the chairs, gaze landing on Coral. "I take that back." He greeted her, hand extended. "Chuck Mays, at your service."

"Coral Winthrop."

Chuck's gaze lingered on her a moment longer, his giant smile rivaling the wall sconces, before turning to Ed. They exchanged names and pleasantries before the big guy took the chair next to Coral.

"So, what's this all about?" Chuck glanced around. "Winthrop. Same as the old New York family?"

"The same. And my great-great-grandfather built this library, but I did not send the invitations."

Jett endured the "Who did?" conversation one more time. By simple deduction, the group, or *society*, awaited one more person. Four of the five chairs were occupied.

"Perhaps the person who belongs in that seat sent them."

Chuck leaned back, curiosity in his eyes. "Why would I get one? I'm not a writer."

"What do you do?" Coral asked. Her voice reminded Jett of thick molasses.

"Drive for Uber." He flipped Coral his card, then one to Ed and Jett. "Also drive for Elite Limo. Call if you ever need to arrange a night out in a fancy car."

"I have a car service," Coral said, handing back the card. Chuck hesitated, almost dejected, before taking it back.

"I ride my bike," Jett said.

"Subway for me." Ed tucked Chuck's card in the chest pocket of his red-and-blue plaid shirt.

Then the Bower went silent, all eyes on the vacant chair.

"I feel like I'm in one of those escape rooms." Chuck leaned forward, slapping his broad hands against his legs. "Or worse, a cheap horror flick." He hunched down, then in a flash snatched at Ed's shoulder.

The old man jumped up, clinging to his Underwood, his breath labored, his words trembling. "Good grief. Give me a heart attack."

"Sorry, old man." Chuck winced. "Just trying to break the tension. I do dumb stuff when I'm nervous. Or angry." He glanced at Jett then his phone. "How long do we hang around?" He tipped his head toward the empty chair. "It's eight fifteen. What if this person doesn't show?"

"Then we go home." Coral sat tall and relaxed. As if she didn't have any place to be.

"Let's give it a few more minutes," Jett said. "Anyone a Giants fan?"

Chuck groused and waved him off. "Broke my heart last season."

"Why don't we at least try to write something?" Ed tapped the side of his typewriter. "The invitation did say *story* society."

"Story doesn't have to be written," Jett said. "It can be told. Every day we tell, listen to, live, and breathe stories. What we're doing right now is a story. People who would've otherwise never met are sharing a moment."

"You two seemed to know one another." Coral motioned between Jett and Chuck.

"It was a series of unfortunate events," Jett said.

"Really?" Coral shifted in her chair. "Do tell."

"Nothing to tell really," Chuck said. "Do you think this is some sort of reality show?" He scanned the length of the crown molding.

"Why would we be in a reality show?" Ed frowned at the ceiling and any possible, invisible cameras.

"Because Coral here left her groom—"

"What?" Coral leapt up and glared down at Chuck. "I'm not the culprit here. If I were to be on a reality show about . . . well, anything, I'd certainly not invite the lot of you."

"Chuck, what are you talking about?" Ed leaned into the conversation.

"Coral." Chuck glanced up at the statuesque beauty. "You are the Winthrop heiress, right? Engaged to a prince in—"

"Is this the story society?"

The door opened, and the discussion crashed to a stop. Jett rose to meet who he believed was the fifth member of this weird, cockamamie "society."

"Lexa?" If possible, the world stopped spinning. His heartbeat slowed, and his thoughts careened together.

She moved across the threshold with ease, hitched her backpack on her shoulder, and raised her sparkling hazel gaze.

"Jett? You've got to be kidding me." She had more heat in her eyes than the flames in the fireplace. "Did you do this? Send that stupid invitation?"

The backpack slipped and crashed down on her arm. She righted it again as she spun toward the door.

"No, I was hoping the person coming through that door had the answers."

"Then I'll say good night."

Wait. Say something. But he couldn't move or speak. Just like all the times in the past.

LEXA

"Wait, whoa." The massive guy in the Queen Anne jumped up with an easy grace, blocking her exit. "You can't go yet. You just got here."

"Trust me. I'm leaving." He wasn't the boss of her and she refused to stay in the same room with *him*. But a spark of ire whirled her around. "So not funny, Jett." She snatched the invitation from her backpack and tossed it at his feet.

The only other woman in the room faced Lexa. "I take it you two know each other."

She glanced at the commanding yet feminine voice. Coral Winthrop? "Oh my gosh, you're Coral Winthrop. CEO, president, owner of CCW." She jutted out her hand. "Lexa Wilder. It's so great to meet you. Wow."

"Likewise." Coral shook her hand. "Won't you join us? Maybe we can figure out this puzzle?"

Lexa hesitated, glanced around the circle, then retrieved the invitation from the floor with a cutting glance at Jett and made her way to the only empty chair.

"I'm not a writer. I don't *do* story. And I certainly wouldn't have invited him." She gestured toward Jett.

"Then why'd you come?" Jett regarded her with his arms crossed, his chin raised, a challenging flash in his eyes.

"A lapse of judgment on my part." Sigh. The large man sat in the chair next to Coral. He had kind eyes with a bit of smolder beneath.

Jett took his seat. "Let's talk. See if we can find something or someone we all have in common."

"I'm Chuck Mays," the large man said. "And this is Ed Marshall."

"Nice to meet you." She sat on the edge of the seat, lowering her backpack to the floor.

She liked the library's warm ambience and scent of precious old books. The wood fire perfumed the atmosphere with memories and the desire for a s'more.

With an exhale, Lexa released the shock of seeing Jett. Without him, the room and the others in the circle seemed perfect. Like a warm group to hang with once in a while.

She didn't have many friends since the divorce. Her friends had been *his* and, well . . .

She pointed to the Underwood typewriter cradled on Ed's lap.

"My grandma used to have one of those," she said.

"Only way to go." Ed patted the side of the machine, smiling.

"Jett, how do we start this society?" Chuck said, perched forward with his arm on his thighs. "See where everyone's from? Maybe we can figure out what we have in common."

"Florida," Lexa said, letting out some of her held breath, relaxing a bit in the alluring hues of the fire and the flickering electric flames of the wall sconces. The hardwoods were gleaming and the rug beneath her feet had to be at least three inches thick. She imagined it to be a carefully preserved Persian.

Chuck was from New Jersey. Everyone else, New York.

"Let's start with the obvious," Coral said. "You two know each other." She indicated Jett and Lexa.

"We're exes."

"Ah, of course," Chuck said. "I recognize the animosity."

"Not on my part," Lexa said.

"I don't know, the dagger in your eyes when you first saw him . . ." Coral grinned.

Did she think this was funny? Lexa certainly didn't, but she admired the woman more than she cared to be offended.

"I was just surprised to see him." Lexa sank deeper into her soft, well-worn leather seat.

While finding Jett here was an unpleasant surprise, meeting Coral Winthrop made it worthwhile. Coral was a captain of industry.

Four years ago she had taken over the archaic CCW, founded by her great-grandmother, and brought it into the twenty-first century.

Lexa could endure the next forty minutes or so for a chance to know Coral better. Maybe work up the courage to ask her advice on heading a company.

"How'd you two meet?" Coral shifted her gaze between them.

"Florida State." Low, and in unison.

Jett took over the story. "I got accepted at NYC for grad school, where I'm now an associate professor. I asked Lexa to marry me and she said yes. And here we are."

"Not married," Chuck said.

"The long and short of it, yes."

Lexa sank deeper, if possible, in her chair. It felt surreal to sit next to Jett as if he were nothing more than a casual acquaintance.

"Lexa, what do you do?" Seriously, could Coral be any more elegant and graceful, charming, and beautiful? Her features were delicate but pronounced, perfectly molded, as if God Himself took extra care to create such a stunning being.

"Executive for Zane Breas at ZB Enterprises." She left off *assistant* because it made her feel like the water girl for the football team where Coral was head cheerleader.

Coral acted impressed. "One of the fastest growing restaurant businesses in the nation."

"Too fast if you ask me, but we're hanging in there."

"I love ZB Burgers." Chuck's voice boomed. "Please tell me you're having Zaney Days in the park this fall. I had a blast there a few years ago."

"We are, yes." Did she see a ghost of something in his eyes? "Best fall event in the city, according to the *New York Times*."

"And it was Lexa's brainchild."

She turned to Jett. He remembered? Ever since his second semester of grad school he had seemed lost in another world, barely raising his head from his books.

Then his brother died and she lost him to grief. Lost him to the world of Mars and characters who lived only in his head.

"Okay, so neither of you sent the invitation." Chuck rattled off names and places where he'd grown up.

Nothing rang a bell with the others.

Coral asked about charities. None clicked. Then she ran down a list of corporate associations. Still no hit.

Jett ran through his connections via the college. Other than the Winthrops being benefactors, there was no known connection.

Chuck had a thousand Uber passengers, but never once had he dropped one off at the Fifth Avenue Literary Society Library.

Ed lived way uptown and rarely came this far south. He was retired from the *New York Times* press plant and now worked as his co-op's superintendent. His daughter was a television producer and lived on Long Island.

"What about Tenley Roth, the author?" Jett said. "Anyone know her? Her great-great-grandfather was Gordon Phipps Roth—"

"Jett's hero," Lexa said.

"And he visited this library with your ancestor, Coral." He shot Lexa a look and she regretted her tone. While she hated sitting next to him, she didn't believe he was behind this clandestine meeting.

"I've met her," Coral said. "But we didn't talk about our ancestors."

"I don't even know who she is." The old man with his typewriter slumped lower and lower in his seat, hugging his machine close.

"Got me," Chuck said.

Another round of "who knows who" and the group concluded they had no common denominator. At least not one they could compute.

"What if this is some sort of cosmic test?" Ed said. "The gods testing us?"

"To what end?" Chuck stood, stretching, pacing toward the bookshelves. "What sort of test?"

Lexa watched him and decided Chuck carried a burden he didn't want anyone to see.

"If it's all the same to Ed's gods, I'd rather not be tested." Coral brushed her hand down her arm, smoothing the wrinkles from her sleeve. "I've been tested enough."

Chuck returned to his seat. "The prince? Is he the one who tested you?"

"Leave her alone, Chuck," Lexa said, low and controlled.

She'd read the articles about the American heiress who left her European prince at the altar. They were not flattering.

"Chuck, you don't strike me as the celeb gossip type," Jett said. "How do you know about Coral?"

"I drive a car all day. I listen to the news, eavesdrop on passengers. Hey, some of them talk really loud. Right after Coral left him, I picked up two women at the airport who'd just returned from Lauchtenland. They'd gone over to see the new American princess, who they called the Panicked Princess."

The more he talked, the more Coral's confidence faded.

"I said leave her alone," Lexa said.

"Sorry, I'm just saying—" Chuck said, hands raised. "It's a pretty big deal when a girl leaves—"

"Chuck, would you please stop?" Coral's stiff posture ended with her hands balled into fists.

Lexa nodded her approval when the beauty icon's gaze met hers.

"I don't know why I'm making a big deal out of it," Coral said after a moment. "I've been through far worse, trust me."

"I'm so sorry," Lexa said.

Coral revealed a side of the elite life most people didn't see or understand. The constant scrutiny.

"What can a girl expect when she leaves a prince at the altar?" Coral brightened by a sheer act of her will. "So, what's our little group about? Are we a one-and-done? Victims of a prank? Failures at solving a mystery?"

"I still want to write my love story."

Ed. All eyes fell on him. Jett started with a low chuckle, then Coral, followed by Chuck and Lexa. Last but not least, Ed.

"Well . . . I do." He held up the typewriter. "The world needs to know about me and my Esmerelda."

"Not sure I can be of help," Chuck said. "I'm divorced. And clearly these two"—he pointed to Jett, then Lexa—"didn't have a happily ever after. Or Coral."

"Maybe that's why we're here," Coral said. "To learn about love from Ed."

Lexa peered at Jett from under her brow. She'd loved him with every fiber of her being. He had been her soulmate. Her best friend. Nothing could ruin, wreck, or penetrate their love.

By the time she realized they were the frog in a boiling pot, it was too late.

"I'd rather learn about business from you, Coral," Lexa said.

"Me?" She pressed her hand to her heart. "I'm not sure I've much to offer. I'm sure I could learn a thing or two from you and your boss. I've never been on the cover of *Forbes*."

"I can help Ed with his manuscript," Jett said. "Chuck, what about you?"

He shrugged. "I can drive people places. Not Uber unless I'm in your neighborhood, but with the limo service. I have some latitude. And I like to eat."

Jett raised his hand. "Me too. Anyone for food at these gatherings?"

"Are we seriously considering another meeting?" Lexa said. "What for?"

"Don't you want to know who sent the invitation?" Ed said.

"We tried to figure it out. We don't know." Lexa's rebuttal bounced about the room. "What would be the point? Besides taking up everyone's Monday night?"

"I wouldn't mind making the time," Coral said. "After the *thing*, I've been sort of socially isolated. All I do is work."

"I work all the time, but come to think of it, I'm pretty much a loner these days." Chuck peered at Lexa. "Can you stand seeing Jett one night a week?"

"I don't know."

"I'm cool with it if you are," Jett said.

"This is how I see it," Chuck began. "None of us knows who sent those invites, but I'd like to see if we can figure out why we're all here. Anyone else?"

One by one, hands went in the air. Coral, then Ed, followed by Jett. With them all staring at her she had to give in. Because she was also a joiner. She wanted to be liked. Even more, she wanted to be wanted.

And this weird gathering of folks seemed to want her. Even her ex.

"I'll give it one, maybe two more weeks," Lexa said.

"Good." Chuck popped his hands together. "I already sort of like you guys."

They'd just decided when a sweet-faced librarian peered around the door.

"Closing time."

Slinging her old FSU backpack on her shoulder, Lexa exited the Bower with Coral, chatting about the strange evening.

"I guess we'll see what the future holds," Coral said as she moved toward the car waiting for her. Ed and Chuck wished Lexa a good evening and headed off together.

Jett rolled his bike up next to her.

"Are you sure you're okay with—"

"I'm fine." She smiled. "This isn't how I ever thought I'd see you again."

"Nor me."

She wished him a good night and headed for the subway. The lights and sounds of the city carried her through the dark.

No question she never wanted to see her ex-husband again. But as the train rattled and shook its way underground toward her Greenwich Village stop, something shook loose in her, and Lexa Wilder felt a little bit more free.

⌒

JETT

Seeing Lexa for the first time in two years knocked him sideways. He had tried to talk to her after the judge banged his gavel, declaring their five-year marriage over, but she bolted before he could shed his talkative lawyer.

She was as beautiful as ever with a touch of summer sun on her freckled skin and an air of vulnerability. Seeing her tonight made him miss her more than he thought possible.

Locking on his bike helmet and anchoring his arms though his backpack, Jett headed home.

He'd imagined their first postdivorce meeting a hundred times. A scene like Streisand and Redford's in *The Way We Were*. Regretful, perhaps still in love, but selfishly ensconced in their own worlds.

He'd see her walking down some New York avenue as he exited his publisher's, where he'd learned his latest book spent a total of sixty weeks on the bestseller list. She'd be decked in her CEO attire with a conquering stride, afternoon sunlight streaming through her hair. Then, as if sensing an unseen force, she'd look around. Their eyes would lock. He'd wave. She'd smile and cross over to greet him, dodging a speeding taxi. They'd exchange a light hug and a kiss on the cheek.

He'd tell her he'd just finished his tenth novel and recently sold an option to Hollywood.

She'd confess she'd read his latest book and loved it.

He'd offer congratulations for her article in *Forbes*. Named to the Top 100 Women in Business to Watch.

She'd tell him she'd married last year. No one he knew.

He'd say he'd just gotten engaged. But it'd be a lie.

She'd reach up and brush his unruly bangs aside and—

A car horn blast jolted him out of the scene. He righted his trajectory and pedaled with focus.

But his thoughts continued to stray. He didn't love her. Not anymore, though he wasn't sure when the flame went out.

Somewhere between "I do" and "Storm is dead."

ED

The Evans family in 211 lost their water heater Tuesday morning and Ed spent the whole day mopping up their flooded kitchen and living room, then prying off wet baseboards and setting up a fan to make sure the walls were dried out before he did any repairs. Dave Evans hired a friend to install the new water heater. Ed was grateful. He'd battled water heaters in the past and been defeated. However, the Evans disaster set off a series of events that consumed Ed's week into the weekend.

So here he was Friday evening, walking around the Romanos' apartment on stilts, patching the ceiling where water from the Evanses' water heater leaked through.

Needless to say, the Underwood sat quiet all week with a piece of paper tucked around the roller.

He wanted to get started, but how? He needed the professor's wisdom.

"Alex," he said, dismounting the stilts, a little unsteady. Being seventy-eight was starting to show. "Tell your parents I'll come check on them this Monday. But looks like the patch work is done."

The teen nodded once. "I hope you make the people upstairs pay for it."

"Not my call."

In short order, he had his tools tucked away in the super's closet and rode the slow-as-molasses elevator up to his third-floor place.

He was tired. Looking forward to a quiet night at home.

He made his way to the fridge, where he retrieved a chicken pot pie and set the oven to preheat. Then he tossed the junk mail he'd brought up during lunch, keeping the one bill in the holder on the counter—right in front of the story society invitation.

The whole scenario puzzled and intrigued him. Who and what brought the five of them together?

Jett struck him as an upstanding young man. Ed looked him up on the internet and discovered he was the son of the adventure guy Bear Wilder, a burlier version of Marlin Perkins from the old show *Wild Kingdom*.

He'd also written a novel, *Rites of Mars*, so Ed ordered a copy.

Chuck appeared to be a decent fellow, too, if not a bit wounded. Nothing popped on the internet for him.

He liked the girls best. They were sweet and reminded him of his daughter, Holly. Stunning Coral's broken heart was reflected in her eyes, and Lexa's in her words and demeanor. She was guarded.

The oven preheat alert buzzed. Ed set the frozen dish on a cookie sheet, slid it into the oven, and set the timer.

He had thirty minutes or so to clean up and maybe type a line or two on his love story. He'd been thinking of what to say all day.

In his familiar old bedroom, he shed his work coveralls before stepping into the shower. After drying off, he dressed in a baggy pair of sweats and his favorite T-shirt—one his father used to own—before passing through the kitchen to his den.

At his desk, he rested his old fingers on the keys and stared at the blank sheet of paper rolled into the Underwood.

Esmerelda was the love of my life. I first saw her on Broadway with my buddies Nick and Sam. It was the summer of '67.

He wasn't Wordsworth or Longfellow. So? It was a start.

Opening his laptop, he checked his email and the sports scores. By the time the oven timer announced his dinner was ready, his stomach was gurgling.

He followed his normal routine, carrying his dinner to the TV tray set up next to his chair. He took a beer from the fridge, flipped off the top, then took a swig.

He rather looked forward to this coming Monday night and the story society, soliciting help and ideas for his memoir.

Wasn't often people had a love story like his and Esmerelda's, one of enduring devotion and affection. People nowadays divorced for no reason. He suspected Jett and Lexa had parted company too easily. Just a gut feeling.

People needed the hope of true love. He'd experienced it. Lived it. Why not tell the world? At the very least his daughter and grandkids.

Esmerelda died so long ago he worried Holly didn't remember her or their love.

All set with his dinner, he aimed the remote and tuned in to *Jeopardy* just as a knock hit his door.

"I'm eating." Steam billowed from the broken pie crust.

"Ed? It's Mabel Cochran."

What did she want? Darn woman was always pestering him about something.

I made a cake. Care for a slice?

I heard a noise in the pipes.

I might walk down to the movies. Care to join me?

"I'm eating, Mabel."

"Well, do you have room for some homemade pasta?" Her voice was muffled through the solid wood door. "I made way too much."

Pasta? Well now that was hard to resist. His taste buds rebelled at the idea of eating a frozen dinner when fresh pasta was available.

He opened the door to find his neighbor empty-handed. "I thought you brought me a plate."

She motioned to her open door. "Won't you join me? The table's all set and everything's hot from the oven."

The aroma of tomato sauce, cheese, and bread wafted down the hall and made him weak. His belly stood at attention.

Holly invited him out to Long Island for dinner every week for a home-cooked meal, but he preferred his place. Besides, her family was busy, going here and there, between her job as a *Good Morning New York* executive producer in Manhattan, her husband's tech business, and two teens in sports.

He angled forward to see into Mabel's apartment. She'd lit candles. Who did she take him for? "Can't you just bring me a plate?"

"Sakes alive, you're stubborn, Ed Marshall." Her scowl almost made him cower. "It's just dinner. I don't bite."

"What am I going to do with my pot pie? I can't just throw it out."

She pushed past him, swept up his dinner, and set it in the fridge. "You can have it for lunch tomorrow."

Back at the door, she waited, hands clasped at her waist. She was pretty, and shapely for a woman in her late sixties, maybe early seventies. Smart too. A former fashion magazine editor. Any man would be lucky to have her. It's just that Ed wasn't *any* man.

"Well?" she said.

"Bring me a plate and I'd be happy to help you with your overload of pasta."

"Ed, why *are* you so stubborn?"

"Why are *you* so bossy?"

She stepped past him and into the hall. "Pardon me. I won't bother you again."

Oh, good grief. "Mabel, wait." He touched her arm. "You, well, you caught me on a busy work week with the Evanses' water heater breaking and leaking through to the Romanos'. Maybe another time?"

She exhaled, her shoulders dropping before she smiled. "Leftovers?"

"Sure. Leftovers."

"One night next week?"

"Okay."

"So, tell me." She motioned toward his place again. "What are you writing? I saw the paper in the typewriter. I used to be an editor, you know. If you need help, I can—"

"I don't need any help." He eased the door closed. "Just so happens I like to collect old typewriters. I used to work at the *New York Times* press plant, you know."

"It's not a collection if you only have one, Ed."

"All right, you got me. I'll confess. I'm writing one of those, whatcha call 'em, bodice-tearing romances, under a pen name. Eloisa Hampersmith?"

She glared at him, then burst out laughing. "Well, that would be the name you'd use. How about dinner Monday? Bring your first chapter. I'd offer tomorrow but I'm visiting my son and his family."

"Monday? I'm actually busy. But check back. And I won't bring the first chapter." He shut the door before she could propose Tuesday, Wednesday, Thursday, Friday, or Saturday.

Rescuing his dinner from the fridge, he warmed it up in the microwave and returned to his worn but comfy leather mission chair he'd rescued from the side of an apartment building on East Eighty-Ninth Street and answered the Daily Double trivia question as he cut into his pot pie.

Eloisa Hampersmith. Ed, you're too funny.

He was jesting about writing a romance, but maybe that's how he needed to structure his story. A romance. Because that's what he and his beautiful, refined society girl Esmerelda Belmont shared.

Ed pressed his fist to his chest, subduing the ache that resided between his ribs and heart ever since she left this world. Dead at thirty-four, but he was keeping his promise to love and remember her until his own dying day.

Of course, he saw Esmerelda every day in Holly. He was right proud of their girl, the executive producer. She married a good man, too, with a solid head on his shoulders. Brant liked to advise Ed on financial matters and how to increase his conservative retirement pay.

And the two of them had given Ed and Esmerelda two fine grandchildren. Drake and Hope.

"You should see them, Esmie. Good kids. Smart. Athletic."

He played along with the *Jeopardy* contestants as he finished the last bite of his pot pie and washed it down with a swig of beer. He figured he was up to about ten grand when he wagered five thousand on another Daily Double and lost.

Well, you win some and lose some. But on such an easy question! Which great American twentieth-century author won the Pulitzer Prize for fiction in 1926?

"Dad?"

Ed jumped up, tipping the TV tray. He caught it before the contents spilled. "Hol?"

"I came up the back elevator." She peered around the kitchen wall, holding up two canvas totes. "I brought you some produce. What smells so good?"

Mabel's pasta. "My pot pie." He schlepped into the kitchen with his clean plate and nearly empty bottle of beer. "What are you doing here?"

Tall and lean, Holly embodied the city in which she grew up—quick, fast talking, fast moving, always in black with the aura of professional ambition.

"Seeing my father?" She kissed his cheek before raising three grocery totes to the counter. "I'm beat. Long day. Did you watch the show? Our first guest was a pain in the rear. She was obsessed with avocados. Had to have a *fresh* one. On warm toast. Like she'd die otherwise. After the fifth run to the bodega, I was ready to smash the whole lot in her face. But"—she speared the air with her finger—"we have Sabrina Fox next week, so that should make up for it."

She smiled as if Ed understood every fast word. Which he did, sort of.

"What'd you bring me?" He peeked into the nearest bag, sniffing out asparagus and potatoes. "I'll make a soup."

"I reminisced with the kids the other night about your famous potato soup. You should come to the house one afternoon, make it for us."

Ed started unpacking the totes, but Holly was distracted by the mail holder on the counter. Every now and then she stole one of his bills and paid it for him.

"Leave that be. I can handle it."

But she bypassed the bill for the story society invitation.

What's this? 'You are cordially invited—'"

"Didn't I raise you not to be so nosy?" Ed tried to snatch it from her but she was too quick.

"I'm a television producer, so no. A story society? Dad, are you writing?" She gazed toward his den. His typewriter.

"Not really." He snatched the invitation from her fingers. "I had an idea but didn't know what to do with it. This invitation came out of the blue, so I thought I might go see what the fuss was about."

"The literary library? On Fifth Avenue? Oh, the one at the old Winthrop mansion. Of course. You never hear about that place anymore. I remember visiting when I was in high school but since then . . . This might be a good story."

"There's no story." He peered inside the nearest tote. Bananas. Good. He'd cut up his last one on his cereal this morning.

"Who's sponsoring this society? The Winthrops? One of the universities?" Holly began unpacking oranges and apples and a head of cauliflower.

"Don't know who's sponsoring it. There were five of us in all, and no one knows who sent this invitation. Even Coral Winthrop is confused."

"Coral Winthrop." Holly stared at him with her blue eyes wide. "The cosmetics heiress. Head of CCW? The daughter of Eric Winthrop III. She was there?"

Uh-oh. He knew the tone, the look. "Now don't go getting any ideas."

"Dad, please." Holly tucked the empty tote under her arm and gripped his hand. "We've been dying to have her on GMNY. Ever since she ran out on Prince Augustus she's been a recluse, a media mystery. She's not even the face of CCW anymore. Every news outlet in the world wants to talk to her. Dad, you've got to—"

"I don't have to do a thing." He directed her toward the remaining tote. "Unload. Listen, Hol, I'm not sure what our little group is about, but I'm pretty sure handing over one of the members to a news outlet is questionable. You're just going to have to find your story another way."

Holly sighed, giving him her rebellious-daughter look. Blue-eyed determination with a hint of "pretty please." "Well if you get a chance, ask her—"

"I won't."

They finished unloading the totes. Holly tucked them away in her oversized satchel, then made her way to the living room. She pretended to reminisce about her childhood home on these spontaneous visits, but Ed knew she was inspecting the place to see if he was living well.

"The place looks good." She smiled at him over her shoulder. "Always feels good to be home."

"You know you're always welcome." He'd been here forty-nine years. Moved in with Esmerelda when Holly was one. Seemed like he'd signed the bank papers and taken the keys just a few years ago. "Needs some updating, but I like this place well enough."

When the building co-op board had caught the former superintendent stealing, they offered the job to Ed. Which he eagerly took.

A year into his retirement, he felt a bit adrift if not stir crazy. The place where he'd raised Holly seemed rather small at times—like when she had her friends over—until he lived in it alone, facing day after day of solitude, memories flooding to the surface.

"We still want you to move out to Rockville Center with us. We bought our house with you in mind. The father-in-law suite is as big as this place, and you'll have a yard for that garden you always said you wanted."

He kissed her forehead. "I know, and I love you for it, but I'm not ready to give up my place." Or his memories and every hope and dream the old apartment represented. He glanced at the ceiling where a thin crack ran through the plaster. "This is home."

She headed for the door. "You know you're my hero, don't you?"

"And you're my princess." Esmie was his queen. But Holly was his princess.

"Plan on coming to the house this week, okay? We miss you. I'll be at the Gottlieb Gala Friday night, but any other time . . ." Holly checked her watch. "Is it after six already? I've got to go. Hope is making dinner tonight." She gathered her things and headed for the kitchen door. "You'd tell me if being the superintendent was too much for you."

"I would."

"Or if you were lonely."

"I know where to find you."

"You're such a good man, Dad." Holly brushed her hand over his shoulder. "Grandpa's old shirt. I miss him."

"Me too. Now get going or you'll miss Hope's dinner. Give my love to the kids."

"Come to the house. This weekend."

When he shut and locked the door, Ed chuckled. He had him a spitfire of a daughter. And she had probably saved him.

He tidied the kitchen and shut off the light, then rewarded himself with an ice-cream bar. Back in his chair instead of the den where the typewriter taunted him, he flashed through the cable guide.

So this was his life. Work. TV. Sleep. He was okay with simple. Peaceful. And the fact very little changed. It kept him connected to his love.

He'd settled on a rerun of *Bonanza* when his work phone jangled from the kitchen counter. Ed frowned at the name on the screen. Mabel Cochran. Now what?

"Sorry to bother you, but my garbage disposal is broken."

"I told you not to shove potato peels down it. Clogs it up every time."

"I didn't, you lug head. I made *pasta* not potatoes. I simply poured water and a few noodles down the drain and *kerplunk*."

"Fine." He sighed, yanked his keys from the hook by the back door, and headed down to the super's closet for his tools.

By the time he arrived at Mabel's, her apartment door stood open, spilling the golden glow of a cozy home over her feet and into the hall, and he wasn't nearly as miffed. Besides, the fragrance of pasta, cheese, and tomato sauce still saturated the atmosphere.

"I *am* sorry to bother you, Ed. Did you have to go down for your tools? Tell you what, I've got coffee on, decaf, and fresh-from-the-oven brownies for your trouble."

Brownies. He stopped short, his mouth watering. He loved a good brownie and vanilla ice cream. His absolute favorite. Used to make them with Esmerelda, then Holly. What happy memories brownies make. Maybe he should start his story there.

You might wonder if a love story can start with brownies. I tell you, it can. Listen to what happened to me.

"The doctor has me off sweets." Was it wrong to not want to share his favorite with Mabel? "And never mind about the disposal. I'll buy you a new one if we need to. Shouldn't run you more than fifty bucks." He crossed her living room toward the kitchen, passed the dining table still set for two. Tall tapers beat their flames against the shadows while ol' Bobby Darin sang "Mack the Knife" from a vintage hi-fi.

Oh, the shark, babe, has such teeth, dear.

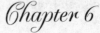

LEXA

She'd developed the habit of leaving her third-floor, walk-up apartment door open when she arrived home on Friday nights. When the weather was nice, music floated up from the streets. Mickey the Irish singer was her favorite.

She wanted to believe she embraced some part of the weekend by living vicariously through the vibe in the Village, through her lively neighbors and the hubbub behind the walls.

Especially Abby, the NYU senior majoring in theater. But tonight, her place across the hall remained dark and quiet.

Lexa turned the heat down beneath her chicken-and-broccoli stir-fry, sipped from her glass of wine, then took a plate from the cupboard.

The weekend was her time to cook. Working for a restaurateur had sparked her otherwise dull interest in culinary arts. But she wasn't very skilled. She overcooked everything.

Pouring the contents from the pan onto her plate, Lexa settled in the low red reading chair under the window of the rectangular living room.

Eight hundred square feet was all she could afford after the split. But she was saving for something bigger. If Zane promoted her, she'd earn enough to move uptown.

Well, not literally uptown. She'd considered moving north after the divorce. Being three blocks from Jett, she feared running into him as they schlepped about the neighborhood.

Then Zane purchased the Tribeca office space and moving didn't make sense.

A laugh bounced off a distant wall. She raised her head. Abby? The occasional laugh or shout, even the muffled sounds of a television show, gave Lexa a sense of belonging. Proof she was among the living and not so very much alone.

That sense was why she loved ZB Enterprises. She belonged. She more than belonged. She was one of the steering forces of the company.

A bit of pride—no, satisfaction—filled her chest. Finding her place had never been easy. And when she did, it usually ended in disaster.

ZB Enterprises was the one place outside her family where she belonged. Where she mastered her own ship and destiny.

Look out, Zane, I'm coming for you.

She watched a show on Netflix as she ate, then washed her plate and returned it to the shelf. Her next place would have a dishwasher.

Beyond the window, the sun had long gone west. She peered down into the street, curious where her Greenwich Village neighbors were going on this Friday night in such a hurry.

After a moment, she changed into her comfy sweats, pulled her hair back in a ponytail, and smothered her face in a charcoal mask produced by her favorite cosmetics company, CCW.

She regarded her reflection, her hazel eyes peering over the muddy concoction.

What was Monday night about? So weird. She'd texted Jett on Wednesday asking once again if he was behind the invitation. He promised he was as confused as she.

So should she go back?

Besides running into Jett, her week had been frustrating. There was no time to talk to Zane about the CEO job. He was busy or on a call, going to a spontaneous meeting not on his calendar. He even took a last-minute flight Wednesday to survey a new location for ZB Burgers in Waco.

Thursday night, Lexa had texted her baby sister, Skipper, the newly minted NASA engineer, for courage.

Do you think he's avoiding me?

No. He's busy. You're not going to get the perfect
moment. Just tell him, "I'm your girl."

Easier said than done.

Then apply for the job like any other candidate. He'll have
to interview you.

True. He posted the job months ago and has yet to
interview anyone.

He's waiting for you.

Then why doesn't he just ask me?

You're killing me here. Apply already. And text Dad.
See what he says. You know he thinks you have a great
business mind.

He takes forever to text back. Never know where he and
Mom are in Zambia. Are you still visiting them in October?

Yes. You should come.

Zaney Days. Too busy. Spring?

"Lex? Hey, you here?"

Abby's voice drew Lexa from the bathroom, her face still
plastered.

"Pardon the mud mask. But look at you." Abby was dressed like
an eighties punk rocker. "Cyndi Lauper. Where are you headed?"

"An eighties party. Obviously. Want to come?" She motioned to
Lexa's face. "You're already halfway to one of the zombies in 'Thriller.'"

"Ha. But I think I'm in for the night." Lexa fingered the drying mask. "Maybe another time." Her head told her to go, try new things. Her heart warned her to stay inside, stay focused, stay safe.

"Abby?" Boy George, followed by Michael Jackson, and what was probably the one-armed drummer from Def Leppard (but you could see his "missing arm" beneath his T-shirt) came in from the hall.

"I'm trying to get Lexa to go with us."

"With that mask on, you could be one of the 'Thriller' zombies." This from the man himself, Michael.

"That's what I said." Abby laughed and slipped her arm though Boy George's.

"I'm honored, Mr. Jackson, but I'm going to stay in and read." Perhaps make her application for ZB's CEO.

Abby shoved her friends out the door. "If you change your mind, Lex, call me. We'll be in SoHo." She drew the door closed behind her. "Pretty depressing to spend a Friday home alone with a book and a mud mask, don't you think?"

Lexa closed the door behind them and twisted the lock. Sitting at home on Friday night used to be the highlight of her week. When she and Jett were first married they'd order takeout, then curl up on the couch for a movie or good book, their legs intertwined. The evening always ended with them on the floor, naked.

Always? No, not always. When the pressure of grad school started taking a toll he barely left his "work chair." Under deadline, he went days without showering.

Those honeymoon days were short-lived but remained so vibrant in her mind.

She shivered. Forgetting the love of her life was not going as well as she'd hoped. Seeing him Monday stirred old feelings and awakened sleeping memories.

Curling up in her reading chair, she picked up the book she'd

found at a used bookstore and tried to read. But Jett's face kept floating across her mind.

After reading the same paragraph five times, she closed the book
and reached for her phone.

I saw Jett Monday night.

Closing her eyes, she waited for Skipper's well-punctuated reply.
A wave of nostalgia crashed against her. She missed her parents
and the camaraderie they shared traipsing from state to state, country to country, air force base to air force base.

If she could go to Zambia with Skip she'd pack her bags in a
heartbeat, but Zaney Days required all hands on deck.

She stared at her phone. No reply.

He looked good. Maybe too good. Still has that wild mop
of hair and steel jaw, and I'm amazed a book nerd dwells
beneath that striking face.

When they met on Landis Green at FSU, her middle flip-flopped.
Honest to goodness flip-flopped. She never imagined Jett Wilder
would give her more than a passing glance, let alone become her
friend, ask her out, then become her husband.

Lexa shoved off her chair to make a cup of tea. The unwitting
stroll down memory lane had her twisted and knotted.

Come on, Skip, answer.

What was she doing on a Friday night in Cocoa Beach? Of course,
she lived in the same coastal county where she'd graduated high school
and college. She had longtime friends. A perk of being the youngest.
She was in middle school and Lexa was a sophomore when their parents finally stopped moving.

Standing at the stove, she waited for the kettle to whistle, then
poured the water in a cup from her grandmother's china set.

Back in her chair, she continued her story to Skipper.

I got this weird invitation to a story society being held at
an old library on Fifth Avenue.

If Fifth Avenue didn't get her attention, then Skipper wasn't near
her phone. It was that simple. She loved the city. Visited Lexa whenever she could get a long weekend.

I was the last to arrive. I walk in and there stood Jett. I
lost my breath for a second. Then got mad. Did he set
this up? There were five of us all together. Chuck, an
Uber driver. Ed, a widower trying to write his love story.
And, get this, the Panicked Princess and owner of CCW
Cosmetics herself, Coral Winthrop. She seemed really
humble and demure. I, however, wanted to fall at her feet.
MENTOR ME! Skip? Did you hear me? Coral Winthrop?
Fifth Avenue?

When Skipper visited Lexa over Christmas they spent an entire
afternoon at the Saks Fifth Avenue CCW counter.

Anyway, turns out we all got the same weird invitation.
No one knows why and we can't seem to find any sort
of connection. We're meeting this Monday to dig a little
deeper. Not sure I'll keep up with the game afterward.

Pausing her story, she set her phone aside, sipped her tea, then
fingered the dry mask. She'd left it on too long. Removing it would
require a hammer and chisel.

As she washed her face with warm water and a washcloth, she
listened for her phone. No ping. By the time she finished her bedtime
tea and watched a rerun of the nineties sitcom *Frasier,* Skipper had
not returned any of her texts.

Okay, you must be busy. Good night.

Lexa climbed the steep ladder to her loft bed—always with the fear of missing a rung and falling backward—connected her phone to the charger, and burrowed under the covers.

In the middle of the dark night, she dreamed Zane gave the CEO job to someone else as a prize-fight bell rang over and over in the background.

Only it wasn't a prize-fight bell but texts from Skipper. Lexa woke and stared at the phone's screen. Fifty-eight texts from baby sister.

What?!?!?!?!?! You saw Jett!!??

Lexa? Hey, LEXA! Wake up!

Rolling over with a grin, she snuggled down.

Serves the girl right. She'd just have to wait until morning.

∽

JETT

Sitting in his office Monday afternoon under a stream of angled sunlight, grading Comm 1 papers, he waited for any one of his many students to cross the threshold during office hours.

But none came. Too bad, because Billy Price in Comm 2 needed help. Maybe he'd catch the kid after class on Wednesday.

"Knock, knock." Renée appeared at his door. "Got a sec?"

"What's up?" He glanced at his watch, standing as she took a seat by his desk.

He needed to leave for the story society in fifteen minutes. He glanced toward the boxy window anchored in the brick wall of his office situated in one of the college's original buildings. The steel plate in the foyer said Built in 1862.

"How's it going?"

Renée didn't typically start her conversations with leading questions. Jett braced for the reprimand he'd been expecting all week. Renée had been at the wedding, but she left the reception early. Before the big brawl.

Two days ago Jett cracked open the faculty handbook to see how many Orders of Conduct he'd violated last Sunday. He counted at least three.

"*The faculty of New York College is held to a high standard . . . Years of excellence and esteemed traditions . . .*"

"Don't coddle me, Renée. How bad have I disgraced the college?"

"Hadley Bennet told the whole story. Said the groomsman had it coming." She sat back, legs crossed, a square white card in her hand. "The dean asked me about it on Wednesday, but I said it was all blown out of proportion. However, if you can, control yourself in the future—"

"Thank you, Renée. I promise, no more drunken outbursts." He opened the middle desk drawer and took out a letter. "Jenn's father sent an accounting of the damage by registered mail. My portion is about two grand. Wrote him a check last night."

She winced. "Two grand? Pretty steep for a man on an associate professor's salary. Is that space-navy tome of yours making any money yet?"

"Kick a man when he's down, why don't you."

He'd emptied all but a grand from his meager savings to clear his debt. Before that, his divorce lawyer cost Jett his savings and every spare dime.

He'd hoped *Rites of Mars* would earn a little bread-and-butter money, but his latest royalty statement indicated no such luck.

"I came in to show you this." Renée dropped the card in her hand onto the desk. "Proof of the Roth Foundation Reception invitation."

Jett leaned to read the Old English script. Another "You are cordially invited . . ."

THE ROTH FOUNDATION RECEPTION
SUNDAY, NOVEMBER 17, SIX O'CLOCK
NEW YORK COLLEGE PRESIDENTIAL RESIDENCE
BLACK TIE

"They're giving us the endowment?" The Roth Foundation had recently partnered with the college to create a school of literature in honor of their patron, Gordon Phipps Roth.

"They are." She reached back to close Jett's door. "Just between us, the reveal will be at the reception. With the endowment money, we're adding a wing to Shehorn Hall. The Gordon Phipps Roth School of Literature."

"The Gordon Phipps Roth . . . Really? Th-that's amazing." *Please do not say this is predicated upon, or due in part to, the upcoming publication of my dissertation.*

"Elijah Roth is eager to quell the fraud rumors that hound his great-great-grandfather. Between your publication"—there it was—"and their endowment plus a building to this prestigious liberal arts college, the reputation of a beacon in American literature will be redeemed."

"Wow. I'm sure Dr. Hanover is . . . Wow." He handed back the invitation. "I guess I'd better put those finishing touches on the book."

It'd been four years since he joined the college as an associate professor. Four years to complete his research on the life and work of Gordon. Four years of peer reviews and revisions, aiming for academic publication.

The doubt started with an article in the *Harvard Review* challenging GPR's authenticity. Renée asked him to look into it. His findings and publication could make him the leading authority on the great American author. Which would be such a win for the college.

Then Storm died and Lexa left. Publishing his dissertation contained no life or joy. So he abandoned the project and buried himself in an epic space-navy novel.

Two years later he was somewhat on the other side of things, though the nagging question remained. Was Gordon Phipps Roth a fraud? If his hero was a fraud, who would remain in his life to admire?

He'd tried to set a meeting with Tenley Roth, Gordon's great-great-granddaughter and distant cousin to Elijah, but she never answered Jett's emails.

"Jett." Renée leaned toward him. "I hired you because you are the new breed of literary minds. You were an outstanding grad student, and I wanted to bring you on faculty from the moment I heard you speak at the literary symposium. You have great literary instincts and a casual, inspiring manner with the students. You see the gems in modern literary voices."

"Th-that's quite a compliment from you." Jett pushed away from the desk and sat forward with his arms on his thighs. He examined the thin threads of his Wise Old Professor sweater.

"I mean it. But I've been waiting four years for you to publish. It's time. Especially with all the money on the line. You've found no footing with the fraud allegations, so let's move forward."

Now in her midfifties, Renée had been a trailblazer in the world of female literature professors in Ivy League schools. She was both compassionate and critical of "good ol' boys" clubs and earned the respect of her peers and elders.

She sat on the Pulitzer Prize committee and was renowned for her insight and expertise.

"Face it, your genre novel, however good, is not going to win us any large endowments." She reached for his book propped against the wall and thumbed through *Rites of Mars*'s 470 pages. "But you know how these things work, Jett. Politics. You scratch my back, I'll scratch yours. It's how we earn the money, stay afloat. The foundation has requested your dissertation be published to, shall we say, silence any critics and prove to the world the great American realist author of the twentieth century is not a fraud."

"No one can prove he's a fraud." He took the book from her and returned it to the bookshelf under the window. "If they could, they would have by now."

The rumors of Gordon's illegitimacy began about three years ago, when Tenley posthumously published a novel written by American heiress and British marchioness Birdie Ainsworth.

No one thought much of *An October Wedding* until a review appeared in the *New York Review of Books.* "Her voice resounds with the likes of Gordon Phipps Roth's." Then the whispers began.

The author's voice, the story setting and era, the heart and soul of the characters, felt so very much like Gordon's. In fact, almost identical.

The article in the *Harvard Review* made the case Ainsworth merely mimicked Gordon's voice. It claimed Tenley dishonored her ancestor and American literature by publishing something so blatantly like her great-great-grandfather's.

Another article revealed Ainsworth's friendship with Gordon, and speculation of her plagiarism spiked but quickly died down.

Still, in the hallowed halls of universities, symposiums, and conferences, the question remained. Did Birdie steal from Gordon? Or did he steal from her?

The latter seemed so implausible. Ridiculous really. Gordon supposedly didn't even meet her until the 1920s. *Of course* he wrote his own books. Suggesting anything else was career suicide.

GPR was a lauded literary genius, and the *thought* of him hiding behind an unnamed ghostwriter was utterly insane. Even shameful.

His publisher, the great Daniel Barclay, was synonymous with integrity.

Jett exhaled. Once again, his imagination ran away with him.

"I'll go through it again." And ignore the tug in his middle to stay after the Gordon rumors. "Submit for peer review—"

Renée looked pleased. "No need for more peer review. Just make your final edits and be done with it. The university press is holding a spot for you in late October. Can you have it to me by the fifteenth? Dr. Hanover wants a printed book in his hand by the first of November. We'll present the book to Elijah at the reception in exchange for his ten million dollars. This is an enormous honor, Jett. And an incredible financial boost."

"So you've said." He rocked back in his chair, his attention fixed on Renée. "New York College has never lacked for funds. Our rich alumni leave millions to us in their opulent wills."

"But this money goes to *us*, the English department. The readers and writers, lovers of the written word and stories. We almost always lose to engineering, or law, or music." She pressed her hand on his arm. "Jett, with this money and a school named after Gordon, we will no longer be the junior Ivy League but a full member of the elite universities."

But what if . . . "You don't think I need more time to track down the allegations? See if there is any truth to the whispers of a ghost-writer?" he said.

Renée stood and reached for the doorknob. "Just make sure the truth is Gordon would've never, ever employed a ghost. Don't let *us* down, Jett." She stepped out with a final word over her shoulder. "Oh, and by the way, I hope your tux is back from the cleaners."

He narrowed his gaze. "It's trashed. I need a new one."

"Then you'd better hurry up and rent one. You're attending the Gottlieb Gala Friday night on behalf of the university." She handed him yet another invitation.

"Me? I'm an ugly-sweater, sneaker-wearing, lowly associate professor. I will not impress. They'll expect Hanover or some other college brass."

"But we're sending you to hobnob with Elijah Roth. He's near your age, interested in literature and everything GPR. You're the reigning expert." She wrinkled her nose and grinned. "Have fun. Be at the Starlight Room, Waldorf Astoria. Eight o'clock, this Friday. I hear the Black Tux shop has great last-minute rentals."

The sound of her footsteps echoed in the hall. But Jett didn't have time to fume or be angry. He was late for the story society.

He hopped on his bike and headed downtown to the romantic, secluded literary library, the thin breeze swirling his emotions.

As much as he wanted the truth, he feared knocking Gordon off the proverbial white horse. He feared that like every other hero in his life who disappointed—his parents, his brother—Gordon would be the same.

While most young men admired superheroes or star athletes, Jett admired literary giants. He had a poster of GPR, Twain, and Emerson on his wall until his older brother, the incomparable Storm, tore them down.

"Find a picture of Britney Spears or Jennifer Lopez. Geez, you're a dude."

A few more blocks and he'd be at the library. As much as he dreaded seeing Lexa tonight, assuming she returned, he rather looked forward to this ragtag gathering and the mystery they shared.

Chapter 7

LEXA

She wanted to leave work early so she could grab the Queen Anne next to Coral at the story society. But Zane detained her, this time with revisions on his speech for Friday night's Gottlieb Gala.

"Sorry I'm late again." She took the only open chair. The one between Jett and Ed. "Zane has a knack for catching me on my way out."

She dropped her backpack to the floor and smiled at the little group.

"He's not used to you leaving so early."

She glared at Jett. "Don't start."

Separated and divorced two years and he dared comment on her life? If not for Zane and work, she'd have been lost and bereft when Jett let her go without so much as a, "Wait, let's talk."

"You two going to nip at each other all night?" Ed said.

"Not me." Lexa sat back, hands surrendered.

"Nor I," Jett said.

"Know what we need?" Chuck pushed back in the large wing-back so the front legs lifted off the ground. "Food."

"In this room?" Coral glanced over at him. "It's too nice. We can't spill on this rug. It's antique. Probably worth twenty thousand dollars."

"We're not barbarians," Ed said. "I've known how to eat over a plate since I was knee-high to my father."

"Me too." Jett raised up to bump fists with Ed and Chuck. "I'm famished."

"Pizza?" Chuck waved his phone with a glance at Coral. Well, look who had a crush. He seemed more amiable tonight than last week. Not as gruff and . . . mad. "On me tonight."

"Guess we're outnumbered." Coral grinned across the circle at Lexa, and in an instant, she felt like she'd gained a friend.

"Guess so."

She'd never had lifelong friends. Just seasonal ones. Then Dad would be reassigned and off they'd go.

She was okay with short-term friends until she married Jett and moved to Manhattan, where they were instantly a family, and instantly "couple friends" with fellow graduate students and the younger faculty members.

When the divorce was final, their friends had to choose. And since almost all of them were associated with the college, Jett carried away the spoils.

While Chuck ordered the pizza, Coral checked with the librarian to make sure it was okay, and Lexa inspected the closet in the back corner. Mostly cleaning supplies, but she was surprised to find a small portable table and paper products. Plates, napkins, and cups. She filled her arms with the treasures while Jett retrieved the table.

His arm brushed hers as he moved too quickly through the narrow opening.

"As long as we clean up, we're good." Coral reached for the long sleeve of cups tipping from Lexa's arm.

Lexa and Coral arranged the plasticware, and Ed demanded to know how to write his love-story memoir.

"Start wherever you want, Ed," Jett said. "You can organize it later. What's the first thing that comes to mind when you think of your wife?"

"She was the love of my life."

"And what made her the love of your life?"

Did Jett just send a sideways glance her way?

"One thing. Many things." Ed cleared his throat and averted his misty eyes. Lexa's own filled with compassion. "She was full of life, fun, even a bit wild. Didn't care a whit about social conventions. But it was the sixties, and my generation wanted to do things our way, a new way. She was beautiful too. Couldn't believe she went for a man like me."

There. Jett did it again. Looked askance at her. *Stop it.* What was he trying to say? Ed's story was nothing like theirs.

At the door, Chuck listened, arms folded, looking back every few minutes for the pizza delivery.

"I took a memoir class when I was at FSU." Jett peered pointedly at Lexa, his blue eyes intense. "Remember?"

"No." Her hard, flat tone rejected his attempt to reminisce.

"How quickly we forget," he said.

Of course he knew she'd lied. They'd stayed up half the night talking about everything but what caused them pain.

"Narrow the story, Ed," Jett said. "Focus in on one thing. Don't tell your whole life but maybe of meeting Esmerelda, some highlights of your marriage, what happened to make you realize the strength and specialness of your love. Use dialog and other fiction tools to bring the reader into your life. And always, always tell the truth."

"Well of course I'm going to tell the truth."

"You have to include a few good disagreements," Coral said. "My great-grandmother wrote a memoir of founding CCW and she spilled her guts. People still buy the book because it's so raw and real."

"What about you, Coral?" Jett said. "Will you ever tell *your* story?"

She shifted around to Chuck. "Pizza here yet? I'm starved."

Chuck checked the progress on his phone. "Almost." He disappeared into the main reading room.

Coral busied herself at the food table, rearranging the plates and napkins. Jett glanced at Lexa. *Sorry?*

"She'll tell us when and if she's ready," Lexa whispered.

A minute later Chuck returned with the rich aroma of pizza pie, and the good smells brought the little society to life. They filled their plates and sat in the circle. Chuck suggested food every week. Ed wanted everyone's number.

"Why would we do this every week?" Lexa said, wiping the corner of her mouth with a thin paper napkin.

"We still don't know why we're here." Chuck glanced at each of them, his attention lingering longer on Coral than the others. "Don't you want to know who sent the invitation?"

"What if the invitations were some promotional thing for the library? Sent to five random people. I get stuff 'to the resident of' all the time," Lexa said, the presence of Jett starting to seep into her skin.

Did she want to punch him? Yell at him? Run away and never clap eyes on him again? Hug him? Yes, yes, all of the above.

"Mine didn't have any address," Coral said.

"Don't believe mine did either." Ed, with a mouthful of pizza.

"Same," Chuck said. "Just my name."

"Okay, so what's the point of our little society?" Jett set his plate with four pizza crusts on the floor by his feet. He never ate his crust. He saved them for Lexa.

"Help me write my memoir." Ed hammered the arm of his chair with his fist.

Lexa reached over and patted his arm. "Write your scene page. We'd love to hear it."

"Read it out loud? To you?" He shied away from her touch. "I don't know."

He went from a grumpy old man to a timid child. He seemed lost without his Underwood. But that thing had to be a beast to carry on the subway.

"Ed, you don't have to do anything you don't want." Jett's smooth tone drew the man back into the circle. "We can help more if we read what you've written. Does anyone else need help with a story?" He surveyed each face.

"No."

"Not me."

"Certainly not me." Coral stood to collect plates. "What about you, Jett? How can we help you? I think we're here to help one another."

"Anyone an expert on Gordon Phipps Roth? I could use some insight into his life and whether he ever used a ghostwriter. I have to submit my dissertation for publication next month. The Roth Foundation is going to use it to quell any suspicions about GPR and give the school a boatload of money."

The circle had nothing to offer.

"If I hear anything, I'll let you know," Chuck said. "I pick up a lot of people from all walks of life during the day."

"The mystery of this gathering wouldn't be about you two, would it?" Coral returned to her chair, gesturing to Jett and Lexa. "Pretty weird that exes would end up here randomly."

"Not about us, no." Lexa's protest contained too much force. "I don't know anyone who wants us back together."

"I certainly don't," Jett scoffed, and she felt it deep in her middle. Heat flashed over her, and her eyes stung.

"Then I guess it's still a mystery." Coral picked up a napkin and passed it around, asking for names and numbers. "I'll have my assistant send you all the list from my phone. Do we want a food schedule? So everyone knows when they're responsible for refreshments?" She pointed at Chuck. "You can't bring pizza every time. Or a bag of chips and cookies."

He laughed. "All right, I'll bring Chinese."

Names and numbers turned into ages. Ed was the oldest at seventy-eight. Same age as Lexa's grandparents in Tennessee.

Coral was thirty-three and Chuck thirty-five. He had twins, a boy and girl, both about to turn six.

"The ex and I waited to have kids. Thought several years together would give us a solid foundation." He rubbed his palms together as if grinding down his agitation. "Guess not."

Jett had just turned thirty and Lexa lingered at twenty-nine, the baby of the group.

A soft knock sounded against The Bower's golden maple door. The smiling, almost glowing librarian peered inside. She was as pretty as Lexa remembered, neat and petite with a mass of wild gray hair. "We're closing."

"Thanks, Gilda," Jett said and faced the group. "I asked her if she knew why we were here and all she did was smile."

"Well then." Coral stood. "Next Monday?"

Lexa hesitated before confessing. "I don't know. What's the point? And don't say to help with your memoir, Ed."

"Does there have to be a point?" Jett slung his backpack over his shoulder. "Can't we just see where this takes us? Maybe the point is at the end of the journey and not the beginning."

"I'm in." Chuck offered a hand to Ed, helping him out of his chair. "I kind of like you guys."

"Me too," Coral said. "Lexa, I'd hate to be the lone female among these handsome men."

Reaching for her backpack, Lexa stepped out of the circle and moved behind Jett toward the door. "I'll see."

"Lexa, don't not come because of me," Jett said. "I know you'd love to learn from Coral about running a company."

"Will you stop talking for me, please?"

"You want to learn business?" Coral said. "I can share what little I know." Her expression both yearned and commanded. *Stay with us.*

"I'll see. Good night."

On the short subway ride home, she mused about her options. Not go, and miss out on something possibly unique, fun, and spectacular. Or go, and possibly have an adventure to tell her friends, children, and grandchildren. Perhaps others would envy her and wonder how she got so lucky.

Or it'd be a bust and she'd have to sit next to her ex week after week, hearing about his life, the one she was supposed to share. Or worse, hear stories of how he met someone fabulous and was falling in love. Or even more devastating, watch him fall in love with the stunning, graceful, and rich Coral Winthrop.

CORAL

Numbers don't lie. At least in theory. If the ones on her screen were anywhere near correct, her company, CCW Cosmetics, was losing money. Loads of it.

And on her watch. She, Coral Winthrop, with her MBA and lifelong history with the company, was failing.

How? She couldn't figure it. Where were the stellar sales from a year ago? The promised ten-percent increase from sales and marketing?

Pushing away from her desk, she retrieved a Diet Coke from the fridge paneled into the office wall and pressed the cold can to her forehead.

She'd launched the preteen lip gloss line, Pink Coral, to glowing reviews. The industry raved about it. But a year later, the sales numbers barely covered the cost of her research and development.

She poured the soda into a glass and took a long drink as she sat on the round leather couch by the window.

From her high perch overlooking the Upper West Side, she was the crown princess to the CCW throne. A reign she inherited with pride and enthusiasm.

But now she was failing. Letting down the family, their history. No one in the Calhoun-Winthrop family had ever failed at this magnitude. *Especially* the women.

Great-grandmother launched CCW Cosmetics at the ripe age of twenty-five in 1934 after being fired from Elizabeth Arden for using products she'd developed at home on her clients.

She was scrappy, if not ribald, a trailblazer and entrepreneur. This was the kind of stock in Coral's bones. The kind that dared her to run out on her royal prince on their royal wedding day.

She took another sip of her soda. It was more than Great-grandma's gumption that prompted Coral to call off the marriage. It was fear. A holy, bone-rattling fear.

She squeezed the memory of that day from her mind, wary that the trembling, shivering, shaking she'd experienced would rev up again if she thought on it too long.

Returning to her desk, she sat in Granny's chair and reviewed the red numbers on the accounting report once more. Pink Coral was in deep, deep trouble.

"What's going on?"

Another swig of her warming cola and she opened another report. Where was the money going? Returns? Expenses? Promotions and marketing? Production?

The whole thing made her head hurt. This would be the fifth quarter in a row CCW reported a loss. Their stock prices would plummet.

Her assistant, Matt, set a stack on her desk. "These are the magazines where we advertised Pink Coral. You okay?"

She smiled. "I'm fine." He was a new hire and she liked him. He was efficient and hardworking, fresh out of college.

"Stop looking at the reports," he said.

"And bury my head in the sand?"

"Sure, why not. By the way, I blocked out your Monday nights. Every week until you tell me otherwise. And I created the contact list and food schedule you wanted. And I've ordered the appetizers for the four o'clock sit-down with the new hires."

"You're the best."

"Can I have a raise?"

"No."

"It was worth a shot." Matt grinned in a way that made her think he was flirting. More likely he'd grown comfortable with her. While charming, Matt was all business and showed no interest whatsoever in her celebrity life. Which was exactly why she hired him.

Blaire Boreland, CCW's aggressive, no-nonsense CEO, had wanted Coral to hire this silly girl from Smith who giggled every time Coral spoke to her. Coral could just see in her eyes, and in her demeanor, she was dying to ask about Prince Augustus.

When Matt had gone, Coral reviewed the profiles on the new hires. But it only tightened her anxiety. New people meant more expenses.

Like her grandmother and her grandmother's mother, she met with new employees within the first month to share with them the history, vision, and culture of the company. Then over the next six months she took each one to coffee and lunch.

Her grandmother didn't want to run a company with strangers and neither did she.

After familiarizing herself with the latest CCW family members, Coral reached for the top magazine and flipped through, looking for company ads. She found one for the charcoal mask and another for their new rejuvenation cream.

Nothing about Pink Coral. And where were the teen magazines?

A message popped up on her screen. The names and numbers of everyone in the society. And the food schedule.

Coral clicked on the group contact, a smile forming in some cavernous place in her soul.

Thank you.

She didn't know until last night she needed this oddball adventure. Until she locked eyes with Lexa and felt she'd found a friend. Until Chuck, who was like the Rock of Gibraltar with a John Wayne swagger, took command of the food. Until Jett asked about her Panicked Princess reputation, then politely backed off.

And dear Ed. *Lonely* came to mind, along with his face.

The same word described her. For whatever reason, by whatever force—and she had her suspicions—the five of them were pulled together for this *story society*, and she was grateful.

The group pulled her back into the land of the living. She'd been hiding from the press for so long, from her family and friends, she'd forgotten what it felt like to be herself, to let go, laugh, look someone in the eye.

Ed's gruff voice rambled through her. "I need help writing my memoir." She laughed to herself. He looked so comical, so serious and desperate.

Opening a new email, she sent the contact list and food schedule to Jett, Lexa, Chuck, and Ed.

Then she returned to the stack of magazines. She wasn't sure Monday night would be a place to sound out her company's problems, but it would be a place to forget. To focus on someone else for a few hours.

She finished her soda and tossed the magazines one by one into the trash. Not one advertised Pink Coral.

Well, really, this was all her fault. She let herself get distracted with a gorgeous boy, and look . . . Everything was falling apart.

"Coral." Dak Denton, her CFO, leaned into her office, laptop under his arm. "We're holding an emergency meeting in the executive conference room."

She sat forward. "Who is we?"

"Blaire, Drew, Sal, me. We've been going over the August report and, Coral, we can't afford another quarter of loss."

"I'm well aware of what we can afford."

Dak crossed the wide, airy office space to her desk. "You know what bothers me? How calm you seem about all this. Is there something you want to tell me, Coral? Tell all of us?"

She rose up, shoulders back, her pulse rising. "Just exactly what are you implying? I left my family company in your care while I was in Lauchtenland with Gus. I come home to find out we're bleeding money." She crossed her arms to steady her demeanor.

"We've known each other for a few years, Coral, so I'll just ask. Are you tanking the company on purpose? So you can take the money and *run*, so to speak?" Dak mirrored her stance. "Running seems to be your thing lately."

The power of his accusation forced her to step back. "I'll pretend you didn't ask that, Dak."

"Too bad, because I think we need an answer."

"Then brace yourself, because I was going to demand an accounting from you and Blaire."

"It's your company." Dak turned on his heel. "See you in the executive conference room. But be prepared." He paused at the doorway. "Pink Coral is tanking us. It's expensive to make and market. Sales are abysmal. We told you not to launch it. Told you it wasn't our brand. Not our demographic. But you insisted. Now we're paying the price."

"Then we're doing something very wrong. Preteen lip gloss is the easiest product in the world to make. Easiest way to break in to the market. And ours, by the way, has been three years in the making. It's why I hired Blaire." Coral unplugged her laptop, tucked it under her arm, and charged toward Dak and out the door. "If you say it's so expensive to make and market, show me."

If CCW couldn't make money in the gold-mine preteen-girl market—which pulled down some ten million a month in US sales alone—then they might as well close their doors.

When she arrived in the conference room, Blaire sat with Drew, director of marketing, and Sal, VP of sales.

Coral marched to the head of the table and addressed her CEO. "Is it true? Pink Coral is the problem?"

With a sigh, Blaire stood, the color on her high cheeks resonating with her fitted, dusty-rose suit.

"I'm afraid so, Coral."

"How?" Coral deflated and sank into the chair behind her. "Drew, are we actually advertising? I can't find an ad anywhere."

"Coral, listen to me," Blaire said. "The product isn't catching on. You hired me for my expertise, so listen to me." True. Blaire brought Glitter Girl from the bottom of the beauty pile and turned it into a multimillion-dollar company with nothing more than glam products—lip and cheek colors, eye shadow, and mascara. "Pink Coral is expensive to produce and—"

"It's lip gloss, Blaire. Oils with color and flavor poured into little tiny bottles."

"Yes, but the most expensive oils, pomegranate and aloe leaf oils, all organically sourced. Don't get me started on the pigments and custom bottles."

"We ran the numbers. We should be killing it." She looked at Sal. "Did you allocate the space at the drug and department stores?" They'd had special racks and signs designed to replace the product they were phasing out.

"We followed the plan, Coral. But some stores aren't phasing out the compact powder yet. We're working on it."

"The marketing has been expensive." Drew turned his laptop toward her and pointed to the spreadsheet on the screen. "We're spending a lot of time developing a campaign unique from our competitors."

"How hard is it? Preteen girls." She sounded like a broken record. "Show a group of girls at a slumber party with shiny lips and we're in."

He scowled. "It's not that simple."

She pulled her chair forward. "Then enlighten me. Tell me how complicated it is to advertise the product I spent three years developing."

"Coral," Blaire said, her soft voice one of a friend. "I'm so sorry. I know this was your baby, but I'm not sure it's working. It's not really our brand."

She blinked back a surge of tears. Her first product launch after taking over was failing. Worse, her team wasn't with her.

"But I think we can salvage it," Sal said. "Let's give it time."

"I'm not sure we have time, Sal." Coral leaned forward, face in her hands.

This was her fault. Love, then heartbreak, distracted her from her priorities. Then she launched the product when she was in a dark, wounded place.

She needed to find her *story*. She wasn't the same woman who met and fell in love with a prince. The journey of leaving him had changed her.

And she was still exploring that road. She lifted her head to the tight, concerned expressions of her executive team.

"All right, let's get to work. Figure this out."

One thing for sure: she wouldn't find her way by quitting and giving up.

LEXA

Another Friday night. Same routine. But she didn't mind. Really.

Schlepping in her comfy sweats past the open door of her apartment, her hair pulled back in a ponytail and her face smothered in a CCW charcoal mask, Lexa settled in her chair and bit into a stacked, juicy ZB Burger.

She'd brought one home from the test kitchen along with truffle fries. *So good.*

With an exhale, she ate and willed the strain of the week to slip away.

She was glad to see the back of it, as well as Zane. He'd been a grouch, anxious, nervous, asking her a bazillion questions about the Gottlieb Gala.

It wasn't like him.

Reaching for her phone, she opened Skipper's text from last week for a laugh. She could see her sister's wide, blue-eyed expression with each line.

Jett! You saw Jett!!!! Did you sock him in the gut? I'd have kicked him in the knee, then the other knee!

Coral Winthrop? The Panicked Princess. Forget CCW. You met an almost-princess. OMG!!!!! What's she like? Tell me everything, I mean everything.

By the way, rocket launch next week. I'm in the command center! I'm trying to be cool but I want to jump up and down. I saw the room where the women from Hidden Figures worked. I was so grateful they paved a path for me.

Jett, really?! I'm still wrapping my brain around it. What
the heck?

What's a story society?

I wish you were going to Zambia with me. Forget Zaney
Days. Are you telling me Zane can't run it by himself? Or
the team? I'm sure you have it all organized. All they have
to do is follow your checklist.

You said Jett looked good. What does THAT mean? Do
you still have the hots for him?

Lexa snickered as she continued to scroll through. Reading this,
no one would know Skipper was a math genius. Graduated summa
cum laude from Florida Tech with no fewer than ten engineering
and tech companies offering her high five-figure salaries and signing
bonuses.

She set her phone on silent, tossed it to the desk, then finished
her burger with another rerun of *Frasier.*

Once again, she'd failed to approach Zane about the CEO job.
But she resolved to next week. After tonight's gala, after Sabrina
returned to Hollywood. No more messing around.

If Skipper could help launch a rocket into space, then Lexa could
ask her boss for the promotion she deserved.

Just this week she lunched with a visiting board member, met
with the quarterly auditors, and reworked the employee handbook
with Lois, the human resources manager.

She picked up Zane's tux from the cleaners, printed his speech
on notecards, tested the final mini burgers recipe her boss was surprising the gala guests with, ordered flowers for Sabrina's room, and
purchased a diamond bracelet for the starlet at Zane's request.

The busywork exhausted her but also kept her thoughts from
Jett and Monday night. She'd decided to go back, then questioned

her sanity. Why would she want to spend any amount of time with
her ex-husband?

He'd talked to her more the last two Monday nights than he did
the last three months of their marriage.

She was on the fence all week about returning until Coral texted
her this morning. *The* Coral Winthrop.

> I could handle Jett and the old man by myself but throw in
> the big guy and I'm doomed. Say you're coming Monday.

Lexa caved. The popular girl liked her.

> See you then.

Then a beauty box arrived from CCW this afternoon. Lexa
accused her of bribery.

> Yes, yes, I am. Making sure you don't change your mind.
> Aren't you curious as to what brought us together?

> Actually, I am.

She'd just finished her burger when she heard sounds of Abby
in the hall. She expected to see her pretty face peer around the door.
Who would she be tonight? Audrey Hepburn for a fifties party?

If Abby invited her, Lexa determined she'd wash the mud off her
face and join the fun. Why not?

But the sound passed without pause at her place. She munched
on the last of her fries, then carried the trash to the kitchen.

"Lex?"

She came around the kitchen doorway to see Zane rushing into
the living room dressed in his custom Armani tux and Bruno Magli
shoes, his hair trimmed and styled, his green eyes wild with panic.

"What are you doing here?" She tugged the hem of her short

T-shirt over the low-riding waist of her sweats. "You're supposed to be at the Gottlieb Gala."

"I've been blowing up your phone. Why haven't you answered?" A frown crushed his clean-shaven, freshly exfoliated face as he barged past her and retrieved her phone from the desk. "Look, missed call, missed call. Text after text."

"I turn it off while I'm eating." Lexa slammed the front door closed and snatched the device from his hand. "What's going on?"

"Sabrina is not at her hotel nor is she answering her phone." Zane paced, pointing to Lexa's device. "Did she call you?"

"What do you mean she's not at her hotel?" She scanned her phone calls and texts. All from Zane. "There's nothing from her. Zane, she's at her hotel. I called and checked this afternoon."

"Well she's not there now. I went to meet her and she never answered her door. When I asked the front desk if June Cleaver had checked in she said no." Zane dropped to the red chair and bounced up again. "June Cleaver is right, isn't it? Her alias?"

"I don't know of another one." Though how many people were named June Cleaver? The name alone screamed "celebrity alias."

Lexa called the starlet's number. After several rings, voice mail came on. So she tried Sabrina's manager, who was also not picking up.

"I don't know what to tell you, Zane. She'll show up. Go to the gala. You don't want to be too late. I'll keep trying Sabrina. She's probably already at the Starlight Room causing a stir."

"We were supposed to go in together, make an entrance." He spread his arms wide as if to demonstrate. "Her idea, not mine."

"Then go to the Waldorf. Go to her room."

"I'm telling you, she's not there." He brushed past her and opened her wardrobe. "Are your gowns in here?"

"Gowns? Zane, what are you doing?"

He riffled through her clothes. Lexa slammed the opened door against his hand. He jerked back, bumping into the wall.

"If you think I'm walking into that gala alone, you've got another thing coming." Zane yanked out her only gown. Blue silk. Years old. The one she wore for a fancy benefit at the college right after Jett joined the faculty. "Wash that stuff off your face. What is it anyway?"

"Charcoal mask." She returned the gown to the wardrobe. "I'm not going anywhere. Sabrina will show up."

"A charcoal mask? Are you Cinderella? And you are going with me to the *ball*."

"What are you? The wicked stepmother?" She pushed him toward the exit. "See you. Your princess will arrive. And your public awaits."

"How do you figure I'm the wicked stepmother? I'm the handsome prince."

"Fine, you're the handsome prince. Bye. Go find your Cinderella."

"She stood me up." He rolled away from the door and back into the center of the room. "I knew she would. I *knew* it."

"She did not stand you up. You just saw her in LA two weeks ago."

"I'm a geeky farm boy from Nebraska. What would a woman like Sabrina want with me?"

"I've been asking myself that for months now."

He spun around. "Really?"

"No, Zane, I'm teasing. You're a great catch. Sweet, successful, decent looking." She grabbed him by the shoulders. "Get ahold of yourself. You're not a geeky high school kid anymore. Women find you powerful and attractive. If you walk in the gala alone tonight every single woman there will be at your side in five seconds flat."

"What will it take?" He yanked his money clip from his inside jacket pocket. "I've got five hundred here, but I can stop at an ATM on the way. How about a thousand bucks?"

"You want to buy me?" She shoved away his money hand. "I don't even want to think of the implications."

"Buy you? No. Hire you. For the evening. As my employee. Nothing underhanded or *weird*." He made a face. "Think of it as a bonus. Please come with me."

"Zane, this is ridiculous. I'm not—" *Wait, Lexa, girl, hold up. He's in a bind. At your mercy.* "Well, there is one thing I want. I'll go if you meet my condition."

"Help you chisel that stuff off your face?" He motioned with his hand toward her hair. "Can you do anything with that mess?"

"Make me CEO of ZB Enterprises."

He stepped back with a long, curious expression. "Just like that? Right now?"

"Just like that."

Over the years, she'd learned to manage her feelings about Zane's subtle ways of dismissing her. It used to drive Jett nuts.

"Quit," he'd say. "Find someone who values and appreciates you."

But she loved ZB. She couldn't help it. She was loyal and devoted to her job. And when her life was falling apart, ZB was her sanctuary.

"All right. CEO, huh? I can put your name in the hopper."

"I've already applied, and as far as I know, I'm the only one. You didn't make the opening public yet, did you?"

"I'll get around to it." Zane turned his back and faced the window. "If I hire you, I'd first have to put you through the entire hiring process. You should know how it works. You wrote the book."

"Fine, put me through the process." She was that confident. "But, Zane, ultimately, *you* are the book. As president, owner, and senior board member you can do whatever you want."

"Fair enough. But let's go by the book. You'll interview like any other candidate."

"There are none."

"There will be." He flashed his charming and genuine grin. "I guess we always knew this day was coming. Now will you go with me?" He walked over to her wardrobe again.

"We can put Quent in my job."

"Will these work with the dress?" He held up a pair of slingbacks.

She took the shoes from him. "Look me in the eye and tell me the job is mine."

"The job is yours. By way of the process."

"Fine, by way of the process, but you and everyone else knows

I'm already doing the job. All you have to do is run my new salary and bonus by the board."

"All right, how fast can you get ready?" He glanced at his watch. "I'll call Clark and tell him to keep circling for what, ten minutes? Lexa, why are you stalling? Go, wash, polish, shine."

She patted his shoulder. "Thank you. For the job. I won't let you down."

"You never do. Now go. Hurry. Clark, this is Zane . . ."

The only way to get this done quick was to jump in the shower. She hollered for Zane to knock on the door across the hall to see if Abby was home.

"Tell her I need help with my hair."

But Abby was gone. So she dried her hair as best she could and hoped the thick, wild, and wavy look was in.

She wiggled into her dress, stashed a lipstick and credit card in a blue pearl clutch, and grabbed her makeup bag.

"I'll polish in the car."

By the time they arrived at the Waldorf Astoria and rode the elevator to the Starlight Room, reality had settled in. She'd done it. Asked Zane for the job and he said yes.

For the first time in a long time, she felt sure about her future.

Chapter 9

JETT

The only thing worse than donning a rented tux on a Friday night so he could rub elbows with Manhattan's rich and infamous was inviting a last-minute date.

In a moment of weakness Thursday morning he invited the lively, energetic Courtney McGuire as they worked out in the apartment gym.

Outside of the weight room, they had nothing in common. Jett discovered the cold truth before they rode the elevator up to the Starlight Room.

She was sweet and cute and filled out her soft yellow gown with spectacular curves and disappeared the moment they entered the room. Jett grabbed a water from the ice-filled barrels along the wall and wished he was home reading.

Elijah Roth sat on the dais with a group of important-looking people. Jett would make his way over in a few minutes, do the appropriate amount of glad-handing, and leave.

"You should've worn your ratty old sweater and high-tops." A familiar feminine voice floated over his shoulder. Coral Winthrop stood behind him in a dark-green, strapless gown with a wide skirt. A distinguished gray-haired man—who wore the air of money and sophistication—hovered off her left shoulder.

"You think they'd have let me in?"

"Considering you'd have looked homeless, yes. These people thrive on those sort of photo ops."

"These people?" He grinned. "Aren't you one of *these* people?"

"Moneyed. Perhaps. Phony? No. Jett Wilder, may I present my father, Eric Winthrop III."

The men shook hands and exchanged genuine pleasantries.

Then the elder Winthrop spotted someone across the room and excused himself.

"This is weird," Jett said. "Seeing you outside the society. Do we talk about how we met?"

"Is it a secret?" Coral reached for a champagne flute floating past on a silver tray upheld by a black-tie server.

"Not a secret, but rather a mystery."

"Then we say we're friends. No further explanation needed."

Jett peered into her eyes. If he were assigned to describe her, he'd declare her a work of art, sculpted with regal features.

Yet beneath her beauty breathed a hurt, wounded, if not confused, woman. He saw it behind her made-up eyes.

"I'd like to be friends," he said.

She tapped his arm with her elbow. "Good, then you can tell me what happened between you and Lexa."

"Only if you'll tell me what happened with Prince Pompous."

"So, how about those New York Giants?"

He chuckled. "As I thought."

"Can we still be friends?" She sipped her champagne as she gazed toward the guests mingling about the ballroom.

"I suppose we have to be, since we're in some sort of society together."

"Do you still love her?"

"How about those Giants?"

She turned to Jett. "I'm serious. Do you?"

"Coral, it doesn't matter. We're divorced. Why do you want to know?"

"Because I think she still loves you."

"She walked out first." He frowned, drawing his lips into a tight line. Only took her ten seconds to draw a confession from him.

Her smile invited him further into friendship. "For the record, I loved Gus. But something changed."

"Must have been a huge something to make you leave him at the altar."

"Indeed. It was a God-size something."

For the next few minutes, she pointed out various New York socialites who tipped back their heads with practiced laughter and moved about in flawless choreography. She told Jett their stories.

"You know your favorite author, GPR, would've dined and danced in the original hotel, perhaps the Octagon Room, and observed the people he wrote about in his novels." Coral swept her hand toward the gathering. "Behold, *your* people. Your society."

"I write about people who travel through space and live on Mars."

"But the interface among breathing beings is largely the same. We want to be seen, heard, and loved. And look at Missy Adock's dress. If that wouldn't survive a landing on Mars I don't know what would."

Jett laughed. "Come on. The food tables have opened up." He offered his arm and buffered his new friend through the crowd of the 1920s art deco room with its high ceiling and swaths of golden light.

Taking a thin white china plate, Jett moved down the line, discussing the food options with Coral, when Courtney tapped him on the shoulder.

"Jett, this is Pete." A stocky, wide-faced man stood next to her. "We went to NYU together. We're out of here. Do you mind?"

"Um, no, not at all." He didn't think she'd abandon him quite so fast. "Thanks for—" She disappeared into the crowd before he finished his sentiment.

"Your date?" Coral said.

"Lives in my building." Jett considered how to add another layer of prime rib to his plate. "We see each other in the gym. Barely know her."

"Why *are* you here if you don't want to be?"

"University business." He pointed to the dais with his fork, his mouth watering for a bite of the tender beef. "I'm supposed to hobnob with Elijah Roth. He and the Roth Foundation are giving the college a bunch of money for the Gordon Phipps Roth School of Literature."

"You sound dubious." Coral popped a bacon-wrapped scallop into her mouth.

"Not dubious. Part of his generosity is tied to my published dissertation exonerating GPR of recent rumors."

"What rumors?"

Jett really didn't want to talk about it. He wanted to try the lean, juicy beef. "Long story, but yeah, I think my research proves GPR was the genius we all believe and want him to be."

He tried to cut his meat with a fork but found the task impossible while standing. He stabbed the large slice and took a bite. "Care to sit?"

"My father's table is by the dais. Won't you join—" Coral leaned forward, staring at the door. "I see the guest of honor has arrived. Zane Breas." She peered up at Jett. "Lexa is with him. Did you know she was coming?"

Jett pushed through the cluster gathered by the food table to see Lexa, dressed in the blue gown she bought for their first formal event at the college, striding in on the arm of the arrogant ZB.

"No, I didn't." The bite of prime rib he'd just tasted turned sour on his tongue.

"She looks beautiful, doesn't she?" Coral said.

"How about those Giants?"

⁂

LEXA

The Starlight Room atop the Waldorf Astoria was a stunning tribute to the fabulous art deco of the past with stained glass on the walls, dark glass on the ceiling, and an etched, patterned carpet that matched the engravings of the upper balcony.

Entering on Zane's arm, a thrill zipped through her. The people parted for them as he moved toward the dais, cameras flashing.

She'd seen Zane's pop-culture rise over the years. Experienced it in small portions during Zaney Days, but never in an exclusive, diamond-studded environment like this. It gave her chills.

He was the man of the hour. The Gottlieb Gala's Young Entrepreneur of the Year.

"I'm a mess," she said under her breath, patting down her frizzing hair.

"You're fine, Lex. Fine." But Zane never looked. Instead, he smiled for a news camera.

Lexa tipped her frown over for the panning camera. She was surrounded by know-it-alls and know-everyones gathered in circles of four and five, retrieving champagne from polished silver trays.

In the background somewhere, the orchestra played chamber music, warming up the room for the dances.

On the dais, Zane was greeted by distinguished men and diamond-crusted women.

"May I introduce Lexa Wilder. Lexa, this is the erudite George Gottlieb, great-great-great-grandson of Franz Gottlieb, a Gilded Age entrepreneur who became rich enough to join Mrs. Astor's Four Hundred."

"But you can call me George." He took her hand with a slight bow. "Welcome." He turned to Zane. "I was beginning to think you'd forgotten us."

He introduced his wife, Shera, along with their daughter, Lyla, and her husband, Rick. Next to Rick was the foundation chairman, Ralph Masker, and his wife, Diana.

"Please, won't you join us?" Shera gestured to the empty chairs on the far side of the table. "Don't be offended Lea, but I was looking forward to meeting Sabrina Fox."

"It's Lexa, and none taken." She sat next to Zane and tried to make her eyes twinkle. Mom claimed she had the gift, but Lexa wasn't exactly sure how to turn it on.

"Shera, really," George said, motioning to the table's devoted server. "Hank, champagne for our honored guests."

While George detailed the origins of the foundation and how

honored they were to give Zane their first Young Entrepreneur award, Hank brought two tall flutes of champagne along with a platter of ZB Mini Burgers.

Lexa squeezed Zane's arm. They were perfect. This event would be their first unofficial test market. They were made with lean organic beef and priced right, and she imagined those watching their calories yet wanting a burger now and then would gravitate toward a five-bite-size gourmet treat.

"ZB Burgers are a weekly meal in our home," Shera said. When she reached for a mini burger, the diamond cuff around her wrist spiraled a kaleidoscope over the white linen tablecloth.

"Maybe I should use you for advertising, Shera," Zane said.

Her expression perked up. "Really?"

Well, he'd done it now. Lexa gazed toward the ballroom trying not to laugh as Zane backpedaled. Their whole brand was good food for everyday folk. Shera was far from everyday folk.

"How long have you two been dating?" The question came from the soft-spoken Diana Masker.

"Dating? Oh, no, we're not romantically involved." Lexa leaned away from Zane. "I've worked for ZB since the beginning. I'm the new CEO."

Zane sputtered a bit of champagne onto the pristine tablecloth. "Nothing official yet, but Lexa wears a lot of hats for us. Very talented."

"CEO? Why not MRS?" Shera tossed a naughty glance at her husband. "George was looking for an assistant when we met, but I soon proved I had skills not listed in the job description."

Lexa choked on her mini burger. "We're just . . . friends. I mean, he's my boss. Have you seen Sabrina's latest movie? I hear it's spectacular."

"I'm dying to see it. Zane, what happed to Sabrina?" Shera fashioned a disappointed pout.

"Unable to make it. She sends her regrets."

Just then the lights dimmed as the orchestra struck up the first waltz. Couples moved through the glitter ball's rainbow of colors to the dance floor.

"Shera, would you care to dance?" George offered his wife his hand and escorted her from the dais.

Ralph and Diana followed, leaving Lexa alone with Zane.

"Don't do that again, Lexa." He dropped his napkin on the table with attitude.

"Why not? You're not breaking your promise already, are you?"

"You put me on the spot. Besides, what if it gets out before we're ready to announce? Shera Gottlieb is a known gossip. And she's a bullhorn to every news outlet in the city."

"Like she cares I'm the new CEO of ZB Enterprises. She called me Lea when we met. She'll forget all about me before the night is over."

"Still, let's just keep our bargain to ourselves for now." He reached for his water goblet. "Is being my assistant so horrible?"

"No, but I'm made for more. Zane, let someone else make your hair and spa appointments, order flowers for your girlfriend. Let me officially run the departments, review the budget, set vision and direction with you. I'm doing it already."

"I know, and I'm grateful." He covered her hand with his and offered a wobbling smile. "Guess I can't imagine anyone else knowing the intimate details of my life. I like seeing you at the desk outside my office."

"I'll still be working with you but, Zane, for the first time in my life, I'm free to dream the dreams I want to dream. I'm not being lugged around the world with my family or following my husband. I know it's a big leap to make your executive assistant the head of the company, but I've been doing the work and—"

"Come on." He grabbed her hand. "Let's dance."

She hesitated. He'd cut her off. "I think I'll just sit here."

He pulled her to her feet. "Forget work for one night, girl." His Nebraskan intonations flavored his words. "We're at a fancy-schmancy gala. In my honor. Let's cut loose and have fun. Maybe show 'em how to do the two-step. We'll talk shop on Monday."

On the dance floor, he stepped around to the music, filling her senses with Lagerfeld.

"Thank you for pulling yourself together for me, Lex." He smiled down at her. "I never said you look beautiful, but you do."

"You're welcome. But don't forget our—"

"That Shera's a piece of work, isn't she?" he said.

Message received. Let it go. For now. "George seems to like her."

Zane peered down at her. "We never crossed any lines, did we?"

"I was married, remember?"

"Think we'd make a good couple?" Zane led her through the box step with ease. He was a line dancer and two-stepper from his childhood.

"What?" She stiffened. "No. I mean . . . Zane, you shouldn't be asking me that. We're coworkers, professionals. You're my boss."

"According to Shera, MRS outranks CEO." His laugh tried to draw her into his joke.

"Don't joke about stuff like that, Zane." Lexa stepped out of his arms. "Or anything romantic between us. Either hire me or cut me loose."

"Lexa, chill, will you? Geez. I'm not proposing anything indecent. Just noting how well we get along."

Through the next song she relaxed a little bit. *Just enjoy the evening.* The Starlight Room was spectacular, and being with the guest of honor afforded her some privileges.

The mayor paused to greet them both, as did the star center for the Knicks.

"I'm kind of glad Sabrina stood me up," he said, turning her to the music. "You should've been here with me all along. You've been a big part of ZB's success. And don't say that's why you should be CEO."

She laughed. "You just said it for me."

"Those early days were wild, weren't they? We just made the grand opening of the Forty-Sixth Street store. Thanks to you."

"It was fun."

When she looked up he was studying her. "Say, Lexa—"

Blame it on the music, the dancing, the glittering atmosphere, but the air between them popped and sparkled.

Lexa was suddenly warm and weak-kneed. "Zane, let's not get carried away."

But his head tipped toward her and . . . Was he going to kiss her? She pressed her hand against his chest. "Shew, I'm beat. Shall we go back to the dais?"

He cleared his throat with a nod. "I could use some champagne. Do you think everyone liked the mini burgers?"

"I've heard nothing but praise." So the awkward moment passed.

As they reached the dais, a commotion rose in the back, by the doors. Oohs and aahs mingled with muffled squeals.

The dancers moved to one side as the orchestra continued to play. Zane instantly released Lexa.

"I don't believe it."

"What's going on?" Lexa peered through the strands of white light streaming from the crystal chandeliers and knew her answer.

Sabrina. She was Moses parting the Red Sea, slinking with cat-like moves toward the dais.

Zane met her in the middle of the floor and scooped her up and kissed her, long and succulent. The gala guests gushed and gasped.

Another waltz began. Zane swung Sabrina around in his arms without missing a beat.

Lexa made her way to her chair. Should she stay or make an excuse and go home? She'd told Zane Sabrina would show up sooner or later.

"Aren't they a gorgeous couple?" Shera came around to sit in Zane's chair. "I hope you're all right with this. Are you in love with him?"

"No, I'm not. And I'm glad Sabrina came." Go. She should really go. Let Zane have his night with Sabrina. "It was lovely to meet you."

"You're not leaving, are you?" Shera pointed to the clutch in Lexa's hand. "Stay. The fun is just beginning. Zane hasn't received his award yet. Or given his speech."

"I wrote his speech, so I know what he's going to say. I was at home in my sweats when he came for me. I think I'd like to go back there, get out of these uncomfortable shoes. Good night, Shera. Thank you for your hospitality."

Just as Lexa made the dais steps, a breathless Zane arrived with the stunning Sabrina.

"Lex, need you to do me a favor," he said.

"So good to see you." Sabrina stepped up on the dais and air kissed Lexa's cheeks. "You would not *believe* the ordeal I had getting here." She hooked her hand in Lexa's and dragged her back to the table, drinking the last of the champagne in Zane's glass. Not that she knew it was Zane's. "But I'm here now, ready to celebrate this guy." She pressed her red full lips on his. "So proud of you, ZB, my bright, shining star."

"Good to see you, Sabrina. I'll say good night."

Once she set her mind on her cozy apartment, comfy sweats, and yes, a pint of ice cream, Lexa almost ached to get to it. She was grateful to be relieved of her duty.

"Wait, Lexa, you haven't heard about my ordeal. It started when the shoot ran late." Sabrina patted the upholstered chair next to hers. "We were filming at midnight. I was exhausted."

She missed her flight. Her phone wasn't charged so she couldn't call anyone. (Lexa didn't ask the obvious question, "Why not borrow someone else's phone?" and just went with it.) Her second flight routed through Dallas, where a lightning storm grounded them for three hours.

"Zane told me how frantic you were when I didn't show. I'm so touched." She batted her eyes at him. "To top it off, the hotel gave away my reservation. Unbelievable."

Oh, the inhumanity. Sabrina had to sit in the VIP lounge to charge her phone while the manager talked to her assistant.

"Finally, I gave up on my room, dressed in the lounge, and joined the party." She held Zane's hand. "I texted you, but you never responded."

"All that matters is you're here now." He kissed her again, then leaned toward Lexa. "I need you to go down to the desk and straighten out Sabrina's room situation. Her assistant got nowhere. They still don't have a room for her."

"You can't be serious."

"Lex, just do it. She can't sleep in the hallway."

"If her assistant couldn't fix it, what am I supposed to do?"

"She's a dimwit. I don't know why I keep her on. Lex, could you? Please?" Sabrina batted her long lashes. The gesture merely strengthened Lexa's resolve. "Work your magic for me."

It was one thing to be his stand-in date. It was another to revert back to his assistant after all she went through to fit into her dress, shower and wash her hair, and walk out the door in less than fifteen minutes.

"This Cinderella has no glass slipper, sorry. If there's no room, she can stay in your guest room, Zane." She gathered her clutch. "Good night."

"Lex, wait. She can't stay at my place. We're not *there* yet, if you know what I mean."

"There are hundreds of hotels in the city. Have her assistant book a room at one of them."

"Lexa, you know the hotels in the city. Can't you—"

"Congrats on your award, Zane."

The elevator doors closed and she punched the down button, getting madder by the moment. She might work for him, but she also had feelings. No one appreciated being thrown aside and then turned into a servant.

She collapsed against the elevator wall, hands clenched around her bag. The nerve of him. Of her.

Come Monday morning, she'd have a few words for him. For now, she steamed.

Dad always said if she didn't like a situation, then she should change it. She'd spent most of her life trying to fit into other people's worlds. High school friends', college roommates', her husband's. Zane's.

If Zane wouldn't recognize her contribution to the company with a promotion, maybe it was time for her to move on, get the experience she needed elsewhere so she could have the career she wanted.

As she stepped out of the elevator, her heel caught in the door. She stumbled and landed against the wall, then retrieved her shoe and slid her foot underneath the straps.

Aiming for the elegant, glass-door exit, Lexa moved past the doorman to the curb. "Taxi."

As the yellow cab approached, she stepped into the street, only her heel snagged a crack in the concrete. Her forward motion halted as her foot twisted, tossing her toward the pavement.

Arms flailing, she tried to stop herself on the back of a waiting limo. But it pulled away and she fell, down, down, down, through a wash of headlights, and landed with her right arm extended on the hard, unyielding pavement.

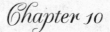
Chapter 10

JETT

He dozed in the chair at the foot of her hospital bed, jerking awake when his head bobbed too far forward.

Adjusting his position, he pillowed his head against his arm and lingered a few feet above a shallow sleep.

"What's going on?" Lexa's voice cracked as she stirred, trying to sit up.

"I'm here." He stretched the kink from his back and moved beside her. Surrounded by white sheets, she appeared pale and ghostly, except for the hideous, creeping black-and-blue bruise on the side of her face. "How are you feeling?"

"Jett? What are you doing here?" She fell back against the pillows. "My head." She strained to raise her right arm, struggled, pushed herself back up with her left hand. "What's going on? Where am I?" Panic and confusion delivered her simple question. And she was loaded with pain meds.

He'd witnessed the whole thing. Her exit from the Starlight Room, her argument with Zane, her hurried walk through the lobby. He'd just made the doors when he saw her fall.

"Mount Sinai."

"Hospital?" Her pale lips quivered. "What happened? What time is it?"

He glanced at his watch. "Ten a.m. You were hit by a car, Lex."

"I what?"

This time when she tried to sit up, Jett raised the mattress with the remote. "You hit your head on the street. You broke your humerus. Your right arm is strapped to your side in a long arm cast."

Sitting at a seventy-degree angle, Lexa was able to confirm his report. "I remember leaving the gala and then—"

"You tripped. Not sure how, but you tumbled into the street just as a taxi was pulling out. You landed with your right arm out." He demonstrated, stiffening his arm and miming a fall.

"Can I go home?"

"We're waiting for the doctor. It's Sunday, so everything moves a bit slower."

"Sunday? What happened to Saturday?" She spoke slow and slurred.

"You slept. You have a pretty nasty concussion, Lexa." Jett pressed the call button beside her bed. The nurse had told him to notify her when she woke up. "And a pretty nasty bruise on the side of your face."

"That explains the percussion section playing in my ears." She sat forward, hand over her lips. "I feel nauseous."

"I called for the nurse." Jett glanced around for a basin or something to catch her distress, should she need to throw up.

But Lexa sat back with a deep breath. "I'm thirsty."

Jett filled a glass from the dispenser in the room and held it to her lips. When she'd taken a long drink, she squinted at him, shielding her eyes from the light creeping around the edges of the window shades. "You're still in your tux."

"It's my new thing, spending all night in a tux." The nurse entered with the doctor following.

"Your new thing?"

"Bad joke. Forget it."

"Morning, Lexa, I'm Dr. Haft." A dark-skinned, dark-eyed man with intense confidence bent over the bed and fired a light in Lexa's eyes. She groaned and turned away. "You're at Mount Sinai. Can you squeeze my hand?" He gripped her good, left hand. "Good. You have a significant concussion. Can you tell me your whole name?"

"Lexa Leann Prescott Wilder."

Wilder. Jett backed away as the staff poked and prodded his wife. *Ex-wife.* Hearing her say her name, his name, plumbed a buried delight. She still had his name.

Seeing her fall face first in front of the cab nearly stopped his heart. He ran to try to catch her, but he was too far back.

When she hit, he yelled for the doorman to call 9-1-1, then sat in the street, protecting her, whispering she was going to be all right, until help arrived.

He intended to go home once they admitted her, but she seemed so vulnerable and alone. He used her phone to call Skipper, let her know what happened.

"Do I need to come up there?"

"Not yet. She can talk to you when she's better."

"Thanks, Jett. I take back the mean things I said about you."

"Can you let your parents know?"

"Yeah, and please, call if anything changes."

Then the admitting nurse kept asking him all sorts of questions, things a husband would know, and he did his best.

By then it was one in the morning and he was too tired to leave.

"You're a lucky girl," the doctor said. "Running into the street without looking usually has disastrous results."

"Actually, she tripped," Jett said.

"You're the husband?" Dr. Haft motioned him forward. "You're going to have to take good care of her. She's going to need a lot of help for the next three to four weeks. She'll be in a cast for six but the last two won't be as intense. I'm sending her home this afternoon but with strict concussion protocol. She needs to be in a calm, quiet place with little to no physical activity." He grinned at Jett. "Take it easy with sex. Wait a few days, a week."

"Yeah, sure, or longer." A lot longer.

Lexa tried to sit up. "Wait, Dr. Hath, Jett is—"

"Let's talk about your arm. The break was clean but severe." Dr. Hath fired off a list of instructions. "I want you resting, no jostling about. I want you off work until I know the bone has set properly and will heal on its own without surgery. Any kind of bumping or minor trauma can cause it to misalign. You'll need to stay away from crowded streets and subways." He flipped

Jett a card. "Can you help her with bathing, dressing, cutting up her food?"

"Um, sure." Bathing?

"Call my office to set up an appointment for a concussion assessment in a week. Number's on the card. I'll check that bruise too." He lightly fingered the brownish-black area around her eye and down her cheek. "In three weeks, I want to examine the arm." He leaned close to Lexa. "A humerus break is very painful. Do not overdo it. Rest. Heal. Let this guy take care of you."

"Dr. Hath, Jett is—"

"Did we give you a pain script, Jett?" He took a pad from his pocket. "Where can we call this in for you?"

"The Greenwich Pharmacy."

He handed the prescription to the nurse, then turned back to his patient. "I'm serious about taking caution with your arm, Lexa. You look as if you don't believe me. A slight bump can cause a mountain of pain. If you fall or trip again, you could inflict greater damage." He clapped Jett's shoulder. "You're her husband. Will she listen to you?"

"He's not my husband." She finally said it.

Jett winced. "I used to be."

"I see. Do you feel safe with him?"

Lexa eyed him around the doctor and his pulse did a one-two. "Yes."

"Can he support you?"

"I can." He fielded that one.

"Is everything okay in your life, Lexa? I can ask Jett to step out if you need to talk."

"Everything is fine. But I can take care of myself."

"When you're healthy, yes. But you're not right now. Trust me, you're not going to be able to manage alone. If Jett's not an option, then who should we call?"

She pressed the fingers of her good hand to her forehead, wincing. "My sister is in Florida."

"I can call her, Lexa," Jett said.

"No, don't. She's supposed to be in the command center for the next rocket launch. She can't be here for three weeks."

"Your parents?" Dr. Haft said.

"They're in Zambia."

"Jett, can you give us a minute?" Dr. Hath pulled a chair around, sat, and gently rested his hand on Lexa's good arm.

Jett exited without a word and leaned against the cool wall just outside the door. Was he really so horrible that she didn't want his help?

She had a good friend, Maria, but he wasn't sure how much help she could be. Most of her friends had been *his* friends, and she lost them in the divorce.

In short order Dr. Haft entered the hall. "She's fine going home with you." He glanced at his watch. "I'll be back this afternoon to check on her before you go."

Jett nodded. Back in the room, Lexa stared toward the window, a tear glistening on her cheek.

"I'm sorry," she said. "I know this is inconvenient."

"Forget it. You'd do the same for me."

"Would I?" She dabbed her cheek with a wadded tissue. "The worst part is I realized I've worked so much I don't really have any friends. I'm twenty-nine and I can't think of one good friend to call."

"What about Maria?"

"She got married and moved to White Plains. They had twins in June."

"I told them I was your husband so I could stay with you." Jett remained at the foot of the bed, hands in his pockets. He'd owe late fees on his tux rental.

"You didn't have to stay." Eyes closed, her emotions walled, he tried to listen between the lines. Even in pain, she held him at arm's length.

She once claimed she'd learned to detach due to all the moving she'd done as a kid. But Jett suspected deeper fears and wounds.

"The doctor said he'd release you this afternoon." He checked his watch again. "If I leave now I can get cleaned up and run by your place, pick up a few things. Would you mind?"

For a good minute she didn't answer. "My toiletries are in the cabinet below the sink. There's a travel case in the wardrobe." She glanced at the cast. "I don't know what I'm going to wear but bring what you can."

"We'll figure it out. You can have the master bed and bath. I'll sleep in the guest room." He reached for her clutch. "Keys in here?"

When she nodded he slipped them into his pocket. "I'll Google some ideas and tips on how to live through this."

A shiny stream trickled down her cheek. "Why are you being so nice, Jett?"

He shrugged. "We're divorced, not enemies."

She sniffed and wiped her cheek with the back of her hand. "I promise I'll be out of your place as soon as I can shower on my own."

On the street, he waited for an Uber ride, trying to imagine the days and weeks ahead.

Never in his wildest imaginings had he seen Lexa crossing his threshold again, much less living with him. Even less that she would have to depend on him.

He'd be helping her bathe and dress, eat, wash her clothes, tie her shoes, brush her hair.

Maybe in one of those awkward yet intimate moments, he might be able to ask a two-year-old nagging question.

Lexa, what happened to us?

CORAL

"Jett, you can't be serious. She was hit by a cab?"

Coral had arrived at the Fifth Avenue Literary Society Library Monday evening with an order of Virgil's Real BBQ and a bottle of Sangiovese.

On this, their third gathering, she was beginning to consider this adventure more than haphazard. But why?

And by whom? She had her suspicions. Someone she'd been getting to know recently.

Already she was starting to see the society members as possible friends. Not deep, heart-to-heart, tell-it-all friends. Not yet anyway. But perhaps . . .

At the gala she'd wanted to speak with Lexa, but Dad involved her in an intense political discussion with Brad Bishop, an up-and-coming New York City political candidate. When she freed herself of that quagmire, her mother, who'd arrived fashionably late, dragged her across the Starlight Room to meet the single son of a friend.

By the time she extracted herself from Sebastian William Ludwig V, Sabrina had arrived and Zane was accepting his award with Lexa nowhere in sight. Nor Jett.

The news Lexa had spent the weekend in Mount Sinai troubled her.

Careful. Don't dive in too deep. You barely know these people.

"You should've called." Chuck set the bags of barbecue on the table Jett retrieved from the closet.

"Sorry, didn't think of it. The whole weekend is a blur. I barely remembered to text her sister." Jett explained about Lexa's concussion and broken arm, how she slept through Saturday into Sunday.

"By the time we got home Sunday afternoon, I was exhausted. I got her settled and went to bed."

"She's staying with you?" Coral raised a brow. "How'd you manage that one? Be honest, did you push her in front of the cab?"

Her attempt at levity fell flat even though Chuck let out a snort. From his chair, Ed gasped.

"No, I didn't push her." Jett's answer contained no offense. "It's just temporary until we know the bone is healing well." He tapped his upper arm. "A humerus break is painful. Takes a while to heal. And she's in a long arm cast."

"Then what are you doing here?"

"She's asleep. The pain meds knock her out. My neighbor agreed to check on her every thirty minutes." He glanced at his watch. "I need to leave right at nine."

"Why'd she leave the gala anyway? Was she upset when Sabrina showed up?"

"Sabrina Fox?" Chuck whistled low.

"One and the same," Coral said. "She and Zane Breas are an item. Imagine, a guy who sells hamburgers dating a woman who doesn't eat meat."

"Match made in heaven," Ed said.

"I didn't ask about Sabrina." Jett started the food line by scooping a pile of baked beans onto his plate. "Though Zane is a putz. Wouldn't doubt he did something to hurt her."

"Please, if you need anything, just ask. Who's with her during the day?" Coral poured a bit of the red wine into a plastic cup. Should she volunteer her place? It was a big and spacious, almost cavernous, penthouse overlooking the park. But no one was home from seven in the morning to seven or eight at night.

She'd dismissed her housekeeping staff after discovering one of them took five hundred grand from a tabloid to tell the "real story" of the Panicked Princess.

For now, she maintained a cleaning crew and a chef, who loaded her up with meals and tidied her space once a week.

"No one," Jett said. "We're still working out a routine. I had someone cover my morning classes today. I think if I can get her set up before I leave for the day, she'll be all right until I get home. I'm not away all day every day either." He carried a loaded plate of ribs, beans, and coleslaw to his chair. "I'm sure she wouldn't mind visitors in a few days."

Coral regarded him for a long, lingering moment. Would Gus care for her the way Jett was caring for Lexa? Even after breaking his heart?

If those two didn't realize they loved each other by the time Lexa was out of a cast, she'd, well, eat a plastic plate.

Picking through the various meats, she lifted her head when Chuck asked, "How's your week been, Coral?"

He eyed her with sincere interest, even tenderness, and she had to look away.

"I've had better." She squirted a small dollop of sweet sauce over a pile of lean pork. "I've had worse."

She'd spent the morning in meetings with her team trying to figure out ways to save Pink Coral. But she ran into the bulwark of Blaire time and time again.

"How much more money can you put into a failing product? As your CEO I can't justify it, Coral."

"Guess we could all say the same," Chuck said. "Especially Lexa."

"Yes, I didn't mean to minimize her ordeal. Jett, please give her our love."

"We could write her a note, tell her we're thinking of her," Ed said.

"How utterly marvelous and old-fashioned." Coral perked up at the idea.

With that, the society minus one ate in contented silence. Coral relished the idea of being there for someone in need. When she was in a desperate situation, she shoved her friends away, afraid of betrayal. Afraid they wouldn't understand.

"You ran out on Prince Augustus?"

"What is wrong with you, Coral? I remember in school you never

went with the in-crowd. Though everyone wanted you in their inner circle. They thought you were a snob of snobs."

In truth, the in-crowd never really accepted her. She was an ugly duckling of sorts. By the time she turned into a swan, she didn't care about any of them. Nor they her.

"Ed, how's your memoir?" Jett caught the man licking his sticky fingers, a dark line of barbecue sauce running from the corner of his mouth toward his ear.

Coral reached for the moist towelettes that came with the barbecue and handed one to Chuck, who passed it to Ed.

"Got it in here." He tapped the side of his head, then tore open the small, square packet.

"Still don't know how to start?" Jett said.

"Letting the ideas ruminate. I was busy this week." He wadded up the soiled sheet. "I'm the super, you know, for my co-op up on Eighty-Ninth. I think about it while I'm working."

"Sooner or later, it's butt in chair, fingers on the keys."

"Can I just say you're doing a good thing, Jett? Helping your ex-wife." Ed breathed life into Coral's private thoughts. "Never hurts to go the extra mile for someone. Even if that someone broke your heart."

She liked the old gentleman more every week. His wisdom, his gruff kindness, the love he still professed for his wife.

"My ex would never do that for me," Chuck scoffed. "She'd rather . . . Never mind."

Coral glanced at him, finding the hardness in his tone displayed on his face. "Would you do it for her?"

"Not in a million years."

"Don't afford me a hero's welcome," Jett said. "To be honest, Lex didn't have any place else to go."

"That boss of hers could pay for help. Or for another place to stay," Chuck offered.

"The less Zane Breas is involved, the better," Jett said. "I think it was something he said that upset her."

"I'm sorry I wasn't there to help keep an eye on her," Coral said.

"Don't tell me she ran in front of the cab on purpose." Ed sounded truly concerned.

"No, she tripped." Jett raised his foot, motioning to the heel. "Her shoes . . . I don't know how women walk in those things."

"I'm with you, bro," Chuck said.

"Because we're trying to look good for you boys." Coral raised her voice in defense of her gender.

"We don't care a whit about shoes." This bold confession from Chuck. "Love us, feed us, and have sex with us. We're good. You wear those shoes to impress other women."

"I don't."

"Trust me, Coral, no man who sees you is looking at your feet."

She gasped and swatted Chuck with the back of her hand. He deflected the move by raising his arm and laughing.

"Men," she said, unable to corral her amusement.

"Women," Chuck echoed.

Ed laughed. "Nothing in the world like the spark between men and women. What a marvelous and mysterious combination. Two sides of the same coin, you know. We both want the same thing, to give and receive love, to be cared for, respected. We just come at it from a different point of view. Points of view we both need, you know."

Coral leaned toward him, her empty plate still in hand. "Your Esmerelda was a blessed woman, Ed."

"I was the blessed one. Yes, sir, I was the blessed one."

Jett and Chuck hit the food table for seconds. Coral moved slowly behind them, one eye on the still-full salad container, one eye on the men.

She saw it now. Even felt it. This society was unto some purpose. Jett clearly fulfilled the leader role. What was her role? Or Chuck's, Ed's, and Lexa's?

Would others show up? She tensed at the idea, not wanting anyone to spoil their young, tender camaraderie. She felt rather mother-hen about this odd society.

Back in the chairs, Ed motioned to Chuck.

"What's your story?"

Coral caught the taut knot in Chuck's jaw as he stabbed a forkful of barbecued meat.

"You know most of it. Divorced. Two kids. Twins. One of each. Grew up in Hoboken. My great-grandfather ran around with Frank Sinatra. Before he was *Sinatra* of course."

"Well, smell you." Coral dug up the old phrase from the Calhouns' southern side, Great-Aunt Lizzy, born and raised in western Kentucky.

Chuck grinned in such a way Coral felt it was just for her. "I never met the man. There's nothing to smell."

"You said the twins have a birthday coming up?" Coral said.

"October. They turn six." Chuck focused on his food, wiping his mouth after every bite with the napkin plastered to his wide palm.

"How often do you see them?" Ed wanted to know.

"Hey, don't let me soak up all the attention. Coral, what about you? Besides being a great heiress and prince smasher." Chuck sat back, stretched out his long, jean-clad legs, and took a noisy sip from the soda bottle he brought in from the corner bodega. "Parents? Siblings?"

"I find your humor droll, Chuck. If you must know, I was hatched under a magnolia tree and raised by squirrels in the park. My grandmother happened upon me one day and carried me up to my mother to raise as a pet." She grinned at his mocking expression. "Of course I have parents. And a brother, Han. Mom and Dad divorced when he was eleven and I was eight."

"I was twelve," Jett said. "When my folks divorced."

"My parents' parting was amiable. We spent Christmases and birthdays together, even some vacations. They tried their best not to disrupt our lives. However, my mother is very eccentric and, to be honest, just plain weird. She was more upset about Gus and me parting ways than I. My dad, though, he's special. My rock. My friend."

She hadn't intended on bringing up Gus, but it was hard to talk about her life and not mention him at least once.

"What did happen with Prince Gus?" Chuck leaned toward her.

"Say, how about those Giants?"

Chuck scrunched up his handsome face. "Is that your way of telling me to butt out?"

"Jett, your turn," Coral said. "Brothers, sisters?"

"One brother. He died two years ago."

"I looked up the story after our night in the clink, Jett," Chuck said. "Died wingsuiting. They say it's the deadliest sport."

"Night in the clink? What's this? Ed, did you know we had jailbirds among us?"

"Nothing. We were at the same wedding and this drunk groomsman was all handsy with one of the bridesmaids so Jett decided to teach him a lesson."

"I was drunk."

"Then somehow I got involved."

"Somehow?" Coral said.

"Okay, I felt like throwing a few punches myself."

"We spent the night together in Central Booking. Released in the morning with no charges." Jett pressed the corner of his napkin to his lips.

"What happened with your brother, Jett?" Ed said.

"He flew off Eiger Mountain to his death. Should've never taken off, but that's a debate for another day."

"What about the rest of your family?" Coral said.

"Like I said, my parents split, but after a few years, they reconciled their friendship. Mom came back to produce Dad's show, *Going Wild*. One set of grandparents retired to Arizona. The other set died within a year of each other when I was in grad school. No hamsters or snakes as pets."

The pet reference moved the stories toward furry companions as kids and adults.

"So is this what we're going to do? Just talk about whatever?" Ed stood, stretching, making old-man moans. "Dole out little bits of information about ourselves until we finally, after ten years, learn our life stories?"

Was that why they were here? To hear from each other, learn from the stories they each had to share?

Coral already yearned for a love like Ed and Esmerelda's. Despite how things appeared on the outside, and the hope she harbored in her heart, her love story with Gus was not a fairy tale. But she believed her own happily-ever-after awaited her.

"Aren't we going to read your brilliant memoir?" Chuck said.

"We can talk about books." Jett gestured toward the loaded bookshelves. "Religion or politics. It's what old Joseph Winthrop used to do in this room."

"A book club?" Ed snorted. "Sounds like a hen gathering. A *society* feels like we should be about more than book discussions."

"We could talk about writing, how stories impact society. Look at the works of Dickens and Twain, Roth, Fitzgerald, or—"

Chuck snorted. "Count me out. I'll go nuts if I have to dissect a book every Monday night. Or hash out the details of my life. I quit therapy because all the counselor wanted to talk about was my childhood. I had a great childhood."

"I quit my therapist because she had zero wisdom," Coral said. "Her only advice was to trick myself into believing I was okay. That I wasn't in pain. And that I should breathe a lot. Can you imagine. *Breathing* being the cure-all to emotional pain."

"We still don't know who invited us to this room." Chuck leaned forward, arms propped on his thighs. "There must be a reason."

"I agree. But we're not a support or writing group, nor a book club." Coral said. "So what *are* we?"

"Friends." Jett. So simple, clean, and pure.

Coral exhaled with a smile. "Yes, friends."

"Okay, friend," Chuck said. "Why did you say, 'How about those Giants?' when I asked you something personal?"

"You mean when you asked about Gus?" She turned to the big man. "All right, here you go. After some conversations with the prince I realized he wasn't the one for me."

Was her confession enough? She hoped so, because the familiar twist behind her breast stole her breath.

She was sorry for the way she ended things. Ashamed, really. And while she'd apologized, she'd not told anyone the rest of the story. The words were hard to find. Her feelings difficult to describe.

Her experience was so personal, so private.

"You couldn't have figured it out before the week of the wedding?"

"Chuck, you seem to know a lot about everyone's business." Ed studied the big man next to him. "Coral's prince, Jett's brother."

"I sit on my brains all day listening to the radio. I have passengers who talk too loud about all sorts of things. Some things I would love to shove out of my head, but I can't."

"So if we are friends, let's respect each other's boundaries for now," Jett suggested. "We really don't know each other all that well. Trust comes with time. With relationship. If we keep meeting, you'll probably get your answers, Chuck."

Thank the Lord for Jett. She could kiss him.

"I'll admit I am guarded." Coral's confession would give the guys a picture of her life. "I had a traitor in my house, one of my staff. Tried to sell access to me for half a million dollars. I agree with Jett that trust comes with time and relationship." She turned to Chuck. "For all we know you're a CIA operative. Ed, a hit man for the mob."

"And you? The black widow?"

"That's right. I'm a superhero." She winked at him. "Don't you forget it."

The tension broke with their laugh.

"So it's decided?" Chuck slapped his hands on the arm of his chair. "We come here and talk about . . . *life?*"

"Why don't we write to Lexa? Before Gilda comes in and ushers us out." Coral rose to collect printer paper and passed sheets to Chuck, Ed, and Jett.

When Jett and Ed echoed her yes, she thought she saw a flash of light in the room. Warm swirls of gold through a gauzy, thick haze.

She'd seen the heavenly veil once before. But it didn't frighten her as much this time.

Only confirmed her suspicions. The invitations to *this* society came from the same source that raised the hair on the back of her neck two months before she was to marry Augustus.

Coral pulled a pen from her bag and moved to the desk in the front corner where the fireplace sat cold and dark. She missed the warm, fanning flames.

"You have to write one too, Jett."

"Me?"

"Yes, you. Every society member is writing her. You're in the society, aren't you?"

> Lexa, I don't know you well but you already feel like a friend. So sorry about Friday night's accident. I'm thinking of you. We missed you terribly tonight. Please call if you need anything. I'll pray for you.
>
> Coral

She folded the page and passed it to Jett. Chuck and Ed were still writing. Jett's page was folded in his hand. If he wrote anything, the note was short.

Returning to her chair, Coral sat with a contented inner sigh.

By the time the diminutive librarian knocked on the door announcing the library's closing, the letters to Lexa were written and collected.

The four of them walked out together. "Can I give anyone a lift?" Coral moved toward the black sedan waiting for her by the curb.

"I've got Ed." Chuck roped his arm around the old man's narrow shoulders. "See you all next week."

"I have a feeling Ed's story might help Chuck." Coral glanced in Jett's direction.

"Maybe. Or Chuck just might help Ed."

"How would that be?"

He shrugged as he strapped on his bike helmet. Coral motioned to Albert, her driver for the night, to wait a moment and she stepped toward Jett.

"I don't know your story, but I think fate, or perhaps God, has given you a second chance."

"With Lexa?" He stared off, shaking his head. "You don't know her very well yet, but she doesn't *do* second chances."

"You never know, Jett. People change."

"And some don't. What about you? Is there a second chance at love with your prince?"

She shook her head.

"See," he said, cutting her off. "No second chances with you either."

"You don't know *me* very well yet, Jett. There is more to the story. And right now, I have hotter irons in the fire than my love life." She turned to the open backseat door. "Good night. See you next week."

"Good night, Coral."

When she looked back, Jett was gone, pedaling his way into the night.

Chapter 12

LEXA

She woke to the muted light of morning peeking into the bedroom around the edges of drawn shades.

Every flutter of her eyelids felt like sandpaper. Her dry lips stuck together, and when she tried to sit up, she toppled left, face first into a thick pillow.

Pain sliced down her head to her arm and out her fingertips. Even the ends of her hair hurt.

With awkward motion, she pushed up with her left arm, scooted to the end of the bed, balanced, then shuffled toward the bathroom.

After she'd spent three days with Jett and exposed more of herself to him than she cared to, he'd rigged one of his oversized T-shirts for easy use. She could finally tend to her private needs without calling on him.

Now, after five days, she felt at home. But this wasn't her home. Not anymore, despite the memories, the familiar surroundings, furniture, and decorations. Jett hadn't changed the place very much. Only pictures and her personal items were missing.

Flipping on the bathroom light, she found the marble sink—the one she'd picked out and helped Jett install—arranged with her face wash, hairbrush, and a prepared toothbrush.

Oh, Jett. He really was being so kind and helpful.

The apartment had been a wedding gift from his parents. A place of their own to begin their *Wilders Move to New York* adventure.

Between his classes and her job hunts, they painted every wall. They ate takeout, laughed, dreamed, and filled their new home with music from Jett's treasured vinyl LP collection.

Gladys Knight and the Pips. Credence. Fleetwood Mac, America, Foreigner. All seventies all the time. Jett was an old soul.

At night they made love on the floor pallet and fell asleep with Jett on his back, Lexa on her side, one hand lightly touching his arm.

She was his true love, his muse. Until one day she wasn't and the bliss she knew faded to nothing.

She brushed her teeth and washed her face—soaking her sleep shirt—careful of the still-dark bruise around her eye and down her cheek.

She reached for the hairbrush, then changed her mind. She wasn't sure she wanted to release the beastly knot twisted and tied together on top of her head.

Turning out the light, she headed back to the bed. Their bed. Short and distant memories surfaced. Of drinking herbal tea and reading, mounds of pillows behind their backs. Sharing a line or two out loud of something clever from the latest bestseller or an obscure author Jett discovered.

Sometimes they discussed their day and planned for the next. Sometimes they said nothing at all. Just rested, hands clasped in the center of the bed.

But by Jett's second semester in grad school, he was sleeping in the Barcalounger. Or the guest bedroom.

"I didn't want to disturb your sleep."

And her days at ZB stretched longer and longer.

Shoving and pushing toward the center of the bed, Lexa settled among the pillows, fighting to find a comfortable position. The long arm cast went from the middle of her hand to just below her shoulder with her arm bent at the elbow ninety degrees.

She felt trapped. Claustrophobic.

And just the simple trip to the bathroom had started her head throbbing.

A shooting pain brought her upright. "Jett?" She listened. Beneath the T-shirt, her belly rumbled. "Jett?" It hurt to raise her voice much louder than a whisper. "You home?"

Lexa breathed through another shard of pain, then inched to the side of the bed and toward the door. She'd have to feed and medicate herself.

After a slow, very slow, journey to the kitchen, she found her meds set out with a bottle of water and a note from Jett.

Meeting with a Gordon Phipps Roth expert. Be home in a couple of hours. There's cereal in the pantry. Milk in the fridge.

Lexa swallowed her morning pills, then filled a bowl with Cheerios and drowned the O's in milk.

Sitting at the banquette, she opened her laptop, but the glare of the screen created an aura so she shut it down.

So, this was her reward for doing Zane a good deed? A concussion and a broken arm.

She slurped another spoonful of cereal and scanned the living area. Jett had taken care to draw the shades and make a place for her to lie on the couch instead of being stuck in the bedroom.

He'd left the remote on the end table. Even lined up a few albums he thought she might like.

"Remember driving up from Florida to America's greatest hits?"

Monday had been awkward, navigating her care as she fought for some form of modesty while Jett treaded over familiar ground that was now off-limits.

Jett *knew* her. Intimately. There was nothing under her loose T-shirt he'd not seen or caressed.

Lexa spooned another bite of breakfast. She had made him turn around while she tried on the night shirt he fashioned. He'd cut the seams and sewn on ties so she could easily disrobe for her bath.

Once he wrapped her cast, she could handle everything else from there.

However, after five days, she desperately needed her hair washed. And that would simply be too intimate. Last time he washed her hair, they'd been honeymooners sharing a shower.

Lexa jumped when the intercom buzzed, spilling milk onto the table. She was not good with her left hand.

"Lexa? You there?" Zane's voice sounded from the foyer speaker. "It's me. Open up."

Scooting out from the banquette, Lexa eased across the living room to the foyer. Zane buzzed three more times.

She pressed the Talk button. "I'm not decent."

"Get decent. I need to talk to you."

"About what?" She hadn't talked to him since the accident. Jett had called HR Monday morning to let them know she'd be out, on doctor's orders, for at least three weeks.

"Let me up. I don't want to talk to you through a box."

"I'm supposed to be resting."

"Lex, come on. I won't stay long. I just want to make sure you're okay."

"You had all week to find out if I was okay."

"Well I'm here now."

Lexa glanced toward the couch and the blanket draped over the arm. She could cover up well enough.

"Five minutes."

She unlocked the apartment, then made her way to the couch and the plaid throw. The short excursion across the room exhausted her.

Truth? She was still mad at him. One, for turning her into his assistant the moment it suited him. Two, for waiting five days to check on her.

The door opened, and Zane appeared around the foyer wall, producing a bouquet of flowers.

"Ah, Lex, look at you." He set the arrangement on the hearth. "I hate to see you like this. Did you really run into the street without looking?"

"Who told you that?"

"The doorman at the Waldorf." Zane perched on the other end of the couch. "He said you were running from some guy."

Yeah, you. She dragged the blanket up under her chin. "I didn't run into the street, I tripped hailing a cab. Jett said I came out of my shoe."

"He was the guy?"

"No, I didn't even know he was there."

"Look, Lex, I tried to get you to stay. I don't know why you left."

"Because you insulted me. Believe it or not, Zane, I'm not at your beck and call twenty-four seven."

"Sorry, I was just trying to help out Sabrina."

"Be her hero?" Lexa straightened the bottom of the throw over her foot.

"No, I don't know. Maybe." He motioned to her right side. "How's your arm?"

With care, she moved it from under the cover. "Painful."

He glanced at her cast, then at her face. "Jett said you have a concussion." He stretched toward her bruised cheek. "This looks nasty."

"You should've seen it five days ago."

"I can't help but feel like this is my fault."

"Good," she said but not really meaning it.

Zane frowned. "I thought you were going to exonerate me. Tell me it was all your fault. Or better, Jett's."

Of course. Because she'd always covered for him, fixed his mistakes, picked up all the balls he dropped.

"It was an accident. No one's at fault. Except maybe the shoes."

His Nebraska-boy grin made her smile. "Are we okay? You and me?"

As much as she wanted to say no, Zane was the most constant person in her life. Her first job out of college. Her stability when her marriage was ending. Her boss and her friend.

"We're fine." She pointed her finger at him. "Don't think this lets you off the hook on the CEO conversation."

He raised his hands. "Wouldn't dream of it."

Pushing up from the couch, he followed Lexa's directions to find a vase, which he filled with water and then the flowers.

Setting the arrangement on the hearth, he turned to her. "Are you sure you want to be here with him?"

"It's temporary."

"I could always—"

"What? Pay for someone to help me? Would you do that for any other employee?" If she was going to be CEO, she needed to behave like one. "I'm fine here. It's weird but fine."

She hadn't told Zane about the story society. How she'd seen Jett twice before she woke up in the hospital to find him sleeping in the chair next to her.

"I mentioned you in my speech. More than what you wrote. I said how you took the bull by the horns and got the Forty-Sixth Street store open."

"Thanks. How's it going with Sabrina?"

He blushed a little. "Good."

"Lois called to check on me. She said Quent was at my desk."

"He's no Lexa Wilder but he's doing a good job."

"Perfect. You'll get used to him while I'm out, and he can stay in the position when I become CEO."

"You are not going to let me forget, are you?" He half laughed and half sighed.

"Are you trying to forget?"

He glanced at his watch. "I should go. Let you rest. Everyone said to tell you hi and hurry back. Don't be surprised if you start getting cards and gifts. Lois is getting it organized."

Lois. The HR manager was a former talent agent who mastered the art of schmoozing. She excelled in winning people over, making them feel a part of the team.

"I'll come in as soon as I can. Say hi."

The front door opened and closed. "Lex?" At the foyer doorway, Jett removed his bike helmet. "Zane."

"I came to check on my girl."

"She's not your girl." Jett hoisted his bike to a hook behind the wall, then crossed the room with a takeout bag. "I brought you an egg croissant, Lex."

"I just ate cereal."

"You need some protein." Jett handed her the brown paper bag. "You want some tea?"

"Green, please."

The microwave door slammed, then beeped as Jett set the timer. "Good, you took your meds." At the banquette, he unloaded his computer. "Don't you have a burger kingdom to run, Zane? People to make fat?"

"I'll call you later, Lex." Zane reached out to touch her head, then pulled back and headed for the door.

"Don't call her with work. She's resting."

As the door slammed, Lexa peered up at Jett. "He was just being nice."

"Nice. Making sure you didn't blame him for your accident and sue him? Or file workman's comp."

"Sue him? For what?"

"Emotional distress."

"If I wanted to sue anyone for emotional distress it'd be you." She unwrapped the croissant as the words fired from her mouth. Bold and unapologetic.

"Me?" Jett glared at her, then toward the microwave as it beeped.

"Forget it." She bit into the hot sandwich. The gooey cheese burned her tongue.

"Forget it? You just accused me of emotional distress." He set the tea on the end table's coaster.

"Which is why we're divorced."

"How? How did *I* cause *you* emotional distress? I was the one in grad school. The one with the dead brother. You were never here for me to distress."

The pounding began at the back of her head and rolled forward. "I said forget it." She rewrapped the sandwich. "I'm going to lie down."

"Lex, wait—"

Head down, eyes covered from the brilliant light of the banquette's chandelier, she moved toward the bedroom.

"I mean it, Jett. Forget it. Let's not talk about the past, go around digging up old bones. It is what it is. Let's try to be friends. If possible. I need to lie down."

She crawled into bed and breathed, quelling the nausea. "What?" she said, sensing his presence.

"Can I get you anything?"

"No, but thank you." Lexa opened her eyes to find Jett at the door. "I'm sorry, okay?"

"About what?" He made a goofy face and she chuckled.

"H-how was your meeting? With the *other* Roth expert?" The pounding began to ebb. The pain pill was doing its job.

"He doesn't think Gordon used a ghostwriter."

"Isn't that good? Don't you want Gordon to be the writer America knows and loves?"

"Yeah, of course, but . . ." He leaned against the wall, arms folded. "I keep thinking of the book Tenley Roth published posthumously for Birdie Ainsworth. The voice, the writing, the story is so much like GPR."

"Then talk to Tenley."

"She's a steel door. Can't get through. The Roth Foundation won't even acknowledge Birdie and Gordon were friends, even though it's documented they were. I think they're keeping a tight leash on Tenley."

"How could they do that?"

"I don't know, appeal to her family loyalty?"

"Are they really looking for your published dissertation to stop all suspicion?"

"Yes, because it would be the first complete work on Gordon since the rumors."

"Hmm, then publish. Sorry, but I'm starting to fade." She rolled onto her good side, her focus landing on the notes from Monday night's story society.

"Get well." Written by Chuck with a bold script.

"We miss you." Sweet Ed.

"*Call if you need anything.*" This from Coral, and Lexa believed her.

Everyone wrote to her but Jett. She wanted to ask but changed her mind. She didn't have the strength for the conversation.

"I'll be at the banquette if you need anything." He reached for the blanket at the end of the bed. "I have a class at four. I'll be gone a couple of hours. I'll check on you before I go."

"Thank you." She forced her eyes open one last time. "I am grateful."

"I know."

He pulled the door to as he left, leaving it slightly ajar.

As she slipped toward slumber, Lexa raised her head to see a thick, brilliantly covered book on the top shelf of the bookcase against the wall.

"*Rites of Mars.*" Suddenly awake, she pushed up and kicked her legs over the side of the bed, waiting for her equilibrium to settle before retrieving Jett's book.

It was heavy. She almost needed both hands to carry it to bed. Crawling back against the pillows, she looked inside.

She'd seen the book online but never read any of it. In many ways, she resisted the novel that he loved more than her. At least for a time anyway.

Using her left hand and elbow she turned past the copyright and title pages, her gaze landing on the dedication.

To Lexa, with all my love.

CHUCK

Friday afternoon he parked his car outside Riley and Jakey's school, paused his Uber app, and ducked down in the seat behind the wheel.

The restraining order prohibited him from being within five hundred feet of the kids' school. But he was fed up. He *had* to see his babies.

All efforts to have the temporary restriction removed got him nowhere. He'd run out of money, so his lawyer stopped working the issue.

He drove the limo for his buddy on the weekends, using the pay and lavish tips to build up his "Get My Kids Back" account.

After the *incident*, he stayed away from them. His first mistake.

But he was ashamed, wondered if the little tykes were better off without him. He'd sort of scared himself with his outburst.

However, driving a car all day gave a man time to think, gain some perspective.

He'd screwed up, but he'd changed. And his kids needed him.

Since the recess bell hadn't rung yet, he distracted himself with the little black Moleskine book he'd picked up from a bookstore yesterday afternoon.

He didn't think it mattered much, but all the talk Monday night about their lives, their stories, their friendship, got him to thinking about his magic book idea.

Already he'd forgotten some of the elements. Jotting them down might jog his memory. For what purpose, he didn't know, but where was the harm?

Taking the pen from the elastic holder on his sun visor, Chuck stared at the book's first page, all pristine and white. Absent of his sloppy, angular handwriting.

With an inhale, he wrote the date in the top right corner and *Magic Book Stuff.*

The sudden crash of children yelling and screaming caused him to toss the notebook into the passenger seat, his pulse energized.

At last, recess. He felt like *he* was in first grade racing to freedom.

He had his mother to thank for this little vignette of his kids.

"Jakey loves the monkey bars," she said the other day. "Riley is the jump rope champion. Recess is at two. Don't let anyone see you."

His eyes stung with emotion. His beautiful Riley and handsome Jake, both of them smart and strong, were fifty yards away. Of course, they had inherited the hearty Mays genes.

His grandfather Mays was a longshore fisherman who survived a hurricane at sea only to join the navy when Hitler invaded Poland. He stood on the deck of the USS *Arizona* when the Japanese dropped their bombs and became one of the lucky survivors.

His grandmother Mays grew up in the Oklahoma Dust Bowl, raising her little brother and sister after her father died of a severe asthma attack and her mother walked off the farm one night never to be seen again.

Years later it was rumored she worked in Hollywood as an actress, but it was never confirmed.

The Mayses were colorful, larger than life. Survivors and thrivers.

He pumped his fist when Jakey swung from monkey bar to monkey bar. Look at him go! He could probably do a couple of pull-ups.

Chuck scanned over to the basketball court, where a couple of girls were hopping up and down, their hair floating and falling.

Riley was holding court, jumping rope while a passel of girls looked on.

Show 'em how it's done, baby.

She was so graceful, a flower in perpetual motion.

Chuck scribbled in his notebook, "I love my kids."

The music of children—laughter blended with screams and shouts—filled his car, his head, his chest.

He *must* be a part of their lives. Must prove to Trudy he'd changed. Yet the only way to remove the restraining order was through the courts.

He was the hamster on the wheel. Running and getting nowhere. The ex never answered his calls or texts.

He was about to fire up his Honda Pilot and get back to work when a shrill, desperate cry broke through the playground din. Chuck scrambled from the driver's side as he watched his son tip backward off the monkey bars and smack his head on the steel ladder.

"Jakey!" He fired across the street, slamming into the chain link fence. "Jakey, are you all right?" Where were the teachers? His kid could be bleeding to death.

The boy sat up, blinking, one hand pressed to the back of his head. The other kids had hightailed it, leaving him alone.

"You all right?"

"Daddy?" Jakey crawled to his feet.

"It's me." Chuck smiled. Darn tears flashed across his eyes again. "Way to take a dive, son." *Sound chipper. Don't scare him. Let him know he's a tough kid.*

"Daddy!" Jakey flew at the wire diamond fence.

Chuck dropped to one knee and wrapped his hand around his boy's. "How you doing buddy? I miss you."

"What are you doing here?"

"Wanted to see you, why else? You were working those monkey bars just like me when I was a kid."

"Where you been? Mommy said you were too busy to see us."

"No, no, of course I want to see you." Trudy, the freaking liar. Threading his hand through the chains, Chuck cupped his son's head and brought him forward for a kiss. "I love you. Very much. Mommy and me are just working some things out, okay?"

"Can you come to my birthday party?" He held up four fingers. "In four weeks. I'm having a magic show, a race-car game, a cake that looks like space Legos, and lots of presents."

"Lots of presents? What about your sister? It's her birthday too."

Look at what he was missing. The twins' childhood. They'd be grown and gone before he'd be allowed back into their lives. By then, they'd hate him.

His jaw tightened at the notion. No. Things had to change. He'd find a way.

Jakey scrunched up his face. "She's having a princess party the next day with just *girls*. Blech."

Chuck laughed and tousled his son's hair. "In a few years, you'll be dying to crash *that* party."

Jake's eyes widened in utter disbelief. "My party is just for boys." His little chest puffed out. "So can you come? Please?" His blue eyes pierced Chuck to the heart.

"Tell you what, I'll see what I can do." He tapped his son's freckled nose. "For now, why don't we keep this little meeting our secret."

"Why?"

"Remember, I told you Mommy and I are working some things out?" Jakey nodded. "Best let me talk to her about the party. And why don't we surprise Riley too?"

A somber-looking Jakey mimicked Chuck's pressed finger to his lips and nodded. "Our secret, Daddy."

"Here," Chuck said with a wink, peeling off a five-dollar bill. "From the tooth fairy for all those teeth you're missing. Have you been in a prize fight, son?"

"Five dollars?" Wonder and surprise flared his sweet expression. "The tooth fairy only gave me a dollar."

"Well, daddies are better and more generous than the tooth fairy." The stupid hedge fund manager could only peel a dollar off his large bankroll? "Tuck the money in your pocket and don't go showing it to your friends. When you get home, put it in your piggy bank."

He and Trudy bought the twins giant pink pigs when they learned there were two babies instead of one. And every night they had deposited their pocket change in each kid's bank.

Chuck kept the routine even now, dumping his change into two large jars at home. One day he'd hand them to his kids.

In the distance the bell rang, calling an end to this father-son tête-à-tête.

"Better go. Have a good afternoon. Study hard."

Jakey thrust his arms through the fence, hugging Chuck as tight as he could. "I love you, Daddy."

"I love you too, buddy." He choked and cleared his throat, clinging to this rare moment. But he'd already risked too much. "I'll see you later."

Back at his car, his tears fell against the ache in his chest. He'd give anything to undo his outburst.

As much as he despised Trudy, he had to give her one kudo. His kids didn't hate him. Jakey wasn't afraid.

Turning on his Uber app, Chuck drove away from the school zone and accepted his first fare as the last rays of the summer sun burned hot against his windshield.

Yet it was the sweet touch of his little boy's hands that warmed him through.

He had four weeks to find a way into the kids' birthday parties. Getting past Trudy would be tough.

So far the only way she wanted the kids to see him again was stiff and cold, sleeping in a casket, about to be buried six feet under.

❧

ED

The calendar had flipped to fall but the temperatures remained warm, good for a dip in the pool.

Sitting on the deck with Holly—who wore dark sunglasses so big they swallowed her face—Ed sipped on the root beer float Hope insisted on making.

A little sweet for his taste but made with love, so he worked on it slowly, laughing as the kids and their friends played Marco Polo.

"Drake, you can't jump in without looking," Holly called, leaning forward. "You nearly landed on Hope's head."

"Here, Dad, maybe you'd like this beer better." Brant set a dripping cold one in front of him, then sat next to Holly. "Drake, did you hear your mother? Be careful."

Between the shouts and laughter, and Brant talking to Holly about an engagement on their calendar, Ed drifted into the background, observing, listening.

"Marco!"

"Polo!"

He felt odd in these homey, cozy family scenes. An interloper. Yet strangely comforted by memories of a similar life he knew long ago.

The smell of grilling meat and fresh-cut grass reminded him of his childhood days at his grandparents' farm upstate.

He'd wanted all of this for Holly, but it wasn't meant to be. They were city dwellers. Then Esmerelda was called away from this world. Too soon. Far too soon.

Holly's soft laugh drew his attention. He caught her smooching with Brant, so he looked away.

"I'm checking on the burgers." Brant tapped Ed's shoulder. "Still medium-rare?"

"If you would be so kind."

Holly reached over and squeezed his arm. "Aren't you glad you came out?"

"I am." He swigged his beer and gazed over the pastoral scene.

They'd shown him a corner of the yard he could till for a garden. Then toured the father-in-law suite connected by a breezeway on the other side of the garage.

"We can update it to your liking, Dad. Paint, new floors."

"Can you make it look fifty years old and add stacks of books and papers?"

Holly kissed his cheek and laughed. "Time to downsize. Out with the old, in with the new."

He liked his *old*, thank you very much. He grumbled and swigged his beer.

"Have you written any more on your story, Dad?" Holly said.

"Been busy."

She smiled at him though her eyes were toward the pool. "Hope, throw the ball for Stella. She's dying to swim." The large golden retriever circled the water, barking and nipping at heels.

"You've done well, Holly. I'm proud of you."

She focused on Ed again and squeezed his hand. "I had a good teacher."

He drowned the rise of emotion with another gulp from the cold bottle. "I like my place. Think I want to stay there as long as I can."

Holly sighed. "I don't know why you won't move out here. You can go into the city anytime you want to see your friends or go to that society meeting. You'll have room out here. We're gone all day, so it's not like I'll be knocking on your door."

"When you're my age, do you want Hope or Drake coming around insinuating you're too feeble to live alone? I'm only seventy-eight, girl."

"I never said feeble."

"You implied it."

"Just know I've got my eye on you." Her smile made him think all those thousands of dollars for braces were worth it.

Holly jumped up with a shout as a wet Stella dropped a tennis ball at her feet and shook pool water from her coat. She kicked the ball into the water, and the retriever splashed in for the rescue.

"It's just . . . I like our place, Holly. It has warm memories for me."

"Me too. Remember the time I tried to cut your hair?"

His eyes filled even though he laughed. "I was bald on one side. And the other . . . I don't know what I looked like. The barber had to shave it all to get me even."

"I mostly remember every Friday night. Pizza with brownies and ice cream." She rested her hand on his arm. "I'd love for you to spend more time with the kids. They need to know what a great man you are, Dad."

"All right, I'll visit more."

"Every Friday night?"

"Every? You'll be sick of me." And really, isn't that what he feared? Just like . . . Well, never mind. "I'll come more often. If you want me."

The kids ran around the deck, shooting each other with water guns. Hope ducked behind Ed's chair.

"Hide me, Grandpa." Then she rose up to shoot her brother's friend. Ed couldn't remember his name. "You can't shoot me if I'm behind Grandpa. He's the safe place."

Holly's grip tightened around his arm. That's what he aimed to be for her. Always. A safe place. And if she ever got sick of him, he'd shrivel up and die.

"Burgers are up. Let's eat."

The kids dropped their weapons and ran to the table as Ed shoved up from his chair.

"The burger with the toothpick is yours, Dad." Brant handed Ed another beer. "Holly says you're writing a book."

"Tinkering." Ed took up a plate and reached for the buns, layering his with lettuce, tomato, pickles, and onion before topping it off with a medium-rare patty.

"What's your idea? Your family history working for the press plant?"

"Hadn't really thought of that, Brant. I'm writing more on my musings of life."

"You could write how you raised Holly as a single father. That'd be a unique story."

"Maybe."

"I have a friend in publishing. I'll ask what he thinks. Holly, can you pass the ketchup? Drake, I left the chips in the kitchen. Run get them."

The tall and broad-shouldered boy dripped past Ed, popping

him gently on the arm, flashing a grin that was sure to weaken the ladies.

"Good-looking kid, that Drake," Ed said to Brant as he sat at the head of the table.

"A little girl-crazy right now but he's keeping straight." Brant clapped the tall neck of his beer bottle to Ed's. "To family."

"To family."

Holly joined them, her burger covered with vegetables and no bun.

"Your dad and I were talking about his book," Brant said. "How he could write about raising you alone."

"He wasn't entirely alone. He had Aunt Faye and Granny." Holly turned to him. "I could help. Maybe add sections from my perspective."

"Let's just see what I decide. I'm not sure I really have the energy or talent for writing."

All this book talk was weakening his will. He wanted his love story with Esmerelda to be a surprise, and he'd almost blurted it out to see if they approved.

"Give it some thought. And Dad, if you can get me an interview with Coral Winthrop—"

"Stop." He raised his hand. "Forget it."

"But Dad—"

"Don't ask me again, Holly." His voice rose with a rare, stern tone. But he would not betray that sweet Coral. By the dull sorrow in her eyes, she'd been through enough.

He'd deal with being told where he needed to live, or what he needed to write, if he wrote anything at all, but not *his* Coral. Not *his* society.

And if he were honest, he planned to die a happy man in his Eighty-Ninth Street apartment, bent over his Underwood, dreaming about Esmerelda.

JETT

September became October with a fury of cold, rainy days, then a blaze as the fall colors crowned the city in golds and reds.

The deadline for his dissertation created a constant pressure. Not because he had much more work to do but because it came with so much money. Because it came with a caveat.

Was Gordon Phipps Roth who he claimed to be? The question plagued him. But why? He didn't believe for a moment GPR employed a ghost.

Jett pushed away from the desk in his English department office, where he'd been reading through his dissertation.

Yes, of course the man was who he claimed to be. Surely if he was not his detractors would've discovered his scheme when he was alive. And Daniel Barclay, his publisher, was known for his integrity and ethical character. He often took the hard line on slipping social morals and suffered for it.

Why was Jett allowing one book, *An October Wedding*, written by a dead woman and posthumously published, stir such doubt?

Because Tenley Roth had brought the project to light. If only she'd respond to his requests for an interview.

The book by Birdie Ainsworth had hit the *New York Times* bestseller list and fallen off two weeks later. And that brief success came from Tenley's rigorous promotion. Otherwise it was hardly a blip on the timeline of classic literature. She was no GPR.

Clearly Jett was bothered by nothing. A rumor. Speculation. No one in the literary community doubted GPR's oeuvre.

Jett poured a cup of coffee from the old machine tucked in the corner on an old table and returned to his reading.

"He wrote more about nineteenth- and twentieth-century life than

any author alive or dead. His insights into the human condition, especially women, was unparalleled. Sigmund Freud wrote, 'I feel I must consult Mr. Phipps Roth when considering and analyzing the female mind.'"

The chapter went on to cite other researchers and authors, quotes from colleagues and academics.

There was no doubt in Jett's mind Gordon Phipps Roth was one of the greatest American authors, if not *the* greatest. His stories intuitively showcased deep human emotion.

Jett often longed for the world GPR depicted on the page. One of struggle, to be sure, but also one of love and faith, failure and triumph. Whether a man was high or low born, GPR ascribed to him respect, a sense of common decency, and charity.

What Jett didn't include in his dissertation, or this final prep for publication, was his personal journey into the lively, vibrant world of GPR.

Beginning with *The Girl in the Carriage,* Jett escaped the pain and trauma of his teen years through Gordon's stories of goodness, faith, and love.

Jett was a romantic at heart.

Gordon became more than a literary hero. He and the characters he drew on the page were his mentors, his counselors, his best friends when his parents were absent in mind if not body.

The man deserved justice. His reputation, defended.

"Knock, knock." Renée leaned around the door. "How's it going?"

Jett rocked back in his eighties desk chair. "Renée, what do you think if I add a personal introduction? Not what GPR means to American Lit, but what he meant to me?"

"I think that would endear us to the Roth Foundation forever. Do it."

Jett nodded. "I'll think on it."

"Think?"

"Yeah, think." Because if he wrote his story, he'd write the whole truth. And he'd wised up enough in his meager thirty years to consider the reputation and feelings of others. Like his parents.

"I stopped by to tell you Harper Franks is ready to roll with the book as soon as you hand it over," Renée said. "I've decided to get an additional peer review for appearances' sake. We'll add Dr. Levi from Harvard to the reviews you already have. You're not making that many changes are you? He'll take a quick look. He's an old friend of mine. We'll just make the reception deadline."

"Dr. Levi's work was a great help to me writing the dissertation."

"Yes, and he loves you for referencing him so much. He's with you, by the way. GRP was a genius, and Dr. Levi finds it implausible he'd have hired an *ink slinger*. His words, not mine."

He heard the subtle whisper beneath her words. *Get it done. We need this.* "I'll have it to you by the fifteenth like you asked."

"I appreciate your attention to this, Jett. I know the college is putting a lot of pressure on you. You still have your class load plus faculty responsibilities, but welcome to the big leagues. Ten million dollars to our school because you timed your dissertation publication perfectly."

"I'm not a fortune teller. If Storm hadn't died, I'd have published a year and a half ago."

"Yes, well, for that I am sorry." Renée turned to go then stepped back. "How's it going with Lexa?"

Jett shrugged. "Well enough."

Renée arched her brow. "Is that good? I'd never live with my ex. Not that I've been married but—"

"I should get back to work." Jett raised his mug for a sip of hot brew, and Renée moved on.

Lexa was still a quagmire to him. For the past two weeks, they'd lived in harmony. He helped her eat, brush her teeth and hair, even dress when she needed it—though she was guarded. He was guarded. She made him close his eyes when he helped her dress.

Every night he wrapped her arm for her bath, and once he'd washed her hair in the kitchen.

She bent over the sink with her left hand braced against the counter, her posture and attitude stiff, flinching when Jett moved his shampoo-filled hands through her hair.

He shook the image from his mind, keenly aware of rising desire. They spoke very little as he washed, rinsed, and towel dried her hair.

Later, he heard the dryer through the closed doors. When Lexa came out to say good night she said she'd go to her stylist next week. After all, it would be two weeks since the break. She felt confident enough to venture out.

He merely agreed with a warning to be careful. "Take a cab."

Jett faced the screen and opened a new document, testing the idea of writing a personal foreword.

"Gordon's books come with a fragrance for me. One of hay and barley, of a warm barn floor and the gentle exhale of a mare in her stall."

The barn. The loft. The corner where he'd tossed an old horse blanket and hidden a flashlight. The holler of their male nanny, Stovall.

"Dinner. Come now or out it goes."

He was gruff. But kind. A steadying force. And the namesake for Jett's *Mars* hero.

Jett rolled his chair to the bookshelf where the spine of *Mars* faced out. He had a love-hate relationship with the story.

Love, because he'd completed what he started. Having written was a great sensation. Hate, because it embodied all of his pain and disappointments. He wrestled through them with Stovall, Colonel Grancy, Amvi, and Raúl, and the cold, barren world of Mars.

Also known as his soul.

Then he dedicated the book to Lexa. Three months after their divorce. Because he'd promised himself he would.

A few days ago, he noticed the copy of *Mars* on his bookshelves had been moved. If she'd read it, she never said.

Back to his laptop. Should he detail his mother's "I'm leaving" announcement? How it devastated him? How his big brother's reaction devastated him even more? Or how he hated her for a long time? How those feelings still spiked every now and then, when the evening twilight faded too fast and shadows stretched too long?

Should he write about reading to Lexa, pausing every other paragraph to break down and analyze the brilliance of Gordon's descriptions and insight? Or how he could close his eyes and recite prose from memory? From his heart?

Should he confess how he trusted love because Gordon proved to him story after story the value and worth of the journey?

His thoughts slipped back toward Lexa. Somehow last night, she let a bit of her guard down. When he was helping her prep for her bath, she angled forward just enough she unwittingly exposed the plump roundness of her breast.

When she raised up, their eyes met. A slight blush tinted her cheeks, and she gently closed the opening of her shirt with her good hand.

"Sorry." He'd backed away and crashed into the wastebasket.

"It was bound to happen."

No use lying—he left the marble and travertine bathroom hot and bothered, realizing she was both sexy and vulnerable in one gorgeous package.

He'd tossed and turned the first few nights she was in the apartment, her presence stirring passionate memories.

Yet he was making peace with his reality. She was *only* his friend, if he dared to even presume.

However, right now he was wasting time. An email notification arrived announcing a response from a notable GPR expert at Oxford. He'd attached a document for Jett to source and quote.

Printing the thirty pages, he vanished into the in-depth insight of Dr. Paulson, exhaling as his analysis and conclusions confirmed Jett's. While the information was good, it didn't add much to what Jett had already compiled in his work.

Nevertheless, ever studious, he pulled out his highlighter just as his phone pinged with a text.

As he reached for his phone, his eyes adjusted to the low, dusky twilight hue filling his office. It was Lexa.

Your mom is here???

Mom? He'd not seen her since the New Year. Not talked to her in a couple months.

At the apartment? When?

Just arrived. Asked for you. Gave me a funny look.

What does she want?

Ask her yourself.

Wilder family relationships ran taut, beginning with his parents' divorce and doubling down since Storm's death.

Jett hesitated with a glance at the document in his hand, then one at the door. Stay with Gordon or see his mom?

He'd rather work. But poor Lex. He couldn't leave her to field Mom alone. She was a force to be reckoned with.

His phone pinged with a text from Mom.

You coming home?

Slapping his laptop closed, Jett packed up, threw his backpack over his shoulder, and headed for his bike.

What was Miranda Wilder up to now? And why was she in the city? Shouldn't she be on location with Dad's show, running *Going Wild*?

Pedaling home, he tried not to imagine her purpose. As much as he loved her—she was his mother after all—her presence always filled him with conflict.

But she was the one who'd walked out. He owed her nothing.

"Hello?" he said as he bumbled his bike through the door and hung it on the hook. "Mom?" He found her on the couch with Lexa, drinking a cup of tea. "What are you doing here? Why aren't you on location?" He glanced at Lexa as he deposited his pack and bike gear on the table.

"We finished shooting for the month. In fact, we're taking off until November."

"Taking off?" The show filmed eight weeks in winter, ten in the summer, and six in the fall. "Is Dad sick?"

"Of course not. He's a beast. In fact, we're expanding to sixteen shows next season. As you know, show prep never ends. Advertising partners must be appeased. I thought I'd run down to the Big Apple and make the rounds. Do people still call it the Big Apple?"

"Old-timers," Jett said with a glance at Lexa. She looked pretty, and the bruise around her face had faded to a brownish-gray.

"Then I guess I'm an old-timer."

Mom lived an hour up the road in Chappaqua. In the house where Jett was raised. Only then it was just Dad, Storm, Jett, and Stovall.

Mom ran away to California for two years when she left Dad. Then returned to a rented farm in Chappaqua. Five years ago Dad sold the family homestead back to her, and Jett's boyhood betrayal flashed forward again, tainting all his childhood memories.

The laughter on the lake, the fall football games in the pasture, the bonfires with his and Storm's friends. The comforting hour after hour of reading in the barn loft, thinking, imagining. Even the feel of Bessy's soft nose under his palm.

Mom didn't belong there. She'd gone. Given up her rights to even be a shadow on his teen homestead where his memories lived.

"I have news, but first, you never said Lexa moved back."

"I told her I didn't move back." Lexa pointed to her arm.

"I'm helping a friend in need."

"A friend? I see." Mom sipped her tea. See? See what? "She was telling me how you helped her when she tripped and fell in front of a taxi." She glanced at Lexa. "Take care, concussions are nasty business. Storm and Jett both suffered with them in their teen years. Especially when Bear started taking them climbing. How's that bruise healing?" Mom started to reach for Lexa's face. But enough.

"Mom, again, what are you doing here?" The subtle tension, along with skipping lunch and the fast ride from the Upper East Side, had him trembling with hunger. "I'm ordering a pizza." He pulled out his phone and searched for Bleecker Street Pizza.

"None for me. I'm heading back home. But I came to tell you something."

Mom waited while Jett consulted with Lexa for toppings. Then asked her if she needed anything from the kitchen. Which she did not.

"Are you finished avoiding me? I want to tell you my news." She smiled as she set aside her tea.

"Well, then, shoot." Arms folded, he stood between the living room and the kitchen banquette.

"I'm engaged." And there it was, said with aplomb as she raised her left hand, showing off the large diamond hugging her ring finger.

Engaged? He lowered his arms. Weakened his stance. "To whom?" He hadn't even known she was dating. Typical Mom. Not a word to anyone until she'd decided and her plans were set. "Who's the poor schlob?"

"Jett." Lexa's rebuke surprised him. "Congratulations, Miranda."

"Thank you." Mom beamed. "The *lucky* schlob is Oz Griffin. We've known each other—"

"Oz? The outfitter?" Jett remembered him. His company was one of *Going Wild*'s first sponsors.

"Yes, the outfitter. You liked him when you met first met him."

"Yeah, sure. Oz?" Jett crashed down in the nearest chair as an image of the angular outdoorsman with the rock-hard features and commanding voice holding and kissing his mother flashed across his imagination.

He shuddered. *Never doing that again.*

"How long have you been together?" Lexa brought in the civility.

"About two years. He came to us with the idea to create the Bear Wilder brand within his Griffin Gear line. Did I tell you the line launches this fall, Jett?"

"No." Oz? His mother?

"Two years?" Lexa's soft voice hammered on. "Right after Storm died?"

"In truth, right before. I'm not sure how I'd have gotten through without Oz."

"You could've called your other son." The confession riffed from his lips with a bitter power.

Mom leveled her calm gaze at him. "I could, yes, but he was as dark and wounded as I. If not more."

"Ever think a call from you would have helped?" Even to him, his bitterness sounded slightly unjustified. But since when did she deserve his loyalty? His benefit of the doubt?

"And what do you think I was doing? The cha-cha?"

"Isn't that what you do when times get rough? Leave? Seek your fun?"

She reached for her handbag and stood. "I'd hoped you'd celebrate my good news, but I can see we are no further down the road than when you were a boy."

She started for the door and he was on his feet before he could calculate what he was going to say or do.

"Mom, wait. Is that all? You just wanted to tell me you're engaged?"

"There's more if you care to hear." She hesitated, then went on. "I would like you to be there, but if you feel it's too much of a strain, I suppose I'll have to understand."

"When is it? I have a lot on my plate. My dissertation is being published at the end of the month."

"Oh, I see. Then congratulations are in order for you as well. Oz and I are finalizing the date. But it will be in a few weeks. At the farm." She smoothed her skirt under her as she returned to the couch. "Lexa, perhaps you can convince him."

"Leave me out of it. I wasn't much good at that when we were married, never mind now."

Both women glared at him. Cleary he was on trial. Yet he was not the unfeeling, selfish parent who walked out. Or the cold, stony-silent wife who filed for divorce.

"I'll come if I can. Either way, I take it you're still going to marry the guy. My presence or not doesn't make a difference." Where was that pizza? He was ravenous.

"There's one more thing." She shifted her fancy bag from one hand to the next. "Your dad has finally agreed to scatter Storm's ashes over the lake. We hope that's okay with you. Did he ask you? He said he would. Anyway, I've been after him for two years and he's come to peace with it, so we're going to do it after the wedding."

"No, he didn't ask me, but it's good. Storm would have liked to rest on the lake."

The lake where they swam, canoed, and fished all summer. Played hockey in the winter. Until Jett went out too far and broke through the ice.

"I'm a bit conflicted about a wedding *and* a funeral. Sounds like a rom-com plot." Mom stared at her feet. Her odd manner, seemingly uncomfortable, forced Jett to see her in a new light. "But I'd like both of my sons at my wedding." A contemplative hush descended. "And if only one attends, frankly I'd prefer the one not in the urn." Her voice warbled a bit. "And everyone who matters will be there. We won't have to draw them back at a later date to put Storm to rest." She turned toward the foyer. "I realize you and I have not been close over the years, Jett, but you *are* my only child. I'd like you to be there. If not for me, for your father and Storm. Lexa, see if you can talk some sense into him. And you are most welcome to come too. Storm saw you as the sister he never had."

"Mom, please, Lexa doesn't need a lecture on what Storm felt about her. She probably won't come anyway."

"I can speak for myself, Jett. Miranda, we'll see."

Mom walked over to Jett and, with tenderness, brushed aside his wavy, unruly bangs. "Have you talked to anyone about what happened on that mountain? A counselor? A stranger?"

Her question froze any sort of reply he might have mustered.

"I see. Well, someday you're going to have to tell someone what happened." She exited with the soft closing of the front door.

Jett fired to his feet and paced the narrow space between the banquette and the balcony, a vise around his chest.

"Jett, what is she talking about?" Lexa clutched the opening of his blue button-down over her tube top and yoga pants as she rose off the couch.

"Nothing. And how do you like her? 'Come to my wedding.' Like she didn't walk out on her first marriage and her two sons. Just burns me up, burns me up."

"It was twenty years ago, Jett."

"And do you know she's never once said, 'I'm sorry'? Not my fault we don't have a good relationship." Pace, turn, pace, turn. "A wedding *and* memorial. Only Miranda Wilder would combine the two. I guess to her, they're the same. Her wedding, Storm's funeral." His angst adhered to his cold anger, coating him with the emotional epoxy of "*What happened on that mountain?*"

No one had ever asked him so directly. Not even Dad, who was there at a distance. Kicking aside one of the banquette chairs, Jett moved toward the door. "I've got to get out of here." Before he suffocated.

"Where are you going?" The door slammed against her question.

Down the elevators and out the lobby door, Jett burst into fall's first crystal-cool evening, jogged down the stone steps, and headed north.

To where, he didn't know. He didn't care.

Chapter 15

LEXA

With her arm cradled against her side, Lexa collected Jett's empty glass and set it in the dishwasher along with Miranda's cup and saucer.

"What happened on the mountain?"

She glanced toward the door, still rattling from Jett's decisive slam.

Storm had died piloting in his wingsuit off Eiger—but Miranda's question probed beneath the physical details to matters of the heart.

Lexa made her way back to the couch, fighting a brewing headache. This one wasn't from the concussion but the tension of Miranda's visit.

She pulled the throw over her legs and aimed the remote at the TV. Then switched it off again.

After Storm died, Jett shut her out as he sank into despair. Then he lost himself in his book, writing when he wasn't working, barely sleeping.

If she asked him what was going on, he snapped at her. Then she'd snap back. The fights escalated before crashing down into a bedrock of silence.

She knew he was grieving, but she was too. She'd lost a friend, a brother. And as husband and wife, weren't they supposed to be there for each other? For better, for worse?

"What happened on the mountain?"

Lexa kicked off the throw. She should leave him be—Jett preferred to process alone—but the exchange with his mom left her unsettled.

She'd always known Miranda's leaving the family had marked him, but this evening she caught a glimpse of how deep and wide the scar.

His phone pinged from the table. She got up to read the screen. The pizza was on its way.

In the bedroom, she wiggled her sock feet into her sneakers and tried to tie them. Failed. Next she wrapped up as best she could in one of Jett's Florida State hoodies.

She'd been cleared from the concussion but still moved rather slowly, careful not to bump or bounce against anything.

Dr. Haft had an emergency and cancelled her past Monday's appointment. Everyone at the story society had been all prepared to celebrate how well her arm was healing, but she had nothing new to share.

The group endeared themselves to her more and more.

Grabbing Jett's phone as well as her own, Lexa headed out, making sure the door didn't lock behind her. Riding down to the first floor, she wondered where she'd start looking for him. He could be anywhere by now.

Maybe she could stand on the stoop and shout, "Jett, pizza is here."

His dad said that worked every time when he was a kid.

"You'd see the boys bursting from the woods like wild animals."

First stop, the gym. But the well-lit room was empty except for a perky girl on the elliptical. Next she checked the media room. But it was dark and quiet.

"Jett?" She scanned the shadows. Looked for any movement in the movie theater chairs.

Through the lobby, she stepped outside, the cold nipping against her face as the sun moved west with the last of its warmth, leaving deceptive fiery ribbons across the passing blue.

Lexa descended to the steps, gripping the iron railing, careful of the clump of men and women brushing past her in the narrow space to enter the building.

Dr. Haft's nurse warned her on the cancellation call not to get bumped. To take all precautions. Lexa embraced every warning with intent.

Jett, where'd you go?

She scanned the sidewalk, busy with joggers and dog walkers, to the stoplight and back again. She searched through the rising street-lights down the adjacent avenue. Maybe he'd walk out of the corner store.

Taking a few steps north, she was immediately boxed in by three boys on skateboards.

Clutching her arm, she backed toward the building and pressed against the rough brick.

"You should be inside."

The voice came from the huddled lump at the base of the stairwell.

"Jett?"

"Go back inside, Lex."

She started to go, then turned around. *Wait.* The wife Lexa would turn on her heel with a huff and go inside, sure of his rejection, and not speak to him the rest of the night. Perhaps even the next day. Which was easy to do when she worked twelve hours and he lived and breathed his grief, his course work, grading papers, and writing his great American novel.

However, ex-wife Lexa was not subject to his moods. She didn't give a flip. His attitude couldn't touch her.

With her good hand against the wall, she lowered to one knee, then dropped onto her backside, barely avoiding a dog walker with no fewer than six scampering Yorkies.

"I realized today my hip is still sore from the fall," she said. "The less my arm hurts the more other body parts demand attention."

"Like I said, you should be inside." He raised his head and peered at her with red-rimmed eyes, shoving back his untamed blond hair.

"Your pizza is on its way." She handed over his phone as a large mastiff sniffed at her feet and wagged his tail before his human moved him on.

"Good. I thought I'd be an old man before it arrived." He checked his phone screen, then cradled it in his palm.

"What's going on?"

"Sometimes I hate her, Lexa, and it knifes me in the gut."

"Why do you hate her?"

"Because she left. Because she's a selfish wench."

"I don't think she meant to hurt you," she said, inching a little closer to Jett's warm body.

Jett shot her a steely glare. "Don't be on her side."

"I'm not on anyone's side. I'm just saying I don't think she meant to hurt you."

"Then what did she mean? 'Hi, boys, I've got news. This ol' life is suffocating me so I'm out of here for California. Check you later, kids. Love and kisses.'"

"Really? That's what she said?"

"Yeah, almost. It was certainly her tone." He twisted his phone in his hands. "I can't believe you'd defend her. Remember our wedding? Huh? She wanted to film everything. Even our honeymoon."

"She's a producer. A communicator. She wanted to gift us a detailed movie of our big day. She knew we wouldn't remember half of it."

"She aired it on the show without asking. She's a money-grubbing, ambitious, self-focused shrew. Hope Oz knows what he's getting into."

"Don't you think people change?"

"Not her."

"Look, at least she was honest." Ex-wife Lexa definitely had different answers than wife Lexa. "And you're adults now. You can have a relationship with her if you—"

"Lexa, just stop talking."

She shrank back against the wall feeling too much like wife Lexa as another canine sniffed her feet. Jett stretched out his hand and the dog settled his head under Jett's palm.

"Where is that pizza?" He checked his phone. "It should be here by now."

"Bear never said anything?"

"About pizza?"

"No, goofball, about your mom leaving."

Jett scoffed. "About a year later he sat us down and asked how we were doing. Said something like, 'I tried to work it out, boys.' We said we were fine. What else could we say? He was making us late for the girls' basketball game."

"Nothing was said when he asked her back as producer of the show?"

"Other than she was 'the best,' no. And she knew him, and what the show was about. Storm started going on-site just to be around her."

"But you refused." She knew the story. He'd told her in bits and pieces throughout their relationship. Yet there were always details missing.

"Until they made me go. Otherwise, give me a book, thank you. Used to bug the heck out of her too. Dad and Storm would be rafting a class-five river and I'd be in the tent with a flashlight and GPR. Or Bradbury. Or Faulkner."

The long-awaited delivery cyclist pulled up and dropped his bike against the stone post.

"Bleeckers?" Jett jumped up. "For Wilder?"

The delivery rider didn't even bat an eye. Handed the large box to Jett with a plastic bag of napkins and seasonings, then rode away.

"Dinner is served." Jett adjusted the box between them and handed Lexa a napkin with a sigh. "Don't tell anyone, but when Mom said she was marrying Oz I realized I'd been holding out hope that Mom and Dad would one day get back together. What an idiot."

"I don't think you're ever too old to want your parents reconciled, Jett."

He passed her a large slice and a packet of parmesan cheese without a reply.

The first bite of warm dough, hot cheese, and sauce with crisp pepperoni was heaven. She hadn't eaten since breakfast, and a mid-morning pain pill knocked her out through lunch.

"We need drinks." Jett wiped his mouth and hollered at the Giovanni kid from the second floor who rode his bike up and down the street. "Brian, can you get two Cokes from the corner market?" He pulled a ten from his pocket. "Keep the change."

"Thanks." Brian popped a spirited wheelie and was off, standing up, swaying his bike from side to side as he pedaled.

"Mom made good pizza," Lexa said. "We had it every Friday night. It was her way of keeping a touch of America in the house no matter where we lived."

It was a repeated story. She must have told him Mom's patriotization stories a dozen times. But they were worth telling.

"I remember your mom's pizza," he said. "For us it was spaghetti. Dad's specialty. Otherwise it was box food, take-out, sandwiches, grilled meat." Lexa listened to Jett's familiar stories, okay that it drew her to him. He needed the comfort of a friend. Friend? Was she becoming his friend? "Though Storm made a mean beef-and-cheese dish. Otherwise we didn't have many traditions. All the traditions left with mom. She was never very cuddly but she liked to do up holidays and birthdays."

"You're thirty years old, Jett. Why don't you talk to her? Man to mom?"

"And say what? 'You hurt me'? Can't change the past. Can't undo what she did."

"You sound like you want to be mad at her."

"Maybe I do. Look, Lexa, nothing she or anyone can say will make what she did okay."

"But you might understand her."

"The big question is why doesn't she talk to me?" Jett passed her another slice of pizza as Brian returned with two cold pop bottles. Jett twisted off the cap for Lexa and set it on her far side. "She runs *Going Wild* like a drill sergeant. Manhandles mega-advertisers. But she can't find the guts to talk to her son."

With a side glance at her ex, Lexa settled against the apartment building and watched Greenwich Village go by as she dined, filling her stomach and perhaps a little bit of her soul. This was the first honest, heartfelt conversation she'd had with Jett in years.

Washing down a bite of pizza crust with a swig of her cold, fizzy drink, Lexa dared a provocative query.

"What did your mom mean when she asked what happened on the mountain?"

He shifted his position, uncurling his legs and stretching them onto the sidewalk. "Other than him dying? Nothing. She makes stuff up."

"Why would she make up something about that?"

"I'm not sure, Lex."

So why didn't she believe him? But it wasn't her burden to bear. She was his *ex*-wife.

"Remember the night I called you at three a.m. to see if you were okay, and found out I woke you from a bad dream?" Jett pulled out another slice of pizza with cheese tendrils dangling.

"How could I forget? It was right after the divorce. It freaked me out that you knew to call me."

"Yeah, it was weird. We talked until five."

"I was so tired that day. First time I left ZB before six at night in three years." Lexa finished her slice and wiped her hand on her napkin. "I'm going in. The chill is bothering my arm." She tried to stand but her left leg collapsed, and she tumbled into Jett's lap. Her broken arm clapped against the stone-and-brick steps.

"My arm." Involuntary tears gathered as she breathed through the piercing pain.

In a Superman move, Jett was on his feet, Lexa scooped into his arms. "I told you to be careful."

"My leg . . . fell asleep . . . sore hip . . . Oh man my arm hurts."

Up the stairs two at a time, he pushed the elevator button with the toe of his high-tops. The doors parted, and Jett pushed in, past a young couple trying to exit. Again, with his toe he pushed the button for floor three.

"Jett, I can walk. Put me down—"

"Quiet." He curled her tight against his chest, so she sank into his embrace.

"Jett, my leg is awake now." But she didn't fight him. She was tired and engulfed in the shards shooting down her arm. A prickly perspiration collected around her neck and ran down her back.

At the third floor, Jett charged toward his apartment. Adjusting Lexa's weight, he reached for the knob. "When did you last take a pain med?"

"About eleven."

He tried the knob again. "Lex, did you lock the door?"

"No, I checked on my way out. I left it open."

He kicked at the barrier. "Well, it's locked now."

Back to the elevator, they rode down to the first floor. "Jett, please put me down."

"Hush, I'm in the groove." He banged on the superintendent's door with his foot. "Billy, I'm locked out. Need you to let me in."

She felt ridiculous yet curiously content as they waited for the super to appear, a five o'clock shadow on his loose jawline, a beer in hand. "How'd you do that?"

"Really, you want to figure out the cause while we still have the problem?"

He pointed to Lexa. "She okay?"

"Yes, I'm fine."

"Hurt her arm. Come on. Let us in."

With a grumble, Billy wandered off for his master keys while Jett called for the elevator.

Lexa pushed against him with her good hand. "Jett, please, put me down."

"Billy, I got the elevator." Jett held it open with his foot, nodding for the sleepy-eyed building manager to get a move on.

He cradled her in his arms as Billy unlocked the door, then he carried Lexa inside, through the living room to the bedroom.

A short snicker escaped her.

"What?" He lowered her against her pillows, his face so close she caught a whiff of citrus and spice on his skin.

"You. Carrying me upstairs, downstairs, upstairs again."

He jerked back. "You were in pain."

"Jett—" She gripped his sleeve and peered into his eyes. "I can take care of myself."

"I never said you couldn't, but isn't it nice, Lexa, when someone steps up once in a while? It doesn't make you less strong to need and accept help." He remained close, hovering over her. "It always crushed me when you were sick or hurt. Even with a cold."

"You never said."

"I didn't want you to think I was a sissy."

"I would never think you were a sissy."

"I know sometimes a woman hurts in places a man can't see." He slid in next to her and slipped his hand carefully around her back and angled her toward him. "Not unless she tells him."

"Sometimes a man is hurt in places a woman can't see. Unless he tells her."

There it was. Their stalemate.

Jett moved slowly toward her. "Lexa—"

His kiss arrived slow, with their eyes locked, their breathing in rhythm. As they sank into the pillows, their bodies responded to the very familiar, pleasurable road.

He tasted like life—the tang of tomato sauce, the sweetness of cheese, and the cool wet of a cold drink.

It made her hungry for more and she tugged on the bottom of his shirt with her good hand.

This kiss. This kiss. She floated, forgetting the pain in her bones. His moves, his touch, were so intoxicating, filling her more than any pizza pie ever could.

Just when she thought she'd forget herself and let her passion carry her away, Jett sat up.

"I'm sorry. I can't"—he turned for the door, leaving her in a sudden chill—"take advantage."

"Who said you're taking advantage?"

"Me." He started out of the room, down the hall. "Helping you these past three weeks, seeing you half naked, knowing you're in here night after night . . ." His low scoff scraped against her. "Lexa, you still press all my buttons. I mean, what are we doing here? I could continue without a thought of tomorrow." He swung his hand in the air between them. "You're vulnerable. I'm vulnerable."

"And divorced." She finished his thought.

"Exactly."

Her confession mingled with his, tossing cold water on their passion. Of course. What was she thinking? She'd regret it tomorrow. Jett knew she would.

She never, ever intended to be in his life again, let alone his bed.

"We know we're not a good couple." She reasoned out loud. "Failed once, why try again? You didn't even write me a note when the other society members did. After I broke my arm."

"Yeah, well, what could I say on paper that I couldn't say to you in person? Why, exactly, are we wrong for each other?"

"Do you not remember the last two years of our marriage? I mean, other than for carnal pleasures, we hardly spoke."

"Yeah, carnal pleasures. Not speaking. Unless . . ." The heat and possibility of his "unless" awakened the rest of her yearnings. "We could, say, take a break from our divorce and—"

"Take a break?" His suggestion intrigued her. But wait, what course would she be taking? No, this was temporary insanity. An emotional response to her physical desires.

"Wilder." An angry voice battered the front door. "Did you leave your trash on the sidewalk?"

"Lexa?" Jett remained fixed on her.

"Jett, I, um, I don't know." But her rapid pulse knew. Yes. Please.

"Wilder! I'm coming in. I know you're there."

Jett released a mild expletive and beelined from the room.

"Settle down, I'm coming."

Lexa slumped, listening.

"Dogs . . . all over. Pop . . . crusts."

"All right, all right, you're right. When Lexa got hurt I just ran inside. I'll clean it up." Jett's voice faded as he exited the apartment.

With an exhale, Lexa scooted to the end of the bed and tapped the door closed. Lying on her side, she tried to drift off, but her dreams stalled as her imagination replayed the motion and feel of Jett's kiss, treasuring it over and over.

Chapter 16

ED

He'd done it. Typed three pages. Yes, sir, he'd actually written down his life with Esmie.

Wasn't much, mind you, just how her beauty knocked him sideways when he first saw her outside the Winter Garden theater.

Luckily for him, the co-op was relatively calm all week, leaving him to peck out a bit of his story.

But as he made his way up the subway stairs to Fifth Avenue, terror sank into his old bones.

Could he share something so holy? What if they laughed? Or worse, smiled politely and muttered, "How nice."

How nice? Would they not feel the love and passion? Last thing he wanted was for anyone or anything to spoil his memories.

By the time he walked through the Bower doors, Lexa had spread out her dinner. Soup and salad.

For pity's sake. How'd she expect him to muster up courage on soup and *salad*? The light fare put him in mind of Mabel's pasta. He never did join her for leftovers. What he wouldn't give now for a rib-sticking, hearty meal.

"Evening, all." Ed set his briefcase in his chair with a nod at Chuck.

"Lexa, I figured you'd bring a couple of ZB Burgers." The big guy took up a paper plate and stared at the rabbit food.

"Me too," Ed said.

"Sorry," Lexa said, stabbing at her lettuce with an awkward left hand, trying to balance the plate with the fingers of her right. "I was hankering for Hale and Hearty's soups."

"Sorry? They should apologize to you, Lex." Coral shot Ed and Chuck a *look*. "She is our wounded sister, boys. Be nice."

"Wounded yes, but she had this delivered from GrubHub. Lex, couldn't you have picked ribs or something?"

"No one said you had to eat it, Chuck."

"You tell him." Coral swatted him with her plate, the color of love, or at least a crush, on her cheeks. Ed saw the same on Holly when she brought Brant home the first time.

What have we here?

"How was everyone's week?" Jett carried a bowl of steaming soup and a dripping bottle of water to his chair. "Any *stories* to tell?"

"No."

"None."

"Not me."

Well, a fine story society they were turning out to be. No one but Ed had a story to tell? Filling his plate with the garden salad mix, he determined not to go first. Someone else would have to burp up a tale or two before he led them down his memory lane.

"How was your week, Lexa?" Coral said, taking her seat, balancing her plate on her lap.

"Boring. I'm home all day."

Well, well, another cloaked glance? Darn if Ed didn't see something in her expression when she looked at Jett.

"Watching any good soaps?" Ed worked the salad tongs and loaded his plate. "My Esmerelda loved *All My Children.*"

"Soap operas? No. I try to read but end up falling asleep. I read work email but since I can't type any replies, I end up frustrated. I finally called Zane today and talked for two hours, telling him what to do with some of the stuff going on. You'd think someone in the office would come up with a solution but it's like they've lost their heads. They try to make it hard."

"You are singing my song, Lexa," Coral said.

"You're supposed to be resting." Chuck poked at his salad, knocking a piece of lettuce to the floor.

"My concussion protocol was cleared, so technically I can work." Lexa motioned to her arm. "But this thing is holding me back."

"When can you go back to work?" Coral again.

"I won't know until I see the doctor later this week. I hope to go back next Monday." Lexa offered a sincere smile.

Ed liked her all the more. She carried her wounds with courage and boldness. Like she'd been kicked when she was down but refused to stay on the ground.

"Here's to your health and well-being." Ed saluted her with his bottle of water as he sat in his chair.

Might as well brave this heap of bunny food.

With a forkful of vegetables drowning in dressing, he commenced eating. Esmerelda used to rag him about eating his veggies. This salad was for her.

"Lexa, this cream of tomato with chicken and orzo is so good." Coral closed her eyes as she savored a bite.

Ed liked her more every week too. She was also strong and bold but cut from a different cloth than any woman he'd ever known. Except Esmerelda. She'd been a society girl. Though not quite as high society as a Winthrop.

Coral had been guarded the first three weeks, but tonight she shoved back the draperies and opened a few windows.

"I'll have to get a cup when I finish my salad. Eating with my left hand is so awkward."

Without a word, Jett pulled around a small table that had been home to a lamp and set it in front of Lexa.

"This ought to help." Then he retrieved a bowl of soup and set it on the corner, leaving room for her to eat her salad.

Ed caught his attention as Jett returned to his grand high-back chair and gave him a slight nod. *Well done, young man.*

"Jett, what about you? How's your dissertation?" Coral turned their attention to the professor.

"Writing an introduction. Going through some more research from a professor at Oxford. Should have it to the publisher by the fifteenth, no problem."

"You're happy with it?"

He shrugged. "Why not? I'm the newest expert on GPR, and the school will get a lot of money because of this publication. So yes, I'm happy. Chuck, what about you? Good week? Hear any fun gossip in your car?"

He shook his head. "Nothing worth repeating."

"Did you see the twins?" Lexa said. "Are you a Wednesday and weekend dad?"

A burly, deep grunt rumbled in Chuck's chest. Ah, the big man had secrets.

"No," he said after a moment, giving his salad the business with a plastic fork.

"Don't tell me you switch off every other night." Coral's gaze followed him. "For Han and I, our parents—"

"Leave it, Coral." Chuck slammed his plate in the trash. Lettuce bounced and floated over the side. Grumbling, he picked up the litter and grabbed a water and returned to his chair, the rumble in his voice still vibrating in the room. "We can't all have the perfect divorce like your parents."

Coral sat back, turning slightly away from Chuck in pinched silence.

"How was your week, Coral?" Ed said, trying to give Chuck space to cool off.

As the senior member of the group, he should ensure good etiquette among the society members. He was no expert, but he was raised in a time when people respected one another.

She wiped her lips with the corner of her paper napkin. "Besides losing my company? Good." She shot a sideways glance at Chuck.

The society collectively gasped, and while Ed was 100 percent interested in how and why this fine beauty might lose her family business, her confession changed the atmosphere and inspired a rather selfish notion he might not get to read his piece about Esmerelda.

Putting it off meant he'd have to wait another week, and he had no assurance he wouldn't permanently change his mind.

"How are you losing your company?" Chuck all but snarled. What was eating him?

"I'm not really sure." She lowered her eyes and Ed almost demanded Chuck step outside so she could have an honest moment without fear of his bark. "We're in the red. In every category." She offered the society a sad smile. "However, my team is convinced the blame goes to our new lip gloss line, Pink Coral."

"How can one product drain the whole company?" Ed said.

"Expenses. Diverted advertising dollars. Brand inconsistency causing concern with long-time customers, the head of the company distracted by a prince . . ."

"But you had a team in place." Lexa exchanged her salad for the soup. Ed rose up just in case she needed help. "They didn't have your back? Once Zane had to go home for three weeks to help his parents. We got more done in that time than in three months when he's in the office."

"Three weeks is one thing, but I was in and out, traveling back and forth, distracted with my wedding. Even when I was here, I was *there*, across the ocean in my mind with him." She tapped the side of her head. "I didn't think I was that distracted, but the numbers indicate I was. I should talk to my father, though I'm terrified of what he'll say."

"What will he say?" Jett got up for another cup of soup.

"That the team is right. I need to kill Pink Coral. But it was my first product launch. I spent months in Paris developing the formula, and another year and a half testing the product, designing the packaging and marketing." She held her soup bowl in her palm. "No Winthrop or Calhoun woman has ever failed."

"Neither will you. You'll figure this out," Lexa said with a bold confidence. "About two years ago we thought ZB was running red. We dug, did some research, and learned our prices were too low. Customers didn't believe we were really organic at the prices we'd set. So we raised them a dollar. Boom. Back in the black."

"We've looked at marketing. It's not our price. It's more like a preteen lip gloss doesn't fit our brand. We're the cosmetic company for adult, even aging, women."

"I love your stuff and I'm not an old lady," Lexa said. Ed loved how the girl with the broken arm tried to encourage the girl with the broken business. "If you want to brainstorm, I'd be happy to think outside the box with you. I know nothing about cosmetics but I love business and marketing, developing strategies."

"She is good at thinking outside the box," Jett said.

"I feel rather like a stone these days. I arrive at work early, ready to go. An hour later I want to quit," Coral said. "I appreciate your offer to help, Lexa, but I wouldn't know where to begin. My own team, I suppose. But I have to do something. This last year has been humbling if not humiliating. I'm not sure I could face another public downturn. Dragging CCW through the mud would be worse than the mess with Gus."

"Coral," Ed said. "What *did* happen with Gus?"

"Not tonight, Ed." She carried her soup bowl to the trash. "Besides, I've taken enough of everyone's time. What about you, Ed? How's your memoir?"

The time had come. "Since you asked—" Ed reached for his briefcase.

"And you two." Coral pointed to Jett and Lexa. "What's going on? There's something different."

"Us?" Jett said at the exact same moment Lexa said, "Nothing." They averted their gazes, and Ed was sure he felt a spark between them. He was somewhat of a "spark detector."

"Are you sure?"

"Yes, I'm sure. Ed, your memoir?" Lexa gave him her best smile. Underneath it said, *"Please read."*

"Jett?" No denying the teasing light in Coral's eyes. "Nothing to add?"

"Not a thing. Ed, so you wrote on your memoir?"

Well, guess he was up. He produced his typed pages, realizing too late he had a drop of coffee on the bottom of the first page. "So,

um, well, what do I do? Just read out loud?" He offered the pages to
Jett. "Maybe you should read them."

"It's your story, Ed. You read."

"Wait, I want more soup." Lexa started to rise slowly from her
table and chair, but Jett jumped up.

"I got it. What kind do you want? The chicken soup is gone.
Tomato basil or spinach artichoke cheddar?"

"Spinach, please."

When Lexa had her soup, Ed stood. Then sat. No, better to
stand. But his legs wobbled. Best sit for fear of falling over.

He cleared his throat once, twice, and a third time, irritated at
the flashing tremors.

"I have to admit, I thought putting my life on paper would be
easier."

"Welcome to every writer's world, Ed," Jett said. "Sportswriter
Red Smith coined the famous line, 'Writing is easy. You just open a
vein and bleed.'"

"Well, I didn't go quite that far, but good to know I have room to
grow." Good, he'd made the society laugh. "Here goes."

But nothing came out. The words stuck to his dry tongue. He
slugged down some water then tried again.

The words swam across the page and he could not command
his lips.

"Ed?" Chuck patted him on the back. "The library closes at nine."

He nodded. Couldn't even manage a simple *okay*.

"You don't have to read if you don't want to, Ed." Jett's voice was
kind. "I understand it's personal."

"J-just give me a sec here, you know." When did that bullfrog
move into his throat? Fist to his lips, Ed coughed and hacked, then
tossed back another splash of water. "My glasses."

The society waited while he fished them from the briefcase. He
began reading before he could change his mind.

"I met Esmerelda when I was a kid of twenty-five. I was a fresh-
man at Queen's College after doing my stint in Uncle Sam's army

and a year in Nam. I worked part time for the grocer on the corner of Seventy-Sixth and Northern Boulevard.

"I'd gotten off early that night and headed to Times Square on New Year's Eve with a couple of buddies. The year was 1966 and I was only a few months home from my all-expenses-paid trip to a war.

"The weatherman predicted snow that night, but we were on fire for a good time. My friend Harold, who liked to say Harold Square was named for him, said he smelled love in the air. He was always saying stuff like that, you know?

"We bought a couple of hamburgers and decided to take in a show. You had to be careful of the theater district in those days due to a lot of unpleasant people hanging around, gangs and such.

"We was making our way down Broadway when I laid eyes on her. She was standing outside the Winter Garden theater with her girlfriends. She wore a fur coat with a matching hat. Her long blonde hair was in curls over her shoulders and down her back.

"I was a goner right then and there. The fellas kept on walking but not me. I had to stop and talk to this vision.

"I didn't know much about art, still don't, but I know a masterpiece when I see it. I had to know her name. Once she looked at me with her baby blues I turned to jelly.

"I called the guys back and convinced them to buy tickets to the show, *Mame*, which they grumbled about but settled down once they saw there was a dame for each one of us. Luck was smiling on me that night.

"My buddies were Harold, Eric, and George.

"So there I was sitting next to this vision. Esmerelda Belmont. During the closing song, I held her hand and never let go. I'd met perfection.

"We married six months later and enjoyed eight years of wedded bliss before she left this world for the great beyond, letting go of my hand for the very first time.

"I miss her every day."

His voice quivered a bit as he finished. He folded the paper and tucked it in the open case. The group was quiet. Too quiet.

"Ed, I can only hope my husband, should I find one, will write such beautiful things about me one day." Coral's kindness made him want to bawl like a baby. So he thanked her with a nod.

"Guess she was something special," Chuck said.

"I can hear how much you loved her in your voice." Lexa angled around to touch his knee with her free hand, her expression so much like Holly's when she was just his daughter and not trying to be his governess.

He waited for Jett's approval. If the professor approved, then maybe he had something. Jett sat back, his Chuck Taylor shoes flat on the library floor.

"What's the rest of the story? How'd she die?"

"The good Lord came for her."

"She died in her sleep?"

"See here, Jett, I want to write about her life and our love, not her death. We had Holly, of course, but this is pretty much the long and short of our story."

"Eight years of wedded bliss? No bumps. No hiccups? No arguments or fights?"

"We didn't always agree, but she was perfect—"

"No woman is perfect."

"No man either," Lexa said.

"Esmerelda was perfect."

"Ed . . ." Jett said.

"Young man, you may find it hard to believe, seeing as you divorced your wife—"

"She divorced me."

"—but Esmerelda and I were perfect for one another. A match made in heaven, if you believe in such a place."

Which he did, if he held any hope of seeing her again.

A cloud crossed Jett's face, then quickly faded.

"Ed, aren't you trying to write a memoir? What you read us was nice but more like a synopsis. 'We met, we fell in love, she died.' That's all well and good, but what happened after you held her hand in the theater? How did you know she was the one? Did she love you instantly too? Did your families approve? Did you fight? Did you have a lot of things in common? Just what made her so perfect for you and you for her? Tell us her side of the story. Can you remember how *she* felt meeting you the first time at the Winter Garden? You have to write the good and the bad, the highs, the lows. There's no interest in a story that's summed up with everyone perfect and everything going well. I mean, dying so young has me intrigued. You can't leave out how you felt when the woman you loved left this world. That had to be painful."

"Very."

"Tell us that story too, Ed."

"I'd like a few years of happily ever after," Coral said. "A decade where everything goes well."

Chuck raised his hand. "Sign me up."

"Maybe that's why we're here?" Coral again. "To share our imperfect stories."

"But why us? Why now?" Lexa said.

"Are we back to a support group?" Chuck said. "Seems we're more than that. Plus I don't want to come here every week and cry over my problems. Or yours."

"Do I have to write about her death?" He'd never considered it. Not for a second. It wasn't what he wanted to say, what he wanted Holly to read. "My memoir is to remember love. To show people how it can be. Not that we didn't nip at one another now and then. But nothing knocked down and dragged out. We cared for one another like we vowed to on our wedding day."

"Ed, I'm not saying you weren't happy, even blissful, but the point of a memoir is to put it all out there. Tell the reader how you loved Esmerelda when it was hard and dark."

"It was never hard and dark. Why do people insist on marriage being so blame difficult? It's 'cause you're too selfish if it's hard. Or too wounded yourselves and can't see it. That's what I say." He was more riled than he cared to be.

"Because sometimes marriage is just hard." So, they were ganging up on him. No wonder Coral left her man, and Chuck, Jett, and Lexa were all divorced.

"I still say people can live selflessly, you know. There are couples who get along, don't argue. Marriages where love conquers all."

"Really?" Jett's expression conveyed his doubt. "I've never seen one."

"Well, you're looking at the remaining half of a solid, giving marriage." Ed glanced around the circle. "Granted, you don't see much of what Esmerelda and I had in these modern times. All I see here is you kids with heartbreak. I don't know what happened to you, Chuck, but I can see pain in your eyes." He patted his new friend's broad shoulder. "Lord only knows what happened with Coral and you two." He waved at Lexa, then Jett. "Esmie and I chose the way of love. It was the sixties, so naturally love was on our minds. We decided things together, and when she was right, I said sorry. When I was right, she made my favorite pot roast." He fell against his chair. "She made the best pot roast."

"Ed, if that's your story, tell it with gusto," Jett said. "Your daughter and grandchildren will be inspired."

Ed rubbed his chin. "I guess I could write down a bit more detail."

"A lot more detail." Jett smiled. "That's all I'm asking. You'll be surprised what you remember as you start to write. What about one of the times she said she was sorry by making pot roast?"

"I'd like to know how your second date went." Coral angled forward, her long graceful arms folded over her legs.

"Romance is for the birds," Chuck said with a quick, sideways glance at Coral. "However, now I want pot roast."

It was good to end the evening on a laugh. Jett volunteered to clean up after the librarian stuck her head in the Bower and told them it was closing.

"Ed, it's your turn to bring the food next week," Coral said as the rest of the group walked out.

"I'm thinking pot roast." Chuck clapped him on the shoulder then offered to drive him home.

"Ed, I want to hear more of your story," Lexa said. "I enjoyed what you wrote. You're a good writer."

Outside on the avenue, he parted company with the girls and walked with Chuck toward his car. Behind him, he heard Lexa accept a ride from Coral.

When Chuck dropped him off he clapped him on the shoulder again. "Keep writing, Ed. See you next week? With a pot roast?"

"Pot roast? Well, why not?"

Nice going, old man. He had exactly six days to figure out how to make the best pot roast a body ever tasted.

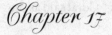

Chapter 17

JETT

Every week he was the first to arrive at the Bower and the last to leave. Tonight was no different.

He put away the folding tables and emptied the trash into the dumpster behind the library, hoping for the chance to talk to Lexa when he got home. The weekend hadn't afforded them a single moment to talk about their kiss.

Friday when he returned from cleaning up the pizza mess on the sidewalk, her closed door was a clear enough message. It also made him realize something.

He was right to pull back from where their kiss had been leading. But he also realized in that moment how much he loved having Lexa back in his life.

Saturday and Sunday he was part of the faculty advising for the upcoming homecoming festivities, which were a big to-do with NYC alums.

She took an Uber to her stylist for a hair appointment.

Just as he was about to bike home on Sunday, she texted she was at her place, watering plants and paying bills.

Abby's new boyfriend has a car. He picked me up.

Monday morning rolled around with the usual blur of getting ready. He started to bring up the kiss twice but words failed him.

Then she said it over breakfast.

"We did the right thing. Friday night. Not letting things get out of hand."

"Yeah, of course. I agree."

So he copped to a half truth, half lie. While cleaning up the pizza, he'd talked himself into a night of amour if she was willing. He'd deal with the consequences later.

Hitching his backpack over his shoulder, Jett aimed for the library exit but was stopped in the middle of the foyer by the sweet-faced Gilda.

"Have you explored the Bower?" she asked him.

"Explored the . . . what?"

"Explored the Bower. There are some very unique books on the shelves."

Jett peered down at Gilda. She was five foot nothing but carried the authority and aura of a giant. "Explored? No, not yet." He started to go, then turned back. "What kind of unique books?"

"So many lovely first editions in here." Gilda headed for the Bower. Jett followed his pied piper. "More than two hundred. Melville, Cooper, London, and Phipps Roth. Even Ray Bradbury." The little book curator stood aside for Jett to enter with fresh eyes.

Lowering his backpack into his chair, he scanned the shelves, taking his first good look at the leather-bound editions from the annals of American literature.

"I didn't realize there were so many first editions." Seeing a Hawthorne, he pulled it down and read the front matter.

Gold leaf, first edition. Signed.

"There are many signed too," Gilda said. "But you should see the libraries where I come from. Endless. Stories you cannot imagine. Some told in ancient times. Some waiting to be told. Waiting for the right one in the right time in history."

Jett glanced back. "What? Waiting? What do you mean? Where do you come from, Gilda?"

"Have you seen this one?" Gilda pointed to *Uncle Tom's Cabin*. Harriet Beecher Stowe. Another first edition. "Now there was a courageous writer who picked up the baton and ran."

Jett opened to the front page.

TO JOSEPH,
SINCERELY YOURS,
HARRIET BEECHER STOWE
MARCH 1855

"This book challenged and changed American culture. See how much the written word can do? See how truth can set a soul free?" Gilda asked.

Jett returned the book to the shelf with a lingering eye on Gilda. Every word caused the hair on the back of his neck to bristle.

Stepping away from her, he examined the shelves filled with literary greats of the last two centuries.

His book would never be in here. *Rites of Mars* wasn't even in the bookstores, let alone a collector's library. Let alone a story waiting to be told. He was no Bradbury.

Was he destined for literary greatness? Jett didn't really care for fame and acclaim. He just wanted the rest of the world to know the beauty and power of a story. How truth woven into the prose could change a person.

Without Gordon's books, he'd have grown up a cynic, never believing in love, much less romance. Not that he was any good at either one. *Ask Lexa.*

But he still hoped.

Listening to Ed's story tonight inspired him to believe again. Even if the old man was sugarcoating his story.

"Impressive, isn't it?" Gilda came alongside him.

"Extremely. A little piece of heaven on earth." In a place like this Jett could feel like himself, not the black sheep of the adrenaline-loving Wilders family. "I know my work will never be in a room like this."

"Jett, you have no idea where your work will go. You're such a young man." He glanced at Gilda. What did she know? "I read *Rites of Mars*. It was good."

"You read *Rites of Mars*?"

"Don't look so astounded. It's my *job*."

"Then you know I'm not equal to the names on these shelves."

"I don't know any such thing. You are far better than you know. Oh, have you seen the Phipps Roth books? We have all of his first editions." Gilda led Jett to the last stack of shelves tucked against the back corner. "Joseph and GPR were good friends. Winthrop was a patron of Gordon's during his writer's block."

"Winthrop? GPR never mentioned the man in his memoir or diaries."

"Isn't it odd? Joseph and Gordon were sparring partners. They loved a good debate. A good many transpired right in this room." Reaching up, she gently shoved one of GPR's books back into place, lining it up with the rest of the gilded leather spines.

"Do you think it's true? What they say about him?"

"That he had a ghostwriter?"

"Yes." Jett retrieved *The House in Murray Hill* for closer inspection. "You seem to know a lot about Gordon."

TO JOSEPH,
MY MENTOR AND FRIEND
GPR JANUARY 1910

"As I said, it's my job to know."

"I've done extensive research on him and have absolutely no reason to believe he was anything but honest, true, and genuine."

"Did you see a marked difference in his earlier work from *The Girl in the Carriage*?" she asked.

"Of course, but he'd aged a decade by then. I see maturity in *Girl*. A man who fell in and out of love. A man who navigated a broken heart. No matter how you strike it, the tone, the pacing, and characters are classic—"

"GPR." Gilda was watching him.

"Yes, very much so." He returned *Murray Hill* to the shelf. "What about the years between *Girl* and his next work? Do you know why there was such a long wait? The book was such a success, but he took five more years to publish."

"You're asking me? You're the professor." She pulled down *Moonlight on the Hudson*. "He was busy, traveling and lecturing, becoming a husband and father."

"And he had a lot to live up to." A feeling Jett knew all too well.

"I've always been curious about this one though." Gilda knelt and retrieved a manuscript sandwiched between two sheets of cardboard. "An unpublished novel."

"Of Gordon's?" Jett reached for the unbound pages. "How long has this been here?"

When she placed the book in his hands, he quivered a little. What a rare treasure.

"Since the early twentieth century, I believe. According to the notes."

Jett glanced at the chair against the far wall and backed up to take a seat. "This is amazing." He flipped through the pages. "Gilda, can I take this home to study?"

"I'm afraid it must stay here." She reached for it and he nearly snatched it back. "Come early next week and you can go through it."

"What do you know about it?"

"Nothing."

An unpublished GPR novel? The Roth Foundation would love to hear about this. Or did they already know? But no one had ever mentioned it to him. What of Dr. Paulson at Oxford? Jett's friend at Stanford? Or Tenley Roth?

"We're closing up." Gilda returned the manuscript to its place and beckoned Jett from the Bower. "Until next week. Good night."

They walked out together and she disappeared behind the door marked Private.

Jett faced the Bower. She couldn't drop a treasure in his lap like an unpublished GPR manuscript and expect him to leave without any initial inspection.

He backtracked for the big Bower door. Just a quick look. But the knob refused to turn. Jett jiggled and tried again. Locked. Gilda had locked him out.

Fine. He'd come back at the first opportunity. In the meantime, he'd reach out to fellow GPR aficionados and see if they knew of this surprising treasure.

Jett locked into his pedals and started his thirty-minute ride home, cutting through Central Park toward Columbus Avenue.

This manuscript could be the very key to quell the nasty rumors and whispers. Besides, anything new of Gordon's should be celebrated. First, of course, he'd have to corroborate the uniqueness of his find, but how marvelous. Renée would be thrilled to know Jett might have something new to add right before publication.

By the time he arrived home, he'd planned out how to get time with the book later this week or next Monday, how he'd tell Renée and Dr. Levi and Dr. Paulson.

"Lex, you here?" He crossed the living room with a glance down the hall toward the open master bedroom door. "Have I got something great to tell you. You won't believe it."

～

CORAL

Late Tuesday evening, Coral stopped by Dad's office. The man sitting at his assistant's desk was new.

Another one? Eric Winthrop III, titan of business and commerce, went through executive assistants like some men went through cars. Or women.

"Is Mr. Winthrop in?" Coral marched toward the massive teakwood double doors.

"Excuse me, miss?" The assistant dashed around the ornate desk that once belonged to their ancestor, Joseph Winthrop's grandfather. Hand-carved in Bulgaria and shipped to New York for a whopping five hundred dollars. "He's asked not to be disturbed." He blocked her just before she reached the knob.

"I'm his daughter."

"Do you have an appointment?"

"I don't need an appointment." She shoved the skinny, perspiring man aside—he'd be gone by week's end—and entered Dad's expansive and bright office. "I see you have a new assistant."

Dropping her bag on the chair by the door, Coral crossed to her father's desk. The plate-glass walls overlooked Manhattan southeast while the two interior sides hosted rare, collectible art.

"Did he look nervous?" Dad remained focused on his laptop.

"Overwhelmed."

"I'm giving him a chance. He just graduated from Wharton." At last he looked up. "How can I help you, Coral?"

"Can't a girl stop by to see her father?" She bent to kiss his cheek, patting him on the shoulder before staring out toward the East River.

"Yes, but you only come to my office when you need something."

"Do I?" Coral sat on the edge of his desk, reaching for the cut of moon rock he bought at a charity auction. "Makes me sound shallow."

Dad gently moved her hand from his precious stone. "I'm happy to help but I have a meeting in ten minutes."

She stared at her manicured fingers. She'd rehearsed this speech a hundred times, almost shared it with the story society, but she'd confessed enough in their short time together.

"Did I tell you I've joined a story society? We meet Monday nights in the Bower."

"The Bower? At the Fifth Avenue library? Is this your own venture? I'm glad to see you're stepping out." Dad moved to the bar and poured a finger of brandy. "Your mother called after the Gottlieb Gala. She believes the worst of your ordeal is over." Dad gestured to an empty glass. Coral shook her head. "Is it? You seem in better spirits lately. Have you been going out with your friends?"

"I am better, yes." But no, she hadn't been going out with her friends. Not her old ones anyway. "This little society has proved distracting enough."

"Your mom thinks you and Gus might start over. She was talking to his mother—"

"What? No. Dad, please tell Mom to stay out of it. Stop talking to the queen. I know you don't understand, but I am confident of my decision."

"Then enlighten me. Why *did* you leave?"

It'd been a year since she left her prince at the altar. Surely her parents understood by now she'd talk about it when she was ready.

"I came to talk about CCW." Spying the fridge paneled into the wall, Coral retrieved a water and took a seat on the imported leather sofa facing the ten-foot windows and stretch of the city.

Dad joined her, legs crossed, arms spread across the back of the couch, the tumbler of brandy dangling from his fingers, and waited.

"Dad." She pressed her palms together. This was hard. None of her practiced words fit the moment. "CCW is in trouble."

"Trouble?" He remained calm and took a sip from his glass. "Define trouble."

"In the red. Bleeding money. I'm flummoxed. Blaire and Dak are sure it's Pink Coral. But sales are steady on other products. Not where we projected, but not enough to make the bottom line so very, very red." She twisted the cap from the green glass bottle and took a long drink. "In the marketing surveys and focus groups the lip gloss was popular, Dad. We did so well. Moms loved the product as much as the girls." She waited for him to reply, struggling to hold his steady, unhanging gaze.

He angled forward. "Is this about Gus?"

"No, Dad, no. Gus? He's ancient history. I mean it when I say it, so don't doubt me." She slipped from the wool-and-tweed-blend suit jacket and folded it over the back of the couch. "It's about CCW."

"Coral, if you're losing money you have to find the bleed and stop it. If it's the new product, cut it. Are you being honest with yourself? You were out of the country, away from the New York office when you were with Gus. Have you gone over every detail? Reconciled sales with returns and profits? What about overhead, expenses, salaries, and taxes? You hired Blaire and Dak for their expertise and wisdom. Blaire turned *Glitter Girl* around overnight. I'd trust her if I were you. Or fire her."

"I've gone over everything. I see the sales and then reconcile with profits and it just seems I've fallen into a black hole. And I've refused to believe Pink Coral alone is the culprit." She sighed. "Maybe I need to face facts, listen to my team. All of them say the product, the advertising, the marketing, is not working. Returns are higher than expected and apparently the website, which was our main storefront, is hard to navigate. Yet when I try it I swear a two-year-old could order product if she had a credit card. Dad?" Her next question merited her frown and furrowed brow. "Do you think I'm not right to lead CCW? Should I hand it over to you? Can Marybeth or Wilma take it over?"

Aunt Marybeth and Cousin Wilma were a mother-daughter entrepreneur duo. Not versed in the cosmetics world but sharp, clever women running a sportswear company.

"I think the girl who found the courage and fortitude to break it off with her fiancé an hour before the wedding is the perfect girl to run CCW. Find *that* girl and confront what's going on."

"Sometimes I think I lost her forever."

"What made you break it off? What motivated you?"

He wouldn't believe her if she told him. He'd scoff. At least at first. Then ask a million questions. But maybe, perhaps, she could return to that source for wisdom.

"Dad, even if I find her, it doesn't mean I'll find what's breaking the company." The conversation made her head ache.

How she longed to just pack a bag and hop on a plane to the Caribbean or the South Pacific.

"Mr. Winthrop?" The perspiring, nervous assistant entered. "Senator Snead to see you."

"Ask him to wait, Miles. And you're sweating again." Dad raised his drink for a long sip and leveled his attention on Coral. "Then you know my rule. Clean slate. If you can't figure out the problem with your team, fire your senior leadership and start over. Hard to believe you're the same woman who convinced me you could run CCW six thousand miles away while fulfilling royal duties and perhaps producing royal babies. Is the company the reason you left Gus?"

"CCW is not the reason, no. But I'm sort of glad I did now. Who knows where we'd be in a year if I were not stateside." She reached for her handbag and water. "I will say CCW wasn't a bone of contention between us. I planned to commute, work long distance with an office set up in Port Fressea. Gus actually supported me. Now I should go. I believe Senator Snead is waiting for you." Coral aimed for the door. "Thanks, Dad."

"Are you ever going to tell me? The whole story? Not bits and pieces?"

Coral paused with her hand on the brass knob. "When I'm sure I totally understand myself, yes, I will."

The senator barged in. "Eric, I'm sorry I'm late. I hope I didn't keep you waiting." His fixed smile only accented the steely ire in his eyes. "Am I interrupting?"

"Stan, you remember my daughter, Coral."

"Of course, the one who bolted on the Lauchtenland prince."

"But you can call me Coral." She shook his hand. "Nice to see you again, Senator. Dad, I'll keep you posted."

"You're a Winthrop," he said. "Never forget."

How could she forget? The family name was carved into buildings, molded into plaques, and scattered throughout Manhattan history. Carved into her DNA.

Her grandmother and great-grandmother were courageous, ingenious women. Their blood ran in her veins. All she had to do was believe.

Believe. One simple word, and the truth about how she'd found the courage to leave Gus on a clear blue, blustery September day.

Chapter 18

LEXA

Dr. Haft was pleased with her progress. No surgery required. However, he still recommended she stay out of work another week.

"Your fall makes me nervous. Let's keep that arm safe."

Lexa objected but he insisted. And she wasn't one to rebel against authorities like doctors or police officers.

Though she kept her plans to visit ZB this afternoon to herself. What the doc didn't know wouldn't hurt him.

She was also well on her way to moving back to her apartment. Once she got hold of the superintendent and had him install a shower hose.

After slapping down her debit for the copay, Lexa was free. Out on the sidewalk, she turned her face to the receding heat of an October sun, texted Jett and Coral the news—they'd both hounded her during the appointment for an update—practically walked backward to the bakery on the corner in order to guard her arm, and grabbed a chocolate croissant and chocolate milk.

Standing on the corner, waiting for a cab, she glanced back at the corner drugstore and saw a sign for Pink Coral lip gloss. She nipped inside to buy one, try it out. Give Coral her uneducated opinion.

There was one left. Diamond Dust. A glittery soft rosy desert sand color.

"We can't keep this on the shelf," the clerk said as she checked out.

"Really? My friend owns CCW."

"Good for you." She was not impressed.

Stuffing the lip gloss in her bag, Lexa hailed a cab and made her way downtown to ZB Enterprises.

She'd been itching all week to check in, make sure Zane and Quent hadn't driven the place off the rails.

Dressed in her broken-arm attire—yoga pants and an oversized shirt—she pushed her way through the steel and glass entrance of ZB, the atmosphere electrifying her dull senses. Angling over the mezzanine railing, she greeted the buzzing Think Tank.

"My people."

"Lex! You're back."

"We miss you."

"Zane is crazy when you're not around."

She gave that one a thumbs-up. "Tell me about it."

Turning for her desk, she yearned to be back in the thick of things. Here is where she felt most like herself. Working, contributing, making a difference.

Being with Jett in their old apartment messed with her concrete reality. Made her want things she'd left in the past.

It had taken her two days to overcome the effects of the kiss. Monday morning in the breakfast silence, she broke through with her little comment. Sort of glad Jett agreed they were heading toward dangerous territory.

Then all day Monday she looked forward to seeing him again. And when he came home from the story society calling her name, so eager to tell her about the unpublished Gordon manuscript, his actions and demeanor, his enthusiasm, were so like the Jett she'd fallen in love with.

As he spoke, describing how he felt holding this rare book, she wanted him to scoop her up, bring her into his joy, swing her around, and kiss her.

But they weren't *together*. Not now. Not tomorrow. Not ever again.

One can undo a marriage but not a divorce.

Lexa slowed as she approached her desk. "Hello, Quent."

"Lexa, what are you doing here?" Quent tucked a large poster under his arm.

"Came to check on everyone." She pointed to the poster. "What's under your arm?"

"The Zaney Days campaign." He held up an image of a smiling Zane holding their number-one gourmet burger, the Zane Train.

"Quent, that's not the ZD poster. Where's the one with the families and the whole team in Central Park?"

"Tossed out. This is the new poster." He walked around Lexa. "I'm late getting this to promotions."

"Since when is *that* the new campaign?"

It was way too late to redesign the poster. And there was no need. Zaney Days was gaining a solid reputation as a must-go-to family event.

"Since Zane hired Tim."

"Tim?"

"The branding consultant. Tim Fraser? You know about him, right?

"The consultant. Yes, of course I knew. His name slipped my mind." She pointed to her fading bruise. "The concussion knocked some things loose."

"Zane's in there with him now if you want to go in." Quent disappeared down the curved stairs to the Think Tank.

Lexa peeked through the glass to see Zane bent over a drafting table with a short, stocky man in khakis and a button-down.

"Lexa, good, you're still here." Lois Watkins came from the direction of HR with a printed form. "I was going to email this to you, but since you're here . . . Zane approved your vacation time." The woman retrieved a pen from the canister on her desk. "You had over three hundred hours built up." Lois wagged the pen under Lexa's nose, one hand on her blue polka-dot hip. Her dyed-red hair, teased into a frenzy, danced above her lined face and squinty green eyes.

"Lois, I'm on sick leave. Not vacation." Lexa examined the form. "We have unlimited sick days, remember."

"Change of policy."

"Since when?"

"Two months ago. You read the revisions, didn't you? We talked about it at the executive roundtable."

"What executive roundtable?"

A soft pink splashed the HR manager's cheeks. "Sick leave is unlimited, but with more than a hundred and sixty hours of vacation on the books, you must use it first before going to sick pay." She waved the pen at Lexa again. "Page thirty-four in your handbook."

Lexa walked around to the desk and with her awkward left hand, opened the employee manual. Sure enough, on page thirty-four, the vacation-sick policy had been changed.

"Doesn't matter. I don't go on vacation anyway." Lexa signed the form with a loopy left-handed script.

"Other than getting hit by a car, how was the gala?" Lois said. "Sabrina looked stunning in the pictures the *Post* ran."

"The mini ZB burgers were a hit," Lexa said. "Lois, when was this executive roundtable again?"

"August. One of Zane's off-site luncheons. Don't you arrange his schedule?" Lois turned for her office. "Good to see you. Can't wait for you to return."

The electricity she experienced when she walked in ten minutes ago ebbed so quickly Lexa reached for the desk to steady herself.

Meetings and policy changes behind her back? Not that he *owed* her anything, but she was a core member of the team.

Trembling, she made her way to his office. "Got room for one more around the table?"

Her boss, her friend, rose up and glanced toward her. "Lexa, hey, what are you doing here? You're supposed to be resting and healing."

"I came to check on you. See how ZD is coming." She stepped toward Tim, offering her good hand. "Lexa Wilder."

"Tim Fraser, Halo Branding Consultants. Nice to meet you. Zane's told me a lot about his amazing assistant."

"Interesting." She glanced at Zane. "This is the first I've heard of you."

"Really?" Zane turned away.

"When did we first meet, Zane?" Tim reached for his coffee. "Last fall? I'm horrible with time frames."

"Last fall sounds about right. Excuse us, Tim. Lexa, can I see you out here?" Zane gently steered her from his office.

"The blank spots on your calendar." With each step, revelations dawned. "You were meeting with him?"

"I didn't tell you because I knew you'd protest." Zane guided her toward an empty conference room and closed the door.

"You hired a consultant without telling me? Why? Consultants charge big money with little to no ROI. We're doing great. We don't need a consultant. People want *us* to consult with them."

"Because we need a plan for growth."

"We have a plan, Zane. And an amazing team in the Think Tank. What more do you need? How much does this *consultant* cost? You need a CEO more than you need him."

He sighed and paced. "I hired him because we're not growing as fast as I'd like."

"Zane, are you crazy? Any faster and our heads will be backward. What's wrong with a solid but steady trajectory? We've been on a rocket ship for three years. Don't you think it's time to slow down, catch our breath?"

"I have franchise offers, airports and malls calling." Lexa could see the tension in his august face. "We could be one of the top restaurants in the nation in five years. A Realtor called yesterday with a primo lot on the water in Melbourne Beach, Florida. Three million. I ran the numbers, Lexa, it's a gold mine."

"Great, let's fly down and see it. But we don't have to decide today, Zane. Why are you so nervous? Why did you change Zaney Days?" She pointed toward Quent's desk. *Her* desk. "That poster of you is ridiculous."

"Tim made a great point about me being the focus of the company, the brand face. Like Dave Thomas from Wendy's or—"

"Ronald McDonald? Cause that's what you look like."

"Will you shut up?" He slammed his hand on the table, his cheeks fire-engine red. "This is *my* company, and I'm a little tired of you telling me what I can and cannot do, Lexa. Believe it or not,

I have personal and business goals you are not privy to, and your constant butting in and objecting is tiring."

The power of his accusation shoved her against the glass. "I-I was only trying to help."

"No, you're trying to run the company."

"Because you asked me to, Zane. You gave me jobs to do and I did them. I sat in board meetings, talked to Realtors, vendors, and suppliers. I dotted I's and crossed T's. I hired and even fired so you could be free to do your magic. I stayed late when everyone else went home. I stepped up when the first store opening fell behind schedule. When we realized we needed a policies and procedures manual, a human resources guide, and an accounting system, I rolled up my sleeves and made it happen. How many nights did you call at ten or eleven in a panic when something was overlooked? Who fixed it? Who found this building and moved us in a weekend? Me, Zane, me. And it cost me. I was here, working, instead figuring out what was wrong with my marriage. Instead of going to Switzerland with Jett when he begged me. I'd have been with him the weekend Storm died. But I chose this place because I thought you needed me more. Thought I was part of the team. The permanent team. And now, I learn you have executive roundtable lunches without me and changed the vacation and sick leave policy. I have to use my vacation time to heal from a broken arm I got on account of you."

"Me? I never told you to run in front of a cab."

"You promised me, Zane. If I went with you to the gala, I'd get the CEO job."

"Lexa, I didn't want to go here, but I have to ask." He looked at her with some sort of sympathetic pinch as his posture collapsed and his voice dropped. "Are you in love with me?"

"Am I . . . what?" She charged toward him. "How can you . . . in love? Why would you—"

"We've worked closely. Been good friends. Confidants. And, I guess, to be honest, we've flirted."

"*You've* flirted."

"Which you didn't reject."

"I didn't want to hurt your feelings. I can't believe I'm hearing this."

"Hurt my feelings?" He laughed in a tone that pitied her. *Poor Lexa.* "I think we both know—"

"I'm not in love with you, you egomaniac." She breathed fire. "Never have been. Never will be. But I did consider myself your partner in business. That one day I'd be CEO."

"You assumed too much, Lex. Do you really think I'd give you a CEO position just because you went with me to a gala?" The raw realities released with the heat of the confrontation. "That's not how to run a company. You're my assistant. No man in his right mind would promote an executive assistant to CEO." He hammered the table again. "You do what I need and if that means you represent me at a meeting or on a call, you do it. But it does not put you on the same level as me. Your name and signature do not carry my authority. You're not the boss, Lexa, I am." For the first time in seven years she saw a greed in his eyes she'd never seen before.

She verged on exploding. The scream in her chest rumbled and rose. Thoughts rumbled, words collided with every late night, early morning, and emergency problem she'd fixed in the last seven years.

She'd brainstormed the brand image, marketing, promotions, uniforms, and store designs, even came up with Zaney Days, one of their best promotional events.

The bile of betrayal filled her. At last, three words escaped her taut lips.

"You used me."

"Used you?" He paced around the table. "You used me. To get your way over mine. Since you've been out with your arm, I'm learning all kinds of things you've done without telling me and—"

"If you'd read your emails and listen in meetings you'd *know* everything. I never hid anything. You just never cared."

"I gave you too much rope, Lexa, and I'm sorry."

With a string of black-and-blue words, she shoved past Zane for the exit, her jaw so tight her teeth ached.

"Not half as sorry as I am."

She rode the elevator down twenty floors to the lobby, kicking the side of the car and simply trying to breathe. At the curb, she hailed a cab.

Zane had dismissed her. Rejected her. Said she was an interference. A busybody.

By the time she unlocked Jett's apartment door, the rage of her tears had boiled to a frenzy. Slamming the door, she threw her bag and keys on the floor, collapsing beside them.

Her moans vibrated in her chest, releasing sob after sob until her wailing cry saturated her entire being.

Somewhere in the noise and pain, she heard her name.

"Lex?" Strong hands caressed her shoulders. "What's wrong? Hey, hey, shhh."

She burrowed further into the floor. If only the wood planks would open up and swallow her.

"Lex, you're scaring me."

But what could she say? Exposing her latest humiliation to Jett would be her undoing.

JETT

"Lexa, talk to me. Please." Peeling her from the floor, he helped her to the couch. "Did you fall? Bump your arm?"

But these were not the tears of physical pain. They were from something deep in her being. She hadn't cried this much when the cab knocked her flat on the pavement.

Examining her face, her arms, her legs and ankles, he found she was unharmed. Gently he touched her chin and captured her attention.

"Zane?" He went with his gut and the rising anger that made his heart hammer beneath his button-down and ugly professor sweater. If he hurt her . . .

Black tears streaked her cheeks, cutting through her makeup. Her hazel eyes, red and raw, hosted a dark glint he recognized.

"He . . . he . . ." Lexa toppled forward, her forehead landing on his chest. Her sobs, softer now, watered his shirt.

"Shh, it's all right." He leaned back against the cushion and rested his chin on top of her hair.

"I tried so hard . . . accepted . . . one of the team."

"I know, I know."

He'd pummel that hamburger-selling jerk.

What if he hadn't come home to go over the notes he left on the banquette table? She'd be here by herself. The notion twisted him with his own pain.

He'd spent a solid afternoon with his dissertation, written and rewritten his personal foreword, even crafted an email to his parents to warn them of what he was doing.

He was ready to send to the publisher early. But the unpublished GPR manuscript gave him pause. If he could include some portion of the unpublished novel in his final product, it would put his work in another class altogether.

Dr. Levi and Dr. Paulson confessed ignorance and delight at Jett's find. Renée placed a few more calls and came back with the same. No one in the literary world knew of an unpublished manuscript.

Lexa shivered in his arms, her energy waning. Leaving his work on the left side of his brain, he checked in with the right.

Maybe this wasn't Zane. Maybe it was her parents. Or Skipper. But she said "he." Zane. Had to be.

Lexa sat up, pushing free. He felt cold where she'd rested against him and fought the urge to pull her back.

"Zane?" he said again.

She nodded, wiping her face on the extra-large shirt tail. Jett reached around her for the box of tissues on the end table.

"He, um, he said—" She hiccupped into another series of sobs.

"Did you go to ZB?"

"After my doctor's appointment. I just wanted to check in, say hi. I really miss everyone. I feel *off* not working." She blew her nose, then struggled to leave the couch. "I don't know what to do with myself."

Jett helped her up, his attention fixed on her troubles as she headed down the hall. "Where are you going? Can I get you anything?"

"Water, please."

He took a cold bottle from the fridge and followed her to the master bath. Setting the water on the sink, he turned to go.

"I'm a mess. Can you help me wash my face?"

"Have a seat." He patted the toilet.

Bibbing her with a towel, he filled the basin with warm water and squirted a dollop of CCW face foam in his hand.

Gently, he washed her face, the sensation of her soft skin beneath his fingers calling to his desires.

"Your bruise is healing nice."

"He's hired a consultant." Her confession was almost breathless. "Changed the Zaney Days campaign."

"Is that so bad?"

Her eyes popped wide. The answer would be yes then?

"Instead of being about the company and the families, it's about him. You should see the new poster. Zane's big fat face dead center. He looks like a cheap mattress salesman."

"You fought about it?"

"It's a waste of money, Jett, and I told him so. He slammed his hand on the table. Told me I was overstepping, reminded me I was his *assistant* and nothing more." Her eyes filled again.

"What about the CEO job?" Jett soaked a clean washcloth in the warm water.

"Surely I didn't believe he meant to give me the job *just* because I went with him to the gala. No one in their right mind would promote an exec assistant to CEO."

"No one in his position would dare ask his assistant to be his stand-in date. Not these days."

"I know, right? But I went to help him out. I'm so stupid."

"No, Lex." He raised her chin to see her eyes. "You are sweet and kind and good. Zane is the wrong one here. He lied to you." Jett bent to his knees and wiped the black stains from under her eyes, her cheeks, and her chin. "Want me to go down there and kick his butt?"

She chortled. A lovely sound that eased the tension in his chest. "Could you, please?"

"Gladly. But I have a better idea. Besides, I already spent a night in Central Booking for getting into a brawl."

"That's right. You and Chuck. What was that about?"

"Drunk groomsman at a wedding. Wouldn't leave a bridesmaid alone." He waved off the story as if it were nothing and rinsed the washcloth. If she pressed, he'd confess weddings reminded him of her.

"You hit him? Doesn't sound like you."

"I might have been a little drunk." On his knees again, he wiped away any lingering soap residue.

"A little?"

"A lot. But that's the last time. Ever." At the sink again, he released the water and rinsed out the cloth a final time, giving it more than the necessary attention.

Hold on to your heart, man.

"Why were you so drunk? So not your scene."

"Just one of those nights." Where he missed her. Wanted her. It started when the bride came down the aisle to the same song Lexa had. He tossed the damp cloth in the laundry hamper and helped Lexa up. "Anything else?"

Her breath brushed his cheek. "Thank you." She reached for her water. "I think I'd like to lie down."

Aiding her to the bed, Jett suggested a sandwich. "My specialty. Ham and cheese." To which she agreed.

The moment of tenderness had turned a few of their brick barriers into chain link fences.

"Want to watch Netflix?" Jett reached for Lexa's Kindle.

"Sure." She slumped down into the pillows. "He asked me if I was in love with him."

A surge of energy gripped him, but he didn't look up from her Kindle. "Wh-what'd you say?"

"What'd I say? Seriously? No. Never. I can't believe you'd ask. He's such an egomaniac. In love with himself. He wishes I was in love with him."

"Yeah, I bet he does. Here." He handled over her Kindle with his heart still pounding, his eyes averted for fear she'd see his question. He'd always wondered if there was something more between them. "I'll go make your sandwich."

"Jett, wait, you don't think I was—"

As if the Divine had dipped down to rescue him, his phone rang. "Be right back."

Was he sweating? He slapped his hand to his neck. Yep, he was sweating. He picked up his phone and shoved open the balcony doors.

The call was a marketer. Hanging up, he tossed his phone to the counter and pulled the bread from the pantry.

At least now he knew. Or thought he knew. She hadn't been in love with Zane. But she was also not in love with him. Otherwise, why walk out, slamming the door so hard the painting over the fireplace toppled to the floor?

"What was your better idea?"

He turned at the sound of her voice. She wore his old football jersey from high school, adjusted for her cast. "Something better than beating up Zane."

"Um, yeah, that . . ." He grabbed the ham and cheese. "I forget—do you like mustard?"

"Please."

She slid around the banquette, exposing the high end of her thigh. When he took two slices of bread from the package they were smashed.

What was his idea? Oh right, her résumé. "I was thinking you could update your résumé. See what else is out there. You may not have the title CEO, but you have the experience."

"My résumé?" She made a face. "I hadn't really thought . . . Do you think I should? I don't want to do anything out of vengeance."

Jett turned from the cupboard where he had reached for a plate. "Lexa, he told you to shut up. Said you'd gone too far, done too much. Put you in your *place* by reminding you of your title. His *assistant*. But you and I both know—he knows—you're so much more. He uses you, Lexa. And he had the gall to suggest you were in love with him."

"I guess I could see where he'd wonder. We did spend a lot of time together."

Her confession slung mud at his own ego. She spent more time with Zane than him toward the end. And he let it happen. He was so lost in himself, in pity, in grief.

Cutting her sandwich into quarters for eating with one hand, he asked, "Do you want water or milk?"

"Oh, milk. Please." She thanked him as he put the plate in front of her. "You know, you're onto something with this résumé thing."

She brightened, sat up straighter, and reached for her laptop. "I mean, yes, I have a lot of experience. I could get a job at a small company, you know? Oh my gosh, why didn't I think of this myself?" She patted the banquette next to her. "Help me. I can't type fast enough."

Sit? Next to her? With her bare leg next to his? "Now?"

"Yes now. Jett, the sooner I get out there the sooner I'm gone." She bit her sandwich, chugged some milk, and hovered over her computer. "Okay, here it is. Wow, I haven't touched this since we moved up here. We're going to have to rearrange a lot. Jett, why are you still standing?"

He sat, squaring up with her laptop, reading her name. Lexa Prescott Wilder. B.A., Marketing, Florida State.

"I'm sure there are great opportunities in the city," he said, typing as she rattled off her duties and experience.

"The city? The world, Jett." She slid from the bench and stepped through the cold air onto the balcony. "The world. I'm a child of the world. I grew up in Germany, Italy, England, California, Colorado, Texas, Florida." She rushed back to the table, eyes wide, a glare in her eye that rattled him. "I've been thinking too small. Holding on. Time to fly. I've never stayed this long in one place. I thought I was anchoring myself but no, I was hiding. Being afraid."

"Okay, then let's fly." *Now see what you've done. You just got her back in your life, now she's leaving. You and your bright ideas.*

"Unless . . ." she said, fading back. "I am running again. I run when times get hard, don't I?"

"Well, you could make a case that you're running, yes." *Stop, let her go. She's not yours. She deserves to find success her way.* "No, Lexa, realizing when it's time to move on from a situation is wisdom, not avoidance or fear." He tried to sound convincing. "But you *have* made a life here, and there are amazing opportunities in the city that never sleeps."

She rose from the banquette and gazed out the French doors toward the cityscape. "But I do run. The moment things get uncomfortable, I hightail it for something I believe will be better."

"Like when you left high school for college? You never did tell me what that was about, but I know it haunts you."

"Just a misunderstanding is all. On the other hand, you've been telling me to leave Zane for years."

"Yes, but not the city. Don't knock down the life you've made here because of Zane."

"Knock down my life? What life? All I do is work."

Discussing her future, her desires, felt like the job a husband, or at least someone who loved her, would do. While he wasn't her husband, he loved her. Didn't he? At least as a friend.

"You have the society. That's a start. No one said you had to work sixty hours a week, Lex."

"Don't preach to me, Jett Wilder. You are no better. No one said you had to bury yourself in books. And if you want to talk about never telling people things, you have plenty of secrets. Like what happened when your mom left. Or what happened on Eiger."

They faced each other, eyes narrowed, lips taut, attitude stony. Then she broke.

"I'm sorry. That was rude. But I won't bother you with my résumé. I'll fix it myself." She stumbled as she reached for her laptop, knocking over her milk in the process, soaking the last half of her ham and cheese. She swore softly. "I'll clean it up."

"Lex, wait." Hopping up, Jett gently grabbed her shoulders. "I'll clean it up. Sit. And we'll work on your résumé together." He forced himself to smile at her. "After all, the *world* is waiting."

Her eyes filled with emotion and words he knew she'd locked inside. "Can I have another sandwich?"

He could kiss her. "Ham and cheese coming up."

"A little mayo this time?"

And just like that, everything was back to normal. The undefined affection between them. It had become their existence.

Yet as Jett mopped up the milk with a dish towel, one thing above all was true. He was in love with his ex-wife.

~

CHUCK

Technically he wasn't violating the restraining order. The writ said nothing about steering clear of his mother-in-law's place.

Yet his nerves attacked, making him edgy as he approached Wanda's door, adorned with a fall wreath.

Arriving just after noon, he counted on Wanda having at least one Bloody Mary in her system. That'd ease her temper.

Squaring his shoulders, rehearsing his greeting, and fixing on a wide Chuck Mays smile, he rapped on the door.

"Why, Chuck Mays." Yep, Wanda had started happy hour early. "What on earth?" Arms folded, she leaned against the doorjamb. "I could have you arrested."

She came out swinging.

"I come in peace, Wanda." He held up his hands to punctuate his point. "But I'd like a moment of your time." She scowled. "Please."

To get what he wanted, he'd have to go low. Humbly low.

"What about?"

"The kids. Specifically, their birthdays."

She hesitated, then motioned him inside. "You have two minutes."

"Thank you." He gushed a little, so she'd hear his appreciation. "I'd like to attend their birthday parties—er, party." He wasn't supposed to know there were two.

"What makes you think we're having a party?"

"It's Trudy. Come on."

Wanda conceded his point with a slight frown. "True. But Chuck, Trudy would never. And if she somehow lost her mind and allowed you to come, Will would refuse."

"Will is not their father."

"Technically no, but more and more every day."

If she wanted to rattle him, it was working. "She might consider it if you asked, Wanda. She really respects your opinion." He'd practiced groveling all week. Ever since the story society, when he'd been so grouchy. Pride had no place in a man who'd all but lost his kids. "I'll be on my best behavior. Better than best. I know a smart, talented woman like you—"

"I smell manure."

Yeah, well get ready, I'm still shoveling.

"You know kids need their dad. Sure, they've seen me at my worst."

"Worst? You terrified them."

"You know I'm not that guy, Wanda. You've seen the real me. I hate the guy I was that day." No truer words. "You've told me I'm a good father. More than once. Please, talk to Trudy. One hour at the party. That's all I ask."

"There are two this year. One for Jakey and one for Riley."

"Then an hour at each. They're turning six. I've already missed half of four and all of five. One hour, Wanda. One."

"Your two minutes is up." She moved to close the door.

"Wanda, please."

The latch clicked. He turned to go but halted when her muffled voice came through. "I'll talk to her. But I promise nothing."

He jogged back to the car, giving the air a solid punch. It was something. A start.

Wanda had been his first champion when Trudy brought him home. Her dad definitely thought she deserved better. Chuck couldn't disagree. But he promised up and down to love her more than himself.

Sometimes he wondered if he didn't still love her from under the rocks of her betrayal. He was darn sure better for her and his kids than the snake that slithered into their lives from Wall Street.

Firing up his car, he mobilized for business and caught his first customer. Just a mile from Wanda's Woodbridge home.

Tuning in to classical music, he settled down. Hopeful. Funny thing about pain, it cut both ways. Going in and coming out. But hope was a powerful salve.

He picked up his ride, a businessman heading to the Newark airport.

It was a quick trip, and when he'd dropped off his passenger Chuck crossed over to Manhattan. The story society met tonight, so he worked that side of the river and thought off and on of Ed's pot roast.

And, if he were honest, seeing Coral. She made him forget about Trudy. Made him glad he was a man.

She was as sweet as she was beautiful. Smart too. Not that he had much proof, but he could smell it. Her vulnerable confession about her business showed her humility.

Out of your league. The truth ground its way forward. If Trudy was out of his league, Coral wasn't even in his stratosphere. *And look how things worked out with Trudy.*

Yeah, he'd have to steer clear of the heiress. The Panicked Princess. So was the story society worth his Monday nights?

Sooner or later they weren't going to accept his grunts as answers. They were going to want the whole story.

Chuck pulled up to a stoplight and connected with a fare on Canal Street that wanted a ride to Brooklyn. The woman talked on her phone the entire time. So Chuck thought more of pot roast.

He liked everyone in the society. Ed was entertaining. Reminded him of his grandpa.

Since he'd already spent a night in Central Booking with Jett, they were practically family. *Ha.*

Lexa was sweet, if broken. Chuck suspected Jett was the cause of her sorrow. But she was in love with him. He with her. Neither one saw it.

Maybe that's what the society was about? Helping those two find love again.

Yeah, he'd stick with this society for a bit. Parts of Ed's story haunted him. He wondered what it felt like to be so in love. Would that ever happen to him? Or anyone he knew?

His parents stayed married. Loved each other despite how much they barked at one another. But a love like Ed and Esmerelda's? Felt like fiction.

Now that he knew Jett was the son of adventurer Bear Wilder, he wanted to hear some adventure stories. Chuck watched a bunch of YouTube videos on his day off last week of Bear and Storm climbing mountains and rafting rapids. Jett was even in a few of the episodes. Bear was a good storyteller. No wonder his son became a literature professor.

Hope. Yep, that was the prevailing sentiment swirling in his chest. He'd like to hang on to it. Since Trudy's affair and realizing he wasn't the man he wanted to be, despair had been his companion.

But after his encounter with this story society and the brief exchange with Wanda, could he dare believe things were starting to look up?

∽

ED

It was nice of Chuck to pick him up for the society meeting. Not so nice of him to mention the pot roast.

Ed spent forty bucks trying to find a recipe. He burned the first hunk of meat in the oven. Overcooked the second in the Crock-Pot. Yes, that's right, overcooked. Apparently twenty-four hours on high is too long.

He'd lost track of time painting the floorboards he'd replaced in the Evans apartment. By the time he was done, he'd thrown his back out. Two ibuprofen and he was sacked out. Forgot all about the roast.

It was a wonder Holly grew up healthy at all. How did he not know how to cook a pot roast? Friday he almost knocked on Mabel's door for help but changed his mind. What chain of events would a conversation with her set off?

Not worth the risk.

By the weekend, he'd made the decision to punt and ordered a roast from the local diner, brought it home this afternoon and dumped it into a roasting pan, then stuffed it in the oven. He bought a couple of bags of salad to go along. Should be enough.

He'd just come from the bedroom, dressed and smelling like Old Spice, when Chuck buzzed up.

"I'm here. Double parked."

"On my way down."

"I'll circle the block."

Ed grabbed a couple of oven mitts and took the roast from the oven. He flung a tote with the salad over his shoulder and decided to leave his new pages at home.

One miracle at a time. Food versus story. He could always *tell* the rest of their story. How they fell in love and got engaged.

But didn't he sort of cover all that last week? Not in detail, but how they held hands in the theater and never let go?

Grabbing his keys and wallet, he headed down to meet Chuck.

As he waited for the elevator—his old legs too tired to take the stairs—Mabel Cochran came out of her apartment.

"Ed?"

"Mabel." Did she hover by her door waiting for him to enter the hall? Seemed like every time he opened his door, she opened hers.

"I made a cake. Care to step inside for a slice with coffee? Decaf if you like."

"Busy, Mabel." He held up his pan. "On my way out. But you have a good night."

"I will. Is that a pot roast?"

"Sure is." He stepped into the elevator, glad to be out of her presence.

Darn woman had gotten to him. Ever since she invited him to dinner, he found himself thinking of her when he should be thinking of Esmerelda. And that would never do.

Chapter 20

LEXA

She balanced a thick paper plate of Ed's pot roast on her lap after Jett cut her meat and dressed her salad.

The tension between them from the other night had faded, but they lived like disagreeable roommates the rest of the week.

"You're quiet, Lexa." Coral addressed her across the circle.

"Just eating." She popped a wide smile. "Good roast, Ed."

"Thank you."

Her argument with Zane lingered in her heart, in her bones. And as Jett updated and uploaded her résumé, she felt something for him. Like she did when they first met. What was *that* about?

Never mind that her arm still hurt and living with a long arm cast was nothing short of a prison sentence.

She wanted to cry. But crying changed nothing.

"Thank you. The recipe is rather simple."

"Jett, you okay?" Coral again.

"Yeah, why?" He shoved a forkful of meat into his mouth.

Lexa glanced over at him. *What happened to us, Jett?*

But why open a coffin to ask the body why it died? There was no answer. The marriage ended as marriages do.

Move on.

She'd decided looking for a new job was not running but advancing. As all people needed to do from time to time.

The Bower clock tick-tocked, serenading the muted sounds of plastic forks cutting against paper plates, and the hum of eating.

The light from the sconces shed a warm light across the walnut hardwood, and for a moment, Lexa could've sworn the sounds from beyond the window were the clip-clop of horse and carriage.

"How are things at CCW?" Ed to Coral.

"I spoke with my father for advice, and today I commissioned an auditor he recommended. We have a sales meeting next week where I'll ask the hard questions. But I'm almost convinced my CEO is right. Pink Coral must go."

"Coral, hey, I bought one of your lip glosses." Lexa set her plate on the table Jett brought over for her. She'd forgotten all about her purchase. "At a drugstore by the doctor's office." Lexa produced the product, still in the packaging.

"There was one there? Where?" Coral reached for the lip gloss. "Diamond Dust. My favorite. And it's supposedly doing the worst."

"The cashier said they couldn't keep the product stocked. She said they sell out."

"She told you that?" Coral furrowed her brow and passed back the gloss.

"Yeah, so there's at least one store where it sells."

Coral tapped on her phone. "I'm sending a text to Blaire, and also Sal, VP of Sales. She really said they couldn't keep it stocked? Which store?"

Lexa told her and Coral sat back with a generous, stunning smile. No wonder the prince had fallen for her.

"Thank you, Lexa. I feel like I've taken my first deep breath in a year."

Coral's relief changed the library's atmosphere and Lexa soaked it up.

"Coral, when did you take over CCW?" she said.

"Four years ago. My grandmother and I were on our way to Paris for the fashion season and she dropped dead in her apartment. Heart attack."

"I'm so sorry."

"Did you want to be the head of the company?" Chuck.

"Someday. But not at twenty-nine. I'd been working with Grandmother since high school. After college I officially joined the executive team, but I was not ready to occupy her corner office. I wonder if that's why the company is struggling."

"You'll figure it out," Lexa said, her cheer genuine. "Didn't your great-grandmother start the company at twenty-five during the Depression?"

"You know my company." Coral's smile shone in her eyes. "Great-grandmother Coral Ruth started CCW in thirty-four."

"Did you know her?" Jett said.

"I did. I have this image of her, larger than life, the grand dame of cosmetics commanding everyone to do her bidding. And they did. Even the men. She died when I was seven. My Dad took me to see her at the hospital a few days before she passed, and there she sat, barking orders at her hair stylist and critiquing CCW's new red lipstick as her assistant took notes." She laughed softly. "I knew I wanted to be just like her when I grew up. But I'm pretty sure I've let both grandmothers down."

"Naw, you haven't." Chuck flicked his hand against her arm. "You just got distracted by being the princess of the wrong kingdom. You're a cosmetic duchess, not a princess of Lauchtenland."

"Chuck, such wisdom," Jett said.

"I'm not as dumb as I look, Wilder."

"You know I applied at CCW when I moved to the city," Lexa said.

"Really?"

"Yeah, but I didn't have much experience, being fresh out of college. And none with the cosmetics world."

"And we overlooked you?"

"Didn't even get called for an interview."

"Our loss is Zane's gain. How are they surviving without you?"

"Well enough."

Detailing her run-in with Zane would spoil the mood. Besides, every time she tried to put the encounter into words, she sounded like she'd been eating bitter grapes.

"Ed, how's your memoir?" Jett said, his gaze meeting Lexa's as he moved his attention to the old man.

Thank you.

THE *Fifth Avenue* STORY SOCIETY   201

"Same. Thinking through what you told me, Jett. I just can't seem to remember any of the hard times. Seems it was always good with Esmerelda."

"Then tell us that story, Ed. Inspire the rest of us. Write about your daughter, your family life, holidays, and traditions. Did Holly get along with Esmerelda?"

"They were thick as thieves."

"It'd be interesting to have her perspective on your relationship in the book," Lexa said.

"She's got a point, Ed. What do you think?" Jett again.

"I just had in mind to tell *our* story. Esmie's and me."

"Tell you what I want to hear," Chuck said, munching on the rabbit food, as he called his salad. "Stories of Jett climbing mountains and shooting rapids with his old man."

"Dude, that's another world." Jett stuffed a dripping, juicy bite of meat in his mouth.

"Don't you want to go with your old man now that your brother is gone?"

Jett looked up, flaring. Lexa felt the heat of his nonverbal response. "No."

"Too scared?" Chuck, merrily eating meat and lettuce.

"Too smart. Can we change the subject?"

Chuck looked up, surprised, a thin pink on his cheeks. "Yeah, sure."

"Chuck, what's going on with your kids?" Jett asked, trying to steer the conversation.

"Nothing. Well, maybe something." He dropped his plate between his booted feet and wiped his lips. "I saw my son."

"Saw your son?" Coral turned her attention on him. "Don't you see him regularly?"

Chuck clapped his hands together, arms on his thighs, head down. "No. The ex filed for a restraining order, and being as her family practically owns Woodbridge, I didn't stand much of a chance."

"She can't file for no reason, Chuck," Lexa said.

Week by week, the group had solidified. Become a bit closer. And lowered barriers.

"What makes you think she had no reason?" Chuck snatched up his plate and moved back to the pot roast. "Can we get potatoes with this next time, Ed?"

"Can we get more than pizza from you?" Jett said.

"You're welcome to take my place. Can't wait to see what you bring, Prof."

"Stop." Lexa said. "We don't need your sniping. We had some good news with Coral so let's soak it up, okay?"

"I don't know if I'd call it good news," Chuck grumbled.

"It's a lead and I'll take it." Coral nodded at Lexa.

"Ed, the pot roast and salad were perfect," Lexa said. "Chuck, I'm sorry about your kids. And just because Storm Wilder died piloting off the Eiger in a wingsuit doesn't mean Jett is afraid." She glanced about the circle. "Anything else?"

"Sorry, man." Chuck popped Jett on the shoulder as he passed back to his chair.

"Yeah, me too."

"Were you there, Jett? On the Eiger?" Coral said. Between her soft voice, her silk blouse, and her wide-leg trousers, she seemed to float.

Jett choked on his food as he reached for his water. "I was, yes."

The confession blanketed the Bower. Coral stretched her hand to Jett's, giving him a squeeze.

"Getting real now," Ed said, more to himself than the others.

"I caught my wife cheating." Chuck's voice broke the reverie. "Didn't go well. That's why I can't see my kids." He raised his gaze. "Guess I'm the mess of the group."

"Don't hog the moniker for yourself," Jett said.

The society fell silent again. Seemed the spirit of confession was moving as it willed.

After a minute or two, Coral began to clean up. Lexa gathered her own trash and started to help.

"In other news," Jett said, "I'm about to submit my dissertation for publication. Tomorrow, in fact. But there's a manuscript in that back corner I'm going to inspect first."

"In this library?"

"Congratulations, man."

"I'll buy a copy," Ed said through gruff emotion.

"I don't think this will be a book you'd want to read, Ed. More for academic eggheads. But thanks. And yes, Coral, an old, unpublished manuscript of Gordon Phipps Roth."

"I bet my ancestors had something to do with that. How nice. Jett, a novelist and a scholar. I feel honored to be in your midst." Even in her compliments, Coral was clever and elegant. And the way she looked at Chuck . . . with tender adoration. Or was Lexa imagining things?

Then Coral turned to her when she joined her at the table, wadding up the empty salad bags and capping the dressing bottles.

"I thought I heard something in your voice when I asked about Zane. What's up?"

"Nothing. Well, we argued." Lexa handed the trash to Jett as he snapped open a garbage bag. "The short of it is I've uploaded my résumé to job sites. Going to reach out to headhunters next."

"You're leaving ZB?" Coral handed Ed the paper products for the back closet.

"If I can find the right job, yes. Maybe." The words tasted like dust. Not so much because she confessed to leaving Zane, although the idea did rattle her sense of security, but because she might leave the city.

Leave Jett.

"But you're staying in Manhattan, right?" Coral said. "Our little society is just getting started. And hey, maybe CCW HR will find your résumé and call you in for an interview. I could put in a word—"

"Coral, no, really, I'm not telling you because I want a favor. I want a CEO position or something executive. And I know food, not cosmetics. You have an amazing CEO in Blaire Boreland. I studied her success with Glitter Girl. And yes, I'd like to stay in New York, but to be honest, I've never lived anywhere longer than four years. I think I'm getting restless. Maybe it's time to move on, spread my wings."

"You moved a lot as you grew up?" Chuck started folding up the food table.

"My dad was in the air force. A doctor. So yes, we moved a lot."

"What was your favorite place?" Ed said.

"Satellite Beach, where I went to high school."

The words *high school* sparked a conversation reminiscing of their younger days, and before Lexa knew it, they'd passed the last half of the hour expounding on stories of friendships and hardship.

It was easier to be honest about the past than the present.

Ed announced he didn't have a lot of friends but was thick with the guys on his block. They ran together all four years of high school.

Chuck was a jock and Mr. Popular with a ton of friends.

Coral, believe it or not, was not popular and often found herself on the outer edge of the in-crowd at her elite private high school.

"I was shy and bookish," she said.

"I was bookish, but not shy. I liked sports as much as I loved studying," Jett said.

"Lex, what about you?" Chuck had relaxed, reclining in his chair, and his easy, loping smile reminded her of an Old Hollywood actor. The kind Grandma talked about when she was a kid. Like Rock Hudson or Charlton Heston. "I bet you were popular."

"Actually, no."

"Jett, is she telling the truth?"

"I'm not sure." Their eyes met and she softened under the power of blue. "She was friends with the in-crowd but left in the middle of her senior year for college. She surfed and made lattes at a coffee shop."

"You surfed?" Coral lit up with fascination. "Out with it, Lex."

"Out with what? I surfed and worked at a coffee shop. Nothing to tell. Nothing to see."

"Surfed? Did you see sharks?" Coral glanced at Chuck. "I've always wanted to surf."

"Then do it. What's holding you back?"

She frowned. "I'm not sure. I can ski. But surfing? Lexa, how'd you learn?"

"Bought a board and went out on the water. Met some kids who were kind enough to show me the ropes. We'd moved to Satellite Beach right before my sophomore year, and I was eager to dig in, make central Florida my home. Dad promised we wouldn't move again before my sister and I graduated."

"You just did it? Hopped on a board and rode a wave?" Coral mimed surfing, wobbling from side to side with her arms out and knees bent.

"I wish. The waves rode me for the first few weeks. But I kept at it, going out early every morning, praying for waves. I stayed out until Mom sent Skipper to bring me home. Maybe eight, nine hours." She grinned at the memory. "I lost twenty pounds in like a month—"

"Those were the days."

"And even with my reddish coloring, had the most gorgeous golden tan."

Chuck whistled. "So, you were the hot new girl?"

Lexa laughed. "Yes, okay, but I was still the new girl."

"You two met in college?" Ed pointed at Lexa then Jett. "Why'd you get divorced?"

"Now that's a dark story," Jett said.

"How dark?" Chuck said.

"Too dark for tonight." Jett again. "Coral, you said no one asked you to your prom?"

"Nope. A couple of my rivals started a rumor that I refused to go with any guy in school. Another rumor said I had a date with a Yale man, which I did not. I was happy to not go but Mom insisted. She fixed me up with the son of a family friend who'd just finished OCS. In fact, she's still trying to fix me up. Anyway, Tom was gorgeous, especially in his uniform, but ten minutes at a high school prom and he was out of there. I joined the wallflowers and ended up having a great time."

"I'd have asked you if I'd been at your school," Chuck said. "I'd see the rumors as a challenge."

"Really?" For a moment, Coral was her high school self. At least to Lexa. She knew the expression she saw on her friend's face. "I'd have said yes."

This story society had just crossed over into friendship. Into the beginnings of trust.

"My senior year, I had a boyfriend who was the most popular kid in school," Lexa said. "Super nice guy. Carnie." She'd never told anyone outside the family the story brewing in her soul. Not even Jett. "But he stood me up for homecoming."

Ed slapped his hand over his heart. "What is wrong with young people?"

A surprising sting of humiliation struck her bones. "I was seventeen and *in love* as you can only be in high school." Each word was like heaving stones. Coral listened with a compassionate expression. Chuck, with large and curious eyes. Ed, poised as if to take notes. And Jett, with a dubious stare as if he didn't believe what she was about to say. "Before me, Carnie had dated Babs—yes, that was her real name—this tall, gorgeous blonde who could've been on *Baywatch*. She was the most popular girl in school. The two of them were destined to be homecoming king and queen. However, they broke up the summer before our senior year. He and I started hanging out, surfing together, and one thing led to another."

"You never told me this story." Jett turned toward her, giving her his full attention.

"My thing was to fit in. Everywhere we moved, I just made myself useful to whoever needed or wanted me. Girl Friday, the second-best friend, the teacher's pet, the organizer, the worker bee, whatever." Once she started moving the stones, the rocks began to tumble. "I remember being so afraid I'd *never* fit in or feel like I belonged. When we moved to Satellite Beach I made up my mind to make the most of high school. And I did. Then when Carnie and I started dating, I was the most popular girl in school. I'd done it. Found a way to be one of the in-crowd. Freshmen and sophomore girls were asking my advice, following me on MySpace."

"There's a blast from the past."

"For the first time in my life, I was not the outsider. Or the foreigner in a small German community."

"Babs got jealous, right?" Chuck knew high school politics well.

"But I didn't know until homecoming. I was supposed to go with Carnie. Since I was the planner of our group, I organized a big homecoming pre-party at the officers club. We were to all meet there, our group of sixteen, have snacks, then go to dinner and the dance. My Mom and best friend Deily invested time and money to help me. It was supposed to be epic. Every event in our senior year was hashtag epic. We wanted to go out with a bang. I'd spent two hundred dollars on a new dress. I had my nails and hair done."

"I've seen pictures. She was beautiful."

Lexa glanced at Jett. "When did you see a picture?"

"Your mom showed me a box of photos when you took me home the first time. But no one told me about Carnie."

"I bet you were stunning, Lexa." Coral leaned into the story. "Go on. What happened?"

"The pre-party was at four. My friends started arriving but by four thirty, most of the gang hadn't showed. Those who did were huddled in corners, texting, whispering." The memory of seeing Deily with her date, Marcus, staring at their phones, knowing what was going down, stung in her eyes. They never said a word. "People started making excuses to leave early. And I realized I was still just the air force kid who moved around and didn't belong. And never would."

"Is that really how you see yourself?" Curiosity framed Jett's expression.

"Where was Carnie?" Chuck demanded.

"I kept texting, asking where he was. He replied once. 'On my way.' By five, I stood alone at the officers club window. I didn't want to mess up my dress, hair, or makeup, so I refused to sit or go outside. Five-o-five, he wasn't there. Five-ten, no limo. I texted him again. No answer. At five thirty, I called. Nothing. Six, six-thirty. I could feel Mom watching me from the loaded food tables. There is no greater humiliation than failing in front of your parents."

"Tell me about it," Coral said.

"Finally, Mom put her arms around me. 'You have to hold things loosely, Lex.'" She imitated Mom's open palm. "I was so focused on not crying I shrugged away from her and ran out. I'd trusted, gotten kicked in the gut, and I had no idea why. Funny thing, we had plans all the way to Christmas break. A bunch of us were going skiing. Carnie had never been." She broke into a soft, reminiscent smile. "He kept promising he'd stand outside my hotel room window under the lights and sing to me while it snowed. Then he'd call me down and scoop me up when I ran into his arms." She smiled at the memory. "It was this idea we had of being our own rom-com or some scene in a Hallmark movie. Got to be honest, I *really* wanted that scene. It sounded so romantic."

She sighed too loud and too long. Clearing her throat, she quickly went on.

"By the time I got back to our house, I was all sweaty, crying, gasping for air. Dad and Skipper were watching a movie and with way too much cheer, invited me to join them, said it'd be great to have a family night. Worse than Mom seeing my rejection was my dad and sister's pity."

Chuck held up his fist. "Makes me want to smash a head or two."

"I'll go with you." Ed gave him a fist bump.

"I went down the hall and walked straight into the shower wearing my dress and shoes, and stood under the hot water for a good hour while I cried. I didn't know it for about thirty minutes, but thirteen-year-old Skipper sat on the toilet crying with me. She said, 'This is like that movie *Never Been Kissed* but you're not Josie Grossie.'"

"That's so sweet." Coral dabbed under her eye with her fingers.

"Then Dad came in. 'I think you and I should go to the dance. Show them how to really have fun.' His trying made it all the harder. When we moved, Dad and Mom did everything they could to make it easy for us. We had dance parties and movie parties. We were our own social group. I knew that's what he was trying to do."

"My father would've done something like that," Coral said.

"When he offered me his arm, I lost it. I'm soaked to the bone, my hair falling out of the updo, my makeup running down my face, but he never said a word. Not 'Get cleaned up' or 'Change your clothes,' just, 'Let's go.' I fell into a heap on the floor. Dad dropped with me and wrapped his arm around my shoulders. Meanwhile, Mom called Carnie's mom. She didn't know what was going on, only that he'd gone to the dance as planned. Key word, *planned*. Only person who didn't know Carnie had broken up with me was me."

"Please tell me that wicked boy made it right," Coral said.

Jett, along with Chuck and Ed, listened with stony expressions.

"He tried. Showed up around midnight. I was alone in the family room watching *Sixteen Candles* wishing I was Molly Ringwald. He tapped on the window and I threw my popcorn bowl at him. Broke the glass." A soft wash of tears filled her eyes. "Dad made Carnie pay for it. Anyway, he texted me to come to the porch. I refused. But he wouldn't leave. He must've stayed out there for two hours. I finally talked to him through the door. He apologized, said he was a jerk. Babs convinced him they should get back together. He wanted to keep his homecoming date with me, but she insisted he go with her. Some bull about it being their senior year, and how they'd always planned to go together, be homecoming king and queen together, which they were, and have the memories for a lifetime."

"What'd you do?" Jett said.

"Nothing. Told him good night. He didn't want me. What could I do? I certainly didn't want him anymore. He was so weak he let his ex-girlfriend bamboozle him. Right then and there, I dried my eyes and moved on. I promised myself I'd never be in that position again.

If someone didn't want me, then I'd go. No sweat. I felt this rock of determination form in my gut. Monday morning, I went to the school office, cashed in my credits, finished the one class I needed to graduate online, and went to FSU in January."

She'd shared more than she wanted, but somehow it cleansed her of a stain she'd not seen.

"So that's why you walked out?" Sadness weighted Jett's observation.

"What? Walked out? When?" Coral glanced between the two of them.

"On me."

"Lex, you walked out?"

The Bower door opened and the small librarian with the vibrant eyes looked in. "Time's up. See you all next Monday."

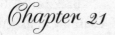

Chapter 21

JETT

With a glance back at the bookshelf holding GPR's unpublished work, he exited the Bower to catch Lexa. At the moment, she was more important than his research.

At the thought, a sensation popped in his middle.

"You never told me." He caught her by the arm as she crossed the main room.

"I told you. Some."

"Never that much."

"I didn't know there was a minimum."

"Lexa, don't." He let go of her arm. "Can we talk later? I really want to know—is that why you walked out on us? Because you felt unwanted?"

Hearing her talk of Carnie brought answers to some of his questions. But why didn't she just say it?

"You make me feel unwanted."

"It's late." Lexa glanced toward the door. "I'm tired. My arm aches. And I've had my fill of confessions for one night. Besides, Coral offered me a ride and I don't want to keep her waiting. See you at the apartment?"

"But you will tell me one day, won't you?"

"I suppose one day I should."

"Lex, I'm sorry."

"For Carnie?"

"For me. I was dark and brooding after Storm died."

"We were all hurting after he died."

She was letting him off the hook. But for now, he'd take it. "See you at home."

She nodded, then hesitated as if she wanted to say something but changed her mind and walked toward the door.

Back in the Bower, Jet gathered himself, shoving aside the churning in his gut about Lexa, and focused on investigating the manuscript. He hoped Gilda wouldn't kick him out again. It was after nine.

Looking back it seemed unimaginable that two people would walk away from a marriage without talking about why. Without fighting for their love.

They'd divorced without a word of protest? Who does that? Verbalizing the truth made it sound all the more ridiculous.

Picking up his backpack, Jett moved down the bookshelves toward Gordon's book. He pulled an overstuffed upholstered chair from the back corner and retrieved the unbound manuscript.

A familiar peace hit him. Happened every time he was with books. And the conversation with Lexa didn't seem so dark. He felt hope.

He was with his heroes. Stories never slammed doors in his face. Or moved to California to "find themselves."

Cradling Gordon's manuscript on his lap, Jett flashed back to the summer Dad took him and Storm on an archeological dig where they'd unearthed old bones.

This manuscript was old bones.

Retrieving a notepad from his backpack, Jett began a thorough investigation of the GPR story the world never saw.

Why didn't Barclay, Gordon's publisher, publish this one? The number of pages fell short of classic Gordon novels, but that shouldn't have been a concern.

Jett snapped a few pictures with his phone and texted them to his friend at Stanford who specialized in manuscript verification. Then to Dr. Paulson.

Unpublished GPR manuscript. Thoughts?

The title, *The Glitter of Gold*, rang GPR true. The man had a knack for great titles. Jett relaxed into the chair and read the first line.

Callie hailed a hansom cab on the corner of Fifth and Fifty-Sixth.

Hmm . . . He read it again. A bit bland. No emotion. Couldn't really get a sense of anything. No intrigue or foreshadowing. GPR was known for his well-crafted first lines that reflected some hidden layer of the protagonist's inner self or theme of the book.

Take note, however, this was a rough cut. Probably never polished. Most openings were boring until the author finished the book and returned to the first line.

He taught students in his writing seminars and courses, "The last line you write is the first line."

In his finished work, Gordon's sentences were lyrical, intelligent, yet crisp and plainly stated. Beginning with *Girl*, he moved away from some of the ornate, wordy prose of his earlier works, but that was typical of authors in his era.

His male protagonists were strong, masculine if not willful, yet kind, loving, compassionate.

His female characters were equally strong and vocal. Not a shrinking violet among them. Atypical for the time in which Gordon lived. Yet each one possessed a feminine allure that made Jett fall a little bit in love.

Especially Elizabeth from *Girl in the Carriage*. In fact, when he met Lexa, Elizabeth breathed to life for him in a new way.

Reading on, Jett found the first three pages were almost academic, as if Gordon was describing a scene for the *New York Tribune*. Where was Gordon's trademark heart and soul?

Jett was beginning to see why it'd never been published. The story was bumpy and awkward with a lot of scratched-out sentences and paragraphs. In some places, entire pages were struck.

The story felt stilted, the characters two-dimensional.

But his 1903 classic *The Girl in the Carriage* was written entirely in the voice of the protagonist, and it changed his career. The emotion was palatable, real, even raw in places.

On page ten of *Glitter*, Jett encountered margin notes. Turning the manuscript ninety degrees, he studied the faded, elongated script. The comments were notated with DB.

So, Daniel Barclay did see this work.

I don't feel you have command of George's journey here. Even in the beginning the reader needs a sense of his purpose.

This exchange with Lady Able meanders with no point.

From then on, every page was marked with Daniel's handwritten notes.

This reference is baseless.

Redundant writing.

Does she really wish him dead? She's heartless.

Flat.

Pointless.

Clearly the publisher did not like this story, and Jett had to agree. Gordon's voice was almost monotone, dragging, unsure, and not one bit engaging.

What happened, Gordon?

Had he written this during the season he lost his fiancée? Or was it just a bad book? Every author deserved grace for a not-on-par tome. Jett certainly appreciated the grace he'd received for *Rites of Mars.*

Skimming to the end, he found a letter tucked between the pages. The envelope was imprinted with the Barclay Publishing logo. The single page was handwritten and signed by the owner, publisher, and editor himself, Daniel.

December 1, 1902

Dear Gordon,

We must put this one to rest. While you've given your best to the multiple revisions, it seems you have not managed to advance the story whatsoever. Clearly my direction and guidance has not engaged your imagination either.

I'm disappointed, as the advertisers and bookstores were looking forward to this spring publication. Perhaps we can meet to discuss further ideas more like your previous works.

I'm sorry to bring you this bad news but The Glitter of Gold is just not publishable.

> Sincerely,
> Daniel

A rejected manuscript. No wonder it was hidden away in this library. Did Joseph Winthrop provide some sort of refuge for Gordon?

What was going on with Gordon in '02? It was well known he suffered writer's block after a devastating split from his fiancée in 1899. He called the years from '99 to '02 "desert years." Then he wrote *Girl* in a two-month burst of creative energy. It released quickly, in the spring, apparently to keep the advertisers and booksellers happy.

Gordon wrote nothing of a rejected manuscript in his diaries or memoir. Nor had Barclay made mention of it in his journals. Was it even important to mention a rejected manuscript? It happened. An author tried something new and failed, moved on.

Yet this book wasn't out of the ordinary for Gordon. It was much in line with his earlier works, which, to be honest, were not highly regarded these days. At least among the academic circles.

His enduring acclaim began with *The Girl in the Carriage*.

"Gordon, what did you do?"

Did he revamp and write a book in the winter? Did Daniel help? Gordon wasn't known for working quickly. He took well over a year to write a novel.

In fact . . . Jett set the manuscript in the chair and paced, thinking. In Gordon's memoir he said *Girl* had brewed for two years. He said he'd muscled through his writer's block and taken the story to Barclay, who loved it and helped him refine it.

Gordon dedicated the book to his publisher and friend.

> To our friendship and partnership.
> I'd not be here without you.

A drop of panicked revelation drained through Jett. Did they cheat in some way? Forge *The Girl in the Carriage*?

Jett was to turn in his manuscript tomorrow to the university press, and he had a brand new, brewing slew of questions.

"But all the principle players are dead." Or not talking. Like Elijah and Tenley.

Did Gordon really rebound in January of '03 and write *Girl* overnight? After such a devastating rejection?

Gordon always claimed his wife, Sweeney, saved him from writer's block by becoming his inspiration, but he didn't meet her until late 1903 or early 1904.

Jett never realized the discrepancies in the dates before.

He continued reading, taking notes in his phone, and sending pictures to his Stanford friend. He pulled out his laptop and logged onto online libraries and resources, searching for any information.

Rejected manuscript. Daniel Barclay. Revisions. Sweeney Roth. Birdie Ainsworth. Birdie Shehorn + Gordon Phipps Roth.

Nothing. There simply wasn't any new information. Other than this manuscript hidden away in a private library.

"Jett?" Gilda came around the door. "It's time to go."

"Gilda, the manuscript was rejected. What do you know?"

"What do you know?"

"What do I—Gilda, you know the truth, don't you? Did Gordon actually write *The Girl in the Carriage*? Or did someone else? The rejection letter I found is dated in December. *Girl* released four months later. When did he write it? How?" The manuscript slipped as he lifted it toward Gilda, and a second envelope fell to the floor.

Another letter to Gordon from Barclay Publishing.

"I'm turning out the lights." Gilda beckoned him toward the door.

"Wait. One second, please." Jett unfolded the handwritten note,

careful of the aged edges. The writer seemed to start in the middle
of a conversation.

> The manuscript belongs to the girl you met in my office. I'm
> glad you found it perfect for your needs. We'll change A View
> from the Carriage to The Girl in the Carriage. It seems to fit with
> your previous titles but brings a spark of life. We can pull it off.
> She's an heiress about to be engaged to a Van Cliff. I doubt she'll
> give us concern.
>
> The advertisers will be most happy, as will the booksellers.
> I believe Barclay is saved.
>
> What do you say? We will edit it together to make it your
> own. You might want to dispose of this when you're done.
>
> DB.

Jett dropped down to the chair with a thud. What more proof
did he need? Gordon Phipps Roth, his *last* hero, was a big fat fraud.

He stole someone's work. A woman's. An heiress. Birdie Shehorn
Ainsworth. The Marchioness of Hapsworth. But instead of provid-
ing answers, this discovery opened a new world of questions.

Did Birdie write *all* of GPR's books post '03? Or did he rebound
and take over from there?

Did the Roth Foundation know? Were they part of the decep-
tion? Jett was convinced Tenley knew the truth. Thus her silence.

What was his next move? Forget? Stop the dissertation's publication? Or would he write what he absolutely knew to be true? What
was corroborated and confirmed?

"Hard decision?" Gilda remained patiently by the door.

"He was a fraud." Jett peered at the petite woman with the giant
stature. "At least I think so. With one book anyway."

"What are you going to do?"

"I don't know."

Suddenly Jett stood on the edge of the Eiger mountain cliff

with Storm, arguing, so angry he literally saw red. He challenged his brother. Accused him. But he didn't believe he'd jump. The wind was too wild.

In this moment he faced a different kind of cliff. Did he jump? Get caught in the crosswinds and commit career suicide?

Defaming one of America's great and beloved authors would make him enemy number one in his small, academic world.

"Jett?"

"A moment, Gilda, please."

Okay. Say someone, Birdie, wrote *Girl*. There was no proof or any indication she wrote subsequent books. None. What did this one little secret matter?

Jett ran his hand through his thick mop of hair. It *did* matter. To him and all who esteemed art and talent. To all who followed a literary path because they admired Gordon Phipps Roth, the man as well as the writer.

"Jett?"

"Yeah, Gilda, sorry." He handed the letter to Gilda, who put it, along with the book, back on the shelf.

Then he collected his things and walked past the patient librarian.

"You'll figure it out, Jett."

"Will I?"

With conflict churning, he rode home through the night chill. Tomorrow was his deadline. Would he tell the truth? He needed a hero's courage to do so.

And he was no hero.

CORAL

After Monday evening's story society, her days moved on fast-forward. The auditor arranged to begin work next week.

Sales reported record returns on the lip gloss. Marketing, promotions, social media, every corner of CCW emerged with trumpets to their lips.

"Pink Coral is sinking the ship!"

Taking her father's advice, she dug deep. Pulled sales reports, consulted with everyone from Blaire to the admins.

Friday afternoon, the evidence was spread across the boardroom table. She'd await confirmation from the auditor, but her analysis left little room for doubt.

The trumpeters were right.

Even more disturbing, CCW's foundation products, Day Glow and Night Refresh, slumped in sales. By comparison, Great-grandma fared far better during the Depression than Coral did now in a thriving economy.

Foundation and mascara reported slightly less than expected. The new charcoal-based Miracle Mask that Lexa loved limped along.

Blaire entered the executive conference room with her laptop and a cup of coffee. "Nice outfit, Coral. Is it new?"

She glanced down at the tiger-print flared slacks and black top. "They were in the back of my closet."

The CEO leaned over her shoulder. "Hard to argue with black and gold."

"Except when it comes to our mysterious revenue shortage." Coral peered down the long table at Dak, who'd just entered. "I take full responsibility for our present state."

Drew and Lacy, heads of marketing and promotion respectively, scanned the pile of printouts.

"We're going old school?" Lacy set down her laptop and took up a stack.

"Coral, we're all responsible." There was an edge to Blaire's confession, as if it pained her to admit the truth. "We are your team and were responsible for the day-to-day when you were in Lauchtenland. Coral, I think I should resign. You brought me on to help steer the preteen line and take the company into the next phase, and all I've done is drive it into the ground."

"It's my fault." Coral darted around the table. "You're the one who kept this *Titanic* from sinking."

"Actually, I've thought the same." Dak glanced at Blaire, then Coral, and yanked his glasses from his face and tossed them to the table. In one move he went from Clark Kent to Superman with his wavy black hair, square jaw, and deep blue eyes. "We've let you down."

"I rather think I let you all down. I am the president and owner. This falls on me. When I should've been here working, I flitted around Paris and Milan for a haute couture trousseau."

Blaire grinned. "Well, you were becoming a princess."

"By the way," Dak said, "why *did* you leave him?"

So, the inquiry finally surfaced. Since her return home, no one had braved the question. But Coral knew of the office pool where almost the entire staff placed bets on why she had left Gus at the altar.

Caught him cheating was number one. Up to almost five grand.

Gus catching her cheating was a close second followed by about six lesser reasons. Cold feet. Didn't want to be a princess. Never loved him. Which wasn't true. Her love for Gus kept her in denial about her fears, about the truth, for far too long.

Coral surveyed the somber faces. Each one waiting for an answer to why she left her prince as much as what she wanted to do to save the company.

"Sometimes a girl discovers something greater and she has to yield her heart. Now, can we move on?" She returned to her place at the head of the table. "Might as well make the call. Despite the glowing reviews, Pink Coral is a failure. Let's pull the plug."

"I don't see another way." Compassion molded Blaire's perfect complexion.

"Numbers don't lie." Of course, Dak trusted numbers.

"Let's just set it aside, focus on our bread-and-butter products," Drew said. "Get them back on the top. Then we can look at Pink Coral again."

"You know my father suggested I fire all of you. Start over." No one stirred. "But I am not my father."

Their slight exhales were followed by shallow laughter.

"Thank you all for standing by me, supporting CCW while I figured out my life. I do value your loyalty." The team gave her light applause as they packed up. "Now let's get to work and put our products back on top. Rachel?" She beckoned the head of human resources. "Raises on hold until we see where we land. Including bonuses."

Rachel nodded toward the exiting executive leadership. "They won't be happy about that, but I was going to email my thoughts on a wage freeze when I went back to my office."

Thirty-year-old Rachel was an HR savant, if such a thing existed. She knew how to manage people and training, how to build a positive corporate environment.

"Please do."

"And Coral?" Rachel said, low and unassuming. "I know you've stopped taking a salary."

"Shhh." Coral pressed her finger to her lips.

"We're going to fix this, I know it."

"One way or another."

Coral strode toward her office with feigned confidence and looked over the railing to the floor below, where more than a hundred people depended on her for a paycheck.

Marketing, promotions, art, sales, administration, finance,

purchasing, human resources, the formulas and new-product department, community and customer relationships, PR. Not to mention
the production site as well as the photographers and models they
contracted every year.

In the middle of the floor, Blaire and Dak talked with Chris, the
head of IT. Blaire caught her attention and gave her a thumbs-up.

With refreshed hope, Coral returned to her office. CCW might
be a cosmetics company but the people, the employees, the customers, were the heart and soul.

It was why her grandmother started developing and selling her
own products. To help women. To create jobs. To give people a better life.

In her office, Coral exhaled against the closed door. "Grandma,
if you're watching, I'm sorry. But I won't let you down."

At her desk, she deposited her laptop and papers, then pulled
open the bottom drawer, taking out the book she'd stashed there a
year ago.

She had one like it at home too. The one she purchased the night
before she told Gus she couldn't marry him.

Flipping through the pages, Coral paused on the words in red,
printed across thin, delicate paper. The page was warped by her
dried tears.

"You got me through the breakup, Lord. Please see me through
this."

With that humble plea, she tucked the book away and got to
work, sending a message to her assistant, Matt.

Schedule Tuesday for Pink Coral shutdown plan. All
executive staff.

Once she got things square, she wanted to go out into the field,
meet the distributors, visit the sales team, tour the production plant.

Then she wanted to peer over the shoulder of every department
and review processes and plans.

Next, she'd haunt the commercial sets. Hover over the art and design departments, comb over every aspect of customer service, administration, and finance.

Then make necessary revisions and redirect her executive team.

She might have lost control over the past two years, but she'd have no excuse going forward. She was taking back the reins.

She'd just made a hot cup of tea when a light knock sounded.

"Enter."

"You busy?"

She whirled around to find Chuck standing in the doorway, so swarthy and broad, seemingly out of place in her glass-and-chrome office with designer furniture, full bar, and bath.

"Chuck, what are you doing here?" The teacup shimmied in her trembling hand. "Can I get you anything? Water, Diet Coke, tea, coffee?"

"Naw, I'm good, thanks." He sat on the edge of the white leather sofa, hands gripped tight, his oversized Ohio State jacket zipped halfway over a dark-blue T-shirt. His thick Italian hair couldn't decide if it was black or a foxy silver. "Nice place, Ms. Winthrop."

"My grandmother remodeled it ten years ago. She had timeless taste." Should she join him on the couch? Or sit at her desk, looking all powerful and executive-like to cover up the fact she had a huge crush? She didn't realize it herself until now.

"Did you drop off a fare near here?" *Couch. Act like a friend.*

"Yeah, around the corner. I was going to break for lunch when I looked up and saw your company name staring down at me from this big ol' building and thought to myself, 'Why not see where Coral hangs her hat?'"

"I'm glad you did." She felt revived in his presence. Even . . . beautiful. How long had it been since she felt like more than a slug?

"Must be a lot of pressure to run a place like this." Chuck stood, glancing around, peering through the glass toward Matt's desk. "How's everything going?"

"We decided to stop production of Pink Coral." His kind inquiry touched her. He knew only a little of her troubles and yet here he was, checking on her. "The pressure is real. Two years ago, I was the leader of a worldwide cosmetics company. We were in the black, making about forty million a year. I'd just been invited to join an international women-in-business organization. While developing Pink Coral, I met Prince Augustus of Lauchtenland, and my life took a road I never imagined." She paused, seeing the irony for the first time. "I never imagined we'd fail and my sweet lip gloss would sink the ship."

"You don't seem like a shrinking violet to me, Coral."

"No, I guess I'm not. Thank you, Chuck. I mean it." She trusted his insight. He wasn't a man of idle flattery.

"My ex loved your products. Didn't get the connection until I walked in here, saw all the posters. Her whole side of the counter was lined with CCW. Too bad about the kid gloss. My Riley would've liked it, I bet. She was putting her mom's goop on her face before she could run."

"I bet she's beautiful. Your Riley."

"She is." After a beat of silence, he tipped his head toward the door. "I won't keep you."

"I'm glad you stopped by." She set her tea aside and walked with him to the door, wishing he'd stay a bit longer. "Would you like a tour?"

He shook his head. "Not my thing. I worked for my ex-father-in-law's trucking company, so I know this side of the business world. A lot of headaches." He was so broad he blocked the hallway light coming through the door.

"A lot of rewards too."

He grinned, making her weak with his old-world charm. "My office was a hole in the wall. Nothing like this." He started to go, then paused and raised his arms over his head, hooking his hands over the doorframe. His strength pushed against the confines of his sleeves. "I was thinking maybe . . . Look, I'm no prince but . . ." She willed him to complete his thought out loud.

Yes?

"I'm glad I met you. At the society."

She deflated a little. "Me too."

"Lexa's story had me thinking all week."

"She told me on the way home she didn't mean to share so much. I think she was kind of embarrassed."

"Embarrassed? She was a victim. Did you notice she never said anything bad about that kid, Carnie? Or Babs?"

"She has a lot of wisdom. But I think it's wasted on Zane Breas."

"I hope she finds a good job in the city. She's starting to feel like a good friend."

"Agreed, and I don't have many good friends."

"Same." Chuck lowered his arms and stepped aside as one of the admins delivered snail mail to Coral's desk. "Guess I'd better get out of your hair. Look, Coral, if you ever need a ride, you have my number."

"Yes, I do." *Is that all?* "But I have a driver. A service."

"Yeah, sure. A buddy of mine runs a car service. Maybe you heard of it? Elite Rides?"

"Afraid I haven't. I'm booked with Car Concierge."

"CC, I know them. Good guys."

"If you want, I could mention you to Lucian, the owner." *Really, he wanted to talk about car services?*

"I'm good with Elite, but I appreciate it." Once again Chuck stepped aside for a second admin, followed by the skinny new geeky kid from IT.

"Ms. Winthrop?" Coral fished for his name. Teddy. "You got a minute?"

"Not at the moment, no. Can I have Matt call you when I'm free?"

"I should be going. I'm in the way," Chuck said. "You got work to do. See you Monday, Coral."

"Yes, Monday." *Is that all? Aren't you going to ask me out?* She'd been holding her breath, hoping.

"Am I going or staying?" Teddy stood in Chuck's place.

"Please, come in." She took a final look at the departing Chuck. He looked as good going as coming.

Gathering herself, she faced the pale-faced young man with long bangs crossing over his forehead.

"What's wrong, Teddy?" She noted his laptop as she retreated behind her desk. "You look concerned." He was a sweet kid, sharp. When she'd taken him to coffee a few months ago after he hired on, they talked for four hours. "Are Chris and the IT team treating you well?"

He twitched like a timid jackrabbit. "Yes, ma'am. They are. I love it here." Ma'am? He was all of twenty-two and she all of thirty-three.

"Good." She pointed to his laptop. "Do you have something to show me?" Something about seeing Chuck filled her with confidence.

"You know I was hired to work on maintenance and stability. Chris has been complaining the servers were slow and the memory shares spiked too often during the day, so I've been doing some tuning."

"Thank you. I've noticed a difference." But why was he telling her this?

"May I?" He pointed to the coffee table and opened his laptop. "I want to show you something, and I hope I don't lose my job for it."

Coral joined him on the couch, choosing the spot where Chuck had perched. The cushion was still warm from his presence.

"What are we looking at?" Two windows. Two open accounting systems.

"A hidden database."

Her skin chilled. "Hidden?"

"Did you know about this?"

Coral rose and shut her office door. "I did not."

"I could tell by the log-in signatures you didn't access this database, but I wanted to make sure you weren't aware."

"Is this what I think it is?"

"Afraid so."

"How'd you find it?"

"Treasure hunting." His narrow face widened with a bashful grin. "I like to dig around, see what people are storing on the server, look for unused data space and clean up drives. I discover things. Usually it's stupid stuff like porn or secret love letters. A lot of people have affairs at work. You wouldn't believe it, Ms. Winthrop."

"Coral. Call me Coral. Is that what this is? Secret files?"

"Secret all right, but worse than illegal downloads. These are two sets of books." He reached for his shoulder bag and pulled out a ream of paper. "I printed these out as a backup," he said, dumping two stacks on the table. "The real financials and the fake. You've been logging into the fake one."

Coral took up the nearest stack and scanned the first page. "This is the real data?"

"Yes, ma'am. Looks like we're doing good. That product PC301 is killing it." He pointed to the budget-vs.-actual lines. "Already exceeded annual projection."

She was on her feet, trembling, flipping pages. PC301. Pink Coral. Her *baby* was killing it.

"Teddy, you're a genius. I'd kiss you if it wasn't against company policy."

He blushed. "Just having some fun. Never thought I'd find a second DB. It was hidden pretty good."

"I bet." Coral paced, shaking. "Let me get this straight. There's a database for me and one for who?"

Teddy flipped to another screen. "Admin1 and Admin2." He pointed to the log-in signatures. "I wasn't sure who they were." He looked at her with round, drooping eyes. "I thought maybe you, but I guess not."

"How do we find out who's logging in?"

He grinned. "I set a trap last night with some sweet code I wrote in college. It sets an alert whenever someone logs in with those usernames. I can pinpoint an IP and take it from there."

"And?"

"Got a hit from last night. Two. Blaire's and Dak's laptops." He handed her another printout. "Shows their log-in time and location. How long they stayed logged in, and the changes they made." He dusted his hands against his jeans.

"What else did you find?"

"Expense reports covering vacations, school tuition, shopping, hotels, dinners out. All charged to the company." He switched screens again. "Here's a list of expenses in the last year. Looks like it started in January."

When she got engaged to Gus.

"The auditor comes next week. I'm sending him to you. Show him what you showed me. That'll save him time. I told the executive team our regular accountant was sending over a new man to get some experience. Blaire and Dak won't worry because they'll think he's too green."

"Even an experienced auditor wouldn't have found this second database."

"But you did. My secret weapon." Coral collected the printouts and carried them to the wall safe. "Keep a strong paper trail for me, Teddy."

"Got it." He closed his laptop. "Better get back before Chris comes looking for me. I have to admit, it's a pretty clever setup. Usually embezzlers don't work very hard to cover their activity, because they want to appear legit. But in order to keep everything straight, and to have some sort of honor among thieves, they have to create a trail. These two covered their tracks pretty well. My guess is someone with database experience helped them. Oh, here's your log-in to the real database." He slid a piece of paper across the coffee table. Very clandestine.

"Teddy, why did you come to me, not Chris? Do you think he's in on it?"

"I came to you because of my grandmother."

"Your grandmother?"

A red hue flashed across his cheeks. "When I told her where I was working, she got stupid excited. Told me how much she loves CCW products. Been using them since the fifties."

"Is she young looking and beautiful?"

"For an eighty-year-old, I reckon so, yeah." He shrugged and tucked his laptop under his arm. "I figure if you helped a woman like my grandma, who took care of my dad and his brothers while my grandpa worked as a bus mechanic, I should watch your back. Besides, yeah. I think Chris is in on it. He's a database expert. The only one who could've set this up for them."

"Tell your grandma her grandson helped save my family's company."

When he'd gone, she collapsed in her chair, relieved, sad, furious, confused. Why? She trusted those two bozos. And they corrupted Chris. Why weren't the auditors, to whom she paid thousands of dollars every year, smarter?

She reached into the bottom desk for her Book and clutched it to her chest. She'd just started to discover the power of her new faith, of her prayers.

Where she'd wallowed in despair an hour ago, she now had the tiger by the tail. Coral smirked at her tiger-print slacks and reached for her phone.

"Dad, I need to talk to you."

Chapter 23

CHUCK

Just call him a gutless wonder. Couldn't even ask a girl out to coffee. But Coral Winthrop wasn't just any girl.

She was beauty in motion. Elegant. An old Knickerbocker heiress running a multimillion-dollar company who also loved and dumped one of the world's most desirable bachelors.

He was a divorced dad and Uber driver with an arrest record. What was his point in riding the elevator up sixteen floors to see her? And hooking his hands over the doorframe like Balboa in the first *Rocky*.

Pulling up along Madison Avenue, he scanned the sidewalk for his next customer—a woman in a red duster coat. He spotted her between two parked cars, her short spikey hair tipped with gold.

She confirmed her destination as she climbed into the back of the car. "One ninety-five Broadway, please."

Chuck pulled into traffic. He knew the place. A publishing house. "You're a writer?"

"Agent." She focused on her phone, the sounds of texting rising from the back seat. "Don't tell me *you're* a writer."

He peered at her through the rearview mirror. "Jaded much?"

The typing stopped. "Sorry. Long week. I'm going to auction with a new book and the author, while promising, has no idea what she's doing yet can't stop telling *me* what to do. 'You work for me,' she says. One more snarky email from her and she can negotiate her own six-figure deal."

"Ever hear of the Fifth Avenue Literary Society Library?"

"Of course. A beautiful old place." She scooted forward, resting one arm on the top of the passenger seat. "My grandfather took me there when I was a girl. The scent of all those books was perfume to me. I almost crave it now. It was part of the old Winthrop mansion."

"I go to a story society there on Monday nights. Five of us. We're not writers, but Jett Wilder is our leader of sorts. He's a professor and wrote a book—"

"*Rites of Mars.* I read it. Loved it. His publisher totally botched the release. Didn't get enough advance reviews, then dumped the marketing money on the girl who plagiarized every teen novel known to man. They lost their shirts on that one. Who's Jett's agent? Do you know? He should've been raising cane with the publisher."

"Don't know. He doesn't talk much about it."

"If you're not a writer, why do you go?"

"I was invited."

"What do you do?"

"Eat. Talk about life. One guy, Ed, wrote a piece about his wife and read it to us. Seems like they were a match made in heaven."

"How'd you come across this little society?"

"Like I said, I was invited." He tapped on the horn, giving the car in front of him a nudge. "We all were. Don't know by who—Come on, buddy, move. Son of a—" Chuck moved into a break in the traffic and escaped the jam.

When he arrived at 195 Broadway, his fare dropped her card in the passenger seat along with a generous tip.

"If you or any one of your society do come up with a story, call me." She tossed another card onto the seat. "Make sure you give one to Jett. If he needs any advice, I'd be glad to help. Not trying to poach another agent's client, but I can always be a friend."

Chuck read the card. Lucy Hughes. "I used to tell my kids a story about a magic book."

"A magic book?" Lucy hesitated, one foot out the back door. "I like it already."

"You don't even know what it is."

"It's high concept. I can imagine it." She tapped his shoulder. "What does the book do?"

"Takes the kids on adventures, see? Anywhere they want to go. All they have to do is jump in and fly. Ride a pony across the milky way. Be a princess with a cloud kingdom." He laughed, remembering Jakey's fourth birthday. "I have twins and one year my boy jumped into the magic book and came out as Joe Namath."

"Who?"

"Joe Namath. You know, the great Jets quarterback." How old was this woman? "The twins' grandfather fascinated them with colorful stories of Broadway Joe, and that's who Jakey wanted to be."

"What's your name?"

"Chuck Mays."

"Send me all you've got, Chuck." With that, Lucy stepped out and ran between traffic into the building.

A shadow crossed his soul as he tucked Lucy's card into his money bag. He didn't have enough stories to send, because he'd scared his ex-wife and kids half to death and got kicked out of their lives.

But hopefully that would all change soon. If Wanda came through for him. He hadn't heard from her since his two-minute visit on Monday.

He'd just connected with another fare around the corner when his phone pinged. A text from Wanda.

You can come. October 25 and 26. Two o'clock. One hour.
Bring your best behavior or this will never happen again.

LEXA

When she looked up, Jett stood in the bedroom doorway.

"Hey," she said, setting her book aside. She'd started reading *Rites of Mars* Wednesday and couldn't put it down.

"Still reading?" he said.

"It's good, Jett. Really."

His smile was so cute. "Good. I'm glad you like it."

"I already want a sequel with Reena."

"How's your week been? Any hits on your résumé?" He'd been busy all week with school and missing his publication deadline, and overseeing homecoming festivities. New York College had lavish, time-honored traditions for their alumni and students.

"A few companies have looked but it's only been a week. I've contacted a few headhunters who were very interested. The right thing will happen at the right time. Who knows, maybe Zane will come to his senses and hire me."

"Has he called?"

She shook her head, slightly pained by the reality. It was time to move on. Even if he did call. No use staying where she was not wanted or appreciated. Life was too short.

"What did you decide about Gordon's manuscript?"

When he arrived home from the story society Monday evening they had talked about the manuscript and all the possible implications instead of the charged question he proposed to her in the foyer after she told her Carnie story.

"Is that why you walked out?"

Frankly, it was easier not to dig up the past, and the matter of the manuscript was more pressing. It wasn't like they were going to change anything about their history and present status, though in the quiet of her heart she'd like closure one day. She'd like to know what he was thinking and feeling when she slammed the door behind her.

But right now, it all felt too close and raw, like her arm. Healing but not ready for use.

Jett sat on the edge of the bed. "I'm three days late submitting. Renée is anxious. The dean is calling. Ten million, Lex. Ten million on the line. I think, well, I have to go with what I have. What I know for sure. The unpublished book in the library doesn't really change anything."

"How could it not, Jett? The publisher wrote a letter admitting to stealing Birdie's story."

"He never said her name. Just that she was an heiress."

"Well, I think we can connect the dots." The "we" was unintentional but she liked how it flowed so easily in the conversation.

"I know, I know." He flopped back on the bed. "There's no evidence of her writing—"

"*An October Wedding.*"

"Or that Gordon wasn't simply inspired by *her* version of *The Girl in the Carriage* and completely rewrote it. Or that he didn't help her write *October Wedding*. No, no, there's not enough to convict." He jumped up and stuffed his hands into his jeans pockets. "I'm emailing my manuscript in now before I get lost in the woods of indecision again."

"Then okay. Do it and stick with your decision."

"You sound like Dad."

"I always liked your dad."

"Speaking of Dad, I was wondering . . ." He moved across the room and looked toward the flares of the setting October sun. "Go with me to Mom's wedding. She set the date for the twenty-sixth."

"That's next weekend."

"I can't handle her, Oz, Dad, and the memorial by myself."

"So you want to take your ex-wife along? *That'll* make it easier."

He laughed low. "It'll be a good diversion. An odd conversation starter."

"Jett, no, I can't. It doesn't feel right for me to go. I'm not family."

"Too late. Mom added you to the guest list and I'm pretty sure Dad would love to see you. And if Storm were alive, there'd be no getting out of it."

"Well, that's true." She laughed at a memory of Storm. "Remember the time he wanted to take us out to dinner and kept getting accosted by fans?"

"Female fans."

"He bought the monkey face and wore it into Delmonico's."

His laugh sparkled. "I still have that mask somewhere."

The moment passed, and the silence claimed their hearts. "Guess I'd better get to work. Papers to grade. Midterms are right after homecoming week."

"I'll go," she said as he entered the hall. "If you want."

"I do."

"Okay, but as your friend."

"What else could you be?"

When he'd gone she sank down into the pillows, more comfortable than she wanted to be.

She should tell him. Not wait until last minute. Not walk out on him like she did before. He'd been so nice to her the past month.

But her building super had called to say he'd installed the new shower nozzle she requested. And the matter of her loft bed had been resolved by Abby, who texted she had an inflatable mattress Lexa could borrow. No surprise, considering all the people who crashed at her place on weekends.

Should she tell Jett that Dr. Haft scheduled her up for a new, shorter cast next week and had cleared her to be on her own?

Should she tell him? "I'm moving home next week."

She tried to read again, but she had the attention depth of a shallow puddle.

Why was she intimidated to tell Jett she was moving home? Other than gratitude, which she planned to express in an expensive gift—yet to be determined—she owed him nothing.

Lexa attempted to finish the chapter, but the turmoil of the epic space adventure's hero and heroine, Stovall and Amvi, hunkering down in their makeshift hut as a Martian hurricane raged over them, seemed like nothing to the turmoil inside of her.

She'd just agreed to a weekend with her ex-husband. And if she was honest, she was falling for him all over again.

⌒

JETT

Since sending his finalized dissertation to the publisher, he couldn't sleep or settle down.

Yet when he assessed his thoughts and emotions, nothing seemed amiss. He believed he'd made the best decision. Done the right thing.

Omitting the manuscript discovery and supporting the academic world's view of Gordon Phipps Roth proved he cared about scholarship and truth.

How dare he imply GPR used a ghostwriter, or worse, *stole* a manuscript from a Gilded Age heiress when he had no other corroboration?

The letters from Daniel Barclay were inconclusive. He could've been talking about anything or anyone.

All right, yes, the letters were clearly addressed to Gordon, still . . .

He'd done the right thing. Especially for his college.

Monday afternoon, Jett reached inside his desk drawer and twisted open a bottle of Tums. Darn hamburger from lunch was burning him up.

Back at his desk, he faced his computer and the first paper of his Comm 2 class. Only seventy-one to go.

He was grateful for the homecoming week where classes were cancelled, and he'd find time to catch up on work.

He was on the first page of the first essay when Renée burst through his office door.

"Jett, outstanding work." She carried a printout of his book under her arm and perched on the chair next to his desk. "Your conclusions are stellar. Dean Hanover just heard from Elijah, and not only is the Roth Foundation giving us the ten million at the November reception but they want to present your book at the annual Roth Awards in February. They want you to be a VIP."

"But the Roth Awards are for fiction." He painted on a smile. "And I'm glad everyone is happy."

"Your work is about a fiction author." She made a funny face. "Why are you protesting? Is this your practice at humility?"

"Just wondering." The more excited everyone became, the more conviction weighed him down.

Someday, someone would find out the truth, find that hidden manuscript and bring it to light. How would Jett feel then? Because he had the chance to set the record straight, but submitted to fear and concern for his reputation.

"Do you want to be on the budget committee for the endowment?" Renée picked a piece of chocolate from the dish he kept on the corner of his desk.

"Not really, but thank you." He'd rather forget about the dissertation, what he left out—yes, *what he left out*, there, he'd said it—and move on.

Renée's gushing didn't bolster his confidence but revealed his cowardice. He'd given the story the ending everyone wanted. All for a measly ten mill. Of which he'd see none.

"You look green." Renée tossed the candy wrapper into the trash. "Go home. Get some rest. You've been working too hard. Get your TA to grade the papers." She selected another chocolate as she stood to leave. "Lexa still with you?"

"Yes." He began to pack up. The story society started in an hour.

"Is that a good yes or a bad yes?"

He flung his backpack over his shoulder. "Just a yes."

"No sparks? No rekindled love?"

"Good night, Renée."

Her snickering echoed in the hallway as she went her way and he went his.

Sparks? Plenty. Rekindling? More than he'd like. He argued that the reason for his attraction to his ex-wife was because he hadn't been with a woman in almost two years. But what a crock. Everything flowing through his veins was all about Lexa.

He hopped on his bike and pedaled toward midtown, growing more agitated with each churn of the wheel.

He wanted more with Lexa. And more for himself. Was Gordon so important that he could make Jett ignore the truth?

Be honest, man, Daniel Barclay's letter leaves no doubt. They stole The Girl in the Carriage. *Lied to the book world.*

And with Jett's omission, he became part of the scheme.

By the time he knocked his bike through the library door and locked it in the foyer, he was grumpy and hungry.

"Where's the food?" he said, dropping his backpack into his chair.

In the corner, the fireplace crackled, daring him to smile, relax, enter into the inviting ambience.

"Exactly, Jett, where's the food?" Coral examined his empty hands.

"Dude," Chuck said. "It was your turn."

"No, I remember it was . . ." He shot a glance at Lexa. "Should've reminded me."

"You should've remembered."

"Let's just order pizza." Coral retrieved her phone from her over-sized bag. "What do we like?"

While she created a menu with Chuck and Ed, Jett stepped toward his ex-wife. "You have a new cast. I thought that was later in the week."

"They called. Had a cancellation, so I was moved to the head of the line."

"What a difference." Jett sat on the edge of his chair and examined the lightweight polyethylene material that embraced her upper arm. "How do you like it?"

"I never thought I'd say this, but I love it. Look, I can bend my elbow." She demonstrated but winced when she raised her arm a bit too high. "I have to have therapy to get back the range of motion, but can you believe it? The ordeal is coming to an end."

"Can I expect a few home-cooked meals this week?" His laugh had barely left his lips before it was killed by her sober glare.

"Jett, I'm moving back to my place." He hated her calm determination. Hated the pit opening in his chest. Hated how he'd not prepared for this at all.

"Are you sure? You're still going to need help with—?"

"My hair, but I've been going to my stylist once a week anyway."

"Can you climb up to your loft?"

"Abby is lending me an air mattress. And the super installed a shower hose. I'm set, really." She pressed her good hand to his. "But I am so grateful. You've been better to me than I deserve."

He shrugged. "You'd have done the same."

"In an altruistic way, I'd like to think I would."

At least she was honest. He left the heat of Lexa's presence and turned to the group. "So what kind of pizza are we getting?"

If he was bothered before, he simmered now. And he'd left the Tums in his office. The feelings, the friendship, the kisses, the subconscious hope they were becoming the people they were before death and divorce was all a facade.

"I'm still on for the weekend," she said after Coral confirmed three large pizzas were on their way. "If you want."

"Yeah, sure, why not? By the way, it's black tie."

"Black tie? I don't have a formal dress any more. Got sort of torn up when I hit the pavement."

"I told mom our high school buddies weren't going to rent a tux for a funeral, but she insisted. The wedding is black tie."

"Can I dress just for the memorial?"

He grinned. "Do what you want. She's not your mother-in-law anymore."

"Who are we talking about?" Coral said. The circle was small, close. Even whispers were heard.

"My mother is getting married. Black tie. Lexa is going up with me and she doesn't have a dress."

"My one gown has tire tracks on it."

"Lexa, girl, I have a hundred gowns. You can borrow one. Come home with me after the society."

"You're a size nothing, Coral. I'm a size something."

"I have all sizes. Trust me. My driver will take you home when we're done. Or stay over for a girl's night."

Lexa's timid smile swept through Jett, nearly making him choke up. "Really? I'd like that."

She always told him she was never good at girlfriend relationships, but she wanted girlfriends very much. After hearing her Carnie story, and, knowing how much she'd moved around, he understood her struggle.

Coral was perfect for her.

"What's your pleasure? Alexander McQueen? Armani? Jenny Packham? Melinda House?" Coral rattled off the designer names with a fluid tongue. "Melinda designs those beautiful country-chic gowns for Princess Regina, the Grand Duchess of Hessenburg. I can call my seamstress to make any adjustments. She's a genius."

Somehow the flow of conversation moved Lexa to Chuck's chair, and Chuck to hers. When he plopped down, he tapped Jett's arm.

"Got something for you." He fished a card from his pocket. "I gave a ride to an agent the other day and she went gaga when I told her I knew you. Said she loved your book *Rites of Mars* and something about how your publisher did you wrong."

Jett took the card from between his fingers.

"Lucy Hughes? You met Lucy?" Good news flowed among the dark and sour reality of Lexa leaving. "I queried her right after I finished *Mars*, and she not so politely said, 'Move along.'"

"She's hot on you now. Said give her a call if you needed advice or anything." Chuck sat back, stretching out his long legs. "She also liked an idea of mine."

"You have a book idea?" Jett tucked the card into the side pocket of his backpack.

"Book, no. Story, yes. About this magic book that takes kids on fun adventures. I made it up for Riley and Jakey when they were little guys. I drew a big book on the side of an old cardboard box and we'd pretend to jump in and go on an adventure."

"I want to try." Lexa entered the conversation.

"How do you go on the adventure, Chuck?" Ed, as interested as any kid.

"Well, you just dream of where you want to go, or who you want to be, and jump, sort of like in *Mary Poppins*. Is that right? Where they jumped into the sidewalk? Anyway, I'd ask the kids what they wanted and boom, we jumped."

Coral stood. "I want to be out of this mess at CCW." She jumped into the middle of the circle, the silly move making them all laugh.

Ed went next, wishing for his Esmeralda. Then there was a short standoff between Jett, Chuck, and Lexa.

"I'll go." Lexa rose up, eyes closed. "A great new job." She jumped and if possible, Jett sensed the earth shift beneath him.

She was leaving. Not just his apartment but this city. His bones knew it.

Before he or Chuck could take a leap, pizza arrived, and hot pizza trumps everything.

When the society had consumed one and a half large pies, Jett refilled his drink cup with Mountain Dew—he'd be up all night— and asked if anything exciting had happened since their last meeting.

"I get to see my kids." Chuck, with a nominal level of excitement, sat forward with his plate in one hand and a folded slice in the other.

Chapter 24

CHUCK

After Lexa's confession last week, he'd decided to be a bit more forthcoming about himself. After all, maybe that's why the society existed.

The gang was excited. Though they had no idea what kind of monster he'd been.

"Chuck, I'm so thrilled for you." Coral's tone shot an arrow straight to his heart. But he yanked it out before it sank too deep. "How'd this come about?"

Chuck detailed the tale of seeing his son at the schoolyard, then visiting his ex-mother-in-law.

"She gave me two minutes. I mostly begged for her to talk to Trudy. Let me come to the twins' parties."

"Good for you. Standing up for what you want." If he didn't know better, he'd think Coral was his personal cheerleader.

"I got a text right after I met the agent. I have one hour on Saturday for Jakey's party and one on Sunday for Riley's." His voice dropped as he pressed his fist to his mouth, coughing and clearing, batting the sting from his eyes.

"Can I ask why you can't see your kids?" Ed said in a tender, fatherly tone.

Chuck reached for more pizza, then dropped back into his chair with another plate full of slices. "I, um, may have—" He set his plate on the floor and ran his hands over his knees. This was the part he dreaded. "I don't want you guys to hate me."

"Hate you? We're not going to hate you!" The others heartily agreed with Lexa's declaration.

"You don't know what I did. In today's world, if we horsewhipped people, I'd have been tied to the post and ripped up."

"Chuck." Coral recoiled at the image he painted. "What on earth?"

"I lost it, you see. Blew up." He couldn't tell the story sitting down, so he jumped up. "Saw her with that adulterating hedgie and lost my mind. I had no idea . . . She never said a word to me. I thought we were happy, you see. I threatened her, tore up the house, threw things, broke things, shouted, maybe threw a punch or two." He raked his big hand through his hair, so the ends stood like exclamation points over his story. "Then I grabbed one of the kids."

As he anticipated, the gasps echoed through the old library, his story tainting the others here.

"By the time I realized what I was doing the cops had me in cuffs." With the story out, he deflated and sank slowly into his seat. "Trudy got the restraining order, and I haven't talked to my kids since. Not until I went by the schoolyard, and that was a big dumb risk."

Coral's touch on his arm electrified him, zapping his next thought. "You were hurting."

"No excuse." He pulled away from her touch. She didn't know the power of her feminine wiles.

"But your son wasn't afraid of you?" Lexa said.

"No. Which means Trudy's not talking me down. Can't say the same of myself."

"This is your chance, son," Ed said. "Make up for lost time. Prove you're not the wild man they last saw."

"I don't even know what gifts to get them. And I'm half afraid I'll show up, see the boyfriend playing the daddy role, and explode again."

"I can go with you." Coral's offer burst into the Bower like a cool rain.

"What?" Chuck glanced at her, his heart on fire. If he walked in with Coral Winthrop on his arm . . .

"I love birthday parties. Didn't you say Trudy loves CCW products? I'll bring her a gift box." She winked at Chuck. "Win her over."

Lexa raised her hand. "I want a gift box."

"I-I don't know, Coral. Trudy can be a bit of a—No, I can't let you do that, Coral. You're good to offer, but—"

"But what? I'm not afraid of a mean-tempered woman. If I backed down every time someone barked at me, I wouldn't be taking back control of CCW. And I'd love to help with the kids' presents."

"Coral, you're busy, I can't ask you to trouble yourself." He couldn't use her for his advantage. It'd be wrong.

However, the idea of spending two hours with Coral Winthrop made him feel clammy and jittery. In all the good ways.

"Please, it will be fun. I don't get to shop for children very often."

Chuck exhaled, allowing a smile to rise from his gut. "Really? You want to go with me to my kids' parties?"

"I offered, didn't I?"

"Then okay, sure, I accept."

Friendship and pizza in a room full of books. Wasn't entirely Chuck's jam, but right now, this place, with these people, was his happiest place on earth. His Monday-night addiction was growing.

Well, talk of birthdays got them all sharing stories. Ed grew up in the old days where kids just had dinner with the family and got one gift.

Chuck, the same. Coral had birthday weekends and trips abroad. Lexa celebrated with her family and maybe her one good friend.

"In whatever city or country we lived in. Mom went out of her way to make our birthdays fun."

"What about you, Jett?" Coral dropped another slice of pizza on her plate. "I'm realizing you're the one who talks about himself the least."

"I agree," Chuck said. "Out with it, Wilder. Tell us about your birthdays."

"I'm the listener of the group." Nice try, but he wasn't getting off that easy.

"Or the avoider," Ed said. Chuck popped him a low five.

"Okay, well, I don't remember ever having a birthday party.

Mom left when I was twelve and it was just us guys. Dad, Storm, and me. We didn't have traditions or do sentimental stuff. When I was sixteen Mom was back working for Dad, so on birthdays she made an effort. Maybe we'd go out to dinner or something. Otherwise she gave us a present. My birthday is in the spring, and usually she and Dad were filming somewhere. Dad wasn't into shopping, so he'd just hand us money. A fifty when we were in high school and a hundred in college."

"I feel a party coming on." Coral tapped on her phone. "When's your birthday?"

"No, please, I'd just feel stupid."

"March twenty-first," Lexa said. "But don't bother, Coral. I tried to throw him a party once and he was so grumpy everyone left within the hour."

"Only because I had a mountain of work to do." Jett wiped his hands on a wad of napkins. "I was finishing grad school."

"Are we going to be here in the spring?" Ed said.

Good question, old man. Chuck glanced around. "Are we?"

"We still don't know exactly why we're here *now*."

Coral announced her assistant would collect birthdays and if they were still a society, they'd celebrate.

"Are we agreed?"

Heads bobbed, lips muttered agreement.

"Come on. This is fun," Coral said.

"You're chipper," Ed said. "I thought you was losing your company. Wanted out of the mess a few minutes ago."

"True, but there's good news about the bad news."

❦

CORAL

She wasn't going to share about Teddy's discovery, but when Ed asked, the words flowed.

"My new tech guy, the one who came into my office as you left, Chuck, found a—"

"You went to see Coral?" Ed said.

"Yeah, I was in her neighborhood, saw her office."

"—second database." She glanced at Ed, then Chuck.

"Coral, no." Lexa tossed her plate in the trash.

"The forensic auditor started today and found even more data. My CEO and CFO are embezzling. Pink Coral is not dying, it's selling lights-out."

"I knew it." Lexa popped the air with her fist. "But why would Blaire Boreland steal? She's a genius. Brought Glitter Girl back to life."

"I'm as perplexed as anyone. Sad, too, because I really liked her. And please, everyone, what's said in the society stays in the society."

"Of course."

"My lips are sealed." Ed threw his pretend key over his shoulder.

"What's your next move?" Jett said.

"Call the authorities. I should have enough data and evidence by the end of the week. They don't know we've discovered the second database. They are logging in all day, sometimes at night."

Chuck whistled and swore softly, his exclamation accented by a soft knock on the Bower door.

"Time, children." Gilda peered inside.

Coral sighed. She was never ready to leave the society's company. Especially now that she enjoyed Chuck's company a bit more.

Jett thanked the effervescent librarian and along with the rest, Coral tidied the Bower.

Chuck closed the fireplace doors and Jett shut off the lights.

"Next week?"

"Same time, same place?"

"Please remember, don't speak to anyone of what I've discovered." Chuck aided Coral with her jacket with one hand while balancing the leftover pizza box in the other. "I really need this to be a secret until I'm ready to move."

Jett and Chuck muttered they wouldn't know who to tell, and Lexa whispered for Coral to call her if she wanted to talk.

"I will." She linked her arm through her friend's good arm and walked out. "I have this gold and peach Melinda House gown that would be perfect for you."

∽

LEXA

"Got a sec?" Jett stopped her before she arrived at Coral's car. "I'll be quick."

"Take your time, Lexa." Coral dipped inside the black sedan with a low word to the driver.

"Jett, if this is about me moving home, then—"

"It's not. It's about the birthday party."

"What?"

"I'm sorry. And, by the way, thank you. After everyone left I felt horrible. You were trying to do a good thing for me and I acted like a jerk. Even worse, I heard you crying but I told myself you'd get over it. I had work to do. I'm sorry. Truly."

Tears collected in the corner of her eyes. She hadn't thought about that party in a long time. Not until she mentioned it tonight.

"You're forgiven."

He held her gaze for a moment, and she wasn't sure she wanted him to break away.

"You'd better go. Coral's waiting."

But she couldn't move from the sweet tension between them.

"Everything's going to be okay with your book, Jett."

"What about with me? When I've convinced myself I've done the right thing, doubt creeps in again."

"What would Storm do?" She'd not referred to his brother since the accident. But they used to challenge themselves, in those good, early days, to be more bold and brave like Storm.

He reared back and regarded her through the streetlight. "What would Storm . . . He would—" A slow smile brightened his countenance. "He wouldn't give a flip about a hidden manuscript and would be on top of the world he helped bring in ten million dollars."

"Exactly." She brushed her hand along the cold plane of his cheek. "You're a good man, Jett Wilder. Never doubt yourself."

"Would a good man let you go, Lexa?"

"Now that," she said, backing toward Coral's car, "is a question for another day."

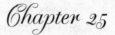

ED

He was nothing if not faithful. Every October twenty-fifth, Ed Marshall donned his best suit and tie, purchased flowers from a street vendor on Eighty-Sixth and Broadway, then hailed a cab.

This year, however, he thought he'd try Uber. Chuck set him up after giving him a ride home last Monday.

If he was unsure about the story society in the beginning, he wasn't now. The oddball group felt like friends. It'd been a long time since he'd had a good friend, let alone four.

Finding his reading specs, Ed opened his Uber app and selected a driver, typed in *George Washington Bridge* as his destination, collected his flowers, and headed for the elevator.

When Holly had popped by Wednesday evening, he showed her how he was up with the times. She grabbed hold of the counter to keep from fainting away. Every once in a while, he liked to blow her socks off.

He had purchased the flowers earlier when he went out for a bite of lunch. Roses, daisies, and lilies. All Esmerelda's favorites.

He hit the down button again. Dang elevator was slower than molasses in winter.

"Don't you look nice." Mabel leaned against the door frame, arms folded over her waist. She wore a pretty floral housedress. "Flowers? Ed Marshall, are you going on a date?"

"Not exactly." He rammed his finger at the down button again. He'd just had the elevators serviced. They should be flying through the shafts.

"Well then, do you have time for coffee and a brownie? I just took a batch out of the oven. I thought I'd take some down to the Canfields. They just had another baby."

"I know. Installed the baby monitor for them." He didn't mean to sound so gruff, but she was messing up his process. He needed to be focused. Her deflated expression almost made him apologize, but the elevator arrived and saved him. "Good night, Mabel."

"Good night, Ed."

His conscience nipped at him. Fine, he'd apologize later. Next week. If he saw her on his way to somewhere.

She meant no harm. Just being neighborly. But tempting him with brownies was not the way to his heart.

At the first floor, he exited the elevator and answered the driver's text asking for a description.

Handsome gentleman in a suit holding flowers.

Chuck had shown him how to see the driver's name, but he preferred to see the license plate so he could confirm he wasn't about to be kidnapped.

When the blue Honda Accord pulled up, Ed slipped into the back. "George Washington Bridge."

"Ed, it's me, Chuck." The man's broad face peered at him through the rearview.

"Chuck, well, you don't say. Did you do that on purpose?"

"Couldn't if I wanted to, Ed. Luck of the draw. Maybe we should buy a lotto ticket."

Ed chuckled but not with a hearty vibration. Having Chuck drive him was not the plan. He'd ask questions Ed would rather not answer.

Maybe he should change his mind, get out and take a cab.

This night was too personal. Even to share with Chuck of the story society. In many ways, Ed considered this anniversary too personal for *him*.

"I hardly ever have fares uptown. But I just brought someone over from the airport." He stretched his hand over the back seat. "Good to see you, my friend."

"You as well." Ed clapped his hand into Chuck's. He should have told him Central Park. Or Harlem. Not the bridge. "Are you looking forward to this weekend? Your kids' birthdays plus the lovely Coral going along?"

"Tell you the truth, I'm a bit nervous. But seeing you has given me a bit of courage. Makes me feel lucky, as if good things can happen to guys like me."

"You're a good man, Chuck." Ed clapped him on the shoulder. "Don't let one dark night haunt you."

Ed knew well the haunt of darkness.

"I'm just an old sinner." Chuck pulled into traffic. "Did you say the GW?"

Ed ran his hand over his jaw. If he said any place but the GW, he'd be untrue and abandon his Esmerelda. He'd promised he never would. And tonight was her night, and oh, she always *loved* her night.

"Yes, the George Washington."

Chuck glanced back. "You mean the park, right?" A horn blasted behind them and Chuck hit the gas. "You meeting someone?"

"In a roundabout way, yes. Esmerelda and I got engaged on the bridge fifty-two years ago."

Chuck's wide grin appeared in the mirror. "That's nice. No wonder you're wearing the fancy suit and carrying flowers."

Chuck maneuvered through traffic with stops and starts, horn songs, and curse words.

"I'm not in a hurry, Chuck."

"Fine, but there's no excuse for these blockheads." Chuck told off the next driver with a series of honks.

Somewhere in the noise, his phone rang, and Ed listened for a moment, then tuned it out. He preferred to be alone on this ride so he could walk through his memories.

Beyond the window, his city, *their* city, flashed by. Born and raised here, he missed some of the Gotham feel of the old days, the grit and grind of the city where every man scrambled for a leg up.

He missed all the mom-and-pop joints. Like Brunelli's on

the corner of Seventy-Fifth and Broadway. Or the drugstore on Amsterdam.

Back then, seemed like everyone in his Upper West Side community was his neighbor. They were family. But they all had secrets.

While Ed lingered in the past, Chuck sped toward the future, making quick time on the Henry Hudson.

As they neared the bridge, he asked, "So who is she? Is she waiting for you at the park?"

"'Tis for me to know and you to find out, my good man. Leave me at the pedestrian walkway, if you don't mind."

Just nearing the bridge made him nostalgic. Tripped him back to his days of wine and roses, of love, desire, and youthful zeal.

He'd proposed to Esmerelda at the highest point of the bridge under the spring stars, the city twinkling at their feet.

The proposal was spontaneous. She giggled and blushed, not quite ready to give an answer.

"Oh, Eddie, you don't even have a ring."

But he bought one in short order—with a promise to buy her an even bigger jewel when he came into his riches—and proposed to her a second time in her father's living room.

She said yes with an approving nod from her father. Later, she let him have his way with her in the dark corners of the terrace garden.

Didn't seem right, taking his woman like that the first time, not even properly undressed, then pulling themselves together in the reflective light of the living room as her mother called them to dessert and coffee.

He waited until their wedding night for the next time. Esmie accused him of being prudish, but he preferred to think he showed her respect. But oh what a honeyed temptress she was, teasing and flirting, yanking at his trousers.

"The old hags are watching TV. They won't know. Let's go hide in Dad's closet."

She never cared much for her old man. But she was a spark of life for Ed.

In the midsixties, he was still fifties straitlaced and square, liked doing things the proper way.

No matter how much he wanted to take his bride-to-be in his arms and ravish her, he held off. For the life of him, he never understood why she chose him. She had Columbia, NYU, and Princeton men seeking her company.

When it came down to it, Esmerelda was a beatnik, a rebel, who wanted nothing more than to sneak away from her family's rich Upper East Side apartment along the East River to the jazz clubs of Harlem. She defined *counterculture*.

After they married, Ed grew out his hair and bought a pair of bell bottoms. She cut her hair short like Mia Farrow and exchanged her skirts and dresses for body suits and hip huggers. With a figure like Marilyn Monroe's, she made the men lust and the women envious.

But she was his. All his.

"Ed, we're here. Did you fall asleep?" Chuck circled the park road and stopped at the head of the bridge. "Do you want me to wait?"

"That won't be necessary. I'm staying awhile." Ed passed a neatly folded hundred-dollar bill to his friend. He did that every year. Gave his driver a nice tip.

"What's this?"

"A little something for your trouble."

"Ed, you've already paid me. Through the app."

"Buy something for your kids' birthday." He stepped out of the car. "See you Monday, my friend."

"How about I text you in an hour, see if you're ready. I'll be in the city all night unless I catch a fare over to Newark. I'll come get you." Chuck bent over the steering wheel to see the bridge. "You're not going to jump, are you?" He opened his car door. "You know every week someone throws themselves off the GW. Or makes an attempt."

"If I were going to off myself, I'd choose a more civilized way than jumping." From the height of the GW, jumping would shatter every bone in his body. Make mush of his brains and organs. "Besides, I can't ruin my best suit. Holly tells me it's vintage, all the rage now. I'm just going up to remember my love."

"You wouldn't lie to me."

"I believe it's an unspoken rule that society members cannot lie to one another."

"But it's okay not to tell the whole truth too."

Ed tapped his nose, then pointed at Chuck. "Good night, young man." He straightened his coat and tie, turned toward the famous bridge, and started the long walk to the apex.

With a final glance over his shoulder, he saw Chuck watching, leaning against his car, legs and arms crossed.

Don't mind him. Go on about your business. With one foot in front of the other, Ed made his annual pilgrimage. The climb got steeper and longer every year.

About a quarter of the way up, he paused to catch his breath, fingers gripped around the quivering bouquet of flowers.

"I'm coming, Esmie."

When he arrived at their spot, the steely waters of the wide, cold Hudson flowing beneath him, the bottom dropped out of his soul. The height frightened him, still, after all these years. Even when he had proposed, his legs shivered and buckled.

But he was with her. And she made him strong.

"I'm here, Esmerelda. Are you?" He raised his gaze toward the slate-gray sky, waiting, yearning for a break in the bleakness.

Somewhere over the billowing clouds, the sun moved west with a tail of fire. But no golden glow appeared.

"I reckon you're busy." Parting the flower arrangement, Ed chose the roses first. Esmerelda's favorite. "Holly fusses over me. But you know that, I imagine. She and Brant want me to move in with them. But I'm rather fond of our place. You'd be proud of our girl, Esmie. Do I say that every year? I suppose I do.

"Hard to believe she was the little peanut I held in my arms and told bedtime stories to. I must've spent ten years at the dining room table helping her with homework."

He chuckled, seeing the golden-haired Holly bent over her math book, chewing on her pencil.

"Seems like another life when I combed and curled her hair, washed her clothes. Learned to iron." A chuckle rose from his chest. "The pleats on those school uniforms were a pain, you know. I burned my fingers every time. But then there were the boyfriend troubles and fights with her girlfriends." The recount was familiar and flowed easy. It comforted him to speak of Holly's youth. And how proud he was of her. "That's where you excelled, my love, listening, with your kind ear and gentle wisdom. Then I walked her down the aisle and gave her to another man. Now she hints at me living under her roof so she can wash my clothes, fix my hair, and listen to my complaints. The cycle of life."

A stiff breeze lifted his carefully groomed yet thinning hair and at last, Esmerelda broke through the clouds with a crack of light.

There you are.

Rain or shine, she always let him know she saw him. Heard him.

A few feet away, another man gazed out over the water, his arms resting on the railing.

"Pretty high up, isn't it?" Ed said. The man didn't look distraught. Or as if he'd hike a leg and send himself over the railing.

"I've been on higher." The man offered his hand. "Justin Rizzo."

"Ed Marshall. Is this your first time to the city?"

"I'm from South Dakota. So yeah."

"Enjoy. There's no place like it."

The man nodded, took another view of the skyline, and started down.

Thank you kindly, sir. "Now I have the bridge to myself, Essie. Just like the night I proposed."

He released the first rose. "Here's to you, Mrs. Marshall."

The flower released into the wind, twisting and turning, jerking down, down, down. Far, so very, very far.

One by one, the roses, the lilies, and daisies took flight, catching the current for a moment or two, then making their way to the water's surface, dotting and drifting across the watery grave of his beloved Esmerelda.

LEXA

"Here you are." She found Jett in the barn standing on the make-shift stage where a bluegrass band had just serenaded sixty guests to a banjo version of Pachelbel's *Canon*.

"What's going on out there?"

"Your mom and Oz are about to cut the cake, and the wedding coordinator announced thirty minutes to the memorial."

He scoffed. "Only Miranda Wilder—"

"Griffin."

"Right, *Griffin*, would host a wedding and a memorial at the same time. It'll be Oz next, the one devastated in her wake."

"Cynical much?" Lexa sat on a bale of hay, the drop hem of her dress draping over the golden straw. "How did you like the banjo version of Pachelbel's?"

"Made me think of our wedding song."

"Unchained Melody."

Jett nodded. "Your dress is nice. I don't think I said earlier."

She'd chosen a fitted bronze-lace Melinda House gown with a flared skirt from Coral's vast closet of designer gowns. And it fit with no alterations.

"I could play princess every day for a month and not repeat a single dress."

"I'm in. When do we play next?"

They'd laughed and talked about everything and nothing as Lexa tried on gown after gown, Coral giving her a story about each dress.

"I wore that one to the Oscars when CCW provided all the makeup for the stars."

"That one, oh, that one . . ." She misted. *"My first royal ball with Gus."*

With each laugh, each story, each ticking minute, something in Lexa healed. She felt it.

"I should've worn cowboy boots." She kicked out her legs, displaying a pair of suede heels on loan from Coral. "These are gorgeous but kill my feet."

"I don't know about your feet, but you look beautiful." He glanced over at her from where he stood among the candles and flowers, hands in his tux pockets.

"So how are you? You've been quiet all weekend." She moved closer, to a first-row seat. "What's going on?"

It was a futile question, but she had to ask. Jett wore his emotions tonight. Between the wedding, Storm's memorial, and the truth he had discovered about GPR, he was decked out.

"I spent a lot of time in here as a kid." He stepped off the low platform, his feet skipping over the clean layer of hay scattered over the wide board floor. He scanned the ceiling and the center poles, trimmed with a million twinkle lights. "Not used to it looking like a fairyland."

"You have to admit the wedding was lovely. Oz couldn't stop smiling."

"I say good luck to him." Jett stopped at one of the stalls. "Did I ever tell you we had a horse for a while? Midas. A former thoroughbred racer. Dad brought him home after Mom left. Thought it'd be a good distraction."

"You did, yes. But he died two years later."

"I curled up in his stall and cried."

"How sad." On the drive up from the city, she sank deeper into the comfortable familiarity that was Jett. When he was her husband. "You never talked much about your parents' divorce."

He pointed to the loft behind her, the one jutting out over the open barn doors. Music from the reception slipped inside and danced with the glowing lights. "I used to hide from the nanny up there and read."

"You and Gordon Phipps Roth against the world?"

"Pretty much." Jett sat on a hay bale at the end of the row. "But now another one of my heroes has bitten the dust."

"But you chose not to expose him."

"Nope." He shook his head. "But the bottom-line truth? I'm a coward. I didn't want to let the college down. Or myself. If I even hinted at scandal, the college would lose the endowment." He hung his head as he joined her on the hay bale. "I said nothing."

"Are you sure that's not a good thing?"

"Yes, I'm sure, Lex. The man was a lying, cheating rat trap. This week I took an afternoon to really study *An October Wedding*, Birdie's book, and except for a few GPRisms, the voice in *Wedding* is the voice in every GPR book."

"You sound sure."

"Author voice is unique. You can imitate stories, but you cannot imitate voice. But did I ponder how to include *that* in my publication? No, I had a pity party about the quandary Gordon put me in. All the way from his grave." His voice rose and fell as he swept his arm through the air. "I turned a blind eye to truth and went with what I wanted to be true."

"You said another one of your heroes bit the dust. What did you mean?"

"Ah, Lex—"

"Storm?"

"Storm, my mother."

"Your mother?"

"Yeah, I know you see her through my adult eyes—"

"I see for myself."

"But when we were kids, she was really funny and warm. She was always challenging us to a game of horse or kickball. Storm Ball came out of a game she started. Mom was a force. I didn't cross her, but I knew she loved us. That's why when she left it was so very hard."

"Doesn't mean she stopped loving you and Storm." Lexa ran her hand over his shoulder and down his back.

"This woman I believed held us all together left because she had to find herself. She wasn't strong. She was weak. And she earth-quaked our lives."

"Did you ever stop to think how it felt for her to leave? That it was hard for her?"

"Then why did she?" Jett jumped up, hands on his belt, kicking the straw beneath his black polished shoes. "I'd never heard Storm cry like he did when she left. Not even when Dad got us for sneaking off one Easter and eating all the candy out of the hidden eggs in the churchyard."

"What?" She laughed. Sounded exactly like something young Storm and young Jett would've done. "All of them?"

"All of them." He glanced down at her. "But when Mom said she was going to California for a while, Storm lost it. Bawled. Fourteen years old, clinging to her, calling her Mommy, begging her to stay."

"Where was Bear?"

"Off in the dark corner, arms folded, mad as a hornet. Probably hurting, but he never showed it. I remember thinking, 'Do something. Make her stay. Make Storm stop crying.'"

"Did you cry?"

"Not then, no. I bucked up so hard the inside of my mouth started bleeding. I refused to cry in front of her. If she wanted to go, good riddance. We didn't need her."

She felt the hitch in his voice, the conflict in his resolve. He *did* need her.

"And I left you too."

"Yep." He tugged a piece of hay from the tight bundle. "Little did we know we were the perfect storm. You didn't want to stay where you felt unwanted—"

"And you'd never ask someone to stay who wanted to leave."

"But your mom came back. Made peace with your dad."

"She never made peace with Storm and me." He rubbed his thumb against his fingertips. "Money. That's all she cares about."

"And you and I are making peace."

He regarded her for a lingering moment. "Thanks to a mysterious invitation."

"Who knew, right? So, Jett, have you talked to your mom about any of this?" Despite the revelation of their opposing wounds, Lexa understood the depth of Jett's bitterness.

"No." He glanced back at her. "What would I say? Tell her how Storm cried every night? How I tried to sneak into his room, but he beat me up, told me to leave him alone. How his face was red and puffy at breakfast. How Dad, lost in his own pain, was no help. How we ate Pop-Tarts for breakfast every morning for a month? How he lost his life and work partner in one fell swoop?" Suddenly he jumped up. "There's a plank in here somewhere . . ." Jett walked toward the barn wall in the back. "Yep, here it is. Can't see it very well. Come here."

Lexa made her way around a row of hay bales and peered at the faded words highlighted by Jett's phone flashlight.

I hate my mom.

"I carved it over the summer with fantasies she'd come visit, walk out here, and see it."

Lexa fingered the gray, deep engraving. "Did you carve something like this about me too?"

His attention snapped to her. "I think I've matured some since I was twelve. But no, I didn't. I loved you."

"And I walked out."

"That's different."

"Is it?"

"Of course. You weren't my mother."

"I was your wife. I made a vow and pledge to you."

"She gave me life. How does a woman walk out on her own kids?" He peeled away a dried piece of splintered wood. "After I heard all of your homecoming and Carnie story I understood a bit more why you left. Not entirely. Why didn't you tell me?"

"Not sure I knew what to say. Telling the story opened up some insight for me too." She smiled at him. "Here we are, thirty years old and just now dealing with childhood wounds."

"Here's a truth." Jett brushed his hand over her shoulder. "Lex, I didn't reject you. I wanted you."

"You had a funny way of showing it."

"Maybe you couldn't see because of your fears."

"Maybe you couldn't tell me because of yours."

"Hey, you two." They turned to see Oz making his way toward them, a tall beer in his hand. "The party's out here. We just cut the cake. What's going on?"

"Just telling stories," Jett said. "Cut the cake? I missed it. Lex, you want a piece?" He offered her his arm to barricade Ox from seeing the etching on the wall.

"Is this it?" Ox walked right past them. "Where you hacked out that you hated your mom?"

Jett lowered his arm. "You know?"

Oz lifted his beer. "Your mom told me about a year ago."

Jett swore under his breath. Oz smacked him on the back. "Don't worry. She understands." The outdoorsman headed back down the aisle. "The memorial starts in ten minutes."

As Oz left, silence filled his wake. Neither Jett nor Lexa moved.

"She never said a word." Jett crushed his hand to his chest.

"Maybe she's not the evil woman you believed." She squeezed his hand and dipped her head to see his face. "But that doesn't take away your pain. Everything you just said here is real, but you can't keep brushing over it. I know. I'm the pot calling the kettle black. I-I need to do more myself. But Jett, you'll pop if you hold all this bitterness in too long."

"What's the point? Won't change how lonely this place was after she left, how nothing was ever the same." The blue in his eyes swam in unhindered tears. "I cried the night you left." He laughed low. "How's that for an admission? The apartment was so hollow without your presence. Everything echoed. At one point I stood in the center of the living room and repeated over and over, 'Lex, I love you. I love you.'"

Regret and relief collided, and she wobbled a little as her fortitude drained. He'd cried?

"Jett, I had no idea. I thought you didn't care at all. I'm sorry—"

"Water under the bridge." Tears glistened in his eyes. "Let's get some cake, maybe move the party toward the memorial." He pulled notecards from his breast pocket. "Mom made Dad and me write down something *meaningful* to say."

"Jett, you do realize everyone can see your emotions. We know when you're upset or bothered. But you don't speak up. You avoid the hard conversation." She squeezed his arm. "You don't have to do everything alone."

"That's some pretty good therapy. I didn't realize you knew me quite so well. Come on, counselor. My hour is up and they are serving cake."

"I have one more question." She held onto him. "Being as it is Storm's memorial—What happened up on that mountain, Jett?"

Suddenly every emotion was reeled in and locked behind a steel door. "Leave it alone, Lex."

"Why? Jett, let it go. Whatever it is. Wouldn't it be nice if tonight, at your mother's wedding and your brother's memorial, you released all the pain that haunts you?" She gripped his lapel. "Don't let another shovelful of dirt cover this, this thing that haunts you. I think it's why you cut me out so drastically when Storm died."

"I'm ready for cake." He released her hands from his jacket. "Come on."

"It was the final straw for me, Jett. I lost you to grad school, but I figured that would end. But when I lost you to grief, I thought I'd never find you."

"What does it matter what happened on the mountain, Lexa? He's gone."

"It matters because you've let it bury you. Even more than your parents' divorce. You've let the guy who loves twentieth-century classic literature and cries at the end of a rom-com because true love triumphs hide behind a wall no one can really see or conquer.

"One day when you're like forty or fifty, you'll look back on your life and wonder what happened to the Jett Wilder who hoped, who dreamed. You'll be completely unaware that your shallow, lonely existence was carved out by a faded, twisted memory of a morning on a mountaintop. That you're haunted by the ghost of your dead brother."

"That won't happen. What you just said."

"In some ways it already has, Jett. Between you and me."

"Don't put the demise of our marriage squarely on me or Storm's death. You played a part."

She stepped back. "You're right. I buried myself in work for fear of rejection. But ever since I told my story at the society meeting, I feel relief. I see what I've been doing. Now I wish I'd gone to homecoming with Dad and walked in with my head high, ready to twist the night away. Twelve years later, Dad and I could reminisce about how much fun we had. I don't even know where Carnie is now. And there's a good chance we'd have broken up by Christmas, or on the ski trip. We were never meant to be. Yet I let his rejection and the opinions of others, all my experiences of moving and trying to fit in, taint me." She raised her chin. "Well, no more. I'm sick of it. I'm commanding my life."

"What if Zane comes crawling back?"

"Depends, but I think my time at ZB is over. I really do. As soon as I get another job, I'll resign." Her confidence came from a real, deep place.

"He always gets to you, Lexa. I'll believe it when I see it."

"Watch me." Lexa marched for the wide barn doors, praying, hoping he'd follow her. Because out there was the real world, the one where she'd have to walk the walk of the talk she just talked. "As for you, Jett Wilder, don't you dare stay on that mountain with Storm, or stuck in this barn reading your books, worshipping dead authors who lied. You were born for more."

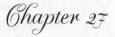

Chapter 27

JETT

Bothered and wrestling with the heat of Lexa's confrontation and his own confessions, he made his way toward the lit area by the lake's shore.

Just to the left of the wedding reception stood a row of thirty flickering tiki torches. One for each year of Storm's life.

An old high school friend, Bobby, clapped Jett on the back and passed over a beer. "I still miss him."

"Me too."

Dave, another friend, had been Storm's high school best friend. Jett clinked his long bottle neck with Dave's and raised it to his lips. One sip and he set it down.

The last time he drank a beer or two at a wedding, he ended up in jail. He felt imprisoned enough with the aggravating revelation that Lexa was right about the pain he retained. Like an old friend. Like the chains he'd earned.

Bobby joined Dave, and Jett excused himself, walking over to where Lexa shivered in the cold.

"Here." He draped his tux jacket around her shoulders.

"I'm sorry." But she didn't look up. "I overstepped. You're not my husband anymore, so your emotional state is not my concern."

"But you're my friend."

She smiled. "Better than enemies. Look, Jett, I am sorry. For everything. I look back and wonder, 'What was I thinking?' I'd like to think I've gained some perspective the past two years."

"Me too."

The reverend who had officiated the wedding gathered the guests.

"Miranda and Oz, along with Bear, chose this night to say a final goodbye to their son Storm. As you all know, Storm Wilder, a wingsuit pilot, died on Eiger Mountain at the age of thirty. He was born Samuel Brian Wilder, son of Brian "Bear" and Miranda Wilder, brother to John Alexander Wilder. Born in Chappaqua..."

Jett drifted from his big brother's eulogy through his memories, seeing shadowy images of the past. The two of them racing across the yard to the lake, running down the dock, and jumping in with a *wahoo!*

A soft, slender hand slipped into his. Lexa.

"Come on," he whispered, pulling her away. He wanted a moment alone with his memories, a moment with Lexa.

They walked over to the lake and the end of the dock. The moonlight cut a swath over the calm, glassy surface where, in due course, Storm's remains would rest.

"Tell me a Storm story," Lexa said. "A good one."

"Can't tell just one. With Storm all the stories are connected." Another reason that day on the mountain was so strange and raw, gut wrenching. Brother confronting brother, discovering a truth that ripped them apart.

"Then your favorite."

"Storm Ball." When he looked down at her, the lake breeze brushed her hair across her face. She was so very lovely.

"The first time I visited, we played."

"Thanksgiving." Their marriage had collapsed so fast he struggled to remember the good days. But there was one. He placed it on the open shelf of his heart.

"What were the rules again?"

"Whatever Storm wanted." He laughed. "But it was a cross between rugby, football, and basketball. And I know what you're doing, Lex."

"Is it working?"

"A little. Why didn't you ever tell me about Carnie and all the implications?"

"And let my hunky new boyfriend know I was a high school reject? Besides, by the time I met you, I was over it, didn't think it mattered. Then you started shutting me out. The first time you didn't come home, but stayed out all night with your classmates, I was so scared. So scared. But Carnie was just the cream on the top of all the times we moved and I didn't feel accepted."

He grabbed her to himself, careful of her new upper arm cast. "I'm sorry, Lex. I am. For what it's worth." He pressed his kiss against her forehead. "I love you."

She shoved out of his arms. "What?"

Those three little words were not casual. They contained a power surge that electrified the air between them.

"I mean, I . . ." He coughed. Cleared. Turned away.

"Jett!" Dave called to him from the shore. "They're looking for you."

They walked back in silence, Lexa's hand swinging free, his tucked into his tux pocket.

He joined Mom, Oz, and Dad, the sheen of Mom's wedding dress catching the glow of the lights.

Dad clapped him with a hug as he faced the crowd and retrieved his notes. *I love you.* How did he let that slip? Because it was bubbling in his heart, that's why.

Jett scanned the wedding guests turned mourners for Lexa as Dad stepped up to the table where Storm's open urn rested.

"Storm," Dad said. "You were a force to be reckoned with from the time you came screaming into this world until the day you died. Both with your eyes wide open. It's been two years but feels like yesterday." He gripped a fistful of his son's ashes, walked to the water's edge, and released them, twisting and drifting, into the wind. "You were my firstborn, my business partner, my friend. I miss you every day. Rest in peace."

The ashes drifted from Dad's open hand. When he returned to his place beside Jett, tears wet his tanned, lined cheeks.

Mom stepped forward.

"When Storm was in first grade he couldn't sit still. His teacher called me in for a meeting and asked me to change his name." A light laugh wrestled through the mourners. "I told her I couldn't change his name any more than I could change his eye color. Storm was Storm. His given name was Samuel, but the moment Bear nicknamed him Storm, we knew we'd captured his true identity. He challenged us and excited us and, now, grieves us. Storm was worth all the aggravation and testing. I am grateful to have been his mother. Lucky, really. He was a good man, a friend, a dreamer, a risk taker." She raised a handful of ashes to the sunset. "May a piece of his adventurous spirit land on us all. I carry you with me every day, son, and every cell in my body misses you."

Jett watched the remains of a man, his brother, float through the light toward the dark water.

An eeriness swept through him. To a stranger, Storm's ashes would be no different from the wood ashes from the firepit. It was as if he had never been flesh and bone, as if he'd never possessed a beating heart or breath in his lungs.

"Jett?" Mom moved aside, dabbing her eyes. "Tell us a Storm story. He has so many, everyone. Our bookworm, our writer." She patted him on the shoulder and he resisted the urge to shrug her off.

Staring at his notes, he started to speak, then frogged out. Clearing his throat, he tried again.

"Storm, you were my brother and my first friend." As he dug into the polished urn, his emotions swelled. The moment he touched his brother's soft dust, Storm's heartbeat pounded in Jett's chest.

He hung his head as his tears splattered on the black ink scribbled over white notecards.

When he looked up, he didn't bother to wipe his cheeks. But he tucked his notes away. He didn't need a script to remember his brother.

"When they recovered Storm from the base of the mountain, every bone in his body was broken. And now, watching his ashes scatter away on the wind, we can't distinguish between the ashes of a man from those piling up in the firepit. Ashes to ashes . . ." He patted the urn. "Hard to image this stone container contains the body of a man who was larger than life. That the ashes inside used to form bone and skin of a man who loved to fly off mountainsides, swim icy rivers, and create nonsensical games with the wackiest rules." A respectful hoot came from the cluster of boyhood friends. "Storm's heart was as large as his courage. He loved hard. He loved deep. He loved in secret. Mom said to tell a story. Well, Storm is the story." A flash of grief clipped his breath. "At six-four, though he claimed to be six-five, my lean-muscled but fiercely strong brother was a force to be reckoned with. I'm not sure he ever knew fear. Except once . . . once.

"He led me down many a dark path of adventure knowing we'd probably get a whupping if Dad found out. But he didn't care. I did and followed him anyway." The laughter from the group was healing to Jett. "He was my hero." When he looked at faces, his gaze mingled with Lexa's. "It's odd how some things have to be broken before their value and worth can be discovered." He hadn't valued his brother the day he died. In fact, he almost hated him. "Storm's broken but free, soaring higher and farther than any man ever could in a wingsuit.

"He loved to make our parents proud. He was his father's son and his mother's rock."

Dad came alongside him with a firm clap on the shoulder.

"I envied Storm's boldness and courage. How he could hang off the side of a mountain for hours just to get the right publicity shot." Jett laughed through his tears. "I was jealous, a little, that he fit in to Dad's life better than I." Dad squeezed his shoulder as he cleared his throat. "Storm left this life the way he lived. Testing gravity. He'd mock us if he were here tonight, giving him tribute, wondering why we weren't throwing a party, causing trouble, playing Storm Ball." A shout arose from the mourners. "He was in constant motion, and now that he's gone, our hearts are still. We miss you, Storm."

Another word and he'd burst into tears. He might show his emotions, as Lexa pointed out, but he'd rather not bawl like a baby in front of so many.

Nevertheless he gathered himself for a final word.

"Let me say this, then I'll shut up." Jett wiped his face with the back of his hand. "Storm was a flawed man, a jealous brother, proud and stubborn—"

"You can say that again," Mom said through a weepy laugh.

"But he gave his heart freely, something I haven't learned to do yet." Jett dipped his hand into the urn. "To my big brother, Storm. I will endeavor to live with more courage, make more noise, and above all, bring back the Thanksgiving Storm Ball tournament." He released his grip of ashes into the small, passing current. "Fly, Storm, fly."

Eyes closed, Jett tried to envision the brother of his childhood, the brother who stood next to him at his wedding, the brother who popped into their apartment unannounced, turning everything inside out, overstaying his welcome, but leaving a void when he finally packed his bags.

For a moment, he heard their laughter, saw their stories. Then it was all gone, clouded by his anger and frustration, tainted by walking away that day on the mountain just before Storm teetered on the edge of his mortality.

As he stepped back between Mom and Oz, and Dad, Mom bent toward his ear. "He'd be proud, Jett. Well done."

He peered at her and drew a long breath. "Can I talk to you before you leave with Oz? It's important."

She hesitated, then nodded once. "So the day has finally come."

Just then a song rose from the middle of the guests as a deep bass started "Auld Lang Syne." One by one, every voice joined in.

"Should old acquaintance be forgot—"

∽

CHUCK

Best decision he ever made was knocking on Wanda's door. How she talked Trudy into letting him attend the twins' parties was a bona fide miracle.

As much as he loved seeing his kids, the cream of the weekend was walking into Trudy's with Coral Winthrop on his arm.

To be clear, his kids were, always would be, commanders of his heart. But showing up with a hot, rich babe . . . How could a guy go wrong?

Sitting at the nook in his little kitchen in his little Woodbridge house, he reveled in his weekend memories.

Coral? Knocked it clean out of the park. Not only was she stunning on the outside, she was gorgeous on the inside.

First time in his ten-year history with Trudy he'd seen her speechless. He played it up too.

"I'd like to introduce Coral Winthrop. Heiress, owner of CCW Cosmetics, and fashion icon."

Trudy's posse of skinny, surgically enhanced Jersey socialites abandoned her immediately to swarm Coral, who, with a sly wink at Chuck, told him to not worry about her. What a pro.

However, his comeuppance enjoyment ended the moment he saw Jakey. "Dad!" The boy flew into his arms, knocking him back.

My boy . . . my boy . . .

Yet it was Riley who sank him. She crashed into his leg, weeping. "I thought you forgot me."

Scooping her up, he held her for the better part of a half hour as her tears soaked his new shirt from JCPenney.

When he caught Trudy watching, she turned away. *That's right, my kids need me.*

On this Sunday evening, he was feeling confident about his chances of getting the TRO dropped. He poured another bowl of cereal and flooded the O's with milk.

He made the most of his two hours on Saturday and Sunday, ignoring family and former friends to focus on his kids.

He hadn't seen any of them since he blew up over the affair, and it felt good to be in command of himself, calm, peaceful, escorting Coral.

After she presented Trudy with a large CCW gift box, she joined

Chuck, stooping down to the kids' level, speaking with them as if they mattered.

Heart, don't go falling in love.

The hedgie, Will—what a blockhead—actually put his phone down and introduced himself to Coral, trying to win favor by naming a mutual friend.

When he flirted with her, she cut him off in less than three words and slipped her hand into Chuck's, playing the role of doting girlfriend.

That's when Trudy cornered him.

"I didn't know you were bringing a guest."

"It was last-minute."

"Coral Winthrop of CCW Cosmetics was last-minute?" She made a face. "Who is she really, Charles Mays? Don't lie to me."

But Chuck refused to battle with her. He was there for his kids.

At one point, Jakey whispered in his ear, "I never told, Daddy."

"I knew you wouldn't."

The hour passed too quickly, but Chuck left without being asked. Coral linked her arm through his as they walked out, never looking back.

Then this afternoon, Riley had clung to him. She insisted Chuck be the king at the head of her royal princess table.

Once again Coral had tongues wagging. She looked like a million bucks coming and going. He owed her big-time for this weekend.

Chuck finished his cereal and carried his bowl to the dishwasher.

Yeah, he owed Coral big. She brought the best present for both kids on Sunday.

Giant, amazingly illustrated and professionally printed magic-book posters for Jakey and Riley.

The kids didn't remember the stories at first, but as he retold the ones he remembered, they went wild. Riley immediately gathered her little friends for a game of "jumping in the book" and Jakey rallied his friends to do the same.

Just remembering choked him up.

"Coral, when, how?" he whispered as she leaned against him.

"This past week. I had our art department work them up. I would've brought them yesterday but there was a holdup at the printers."

He wanted to kiss her smack on the lips and not *just* for the posters.

Each poster featured a book boldly titled *The Magic Book* and had a perfect depiction of the kids. Coral said the artist stalked Trudy's Facebook profile for pictures.

Jakey's poster was of a train engineer chugging over the Rockies. Riley's depicted a princess riding a pony over the clouds.

The artist added the words, "Whenever you want to dream, jump into a book."

In addition to the posters for the twins, Coral had smaller versions made for the party guests.

Seeing her outside of the society, and not as a headline on a tabloid, Chuck wondered how the prince ever let her go. He'd have sailed the high seas to get her back.

She was real, genuine, and *hot*. Did he say that already?

As if the posters weren't enough, she brought more CCW gift boxes for the moms and cases of Pink Coral lip gloss for Riley and her friends.

He offered to pay her back, but she refused.

Now that the day was over and he was back in his little house, he relived each hour, trying to remember every detail.

He shut off the lights and jogged the narrow stairs to his room, stepping over the drop cloth and paint cans he'd left out to finish painting the hallway.

He'd completed remodeling his bedroom and bath two months ago but ran out of energy for the final touches.

In the bathroom, he dropped his clothes in the hamper, stepped into his sleeping pants, and brushed his teeth.

Flopping down on his bed, he linked his hands behind his head and stared at the ceiling, hanging on to the hope he felt. Did he dare to believe his days of estrangement were going to end?

He'd apologized to Trudy many times. Even sent her a text after Riley's party, apologizing again and thanking her profusely—swallowing whatever pride he had left—for allowing him to see the twins.

He submitted himself to her mercy, if she actually possessed any, for a chance to remove the restraining order. They'd have to go to court together. She'd have to convince the judge on his behalf.

Tomorrow night's story society would be interesting. This had been a big weekend for them all.

Jett and Lexa had attended his mom's wedding and brother's memorial. A wedding at a funeral? Now there was a story waiting to be told.

Then there was Ed's trip to the top of the GW. Chuck had watched to make sure he made it to the top okay, then picked up a fare.

Ed never called, so Chuck assumed he arrived home safely. And there was nothing in the news of an old man leaping from the GW. He checked.

However, he felt certain there was more to Ed's bridge story than he let on.

Laundry. The random thought shot him out of bed. If he didn't toss a load in he'd be wearing dirty underwear this week.

Filling the washing machine, Chuck considered his work schedule. He'd agreed to a couple of evenings with Elite Limo. While he preferred driving for himself, the limo tips were incredible.

Back in bed, he picked up *Rites of Mars* hoping to get to the end of the chapter before falling asleep. Jett was a good storyteller. Really good.

He'd just started chapter twenty when a text came in. Coral.

Is it weird I'm still floating from the weekend? I really had fun. Thank you for letting me horn in and be a part of your kids' story.

Are you kidding? Thank YOU for coming. For the posters.
Best gift ever. I'm still floating myself. You were the hit of
both parties. Trudy was impressed.

Maybe too much? I took away some of her attention.

Ha. Don't worry. Not your fault. She does like to be the life
of every party. Center of attention.

Did you know she invited me back? I think you'll see your
kids again soon.

She what!? Well, that's bonus, good news. I'm working up
the nerve to ask her to remove the TRO.

I'll say a prayer.

Please. See you tomorrow?

Story Society. 8:00.

Smiling, he tried to go back to Stovall and his plight on Mars,
but Coral filled his imagination. When he'd read the same sentence
five times he closed the book and called her.

"Chuck? Is everything all right?" she said.

"Yeah, sure, I just..." He sat on the side of the bed. *Just what? Say
something.* "The posters... How much do I owe you?"

"Owe me?" Her voice dropped. "Nothing, Chuck. I told you, it
was my pleasure."

"Are you sure, because I didn't bring a gift. You were going to
help me..."

"The entire art department had a blast working on the concept."
Her tone was flat. Insulted. "Don't worry about it."

"Okay, and, um, thanks. Really."

"Is that all?"

Don't hang up ... Don't hang up. "I was wondering about you. Any news on your double databases?"

"Oh, that, well, yes, my mole Teddy tracks their activity. If they move money to another account, I'll have to act fast, but so far they are letting their account build up."

"Any idea why they'd do this to you?"

"Besides greed? No."

"Who can understand a criminal's mind, right?"

"That's just it, Chuck. I don't think they are criminals. Greedy, yes. Stupid. For sure. Calculating. But criminal? I don't see that in either one of them."

"Betrayal is the worst. Especially by people you trust. Hard to like or respect betrayers. It's the worst kind of selfishness."

Her silence lingered long enough for three heartbeats. "Yes, I suppose it is."

After that the conversation stalled and he wished her a good night. It was when he hung up he realized what he'd said.

"Hard to like or respect betrayers."

The prince guy ... Coral had betrayed him in some way by running off. It was a wonder Chuck wasn't choking to death, since he stuffed his fat foot into his mouth.

He grabbed *Mars* and tried to read but couldn't, so he snapped off the light. *Think, Chuck, think before you speak.* His mother preached that almost every day.

Snatching up his phone, he texted Coral.

Sorry. Wasn't thinking.

Lying back, phone on his chest, he closed his eyes and waited for her to respond, desperately trying to recapture the joy from the day, the joy from five minutes ago.

Don't let one misstep sour the whole weekend. But he'd inadvertently insulted the woman who made the two parties sparkle.

He'd just drifted off when his ringtone blasted, jolting him upright. *Coral?* But no, Trudy's number filled the screen.

"Trudy? Are the kids all right?"

"They're fine. What I want to know is what you're up to?" Her hard tone pelted him.

"Up to? Nothing. Just want to love and help raise my kids."

"Behind my back?"

"Behind your . . . ? Trudy, just say it. No games. I'm tired."

"Did your snooty heiress *wear* you out?"

"Don't be vulgar." He capped his temper. If he lost it with her, she'd use it against him.

"Did you go to the twins' school?"

Oh boy. "What? No."

"That's funny because as I was tucking Jakey into bed tonight, he regaled me with magic-book nonsense and how he wanted to jump in and pretend his daddy would visit him at school again."

Jakey, oh, Jakey. "He's six, Tru. Sometimes pretend and reality are the same."

"You didn't visit him at his school?"

"What did he say exactly?"

"You tell me. What did he say?"

"I don't know. I wasn't the one tucking him in." *&#@!&.* How was he going to get out of this?

"Chuck, tell me the truth. So help me, you and your stupid magic book have him all turned around."

"Jakey knows how to tell the truth. At least he did when I was in the house. Or has Will taught him to lie?"

"I won't dignify that with an answer." Her breath was fire in his ear. "He said he invited you to the party when he saw you at the playground fence. Is that why you went to my mother? Huh? If you showed up at their school I will file for a final restraining order. You'll never see them again."

"Really? Is that what you want? To take their father from them?" *Shut up, man. Shut up.* "You cheat on me and I end up watching from the outside. You saw how Riley clung to me. She thought I forgot her. Is that what you want? For your daughter to have this, *this* rejection, just to get back at me? I lost my temper and I'm sorry, but don't make them pay."

"You waved a gun at us and terrified the children."

He sighed and ran his hand over his face. "It wasn't loaded. I would never hurt you or the kids."

"I don't care. You threatened our safety and I'll never forgive you."

"You cheated on me, Tru. I loved you and you brought another man in to *my* home. How is that any better? Lust is still one of the seven deadly sins, I believe. Waving an empty gun around never made the list."

"You broke the law. And I believe anger is on that list."

"So did you. The law of our marriage vows. We got married in the church, for crying out loud. Now you're hurting the kids, punishing them by keeping me away. Even worse, by subjecting them to that slick-haired-money-grabbing-phone-addict of a boyfriend."

"What do you call bringing Coral Winthrop to my house? Huh? I ought to file for the FRO just because you're such a liar. How much did you pay that model to mimic Coral Winthrop?" Proof. His ex-wife was certifiable. "And the CCW products and those posters—you'll be driving twenty-four seven to pay for those. How would you even know the real Coral Winthrop, huh? You drive Uber and limousines for prom nights and drunk businessmen."

"Trudy, as much as I love the sound of you shrieking in my ear, do you have a point? I have an early day tomorrow." Not that he'd fall asleep anytime soon.

"Is she your girlfriend?"

"No."

"Did you bring her just to show me up?"

"How did Coral Winthrop show you up?" He hadn't planned on showing up his ex, it was just an unexpected perk.

"Everyone whispering how great you are if you won over the real

Coral Winthrop. And wasn't I so mean to keep the kids from you. But they weren't there that night. I have nightmares about it."

"So do I. Believe me, so do I. I have the added bonus of seeing you in our bed with another man."

"You listen to me, Chuck Mays. Stay away from the kids' school. Stay away from me."

"Do you hear yourself? You're mad because I did something nice for the kids? This is all about you."

"I'm warning you. Don't let that long-legged blonde Barbie come sniffing around here either."

"They're my kids, too, Trudy. I'm not too thrilled your cheating hedgie—"

"Stop calling him that, Chuck."

"—is in their life."

"I'm calling the shots. And don't you forget it."

She hung up and Chuck fired his phone across the bed. He got up and started pacing, hands flexing into fists, releasing, and flexing again.

She was an evil, jealous witch.

He ran downstairs for a water, but his middle was full of burning coals. He tossed the bottle back into the fridge, then ran upstairs again, stopping at the paint cans and drop cloth.

Might as well work. He was too mad to sleep. He pried the lid from a can of paint, then slumped down against the wall.

The house built for one was suddenly too small. He had to get out of here before the old walls closed in.

Yanking his gym bag from the closet shelf, Chuck threw a few things in and hammered down the stairs. He locked up and burned through the cool air toward his car.

He fired up the engine, then made a call.

"Feel like company?" he said. "Naw, just Trudy the nut job. Tell you when I get there."

Chapter 28

ED

The morning light brightened the kitchen as he washed the cast-iron skillet he'd used to make a hearty breakfast of eggs and bacon.

His very own granny used to cook for him with the same skillet, and he sometimes imagined he could still taste her fried pork chops.

She'd be 121 were she alive. Born in 1898, in a world on the verge of a new century, in a city ripe for industrial and moral revolutions.

"Ed, thanks again, man." Chuck dropped his bag on the kitchen counter.

"Did you sleep good?" The circles under his eyes said he did not.

"Too much going on in my mind."

"You did the right thing, reaching out to a friend."

Chuck dug a tumbler out of his bag and motioned to the coffeepot. Ed nodded. "Finish it up. I've had my two cups."

"Trudy knows how to get under my skin." Chuck fell against the counter and peered around the large airy kitchen that hadn't been updated since the eighties. "How long have you lived here?"

"Almost forty-eight years. A lifetime. Holly was a toddler when we bought the place. You know, you shouldn't let her get to you. If we love when it's easy, it's of no credit to us. Anyone can love when it's easy. But if we love when it's hard, then we are all the better. We gain what we cannot see."

"Clearly you've not met my ex." Chuck glanced back as he meandered into the den. Toward the typewriter. Too late for Ed to stop him. "You didn't have a difficult marriage. Didn't get cheated on and threatened." The big guy hovered over Ed's Underwood and the stack of paper. "How's the memoir?"

"Turns out writing a book is a lot harder than I imagined." Ed made a racket of putting the iron skillet away in the oven drawer. "Can I get you anything else?"

"I should be going." Chuck snatched up his duffel bag. "Thanks for letting me crash. I just had to get out . . . My place was closing in. Driving clears my head."

"Are you ever going to tell us what really happened with your ex? Why she won't let you see the kids?"

"I told you. I caught her in an affair and lost my temper."

"Is that why you had to get out of Woodbridge at eleven o'clock at night? Your temper?"

Chuck's big frame moved with wildcat grace. He snapped up his bag. "Sorry to have bothered you, old man."

"Chuck, facing the truth is the only way to heal and move on."

"From what I can see, I'm not the only one lying to myself. What was that trip to the GW really about?"

Ed turned back to his dishes as the door slammed behind Chuck. He wilted against the counter. He'd meant no harm. But it was his flaw. Pointing out things other people didn't care to see. Esmerelda used to get on him about it.

"Just keep your opinions to yourself, Ed."

"Ed?" The knock on his door came with the sound of Mabel Cochran's voice. "I made a coffee cake."

"Do you stand with your ear against your door waiting for me to come out?" He jerked open the door Chuck just slammed to find Mabel with a flash of shallow pink on her cheeks.

"No, but I heard a slam." She turned to go. "I'm sorry to have bothered you."

"Mabel, wait—"

For the second time in two minutes, he had a door slammed on him.

He was just trying to help. Well, help Chuck. Mabel he wanted out of his hair and to quit plying him with sweet cakes.

Back in his place, Ed banged around the kitchen, taking out meat for dinner, then realizing it was story society night and someone else was in charge of food.

He stepped into his coveralls and checked his list of repairs for the day.

What did Chuck mean he wasn't the only one lying to himself? Ed wasn't lying. No, he was loving. Something the world could use a little more of about now.

❧

LEXA

Trouble had come to their little society. At nine o'clock when Gilda announced the library was closing, she found herself sitting alone with Jett ten seconds later.

"That was weird," he said.

"Very. No one talking."

To be fair, Coral, Chuck, and Ed were speaking but not communicating. Then as soon as Gilda announced, "Closing time, children," the three of them bolted for the door.

Coral informed them her auditor had found an off-shore account. But no money had been transferred.

Chuck smiled only when describing what it felt like to hug his kids for the first time in over a year.

Ed muttered something about his neighbor Mabel trying to make him fat and how the co-op residents needed to read the instructions on the proper use of a garbage disposal.

"Chuck and Coral were barely talking." Jett stretched as he stood.

"Do you think something happened between them?"

"Or perhaps *didn't* happen."

"I'll try to call her tomorrow."

Jett set his backpack on his chair. "What about you and me? We good?"

"We are good."

"I thought a lot about our conversation in the barn," Jett said. "You're right about me being stuck. I don't want to be an old guy who looks back and wonders what happened to his life. Who wears his emotions on his sleeve but does nothing about them."

"Weddings and memorials put life in perspective," Lexa said. "What you said about Storm's ashes being undiscernible from those in the firepit hit me." She shivered. "We really are made from dust."

"And yet he lived with the breath of God in his lungs."

"Makes me wonder what I'm doing with that breath in mine."

"What'd you conclude?"

"The past is the past. I'm wasting time carrying a wound from twelve years ago. Why does Carnie get to live in my emotions when I knew him all of six months? I accused you of being stuck, but I'm not much better."

"You put your résumé out there."

Yes, and when she checked her account after arriving home from Chappaqua, she had several inquiries.

"When you and your parents spoke of Storm," Lexa said. "I dropped my own bones, so to speak, into the firepit." She looked at him with intention. "What happened between us in the past is over. Time to move on. Carnie? Moving on. All the little rejections and disappointments from moving so much, burned in the fire."

"I'm sorry for my part, Lex."

"Me too. For mine."

In her imagination, the light on the walls, in the fireplace flickered as if happy. Gilda looked in again.

"Time, children."

"On our way." Jett hitched his backpack over his shoulder and spun around. "I have to say this, Lex. I should've never let you go."

"Jett, I—" She'd been waiting so long for this sort of confession. But it was too late. Too late.

"I'm just being honest." He picked up a napkin under Ed's chair. "I don't expect anything."

"We both made mistakes. We should learn from them."

"No more running when things get hard?" He shot the wadded napkin at the trash bin like a basketball. "Wilder for three."

"No more running. At least not out of rejection or pain." She smiled. "From now on it's calculated leaving, or moving. However, if I'm being chased down a dark alley, it's all elbows and heels."

"Or if some handsome man asks you to dinner, you hightail it."

"Really? Toward or away?"

"Away, of course. You can never trust handsome men. Too shallow."

Her eyes met his. "I trusted you."

"And your point is?" Every once in a while, Jett made self-deprecation work.

"I wouldn't change anything." She was finally comfortable with some of the little confessions. "Only wish we'd been more mature."

"Yeah, me too." The soft light in his blue eyes reminded her of why she fell in love.

"Are you ever going to tell me what happened on that mountain?"

"What happened to letting the past be the past? Letting things go?"

"Because this is one thing that still feels like the present. Storm's death did more than grieve you, it broke you. It broke us."

He paused, hands in his pockets, his backpack slipping from his shoulder. After a moment he looked up, glanced at the door, then motioned for her to follow him to the back of the Bower.

"Want to see the unpublished GPR manuscript? It's really fascinating."

"You're avoiding the question again." Whatever happened that day remained hooked in Jett's soul, refusing to let go. She touched his arm. "Jett, you don't have to tell me, as long as you're honest with yourself about what happened. Don't keep ignoring it. And tell someone."

"Did you ever consider I let it go during the memorial?"

"Did you?"

Without answering, he dropped to one knee and reached for a book on the bottom shelf.

"Here it is. Written by Gordon's hand. One he held and touched. Look, here are his publisher's margin notes."

Kneeling next to him, she let the question of the mountain go and trusted the melody of his voice. He'd have to slay his giants his way.

She'd treasure this moment along with him, because it was the perfect ending to the long chapter of their short marriage.

❧

CORAL

The assistant at the desk outside Dad's office was new. The nervous, sweaty one hadn't lasted a month.

"Is Mr. Winthrop in?" She marched toward the door.

"Coral?" The man stood, his thick arms bowing by his side, the pressed fabric of his shirt straining against clichéd biceps.

"Yes." She offered her hand. "His daughter."

"Dallas Scott."

"You're new."

"Started yesterday."

"And you know me?"

"Yes, ma'am." His military training was evident. "Made it my business to know your father's family and associates."

"Then you and Eric Winthrop III must be getting along fine."

"That's my goal, ma'am."

She met Dad in the middle of his office. "Where did you find him? And what took you so long?"

"Retired marine. Logistics officer. I finally listened to the advice of my friends and went to the VA." He handed her a blue folder. "You should give your tech guy a huge bonus."

She'd sent over the initial findings of the forensic auditor. Today she and Dad would review together and come up with a plan.

Coral carried the folder to the couch and sat just as rain splattered against the windows.

"What should I do?"

"Call the authorities. And before I forget, I'm having brunch with your mother and brother on Sunday, eleven thirty at Daniel. You should join us."

"I'd rather eat at your place. I hate going out." She opened the folder and scanned the data.

The embezzlement had started when she was in Lauchtenland. An expense report here, a vacation there, kids' dance and karate lessons. Then it was low-hanging fruit, starting with a concealer they'd discontinued but Blaire managed to sell through discount channels. She siphoned all of that money into the second account.

It was as if they were testing the waters.

"You need to be seen out and about, Coral. Let the world know you are not just a runaway bride in hiding."

"Did you see the PayPal account where they're diverting some of the money? It belongs to Dak. You'd think he'd be smart enough not to use one of his personal email accounts."

"Are you?"

She glared at her father. "Am I what?"

"Still the runaway bride in hiding?"

"Dad, my company is being hijacked, and you're concerned about my personal life?"

"I am your father first and your business adviser second."

Coral dropped the folder onto the coffee table. "If you must know, I had some time 'out and about' this weekend." Technically, it was not a date but, in her heart, she wanted to be Chuck's girl. Which was crazy. She barely knew him. "I went to a birthday party with a man I met at the story society. He has twins and in the process of his divorce ended up not being able to see them. I volunteered to go as moral support."

"Not see his kids? What happened?"

"Not really sure, but he's a very nice man." Initially she played up their relationship just for his ex-wife, hoping she'd see Chuck in a new light.

But deep down, she did it for herself. To freely touch him and hold his hand.

Then he called, and things got weird. But only because his comment about betrayal caught her off guard and, yes, hurt. A lot. She knew all too well she'd betrayed Gus.

Yet she wasn't sorry. Her betrayal was also her salvation.

She wondered, though, if Blaire and Dak's betrayal wasn't her just due. Did she deserve it for what she'd done?

God, was I wrong? And please take care of Gus for me.

After she walked out of the abbey—technically she did not run—she tried to text him over the course of several days, but Gus never responded. He liked to block people. She'd been added to his list.

All day Monday she battled fear of Chuck doing the same. She had every intention of talking to him at the society meeting about his comment until he walked in like a grumpy bear after winter. He barely looked at her.

"He's so nice he makes you frown?" Dad said.

"What? No, no, not at all." She raised her head, tears bubbling. "Just want this business with Blaire and Dak over."

Let him go. You're imagining things. She didn't need romance in her life right now.

"Your grandfather had an embezzler. The man took more than a million dollars before he was caught."

"Really? I never heard that story. What'd he do?"

"Threw him in jail. He'd been a good friend too."

"I don't get it," Coral said. "They are both well paid with excellent bonuses and benefits."

"Those things don't make up for lack of character. Sometimes corporate execs, or admins with access to the money, believe they are entitled, taking what's due them. If you asked, they'd swear up and down they are honest, good people." Dad crossed the office to the coffee bar and poured himself another cup. "But with Blaire and Dak, I think they want CCW. Blaire was a founder at Cosmo Glam until they shoved her out. Then she walked into a faltering Glitter Girl with stock options. She could've owned it in ten years if the other shareholders hadn't bumped her. She's gunning for something, and I think she has set her sights on you. I remember meeting her at a luncheon. She clearly thought being a CEO was beneath her. She wanted to *own* a company."

"But CCW is a well-established, historic cosmetics giant. How does she plan to oust me? I may have been out of the country with Gus, but I was not absent from the business."

"Come on, Coral. You can see what she's doing." Dad rocked in his chair, Yoda to her Luke Skywalker.

Use the Force.

"Besides stealing from me?" Coral picked up the folder and flipped through the pages. "Most of this is about Pink Coral. She recorded all the sales and revenue here instead of our main database." A ping of revelation. "Oh, she wanted my lip gloss."

"They've advised you to discontinue the product. When you do, they'll either steal the formula or offer to buy it—"

"And start her own company." Thunder rumbled beyond the window. "Who do I call? I know you have a contact with the FBI."

Dad handed her a card. "Agent Tagg. He's expecting your call."

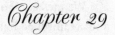

LEXA

Tuesday after the wedding Lexa returned to work at her usual seven-o-five, sat at her desk, and resumed a routine that felt stale and dull after five weeks off.

Quent moved back to the Think Tank but ran in and out of Zane's door ten times a day.

Zane came in early with two lattes and a bag of donuts. He called her into his office and they sat by the window, looking out over the city.

"Are we good?" he said.

"You tell me."

"I said some harsh things."

"You did."

"I'm sorry."

She locked eyes with him and saw his sincerity. "You're forgiven. And look, Zane, if I overstepped it was only because I was trying to do what you asked and needed."

"I know, and I'm as much to blame as you. But Lexa, you are very valuable to me. I appreciate all you've done for ZB."

They talked for over an hour, apologizing, catching up, and reminiscing all at once. She almost asked if he was still set on not considering her for the CEO position but decided to wait for another time.

On his own, he admitted he wasn't sure he wanted to fill the job just yet.

"I think I make a pretty good CEO and president."

Nevertheless, she had a hard time getting back into the groove. While all of her tasks were very familiar—she could do them in her sleep—she felt as if she were pulling bricks through mud.

Wednesday she arrived closer to seven thirty than seven-o-five and steamrolled her way through the morning. Then during lunch she responded to an inquiry about her résumé that had shown up over the weekend.

It was from a Seattle company, The Glass Fork, an up-and-coming organic bakery that had seen rapid growth, much like ZB. They liked her for their newly opened CEO position.

We believe you'd be perfect for us.

Seattle. It was one of her bucket-list cities but . . . *Seattle*. The opposite side of the country. So far from Skipper. From . . . *Don't say it. Don't.*

Jett. Her ex. Her no more. Her once-was-but-not-now.

Yet ever since the barn conversation, she thought about him. A lot. All the time.

If she said yes to Seattle, she'd be a West Coaster. A six-hour flight from New York. Five from Orlando.

She glanced at Zane's office. The door had been closed since before lunch, and the wooden slat shades blocked her view through the glass interior wall.

What was going on in there?

She peered at her computer again. Change required courage.

"He in?" Quent walked past her desk for Zane's office.

"The door's closed."

Quent didn't even slow down. He rapped once and walked right on in, closing the door behind him.

Okay, Glass Fork, let's talk.

It couldn't hurt to learn more about them. Take an interview.

But Lexa knew from experience. Once she started the process, she'd have to see it through. Replying to their inquiry meant she was willing to move to Seattle.

She startled when her phone rang. Seeing Jett's name and number added a nervous shiver to her unease.

"Just checking in." He'd called Monday and Tuesday as well.

"You didn't call me this much when we were married."

"Making up for past oversight."

She paused, wondering if he was whispering something to her between the lines. "How are things in academia?"

"The usual. I'm heading into the staff meeting. And the publisher dropped off a proof of my book."

"How's it look?" She liked the buoyancy in his voice. Maybe he'd finally settled the debate within himself.

"Beautiful. Lex, thanks again for this weekend. For the things you've said. I've been thinking about them."

"Yeah, me too. I'm glad I went. It was good to say goodbye to Storm." She looked up as Zane rapped on her desk and pointed to his office.

"Meeting," he said, low.

Now? "Jett, got to run."

"Want to grab a bite? Burgers or something?"

"Um, I don't know . . . When?"

Zane wore a mask of impatience. What was going on?

"Tonight. Paul's Da Burger Joint."

One of their favorite Greenwich Village spots. But Lexa had always hesitated after she joined ZB, considering Paul's a competitor.

"Paul's? Sure. It's been a while." She could do some recon. See what the competition was doing.

"Lexa, let's go." Zane's command startled her.

"Jett, I have to go, but see you at Paul's."

She hung up wondering if she'd just agreed to go on a date with her ex-husband.

Spending the weekend with Jett and his family opened her heart just a little and reminded her of what she craved most. Intimacy with a man she loved. Community. She'd tried to fulfill her cravings with work, but after two years, she was dry, dull, and starved.

Grabbing her iPad, Lexa met Zane at his office door, surprised to see a small company around his conference table.

"I think you know almost everyone," Zane said.

"I do. Hello."

To her right was Quent and the consultant Tim Fraser. Next to him sat board member Isaac Stokes. Across the table was the CFO, Albert Bernstein, and an exquisitely dressed woman in a cream suit with a brilliant silk blouse, her sleek brunette hair flowing over her shoulders.

"This is Kathryn Buck." Zane motioned to the woman who rose to shake Lexa's hand.

When they touched, a chill crept over Lexa despite the afternoon sun burning through the window.

"I've heard a lot about you, Lexa." The woman held onto her hand, almost challenging. "I'm looking forward to working with you."

"Working with me?"

"Yes, I'm the new CEO."

Well, finally. Now she knew. Lexa dropped to the chair with a glance toward Zane. *This is how you tell me?*

"C-congratulations." Wasn't it good she'd responded to The Glass Fork?

"Kathryn is an expert on branding and taking struggling startups to the next level."

"We were struggling?" Lexa said.

"In many ways, yes, but with Kathryn on board we can steer toward a solid future." Zane also sounded stiff and flat to her. "Kathryn, why don't you say a few words?"

She stood, smoothing imaginary wrinkles from the pristine skirt, and cast her shadow over Lexa.

"First of all, thank you for inviting me to be a part of this great team . . ."

As she spoke, Lexa stared out the window. Far below the fall colors were beginning to fade. The glorious red, gold, and umber were now a dull, dry brown.

She was sad at this outcome, even a bit humiliated. But she was all right. Truly. Maybe she'd brought back a bit of hope and courage from the farm.

It'd been good to see Miranda happy and in love again. Healing to say goodbye to Storm and remember how boldly he lived life.

And shocking, if not alluring, to hear Jett say with a bit of conviction, "I love you."

"Lexa?" Zane peered at her. "What do you say?"

She brought her gaze from the window to the gathering around the table. "About what?"

"What we've just been talking about. The new brand. The updated Zaney Days."

"I think I don't really care." She gazed at Kathryn, then the goofy poster of Zane and Zaney Days. "It's horrid, but it's not my call. It's not the brand that gave you such rapid success. Looks like you're going for the fickle Millennials. Good luck. But we built this company to this point with families." She pushed back from the table.

"You're right, Zane, she does speak her mind."

How true. But with everyone except Jett.

Lexa stood and pushed her chair under the table. "I quit."

"Oh, Lexa, come on." Zane popped up. "This is no time for a tantrum. You know we need someone with Kathryn's experience."

"This is not a tantrum. This is me moving on. Good luck to you all."

"Lexa, stop it. Sit down. We need you. Kathryn needs you. The vendors love you. And you know every supplier and—"

"Let her go, Zane. If she's not happy she'll make trouble."

"It's not an issue of being happy, but becoming who I'm supposed to be." She walked around the end of the table with more grace than she imagined she possessed. She kissed Zane on the cheek. "It's been real. An amazing seven years. All the best luck going forward, and I mean it."

She nearly skipped on her way out, her bravado turning into real courage. Which change required.

As she packed up her desk, she began to tremble, to waver in her resolve. Endings were so very, very sad.

With her box tucked under her arm, she made her way to the elevator bank and pressed the down button.

She was leaving the twentieth floor for the very last time.

❧

JETT

For a man who didn't believe in luck or fate, the last month was shot through with kismet.

Kismet that Mom chose to marry Oz during the season Lexa lived in his apartment. Kismet she and Dad chose the same weekend to bid a long overdue, final farewell to Storm. Kismet Lexa went with him. Kismet how they opened up and shared their hearts after so much silence.

Kismet that he and Mom talked. She listened to how she broke his heart when she left, tears streaming down her cheeks. Not once did she interrupt or make an excuse.

She apologized and asked forgiveness. Then left on her honeymoon with a bit of her heart, and Jett's, healed.

It was kismet that he finally, after four years, published his dissertation. Kismet that the book brought an extraordinary endowment to the university.

It was kismet he'd been at the Waldorf gala the night Lexa tripped in front of a cab.

Kismet he cradled her limp body in the street while waiting for the ambulance. Kismet he'd received a mysterious invitation to the Fifth Avenue Literary Society Library and the curious story society.

Looking back, the night in Central Booking with Chuck smacked of kismet. Or at least a close cousin, coincidence.

Kismet, kismet, kismet. His life had become one of his beloved novels. But *who* was writing his story?

With kismet on his mind, Jett made his way to the faculty

conference room, a proof copy of his published dissertation tucked under his arm. It was thick and heavy, heavenly.

"Afternoon, all." He plopped down in the first open seat, grinning, gazing around the table at his staunch, stuffy-looking colleagues. "Why the long faces? Who died?"

Jett stretched, propping his long legs on the corner of the table. Life was good. *Kismet.*

With so much kismet on his side, he was going to tell Lexa how he felt. Tonight. Over hamburgers at Paul's.

His skin tingled with anticipation. *"I'm still in love with you."* He buzzed with desire. Their next kiss would be intentional, deep, and passionate.

"You haven't heard?" Hardin Jones, tenured professor and resident Oscar the Grouch, reached over to shove Jett's feet from the table. "There's a rumor Tenley Roth has finally spoken about GPR. She said he was a fraud."

Jett's feet landed with a thud. "What? How? When?" He glanced back at Renée as she entered with Dr. Hanover. "Tenley said something about Gordon? After she refused all my requests for an interview?"

"We just got off the phone with the Roth Foundation. They say it's not true. Tenley has no intention of making a statement about her great-great-grandfather. Apparently an old rumor resurfaced from a few years ago. After she published *An October Wedding*. An article in the *New Yorker* online raised the question. Probably based on the advance copy of your book we sent."

With an exhale, Renée sat. "If I never hear another word about GPR being a fraud it will be *too* soon."

"Jett, did you address the rumor at all?" Dr. Hanover reached for the proof copy and flipped through the pages. "Three weeks and we're ten million richer. The Roth people want a school named after Gordon as much as we do, so let's get this book printed and on the shelves. They just showed us their ten-year plan for partnering with high schools, universities, and libraries to expand the love of literature." He dropped the proof in front of Jett. "We want to start a summer writing intensive. We thought you'd like to head it up."

"Are you kidding? Yes. Absolutely." Dividends on his hard work and loyalty already.

"We're also partnering with Roth to hire a PR firm to promote your book and their upcoming programs. I hope you like radio interviews and talk shows, Jett."

"Of course, and yes, I addressed the speculation among our peers and GPR detractors." There were always detractors. "I added a short paragraph in my conclusion. No need to prattle on about something unfounded to start with."

If he spoke up, brought the rejected manuscript to life, he'd open a horrific Pandora's Box.

Years and years of debate and discussion would ensue. Questions with no possible answers.

It was a rabbit hole of *Alice in Wonderland* proportions. He was right, even smart, to leave out his finding. He wasn't even sure the Fifth Avenue library would let anyone in to see the book, tucked away, hidden on the bottom shelf. No one had discovered it for 117 years. If they had, they remained quiet. Like Jett.

"Here are your official invitations to the reception. You each have a plus-one." Renée nodded at Hardin as she distributed envelopes. "Since you never bring a plus-one, I'm taking yours. Bringing my nieces."

THE ROTH RECEPTION
SUNDAY, NOVEMBER 17, SIX O'CLOCK
NEW YORK COLLEGE PRESIDENTIAL RESIDENCE
BLACK TIE

Jett tapped his invitation against the tabletop, ignoring the pebble stuck in his craw. He'd done the right thing. Absolutely. No regrets. And also, he was bringing "plus four" to the reception.

Someone always dropped out last minute or left a significant other at home.

"Elijah Roth will present President Gee and Dr. Hanover with the check. Afterward, Jett, you'll give a fifteen-minute talk on the value and worth of literature, highlighting Gordon of course, and present your book to Elijah. Then we party like we're ten million richer."

The faculty applauded and cheered, high-fiving Jett and talking all at once about what they could do with the money.

Then Dr. Hanover excused himself, and Renée moved to the regular staff meeting. Jett sank back into his mental debate, annoyed by the growing unease in his gut.

His manuscript was done. Approved. Endorsed by Dr. Levi. Gone to print.

Stop second-guessing.

Wasn't he just reveling in the power of kismet? How *fate* intervened in the last six weeks?

Wasn't it kismet that brought him to the inner recesses of the Bower where he discovered the rare, unknown manuscript? And he just ignored it.

A flash of heat slithered though him.

He discovered the manuscript just when he was about to publish. So what? It was, was . . .

Kismet.

Because if it wasn't, then neither was the mysterious invitation. Or reconnecting with Lexa. Or spending a night in Central Booking with Chuck.

He needed to get out of this meeting. Burst into the cold fall day and clear his head. For crying out loud. He didn't actually *believe* in kismet. Nor that his story was being written by some divine hand.

"Jett, we'll have someone cover your classes, so you can go on a short book tour." Renée stared at him. "You all right? You look green."

"I'm fine." *Focus. Pay attention.* "Book tour, you say?"

"Yes, book tour. Hardin, you can cover Jett's writing courses as needed." Hardin fumed. "I'll assign a TA to his Comm classes. Now, on to the faculty senate notes . . ."

"Renée, if you'll excuse me."

Jett barged from the conference room and down the hall, out the door, and into the afternoon chill. Gray clouds hovered overhead.

With long strides, he aimed for the quad, for some sort of peace of mind, for the joy of his fantastical kismet.

⌇

LEXA

Dinner Wednesday evening with Jett was a blast from the past. And not the fun kind.

He sat across from her and sulked in silence. Once again wearing his feelings and saying nothing.

"Everything okay?" She dipped her fry in a puddle of ketchup, feeling pretty good to be eating at *another* burger place.

Take that, ZB.

Jett stuffed a fry in his mouth. "Yeah, why?"

The question required no answer.

She'd shown up tonight with her own resolve to tell him she'd quit ZB Enterprises, and tomorrow at noon EST she was Skyping with an organic bakery in Seattle.

If all went well, she'd be heading to Seattle after Thanksgiving. At least that was her tentative plan. And as luck would have it, just before her apartment lease renewal.

"Have you talked to anyone in the society?" she said.

"Should I?"

"I was going to call Coral, see if I could find out what happened with Chuck, but some *things* happened today." She inched toward telling him about her day.

Jett didn't bite.

On her way to Paul's, she'd convinced herself she'd be raw

and real with him, keep her heart open. But when he grunted his responses as he shoved food into his mouth, she slammed her willingness closed.

Wife Lexa would be fretting about now, or worse, fuming. Ex-wife Lexa was thinking of ordering a chocolate shake and walking home.

"Everything good at the college?"

"Never better."

Liar. What was eating him? His book? Her phone pinged with a text from Skipper.

This dress or this?

Two images popped up on the screen, with baby sister in a department store changing room.

She wore a purple silk number with drop sleeves in the first image, and a cream dress with large printed flowers in the other.

Neither.

Really?

Too slutty. Too old lady.

You're ridiculous.

If you don't want to know, don't ask.

I'm putting them back. But I need something for my date Friday night.

Go to the shops in Cocoa Village.

Speaking of date, when are you jumping back in the pool?

I quit my job today.

WHA??????!!!!!

Jett looked up when her phone rang.

"Hold on, Skip." Lexa grabbed her bag and took a ten and five from her wallet. "Here's for my dinner." She pushed back from the table. "I'll see you later."

Jett straightened, eyes wide. "You're leaving?"

"I hate to break up our vibrant conversation but yes, I'm leaving."

"Okay, har-har, I've been a bit quiet."

"Quiet? That's what you call it? Break out your thesaurus, professor." She made her way to the door.

"Lex, come on. I have a lot on my mind."

She turned back, Skipper still holding. "Jett, let's not make more of last weekend than we should. We had a nice time. Said some honest things. But we're not meant to be together. You know it, I know it. Find a woman who doesn't care when you get in your moods and clam up. I'll find a man who can be honest with me, share what's going on in his heart. I don't want to be cut out of my partner's life. Not that you and I are partners." *Not anymore.* "I'll see you Monday at the story society."

Without a backward glance, she walked toward the door, passing the cashier and forgoing her chocolate shake craving, hoping upon hope—

Would he come after her? Not that she expected him to, but—

However, when she stepped outside, the only thing reaching for her was the sharp chill in the night breeze creeping down the avenue.

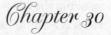

Chapter 30

CORAL

She was exhausted. So much she almost blew off the story society, but it was her turn to bring the food. She'd ordered from Mexicue, and while she didn't have to be there to partake, she'd been craving it ever since she rattled off her credit card number.

Nevertheless, she arrived late, wet, and cold. Discouraged. Running from her car to the library door through a chilly deluge.

"Sorry I'm late." She shook the rain from her jacket and hung it on the rack by the door. "The underbelly of fall has arrived."

"Yep," Jett said, phone pressed to his ear.

"Is it raining again?" Ed said.

"What'd you order? I'm starved." Chuck.

"Mexicue." She made her way to the fireplace and the romance of the flickering flames. And apparently the only warmth in the room. "The food should arrive soon."

Lexa and Jett were both on their phones. Chuck walked the length of the bookshelves, reading the spines. And Ed stared straight ahead, hands in his lap, a folder on the floor by his chair.

Oh, what was happening to them? She needed her society, ached for them to be okay with one another. Her company was about to go through it, and the idea of Monday night story society anchored her.

"Ed, did you write more of your memoir?" Slightly warmer, Coral returned to her seat with a glance toward Chuck.

They'd texted a few times this week and she confessed the word *betrayal* caught her unaware. He said he was sorry. She said it was her issue, not his. They seemed fine. But clearly they were not back to where they were the evening of Riley's party.

She'd had a rough week. The FBI was involved in her problems now. But she was willing to set it aside to enjoy the society. She feared she was alone in her quest.

"Yeah, some."

"Are you going to write about the GW?" Chuck spoke from the back of the room.

"Of course, that's where I proposed." Ed frowned. His reply snapped at what little peace existed in the Bower.

"I saw you drop flowers over the side." Chuck made his way forward with barely a glance at Coral.

She didn't have time for any pettiness. Or the energy to deal with Chuck's issues. She was about to turn her company inside out.

"Can't a man drop flowers if he wants? I told you I proposed up there. How did you see me anyway? Were you spying?"

"I stayed for a while, yes. Then I caught a fare."

"Should've never let you drive me. I broke my routine and now look, got some nosy boy butting into my business."

"Well pardon me, Ed."

"Coral, did he tell you he came to my house after your argument last week? After Trudy got all into his business."

"Did we argue?" She peered up at Chuck. He told Ed they'd argued?

"Ed, do you know what *confidential* means?"

"Chuck, we talked about your comment. It just caught me off guard is all. Ed, we didn't argue."

The big man with the sexy eyes dropped to his chair with a heavy sigh. "He means Trudy. I fought with Trudy. If you're going to tell the story, Ed, know the players."

The tension was weakened by a knock on the door. Thank goodness. Food. Coral answered while the others, in practiced motion, set up for dinner, the conversation centered on nothing more than verbal directions.

Then they filled their plates and ate their tacos, cornbread, and poblano mac-n-cheese in silence.

Besides the grumpy sobriety from Chuck, tension buzzed

around Lexa and Jett. So thick Coral could have spread it across her cornbread.

What a difference a week makes. Last week those two had talked about the wedding-slash-memorial in rotating dialog. Like an old married couple. He said. She said.

"I dumped the flowers as a memorial to Esmerelda," Ed said out of the blue as he wiped sauce from his whiskered chin. "That's all."

"You do know flowers grow better in dirt, Ed?" Lexa's comment drew a reserved laugh from the group.

"Yeah, Ed, try dirt next time." Chuck got up for seconds.

"Mind your own business, you fat-faced mule." Ed's blue gaze snapped red, and he quivered so his plate rattled against his lap. "I don't know what's eating you but don't bring it to the Bower. Think I want to read more of my story to you now?"

"Fine, no one wanted to hear your sickly sweet love story anyway."

"Enough." On his feet, Jett commanded their attention. "Why are we turning on each other? We're supposed to be friends. A society."

"A society of what?" Lexa said. "And how can we be friends if we're never really open and honest with each other?"

She glared at Jett in a way that gave Coral a clue about their week. What'd he do? Or not do?

"Sometimes friendship requires patience," Jett said. "Giving. Serving."

"Sometimes it's just not worth the effort." Lexa didn't even pause. Just fired right back.

"Can we stop?" Coral raised her hand. "Start over?" She exhaled, waiting for Chuck to sit again. "Okay. Hi, everyone, how was your week?"

"Rotten," "stinky," "who cares" bounced around the circle.

Not good, but it was a start. Recently her life journey had taught her if she wanted something from someone else, she had to be willing to go first.

Setting her plate aside, she faced her friends. "My CEO and CFO have been embezzling. I've called the FBI, and probably sometime this week, they will be arrested. The evidence is there."

"I knew it wasn't the lip gloss." Lexa, with boldness.

Coral gave them the social-media version of her troubles, each member rapt with attention.

"So that's my life. Anyone want to top it?"

"Trudy bawled me out for bringing you to the party." Chuck glanced sideways at her. "Threatened me with taking the kids away. Jakey was so excited I came, so excited about his Magic Book poster, he let slip that he saw me at the schoolyard."

Coral pressed her hand over his.

"I tried to bluff my way out of it but I'm pretty sure she knows. I wake up every morning wondering when I'm going to hear from her lawyer that they filed the final restraining order." He jumped from his seat. "Those are never removed. It would take years and thousands of dollars to try. I'm not going to see my kids grow up. Ah, serves me right."

"What did you do, Chuck? I can't imagine," Lexa said. "How does it serve you right?"

At the food table, he picked up a wedge of cornbread, then put it back down, his jaw taut, his posture stiff and unyielding.

"If I say, you'll hate me."

"Maybe we'll understand," Jett said.

"Let someone else talk." Chuck returned to his chair and slumped down, legs splayed.

"Do you want to know why I left Gus at the altar?" She'd been thinking of confessing for the last two weeks. It was time. Plus, recently she ached to share good news. *The* Good News.

Chuck sat up. Lexa leaned in. Jett and Ed ate, watching her and waiting.

"I, um . . ." She inhaled, her unspoken confession manifesting in tears. "I met Jesus."

"Jesus who?" Ed's curled lip accented his question.

"And you called me a fat-faced mule?" Chuck said. "You know, Jesus, God. Didn't you ever go to church?"

"Don't call me a fat-faced mule. She may have met a Latino gentleman. A Jesús."

"Will you two hush?" Jett, sounding like a father. "Let her tell her story."

"Start from the beginning, Coral," Lexa said. "Leave nothing out."

"My journey started a few months before our wedding, when we were finalizing the ceremony. I kept reading all of these references to the Father, the Son, and the Holy Spirit as part of our wedding vows. We were to honor God as much as each other. To serve God. To recognize Him as the head of our home, our family, our nation. Gus vowed to serve Him.

"One evening, I asked him about it. I thought we should change the wording since neither one of us were religious. I do think a man's word is his bond and if I'm going to vow something to God, I want to mean it.

"Gus said I was reading too much into it. That the vows were the rites of the church and nothing more than custom. He said no one expected the bride and groom, the royal family, to actually follow Christian truths and morals. I asked how I would know which vows he intended to keep.

"We fought about it but the more I considered what we were to pledge, the more I wanted to know. I talked with the archbishop. I read a book. I actually picked up a Bible. I didn't want someone telling me who God was without seeing for myself.

"I didn't want to say vows at my wedding then toss them the moment we walked out of the nave. As I read the New Testament, I couldn't believe the love and hope I saw there. I cried myself to sleep every night. I had to know this Son of God, Son of Man. Gus thought I was being silly, and too literal. He had no interest in studying the Bible with me.

"So I asked him who steered his moral compass. Who or what

was his moral and spiritual governor. He said himself. He was his own highest power, supreme commander, and chief architect of his life." Coral pressed her hand to her chest, reliving the magnitude of the moment. It had been horrendous. "In an instant, this fear hit me. Not like anything I'd ever felt before. As if God heard and wrote down what Gus claimed. I begged him to reconsider God as part of our life. To read the Bible with me. He refused.

"The fear increased daily. I know now it was the fear of God, the good kind that makes you want to know Him, obey Him, love Him. If Gus's highest authority was himself, then to whom did I appeal when I had an issue with him? When we didn't get along? When I was worried about the choices he was making and could not get him to see reason? If he was his own boss, then I was at risk. How was I to know his self-convictions would keep him faithful to me and our family? He respected his father, and his brothers, but Gus *was* his own lord and master. I started to see it more and more. I didn't want to be my own lord and master, so I surrendered." She wiped her cheeks as she scanned the circle. "Do I sound like a TV evangelist if I say I was 'born again'? All I know is I met Jesus and my heart is not the same.

"Gus wanted no part of my religious experience. Meanwhile, we were speeding toward the wedding. Parties, fittings, plans, portraits. A month before the wedding I was going over the RSVPs with the wedding coordinator and the head of the king's office, and I knew I couldn't marry him. But I convinced myself I had cold feet. I buried myself in the preparations. My mom came over for the last month. Then my dad and brother showed up for the last two weeks. My friends were flying over. Gus's family and friends were celebrating. I loved his family, I truly did. Still do. How could I walk away for fear of a God I barely knew? We were both so invested in the relationship, the wedding."

"You needed the society, didn't you?" Ed was at her feet, bending to one knee, patting her arm. "We're here for you."

She laughed through her tears. "And I'm grateful."

"How'd you manage the courage to leave?" Lexa said.

"On *the* day, I woke up excited. Gus and I had been getting along so well. He'd been super sweet. I'd been praying for him, for us, every night. I just knew we'd come together on the issue of faith. But when I put on my wedding dress, my beautiful, exquisite gown with five thousand hand-sewn pearls, I felt sick." She pressed her hand to her middle. "I could not marry His Royal Highness Prince Augustus of Lauchtenland." Fresh tears dropped to her skirt. "You cannot imagine the horrible, horrible feeling that claimed me. I either had to marry him knowing it was wrong, or break both our hearts. Humiliate both of us. We had over a thousand guests from across the globe making their way to the church. Millions of dollars had been spent. There were two wedding dresses, two receptions, not to mention the wedding rings, my tiara. People say Christianity is for the weak but let me tell you, it takes courage to follow God. To obey Him."

"So you ran?" Chuck said.

"Yes, because if I saw Gus I'd never go through with it. And honest to goodness, I've never told anyone this, I heard the audible voice of Jesus saying, 'Coral, follow Me.'"

⁓

CHUCK

Hearing her story humbled him. He'd been working so hard to diminish her in his eyes, to quell his feelings, he'd set aside her strength, her kindness, and her vulnerability.

"I'm sorry I've been so rude," he said.

If she could leave her prince for the sake of faith, he could be a bit more tolerant of Trudy.

"Yes, you have been." She dabbed the mascara from her face with a greasy napkin. Chuck dug his clean handkerchief from his pocket and passed it over.

"You can keep it."

"Thank you, but I'll return it, clean. And if I had the courage to leave Gus and confront embezzlers, I'm quite certain I can handle you. But stop being so grouchy. I'm on your side."

"Me too." Sweet Lexa. Still hiding her torch for Jett. Something had been different between them, but this week it was the same ol' same ol'.

"You know I have your back, Coral." Jett pounded his fist with Chuck's.

"Chuck, I have a question," Lexa said. "If Trudy cheated on you, why is she calling the shots?"

So they were back to his story.

"Well?" Ed. Good ol' Ed.

"Because." For a guy not afraid to jump into a fight, he was a coward. Sure, he rolled up his sleeves and threw a few punches at a wedding reception brawl. Sure, he unleashed his temper on Trudy and Will when he caught them a second time.

But share his fears and failures? Confess the things that made him weak? It physically pained him.

Jett passed around cold waters while they waited. Chuck twisted the cap from his and drained the bottle in one tilt.

"We had this cat named Red when I was a kid." He wiped his mouth with his wadded-up napkin, then crushed his plastic bottle. "A sixteen-pound red tiger tom. Sweet but with a devilish mean streak. He clawed half of our family and friends. It became a rite of passage to get scratched by that cat. I can still see my two-year-old cousin sitting at the sliding doors looking out. Red sat next to him. They looked at each other and next thing we know . . . *swack*. And Seth was screaming.

"Red loved dogs though. Weirdest thing to see him in our back-yard sitting under the nose of a hundred-pound Akita. Have you seen that breed? Got heads as big as a bear's. But bring around a two-pound kitten, and Red hightailed it. Hid under the bed." The society's laughter fed his courage. "You guys are the kitten to me. You scare me. I'd rather arm wrestle than tell you how I *feel*."

Jett and Ed nodded, agreeing.

"Here's the facts between Trudy and me. I hope you don't hate me for this. But I beat the stuffing out of her hedge-fund boy-friend." Head down, hands loosely linked between his knees, he went on. "Destroyed furniture, vases, Limoges, and crystal. Took a sledgehammer to his Beemer, then hers. Word to the wise: Carrie Underwood can sing about scratching up a cheater's car, but it'll land you in jail. What I didn't know is I knocked over Riley in my ram-page. Jakey was hiding behind the couch and saw it all. And I might have waved a gun around." He stopped their surprise with raised hands. "Unloaded. I didn't fire at anyone. I was arrested."

There. He'd confessed his anger and lack of self-control. How jealousy and pain made him blind with rage.

"Makes more sense why you helped me at the wedding," Jett said.

"I might have been aching for a fight."

"Still, Trudy let you come to the parties. Isn't that a good sign?" Lexa said.

"Not if she figures out I saw Jakey at his school." He motioned to Coral. "She claims I upstaged her by bringing Coral around, which added to her venom."

"I take it she's not going to invite me over again?"

Chuck appreciated the light tone of her question. "No, and probably not me either. I thought I'd gotten somewhere with her. Proven myself. If she files for the final protective order I won't see the kids until they're eighteen. Maybe not even then."

"Is there anything we can do?" Jett said.

"Like what? Trudy has the connections, the money, the support. I'm just an Uber and limo driver with a record."

"There is a higher authority," Coral said.

"Don't preach here, Coral. God and me, not on speaking terms."

"It never hurts to ask Him for help, Chuck. Humility is a magnet for His affection."

"I don't know." He squirmed, feeling like Red the cat facing a one-pound kitten. "Feels fake."

"I felt that way in the beginning too. And none of us hate you."

"I'll think on it." With his confession, he decided he had more room for the last bit of cornbread. "Anyone else want cornbread?" *No?* He reached for a new plate and the last large piece.

"Jett, how's your dissertation?" Chuck said.

"Good. All set to publish." He reached into his backpack and passed around embossed invitations. "The Roth reception is on the seventeenth. I stole these from faculty mailboxes."

"Jett, aren't you a rascal." Coral tucked hers into her large fancy handbag.

"Don't worry. New York College is ripe with absentminded professors. They'll get in without the invite."

"So, another invitation," Ed said. "Wonder what mystery this one will unlock?"

∽

JETT

"Good point, Ed. We still haven't unlocked the mystery of the society's invitation."

"Guess I'm in if you guys are," Chuck said. "I've been reading your Mars book, Jett. It's good. I want it to be a movie."

"From your lips to God's ears. But since no one but you and ten other people have read it . . ." Jett passed an invitation to Lexa, but she refused. He returned it to his backpack with a flare of ire.

She was one person he really wanted there.

Since their failed burger date, he'd given her space. But he was going to try again. To tell her how he felt. Tell her about the faculty meeting, how it raised his fears.

Tell her they weren't wrong for each other. They just needed to learn to communicate.

"Did you ever call that agent?" Chuck again.

"Not yet." Jett swigged from his water bottle. "Maybe when the semester is over."

"Coral and Chuck were honest tonight, Jett." Lexa angled toward him. "Why won't you tell me, us, what happened on Eiger with Storm?"

She wasn't going to leave it alone. "You know what happened, Lex. He died. Jumped and plummeted to the ground."

"Ed, did Esmerelda jump?" Chuck's question shot a line drive through the conversation. "From the GW?"

"Young man, your persistence is hindering my enjoyment of the society."

"Did she? You can trust us, Ed. Why did you really drop flowers off the bridge?" Chuck wasn't letting up, and to be honest, Jett was relieved. Get the focus off of him.

"Ed?"

"Chuck, leave him alone. He's told you he proposed up there." Coral squeezed his hand. "Besides, Gilda will kick us out soon."

"Indeed, Gilda will be here soon." Ed cradled the thin folder against his chest, his eyes flooded, his chin quivering.

Coral moved over next to him and the pressure of emotion rose in Jett's chest.

They were wrestling with one another tonight, getting to the heart of issues.

"It's okay," she said. "We're here."

Ed peered at her, shaking his head. "I can't. I can't."

"Did she jump, Ed?" Chuck repeated with a surprise tenderness.

"No, no, she just, she just leaned too far. That's all. She liked to climb the steel suspension and spread her wings. She fell, that's all. She fell." Chin to his chest, his soft sobs echoed. "She loved me. She loved me."

Out of her chair, Lexa wrapped her arms around the old man and rested her head against his.

"It's okay, Ed. It's okay."

Jett glanced at Chuck. *You happy?*

Chuck stood and clapped Ed on the shoulder. "I'm sorry, Ed."

"Are you?" Tears spilled from Ed's eyes when he looked up. "I miss her. Every day."

Ed's sobs filled the Bower. Jett remained seated, head bowed, wishing for a moment he knew how to talk to the God Coral mentioned.

After a few minutes, a hush, a peace coated the room and Ed collected himself, blowing his nose on the handkerchief Chuck gave to Coral.

Then, without asking, the heiress released her faith over them, praying softly, asking God for things Jett never dared ask. Peace. Comfort. Help. Wisdom. Love.

Gilda knocked on the door. "It's time, children."

They filed out slowly, Chuck with his arm about Ed, Coral and Lexa whispering together.

And Jett was alone in the Bower. Alone with his thoughts. Alone with evidence of the truth. And not just the manuscript on the bottom shelf. But within himself.

"It's time, Jett," he heard Gilda say. "And I don't mean the book."

He hooked his backpack on his shoulder. "Time? I don't know what you mean."

"I think you do." She nodded toward the manuscript. "Gordon couldn't confess the truth. It would ruin his career, his life. But in doing so he defrauded Birdie."

"How do you know all of this?"

"It's my job to know." She patted his arm. "Tell Lexa the whole story."

"She already knows about Gordon."

"I'm not talking about Gordon, am I?"

"Aren't you?" He followed her from the Bower. "Gilda? What are you talking about?"

"Good night, Jett." Once again, she disappeared behind the door marked Private.

LEXA

Her Skype interview with The Glass Fork owners, Jenn and Ki Lee, went long into the afternoon, the time flying by.

When the call finally ended, the shadows of the short November day draped over MacDougal Street.

Three thirty. Lexa glanced about her apartment, famished. Excited. Churning with ideas.

"Tell us about yourself, your experience with Zane. We think he's a genius."

She spoke of her former boss with enthusiasm, not glossing over his accomplishments but making no bones about her part in his success either.

"I've actually separated from ZB to seek other opportunities."

No use hiding the truth. They'd find out sooner or later. They understood her reasons completely and were relieved not to steal her out from under Zane.

The Lees shared their dream and vision, how they got started, thrilled with Lexa's start-up experience.

Through the power of the internet, they toured her through their offices and the bakery. Ki promised to overnight samples of their most popular products.

A double-chocolate raspberry croissant with organic wheat and oats? She felt inspired just hearing about it.

Midway through the conversation, Jenn's assistant sent housing information and Ki walked Lexa through the best places to live.

"We want you on our side of the city, so your salary will compensate for rent prices."

The high-rise in Belltown with a view of the water had her mouth watering more than the double-chocolate raspberry croissant.

I'm in. I'm in.

She met the admin and HR rep, as well as the director of production and head of sales.

Conversation and ideas flowed. Lexa actually started taking notes, as did Ki and Jenn.

When they finally wound down, Jenn looked at Ki. Lexa held her breath. Were they going to make an offer now? Should she fly out to see the place, or was the connection she felt enough?

She was ready for this. She knew it.

"Lexa, it's been great talking to you. Never thought this call would last over three hours. We should talk here and give it a day or two. You think it through as well. Email if you have questions and let's connect again at noon your time on Friday."

So here she stood in her eight-hundred-square-foot studio with a single-wide window looking down onto infamous MacDougal Street.

She hated endings. But if things didn't end, where would all the amazing beginnings be?

While she'd loved her time in Greenwich Village, she was on the verge of a new decade—her thirties—and it was time to move on.

Seattle would be a fresh start in a new city. With a cool new job, a chance to contribute again. She'd be a CEO, thank you very much.

She'd make new friends on her own. Ones she wouldn't lose in a divorce.

She could take up hiking and eat more granola. Maybe even go on a date. The idea landed hard.

She would miss Jett. No use lying to herself. He was her first real love. Her forever love. Or so she had thought.

She didn't resist the rush of tears. If there was no sadness about leaving New York, then her time here would've meant nothing.

Slipping on her coat, she grabbed her wallet and keys, thinking of falafel from Mamoun's.

She paused at the window and stared out. Beyond the square

glass pane, the shadows had brightened to a soft gray and shook a gentle snow over the village.

Lexa leaned around her desk and peered into the street. A couple of kids raced down the sidewalk with a dog in tow, arms wide, tongues trying to catch a taste of winter.

Her attention drifted toward the lamppost. Where did she ever get the idea she wanted to be serenaded from the street while it snowed?

Probably one of Mom's Golden Age of Hollywood movies. *Singing in the Rain*, maybe? Or *My Fair Lady*?

Another dog walker paused by the lamppost, and his leashed beast hiked his leg and did his business.

Lexa stepped back with a laugh. What a poignant metaphor. She took a twenty from her wallet, checked for her keys, and started for the door, then halted at the sound of the Skype call tone.

It was Jenn.

"Do you miss me already?" Lexa sat in her chair and smiled at the face on the screen, donning her CEO posture.

Jenn laughed. "How'd you know? Lexa, we don't need forty-eight hours to think about it. We know you're the one. Ki just got off the phone with Zane Breas, who sang your praises."

"Great . . . Wow." So now he knew. Now it was happening. She was really, truly, no-take-backs gone from ZB. And New York.

"I know this might be quick for you, but we're ready to close the deal. We're offering you the job of chief executive officer at The Glass Fork. A big title for a small company but we think we'll grow into it. Ki is emailing you the offer as we speak, and Lexa, I think you'll be pleased." Jenn cupped her hand around her mouth and leaned toward the screen. "Counteroffer. We'll pay whatever you ask." Then she glanced over her shoulder and spoke in her normal tone. "Our offer is more than fair."

Lexa could not hold down her smile. She was wanted. Appreciated. Sought after. Accepted.

"I'll read the offer but I'm pretty sure it's a go from my end, too, Jenn."

The woman slapped her a cyber high-five. "Let's make it official on Friday at noon. In case you haven't figured it out, Ki is a huge Gary Cooper fan. In the meantime, look for flight times that will allow you to come out and apartment hunt. Send Suki the details. She'll make the reservation and set you up at a hotel. Do you want a car? But Uber will be easier. Ki and I will go with you to find a place. It'll give us a good chance to build a relationship."

A relationship. They didn't just want to be her boss.

After a few more details and a final "I'm so excited," Jenn hung up.

Lexa exhaled, then jumped and spun around her tiny apartment. But the jarring bothered her arm, so she settled for a subtle, "Yes!"

Meanwhile, she was still hungry and still in the mood for a falafel. But she couldn't resist checking her email.

The offer was in her in-box. She opened the document and gasped, tumbling back to her chair. Triple her ZB salary, plus bonus.

Hands shaking, she clicked the link Ki added. It opened to a penthouse in Belltown overlooking the bay. She could afford it as well as a new car.

Reaching for her phone, she texted Skipper.

Job. Seattle. Big money. CEO bakery. WAAAAA!

What?

Her door rattled with a solid single knock. "Abby? It's open. Girl, you're not going to believe what just—"

"You shouldn't leave your door unlocked."

"Jett." She stood as he entered, shaking a small fluff of snow from his shoulders.

"Can I come in?"

"Yes, yes." She pointed to her red chair. "What are you doing here?"

He sat in the chair, then stood. "Look, I'm just going to say it. I've been thinking about us ever since Mom's wedding, and I know you said we're not right for each other, but I think we are, Lex. I mean, yeah, I was a jerk at Paul's. Renée had just informed the faculty of a rumor that Tenley Roth was going to out Gordon, but in the end she wasn't. It just brought up all my doubts again. Anyway, I'm sorry."

"But you know about the manuscript, Jett. I think you want to doubt. You should doubt."

"Tell me something I don't know. But it's too late." His sneakered feet made soft echoes on the hardwood as he paced. "But I'm not here to talk about GPR and his moral failings. I'm here to talk about us."

"I'm moving to Seattle, Jett." She cauterized his brewing confession before it spilled into the room and made a mess.

"What?"

"I spent the afternoon interviewing with an up-and-coming organic bakery in Seattle. They just signed a deal with Whole Foods. They've been around ten years and just built a new plant. They're growing faster than they can handle. They need a CEO. I'm it."

"Seattle? But that's a six-hour plane ride."

"I know." Her phone vibrated in her back pocket. She glanced at the screen. Skipper.

OMG. You have to take it. Yes!

"Five hours for Skipper." Lexa held up her phone. "She's excited. Said to take it."

"So that's it? You're leaving?" Jett sank into the red chair. "Congratulations, I guess. You're a CEO."

"Thank you." She perched on her desk chair. His posture, his tone, reminded her of who they used to be.

"You know we could never return to who we were when we got married, Jett. I think you're only remembering the good."

"I remember the bad, believe me. It's just—" He stared toward the kitchen. "Being with you the past month and a half reminded me what an amazing woman you are." He flipped his gaze to her. "I don't want to lose you."

"I don't know what to say, Jett. Can't I be your amazing friend?" The afternoon interview and extremely generous offer was making her immune to his sentiment and overtures of love.

She was Wonder Woman.

"Watching your life from the sidelines? Getting a Christmas card where you announce you're getting married?"

"I don't send Christmas cards."

"Well, you should." Jett shot from the reading chair. "I want you to be my wife, Lex."

"Take that back, Jett Wilder."

"It's the truth."

"You should go." Her heels thudded over the hardwood as she walked to the door.

"You're not going to even give me a chance to make my case?"

"There's no case. Weren't you *there* last week, sitting at Paul's, barely talking? I tried to break through your moody wall, but you knocked me back. I don't want to live that way, Jett. I don't want to come home every night and wonder if we're going to laugh or walk past each other in silence. You weren't like that before grad school, before Storm died."

"I know, I know. I'm working on it. But what about the times I reached out to you and you shut *me* down? The times I tried to explain the pressure I was under during grad school and you—"

"Understood. Yes, and left you alone. Now I'm wondering if I shouldn't have. Instead of bringing you to our bed, I covered you up when you fell asleep with a book on your chest. I gave myself to my job, so you didn't have to worry about money."

"And when I tried to make time for us, you were too wrapped up with ZB. I knew I'd lost you to him."

"You never lost me, Jett. But yeah, I stayed where I was wanted and needed, useful. Where I could carry on a conversation, for crying out loud. And when did you ever try to make time for us?"

"Tickets to Broadway. Dinner at the faculty club. Oh, the night I finished exams and made a picnic for us in the living room. I called you six times and you never answered. Came home at midnight as I recall."

She grinned, then snickered. "You were so cute, lying on the living room floor, naked, a rose in your hand."

"Fat lot of good it did me." His demeanor changed with his firm laugh.

"If you recall, I woke you up." She arched a brow.

"Oh, I recall."

"But we cannot live in the past. I don't know how our final two years were for you, but they were hell for me."

He gazed at her. "Look, can't we just try? We're still that couple who made love at midnight in the living room. Who laughed at the same jokes. Who scoured vintage record stores for a copy of Fleetwood Mac's *Rumors*. Who hiked the Catskills and dreamed of a house with kids and a dog. We just have to figure out—"

"I'm moving to Seattle, Jett." *Steady. Stay focused.* She couldn't be lured into the woods by Jett's idyllic memories.

"Just like that? No discussion?"

"And what if I pass on the job and we don't work out? Again?"

He left without a word, the door closing softly behind him.

Trembling, she collapsed in the red reading chair, a single sob multiplying to two, then three, filling her soul to overflowing. And while the snow twisted and twirled outside her window, she mourned her past and hoped for her future.

Chapter 32

CORAL

Friday afternoon, she closed her office door and messaged Matt: DND.

Do not disturb.

Today was *the* day.

Wringing her hands, she sat on the couch, then stood, pacing. Her heel caught on the threads of the Italian rug and she moaned, stooping to pat her hand over the obvious loose thread.

"This was Grandmother's."

Was everything she touched going to stain, rip, tear, shred, fall apart?

"Coral?" Matt peeked through the side office door. "I know you don't want to be disturbed but—"

"Here you stand." She reached for the outstretched iPad, regretting the slice in her tone. Matt never interrupted unless it was an emergency.

"I thought you'd want to see this. Especially going into the all-hands." She'd brought him into her confidence this morning, so she trusted he had her back in some way.

Coral stared at the headline on the screen. HRH Prince Augustus Carwyn George of the House of Blue was engaged to Lady Robbi De Smet, daughter of Lord and Lady Largess De Smet.

The picture showed a smiling, very handsome, and happy Gus on the palace steps beaming at Robbi, holding her hand, presenting his new love to the world.

He'd presented Coral to the press on those same steps.

"He's engaged." She returned the iPad to Matt with no small number of tears bubbling in her eyes.

"Was I wrong to show you?"

"No, of course not. I'm happy for him." She was, truly, but seeing the man she once loved and adored with another woman wasn't easy. And on today of all days.

Be blessed, Gus.

She'd tried to make him understand her reasons for leaving, for needing God more than him, but hurt made him blind and dull of hearing.

The God-size hole in her soul was too vast and deep for any one man to fill. Except her Savior.

Had she let Him fill it? Not entirely. But she was sipping and drinking from His well.

Matt entered again without a word, crossed to the paneled fridge hidden in the wall, and took out a Diet Coke. Filling a glass with ice, he set it on the coffee table.

"Fortification," he said with a wink and headed out.

"By jacking me up on caffeine?"

Nevertheless, she sat on the couch and took a long, cold, fizzy drink.

In thirty minutes, she'd march downstairs to the four o'clock all-hands. At four-o-five, the FBI would enter to arrest her CEO and CFO.

"Lord in heaven, give me wisdom."

She understood He was with her. Lived inside her, according to the writer Paul. He called it an age-old mystery. *Christ in us.*

Yet Coral had never felt more alone. What if everyone turned on her? What if Blaire and Dak's corruption ran deep throughout CCW?

Dad offered to stand with her today, but she declined. This was her company and her mess.

However, in hindsight, she wished she hadn't been so independent. His presence, or *someone's*, would be a comfort.

Chuck.

Coral's hand chilled as she set down her soda glass. They'd cleared the air, but the titillating vibration between them died.

The last two story societies ended with polite conversation.

Nothing more. She'd pieced together that he feared their relationship would drive Trudy to file for the final restraining order.

Another sip of soda. Coral warmed her chilled hand in her lap. The hand that had wrapped around Chuck's thick arm. The hand that knew the pulse in his veins when he saw Jakey and Riley. The hand that ached to hang on to him for the rest of her life.

Coral, Coral, Coral. Do not be distracted. At her desk, she reached for her handwritten notes.

"I'm pleased to report... CCW... exceeded quarterly goals..."

This was to be an epic all-hands. She'd called in the regional sales directors and senior reps. With Teddy's help, she set up video conferencing for the European team.

She silenced their complaints for the late hour by promising to keep the meeting short and to the point.

Dad suggested the all-hands to put the fear of God—his words—in every employee and root out any co-conspirators.

"Anyone on the fringe will talk, hoping for a deal."

Another gulp of caffeine and she circled the office again.

"You helped me choose You over Gus, so please give me wisdom today."

Pouring out her heart to what seemed like *air* always felt awkward, but when the air spoke back in the form of peace or confidence, her faith grew.

If confession was good for the soul, outing herself as a Believer Monday had cleansed some of her fears.

She had no idea where Chuck stood on issues of faith. Was he like Gus? His own master and highest authority?

Yet for the first time in over a year, she spoke out loud about her faith journey, pleased at her genuine tone.

Setting aside her notes, Coral whispered prayers until her phone alarm announced it was time to go down.

Finishing her soda, she headed for the door. Her phone pinged with a text from Lexa.

Thinking of you.

Headed down now.

Can we talk later? I have a job offer from a bakery in Seattle.

Coral froze. What? Lexa leaving? Why, she couldn't. No.

Absolutely. Seven o'clock? My place. I'll send my driver.

Really? Thanks.

Matt knocked and peered in again. "The media room is standing-room only."

"On my way."

If Lexa left, what about their society? She hadn't heard all of their stories, and her heart needed them.

Rounding the walkway toward the stairs, Coral practically ran into Blaire. Her heart plummeted, taking the last of her nerve and strength.

"Coral, what's this big meeting about?" Blaire fell in stride, the legs of her flared black pants swaying over a pair of red Manolo Blahniks.

"Team building."

Blaire rolled her eyes and sighed with exaggeration. "Please don't tell me we're doing some ridiculous trust-one-another game. We've all done those. Team is not our problem. Sales are our problem. What we need is to get back to CCW's core brand and do our jobs."

"I hear you, but this is no team exercise you've ever done before."

"Bringing in the regional staff will hit our bottom line. You should've videoconferenced them in like Europe. By the way, the

London and Paris offices were none too happy. It's ten o'clock p.m. their time."

"They'll survive," she said with a glance at Blaire, the woman she had believed was her friend. "I've never had a four p.m. all-hands but I've had two six a.m. conferences with both London and Paris this year."

"I just have no idea why you're wasting *everyone's* time."

She marched down the center steps in unison with Blaire, amazed at the woman's charade *and* conviction. For a moment, Coral almost doubted what she knew to be true.

Like Matt said, the conference room was filled to capacity, every seat taken and a standing line along the wall and around the back.

"Good afternoon, everyone." Coral moved to the front of the theater. "This will be short and painful." The light laughter rippled around the room.

Most of the staff were on their phones, however, unaware she'd entered.

Blaire sat on the end of the second row behind Dak and whispered something over his shoulder. He nodded with a sly grin.

So it began. The "take-down" as Dad called it.

She welcomed everyone, including those videoconferencing in. With Teddy's help, she swiftly presented the *actual* year-to-date financials, using every muscle not to glance at Blaire and Dak.

"Our new launch, Pink Coral, exceeded our first-year projections in the third quarter by twelve percent." She clicked to another slide. "So far this quarter we've gained another three percent in the North American market and six internationally."

Dak shot out of his chair. "Coral, where are you getting these numbers?" Perspiration glistened on his forehead.

"From our database, of course." She smiled. "Since Pink Coral is killing it, I've decided to launch Crimson Coral for the holidays, a limited-edition lip gloss."

This time it was Blaire launching from her seat. "Since when? We've not even talked about Crimson Coral. Coral, what is going on?" She stepped out of the row and headed down to the front. Dak followed her.

"We don't have the revenue," he said. "Coral, what database is feeding you these numbers?"

"The financial database you and Blaire hid from me."

The side doors opened and uniformed agents with *FBI* printed on their jackets cruised into the room.

A hush fell. Coral could hear Margo Chapman and her cold breathing in the first row.

Everyone heard the click and snap of handcuffs as Blaire and Dak were arrested and read their rights.

"This is an outrage." Dak fought the man steering him toward the exit. "It isn't true. You have no proof."

"Dak, shut up." Blaire squirmed against the cuffs. "Coral, let me explain. We were going to pay you back."

"She wanted Pink Coral," Dak shouted. "To create a new Glitter Girl. But she was going to pay you back. Honest."

Blaire kicked at Dak as she was led away. "I said shut up."

"I can't go to prison." Dak dug in his heels. "My wife will leave me. It was Blaire's idea, Coral. All her idea." Dak pleaded with the arresting agent, assuring him he'd talk, sing, spill the beans, whatever, just so long as they didn't put him in prison.

The hush deepened after the agents escorted a few other persons of interest to the upstairs conference room for questioning.

With a steadying hand on the projector table, Coral detailed the embezzlement and fraud.

Right then and there she fired Chris, head of IT, and promoted Teddy. She also promoted Mark Peeters, a long-time CCW employee, to CFO.

"I should've given you the job in the first place, Mark."

For now, she'd take on the role of president *and* CEO.

Then she glanced at her watch. Four twenty. And she was exhausted. Matt stepped forward to close the meeting.

"When you return to your desks, please read the email that just went out. If you have any further questions, please see me for an appointment."

The room emptied without a word. The heavy reality of what just went down settled over them all.

After the room emptied, Coral sat in the grand octagon-shaped theater alone, too drained to move.

At last, she pushed up and made her way back to her office one step at a time.

Matt met her there. "London's on the line. This is the third time Ian has called." He made a face. "He said everyone is blown away."

"How'd he sound?"

"Honestly? Elated."

"Is he on phone or video?"

"Phone, but Coral, there's a man in your office." Matt jerked his thumb over his shoulder. "I tried to tell him you were busy, but he refused to leave."

Coral rounded the corner to see Chuck waiting in the shadows caused by the shift of the late-afternoon light.

"Something told me to come." He fidgeted with a nervous smile, digging his hands into his jeans pockets.

She almost collapsed as she made her way to him. Weeping, she fell into his arms and buried her ordeal in his strong, broad chest.

∽

ED

When he really thought about it, the story society made no sense. He was the odd man out.

Jett and Lexa, Chuck and Coral, and then him. Ed. In his mind, his name dropped like a brick. Ed. Boring old Ed.

He missed the way Esmerelda said it. Ed, or Ed*die*, with a lilt and a bit of va-va-voom.

Sitting at his desk, hands on the Underwood, the paper in the roller, blank, he squeezed his eyes shut and tried to concentrate.

If he was going to continue with the story society, then he must work on his memoir. Otherwise, he might as well stay home, watch *Jeopardy* and *Monday Night Football*.

However, no words came. What was it Jett said? Remember the good *and* bad times. Be honest. Real.

Well, he'd climbed into the co-op's attic this morning and carried down the Christmas decorations. With Halloween behind them now, the Christmas Cheer committee wanted to start planning, going over the lights, the fake holly wreath and garland, see what they needed new for this year.

Christmas. Hmm . . . Esmerelda sure enjoyed the holy season. Mostly because it came with doctored punch and spiked eggnog.

A memory suddenly surfaced, and Ed hammered at the keys. Oh boy, this was a good one.

On December 4, Holly came smiling into the world. I'll never forget riding home in the back of a taxi through a thick snow, holding her so close.

Esmerelda had the idea to go all out for the holiday. You know, set up a big tree with lots of ornaments and lights, use our new credit card to buy presents and throw a big party.

We had the prettiest baby in the world, why not show her off? I invited the boys from the printing plant and she invited her society friends.

The party was going to be a humdinger. We'd set it for the Saturday before Christmas, so the Friday before, we cleaned and polished the house.

Around nine, we collapsed on the couch with a glass of wine and cuddled up, enjoying the pretty tree, a bit of Bing on the hi-fi and Holly sleeping close by in her bassinet.

"Thank you, Eddie," Esmerelda said. "For Holly, for this lovely Christmas."

I can still taste her lips.

"Anything for you, my love. Anything for you."

Ed sat back, a bit drained, and reread his words. Should he go on? Write about the party? Maybe tell the truth?

"Dad?"

He glanced toward the kitchen as Holly entered with her usual tote bag full of fresh fruits and vegetables.

"What are you doing here?" He ripped the page from the typewriter and tucked it inside his story society folder. Then put it in the drawer.

"Same as I do every week."

"You come on Wednesdays. This is Monday."

"Dad, see this avocado? Eat it soon. It'll go bad." She smiled and began unloading, her eyes on him.

He glanced at his watch—seven fifteen—then peeked inside one of the totes. "I've got to go."

"Go ahead. I'll lock up. Can I meet this society sometime?"

"I-I'm not sure." He felt nervous, jittery, like he'd been caught with his hand in the cookie jar.

Someone knocked on the door. *Please, do not be Mabel.* "I'll call you later, Hol." He kissed her cheek then took his jacket from the coatrack in the corner.

When he opened the door, Chuck stood on the other side.

"I had a fare up this way and thought I'd see if you needed a ride. If we're going to get downtown by eight, we need to roll."

"Well, I'm ready."

But Holly was right behind him. "I'm Holly, Ed's daughter." His confident girl reached around Ed for a handshake.

"Chuck Mays, Ed's friend from the story society. You're on *Good Morning New York*?"

"I am." She turned to Ed. "So, what do you do at this society? Dad hasn't said much."

"Talk, mostly." Ed shoved Chuck toward the door. "Lock up on your way out, Hol."

"Talk about what?" Holly said like a nosy reporter and producer.

"Life," Chuck said. "Our troubles. Broken relationships."

"We eat, too, Chuck. Don't forget. Lexa's turn this week, I believe?" Ed turned to Holly. "This one eats like a horse."

He had to calm down, stop acting so jumpy. It's just he didn't want to bring up Esmerelda in front of Holly. Not yet.

"I'm standing right here, Ed," Chuck said. "Have you seen Jett eat?"

"Well, Dad has a lot of wisdom to offer."

"We love your dad's stories about your mom."

"My mom?"

Well, he'd said it. Dropped the grenade in the room. "We best be going, Chuck. We'll be late."

"He tells us every week how much he and your mother loved each other." Chuck bumped Ed with his elbow as he made his way from the apartment into the hall. "Gives us all hope. He's even read some of his memoir to us."

"About my mother?"

Ed's eyes pleaded with her. *Don't . . .*

"Your mother is Esmerelda, right?" Chuck glanced at Ed's empty hands. "You're not bringing any more of the story with you?"

"I've been kind of busy." With that he shoved Chuck toward the elevator. "Good night, Holly."

"Night, Dad."

"She seems nice," Chuck said, pushing the button for the lobby.

"A peach." Ed exhaled when the doors closed.

Close. Too close. Where his real world almost destroyed his pretend.

Chapter 33

JETT

Parking his bike inside the literary library foyer, he removed his helmet and jacket, then stooped to retie his Chuck Taylors.

The snow from the weekend had melted when Sunday jumped into the fifties. But this afternoon, the sun disappeared behind a blanket of clouds, taking yesterday's warmth with it.

Heading toward the Bower, he hoped against hope it wasn't his turn to bring the food.

Meanwhile, the jitters of seeing Lexa filled him. She was heading to Seattle this week to find a place. He sort of prayed she'd hate the city. Hate the long flight. But who was he kidding? She was the girl who'd traveled the world as a kid.

He also considered her assessment of their relationship. She was right. They were all wrong for each other. He didn't exactly see it, but between the mess with Gordon, Mom's wedding, and Storm's memorial, he was primed for emotional hogwash.

Just before he reached the Bower door, Gilda intercepted him. "Have you spoken to her, Jett?"

Her cloaked comment pricked his patience. "Just say what you have to say, Gilda. And how do you know so much?"

She adjusted the stack of books in her hand. "One truth. Opens a whole new world."

"What truth might that be?"

She tapped his chest. "The one lingering in here."

Jett nearly slapped her hand back as he sidestepped her touch. "You don't know me and my truth."

"Ah, well then . . ." Gilda moved around him, humming a tune that disrupted his inner man, and disappeared behind the door marked Private.

One day he was going to barge in and see exactly what went on behind that door.

Jett entered the Bower with an edge. "Sorry I'm late. A student stopped by my office—" The society stood by the food table, plates in hand, eyes on him. "Was it my turn?"

"Dude, I just texted you an hour ago," Chuck said.

"I know, I know, and I was about to order subs when the student came in, distressed over her grade." He pulled out his phone. "I got it. Pizza?"

"I was thinking Ed's pot roast." Chuck said.

"Or a nice, creamy squash soup," Coral said.

"From now on, the four of us will handle the food," Ed said. "Jett, you just be our fearless leader."

"Sorry again. Maybe I truly am the absentminded professor."

"Actually, it will just be the three of you," Lexa said, returning to her seat.

Jett's fingers trembled over his phone and he fat-fingered his search for pizza.

"Already ordered," Coral whispered, leaning close. "I have people."

He gave her a sheepish grin of thanks and lowered his backpack by his chair.

"What do you mean, three of us?" Ed was in his seat, propped up, looking wise and aged. Like a good grandpa.

"Lexa has a job offer in Seattle, Ed." So, Coral knew too. "She's flying out tomorrow to look at apartments."

"Won't be the same without you, Lex. What if another mysterious invitation goes out and we have to accept a new person?" Chuck frowned and deflated a little. "I was just getting used to you weirdos."

"It's what she does, you guys," Jett said. "Times get rough, Lexa leaves." He regretted his words the moment they hit the air.

She speared him with a glance. "This is not the same thing. This is me growing up and moving on. I've never done this on my own before. My moves were with my family or you, Jett. But this company is super excited to have me on board. It's a good opportunity."

"It's a great opportunity," Coral said.

Coral, don't back her up.

Ed reached over and patted her arm. "Lexa, girl, we'll miss you. This company must have impressed you an awful lot to leave us. We'll make your last story society a slam-bam goodbye party. Now, did someone order pizza? I'm a bit peckish."

"On its way," Coral said.

Jett noticed her hand resting on Chuck's. At least someone in this silly society found love.

"What's going on with you two?" He pointed to their touching limbs.

Coral giggled. The elegant, sophisticated beauty giggled. And the big guy's cheeks turned a brick red.

Coral spoke first, then Chuck. "I think we're in love."

"Something told me to go by her office Friday afternoon."

"He had no idea the takedown was happening."

Together they detailed the arrest of CCW's CEO and CFO during an all-hands meeting.

"Holy Toledo," Ed said. "How humiliating."

"I needed to scare honesty back into my troops. Lex, so after you and I talked the other night, five people have come to me privately to admit their part. They're going to testify against Blaire and Dak in order to save themselves."

Chuck and Coral, Lexa and Coral, Ed and Chuck. The group was melding. Bonding. Jett cut a glance to his ex-wife. And she was leaving. He hated to say it but this was typical. He'd thought she'd changed.

And just what truth was Gilda going on about?

"When I came back to my office and saw Chuck, I fell into his arms." Coral's fingers intertwined with his as she peered up at him. "My rock."

He blushed again. "Don't know how I can take the place of a prince but—"

"I asked him to come to church with me on Sunday and he said, 'Why not? I've been meaning to check out this God thing.'"

"G-good for you two."

"Enough about us. Jett—your publication, the reception." Coral raised the hand laced with Chuck's. "I'm in plus one."

They laughed in harmony. Heaven help him, if they kissed, he'd puke. For real.

"I'm in too," Ed said, tapping his heart. "Esmerelda will come with me."

"I met Ed's daughter tonight," Chuck said. "Holly."

"A good girl, but we don't need to talk about Holly." Ed made a *pffbtt* sound.

Jett turned at the knock on the door. "Food. Coral, what do I owe you?"

When he opened the door, a stunning blonde from morning TV stood on the other side.

∼

ED

"I'm looking for my father, Ed Marshall."

Holly? Couldn't be. She was home with Brant and the kids by now. Ed braced himself as Jett stepped aside. She had his memoir folder in her hands.

"Hol, you're interrupting our meeting." Ed reached for the folder. "How'd you find me?"

She flashed the original invitation. "I also found your memoir." She pointed to the folder now safe in his hands. But the stuff inside was personal and private. "Dad, are you okay?"

"Do I look okay?" Ed turned her toward the door. "I'll talk to you later. Best get on home to your family. Give them my love."

"Can't she stay?" Lexa said. "I'd like to meet her."

"Yeah, Ed, let her stay." Chuck pushed the Bower door wider. "Come on in. Jett can find you a chair."

"But this is our private club." Ed huffed and puffed in his best "Dad" tone. "Hol, Brant will be wanting his supper."

"Then he can cook it himself. Hi, I'm Holly."

She shook hands with Lexa and Jett, then Coral.

"I don't know if Dad told you but if you ever want to tell your story, *Good Morning*—"

"Holly, no panhandling with my friends. If you're going to stay, be quiet." But why would she stay? No one would speak in front of her. Not openly or honestly. They were just beginning to open up to one another.

"I've been to this library before but not this room. It's charming. So old-world and cozy." Holly settled in as if she'd been here from day one.

She laughed at Chuck's flat jokes. Talked makeup with Coral. Praised Lexa for her stint at ZB Enterprises and gave her a half dozen restaurants she "just had to try" once she moved to Seattle.

With Jett, she talked academic shop as if she, too, had a PhD and expert knowledge of classic literature.

Ed was beginning to see firsthand why she was so good at her job.

"Jett, here's my card." Holly reached for a card case in her bag. "Call me. I think I can get you on the show. We can do a little literature corner."

"I'm not sure a stuffy book written for scholars will entertain your audience."

"No, but you will. And you are Bear Wilder's son. I like the contrast. Adventure man raises a bookworm. And Coral, no pressure. But if you want to talk ideas, just let me know. I saw Prince Augustus just got engaged."

"He did. I'm happy for him."

While Coral kept her feelings close to her chest, Holly managed to own the room. And before he knew it, Ed's buttons were popping.

"So tell us what you remember about your mom," Lexa said. "Ed's inspiring us with their love story. What do you remember most about her?"

And there went all his pride.

"My mother?" Holly glanced at Ed. "I, um, I really don't remember much. She left when I was young."

"That's right," Ed said. "Hol was so young."

"My grandmother died when I was ten. I have a lot of memories of her." *Thank you, Chuck. Kindly don't help, please.*

"Ten? I was two when Mom left. Or not quite."

"Numbers. Two, ten, who cares." Ed forced a laugh. "I get mixed up, can't trust my memories either."

"So you know about the bridge then?" *Chuck, will you please be quiet.* Ed fussed and twisted in his chair. *Say something, man. Say something.* But what?

"The bridge?" Holly looked at him with those big blue eyes and for a moment, she was two again with tears in her eyes, crying for Mommy, but all he could do was hold her and rock her, promising Mommy would be right back.

"Where your dad proposed to your mom."

"Daddy, you proposed to Esmerelda on a bridge?"

Ed cleared his throat. "I did. I never told you. On the GW."

"The GW? But she jumped from the GW." *Holly, so honest, telling the only story she knew. Thanks to Aunt Faye.*

"Ed?" Chuck had more ammunition now and Ed figured he wouldn't hesitate to use it.

His pulse thumped through his chest. *Tell them. Tell them. Tell them.*

"She jumped? What's this?" Lexa's, Coral's, and Jett's voices blended and mingled.

"Dad?" Holly pressed her hand to his. "Why didn't you tell me you proposed to Esmerelda on the bridge?"

"Because, I, well—" *Tell them.* Glancing around he met five sets of eyes, all intent on him. "I, um, didn't. I meant to but I actually didn't propose on the bridge."

"I knew it."

"Chuck, will you be quiet?" Lexa said with enough force to make the big man's cheeks blush.

But he did propose in her father's living room. And did make love to her for the first time in the garden under the glow of kitchen lights.

For a long time, no one said anything. When a warm drop of water hit Ed's hand, he realized he'd been crying.

"She was a drug addict," he said slow and low, more to his chest than his friends. "And a perpetual adulterer." Holly gripped his hand for dear life. "She left once before Holly was born, then again when she was two. I thought she'd come back. She adored Holly. Everyone said she just needed a break. She was always a bit of a free feather. Except her father knew. He said, 'Never could control her. Sorry to have dumped her off on you, Ed.'" Someone stuffed a large soft tissue in his hand. "In '80, she fell from the GW."

"Oh, Ed—" Coral said in harmony with Lexa, who scooted her chair over and set her right hand on his left.

"She never meant to fall. She just wanted to fly." He tried to compose himself but he shivered and shook, slipping from the soft leather chair to the floor. Chuck caught him as his knees knocked the hardwood. "Why wouldn't she let me love her? Why wasn't I enough? Holly, you were the light of our lives. She loved you, she did, I know she did. If only I'd been enough."

"Daddy." Holly gathered him and brushed her hand over his hair, whispering everything was going to be all right. "Esmerelda loved you in her way, I'm sure. But she loved herself more. She needed help, but no one could reach her. Not even Aunt Faye. Her life was not your fault."

The daughter he'd cradled, cradled him. The young girl he'd comforted, now comforted him.

"I loved her. I always loved her. Why couldn't she see? Why?"

"Dad, please, don't blame yourself. Esmerelda lived her life her way."

Forehead to the carpet, Ed wept for the past forty years. For what he'd lost. For Esmerelda's bound up and hopeless existence. For Holly.

Somewhere a door opened and closed. The aroma of tomato sauce and melting cheese wafted on the air.

But for a long time no one moved while he, an old man, finally came to terms with the past.

Sitting up, he blew his nose and tried to collect himself. Well, he'd told them. The truth was out.

"A hand, Chuck?" Ed used the man's strength to leave the floor.

While Lexa and Jett passed around plates with pizza slices, Ed retreated to his chair, trying to find himself, trying to see what the world looked like from behind his wall.

Brighter. Much brighter.

Nevertheless, the pieces he'd used to build his memories were scattered. When he tried to gather them back, he realized they were nothing more than moth-eaten cardboard.

He couldn't rebuild his memories of Esmerelda, because they never really existed.

And his friends . . . They said nothing. Just showed kindness and understanding. He took a bite of pizza, then set his plate aside.

"I'm sorry, everyone," he said. "I was just making up my love story with Esmerelda. Jett, you were right when you said I needed to tell the good and the bad. But there was so much bad I wanted to make up the good. Pretend we lived the life we pledged to one another. I know. She was never really what I saw. Faye used to tell me, 'Take off those love goggles, Ed.'"

"But you and I had a good life, Dad, didn't we?" Tears tenderized Holly's soft tone. "You were there for me and I will always, always be grateful." She gave him a shoulder hug before turning to the circle. "When I was a teenager I used to tell him to date. But he said I was his priority and—"

"I'd convinced myself Esmerelda was coming back. That she'd figured out I loved her, and that you were an amazing kid, Hol."

"Sounds like Hosea," Coral said. "The man who married and loved a prostitute."

"Well, my hat's off to him. It's not an easy row to hoe."

"So Esmerelda never found what she was looking for?" Jett said.

"She found it all right. It just didn't include being a wife and mother. Esmie was all about the counterculture of the early seventies. She partied her way through her trust fund. Somehow she met a Hollywood agent and ran off with him. He took the last of her money and dumped her. Her mother sent her money to come home, hoping she'd grown up, learned her lesson, and settled down. But she just found someone else to distract her from real life. She'd only been back from California for six months when she fell from the George Washington."

"Why did she jump? Do you know? Did she leave a note?"

Ed shivered, his hands curled into taut fists, his jaw so tight his head ached. "It was me. I am the reason she jumped."

"Dad, no," Holly said. "What are you talking about?"

"I found her. In Bryant Park. You kids don't know how rough the city was in the seventies. Gotham was a rough place with high crime, drugs, and prostitution from the Bowery to Times Square. When my parents kept Holly, I'd look for Esmerelda. If not for my sake, for hers. Bryant Park was the biggest drug hangout, so I went, you know, just to see." He glanced at Jett. "If I wrote about what I saw that night, no one would believe me. Kids passed out with needles in their arms, couples copulating in the open, a man screaming, running naked toward the street. I was about to give up when I saw her. She sat up and looked straight at me. 'Eddie,' she said.

"She was so helpless and frail. I washed her face and bought her some dinner. She was high but manageable, and almost seemed like her old self. Out of nowhere she asked me to tell her something good. So I did." His eyes puddled when he looked at Holly. "I told her about you. Then I hailed a cab and took her to the GW. We used to go there and watch the city lights, talk of a big life. I thought if I reminded her of our dreams, she'd want to come home, accept the security I offered. I told her over and over Holly and I needed and wanted her." The truth made him breathless.

"Dad, you never told me."

"She was so calm on the walk up, listening to my stories. Then she changed. I don't know if the drugs were kicking in or waning, but she became irrational, accused me of wanting to kill her. She ran off. It was dusk and I had a hard time seeing her between shadows. When I caught up to her, she'd climbed up on the suspensions."

"You were there when she jumped?" Lexa said.

"Yes." The heat of his confession soaked him with perspiration. The Bower door opened and closed. Jett and his backpack were gone.

"Ed?" Coral said, leaning forward. "You actually have a great love story. You loved when it wasn't easy. You rescued your wife from a drug park, gave her something to eat, reminded her of your love."

"Then why does it feel like I failed? That her death is on my hands?"

"Love isn't love just because someone receives it or reciprocates," Coral said. "Loving someone who doesn't love you in return is perhaps the greatest kind of love. Sacrificial. Without demand or condition."

"Yet it led to her death." He exhaled. The truth became easier to tell as the shadows of his fantasy faded. "And I'll be honest, I hated her for the longest time. Sometimes I still do."

"Dad, thank you for giving everything to me. For being so selfless." Holly's makeup was a watery mess.

"I'd do it over and over." Ed touched his daughter's chin. "You made my life worth living. We had a happy home. I just thought you deserved your mother to be a part of it."

"Ed, if you spend all your time trying to fix your past, you'll miss right now." This fine wisdom came from Lexa.

"Guess I'm a bit scared. I got it so wrong the first time."

"But you have me to help this time." Holly picked up her slice and took a hungry bite. "I really like your neighbor, Mabel."

"Oh, pshaw. That nosy old biddy."

"She's beautiful. Smart. You guys should see her. Coral, she used to edit *Fashion Weekly*."

"I loved that magazine," Coral said. "My grandmother knew the editors well. I bet she knew Mabel."

Ed bit into his pizza, suddenly famished, suddenly free for the first time in forty years. He had more threads to untangle but this felt good. Really good.

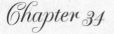

LEXA

"Good night."

Standing on Fifth Avenue, the night chill sinking in and causing her arm to ache, she bid farewell to her friends. Holly and Ed accepted a ride with Chuck and headed north.

Coral stood beside Lexa, her car and driver waiting on the corner. "What's up with Jett?"

"I'm not sure, but Ed's story touched something. Jett was on the mountain with his brother when he died. That might be it."

"And you don't know what happened?"

"He won't tell."

"Lexa, I know you two care about each other, but it's not your responsibility to fix him," Coral said.

"What makes you think I'm trying to fix him?"

"Lexa, please, I may not have known you long but I've figured out you're a fixer. An organizer. A helper. I get it. Being needed is a high value to you, but you cannot make Jett face something he's not willing to face. Look at Ed. Took him almost forty years to admit the realities of his wife."

"Jett and I had a similar conversation at his mother's wedding."

"What exactly happened between you?" Coral tied the belt of her leather coat when the wind took an icy turn.

"We fell apart. Neither one of us stopped it. When Storm died, he disappeared into a place I couldn't go. I got fed up, never said anything, and left. He never came after me." With each retelling of their story, the truth became so clear. They were not meant to be. "We had issues. I was the girl who wanted to be chased and he was the boy who didn't want to run."

"Will you come to his reception?" Coral pressed her hand on Lexa's arm. "I think it would mean a lot to him."

"I may be in Seattle."

"Which makes me sad. For me," Coral said. "I'm happy for you but I'll miss you. I'm scared to think who will fill your chair."

"Maybe Holly."

Coral flipped her coat collar against the thickening chill. "Maybe."

"You should do it, you know, Coral," Lexa said. "Tell your truth. Your story."

"I don't know what you mean."

"I think you do."

"But I'll pretend I don't." Coral slipped her arm gingerly through Lexa's. "Come on, gimpy. I'll take you home. When does this final cast come off?"

"Gimpy? And my *brace* comes off next week."

In the back of the Range Rover, Lexa and Coral settled down with their phones. After a small debate with herself, Lexa texted Jett.

You okay?

By the time the driver turned down her MacDougal Street, he'd not responded. Nor by the time she'd readied for bed and checked her suitcase for tomorrow's apartment-hunting trip.

She dragged Abby's air mattress across the hall. Lexa was finally well enough to climb her loft.

When she made a cup of tea and settled on the window seat and looked out on the city of 1.2 million, he'd still not texted.

She'd grown up here. In Greenwich Village. Found a piece of herself in the city that never slept. She'd known success and failure, love and heartache.

When her phone pinged, she snatched it up from the bench. But it was Skipper, not Jett.

Good luck tomorrow. Text me LOTS of pictures.

Will do. Love you.

Resting against the windowsill, music rising up from the street, she sent Jett one last message.

Why'd you leave, fearless leader? You should've seen Ed's change after he finished his story. And he chowed down on some pizza. Holly's cool, don't you think?

Just as she was about to press send, Coral's observation echoed. *You're a fixer. Jett has to work this out.*

Hitting the back space, Lexa deleted the message and carried her phone up to bed. He'd text her when he was ready.

She tried to sleep but found herself dozing between images of the life she had in Manhattan and the life she anticipated in the Northwest.

Then she saw Jett, felt him, sitting at his banquette alone, wrestling with his painful, untold story.

Oh, Jett. And she knew. She loved him with every fiber of her being.

❦

ED

Mrs. Thompson in apartment 2A said he had a skip in his weary old step. He was inclined to agree. Even with his heavy toolbox in one hand.

"Take me up," he said, patting the side of the ancient elevator box. He'd called the head of the co-op association this morning and told them it was time to upgrade. "Last thing you want is a tenant getting stuck between floors."

The woman miraculously agreed. Work on a replacement would begin next week.

Unlocking his apartment, he gazed toward Mabel's door. She hadn't popped out at him since he groused at her a few weeks ago.

But ever since Monday night, since the healing, he had a mind to chat with her. Dang it, he *was* free. For forty years, he'd clung to a lie, to guilt, to a fantasy of if-onlys.

He wasn't responsible for Esmerelda's death or for ruining her life. God, should He exist and care about ol' Ed Marshall, had finally shown him the light.

Setting his toolbox down with a bang, he glanced toward Mabel's closed door once more. He had a plan. If it failed, well, he'd come up with another plan.

Inside, he put his tools away and checked the pot roast he'd put in the Crock-Pot before breakfast.

The aroma of the meat along with the garlic, onion, olive oil, and smoked paprika made his stomach grab his ribs, trying for a look-see.

He checked to see if the wine was properly chilled, then headed for the shower. Dinner would be ready in a half hour.

Donning his blue suit and matching tie, he checked his appearance, smoothed back his damp gray hair, and leaned toward the mirror.

Ed Marshall, you're not a bad-looking cuss.

Holly said there was something different about him. She was right. He could finally see for himself. The lie was gone.

She had stayed with him Monday night and again on Tuesday. They talked a lot, especially about Esmerelda. He told Holly the cold, hard truth from their first meeting to their last.

Even the Christmas memory he'd penned ended with what really happened. Not what he wished had happened. Esmerelda drunk in the stairwell, high on reefer.

He could admit it now, but that night he realized the kind of woman he'd married and lost a bit of hope.

But this Friday night, he charted a new course. Never too late to begin again. As long as he had breath in his lungs.

He buttoned his jacket, then unbuttoned it. Buttoned was too formal. And he could finally admit Esmerelda hated him in suits. She'd never even *seen* him in this one.

Hearing a sound in the hall, he scooted out of the bedroom, around the living room wall, and jerked open the door.

"Mabel."

"Ed, sorry, I didn't mean to disturb you." She carried a loaded tote toward her place, a thin weariness in her voice. "I'll be out of your hair. Don't worry. I won't invite you in for brownies."

"Mabel?"

"What is it, Ed?" She worked her key into the lock without looking back. "I've had a long day babysitting my grandkids."

He ran to carry her bags inside. She looked frazzled but very pretty. "How were the grandkids?"

"Energetic." She set her pocketbook on the counter. "What's going on?"

"Will you have dinner with me?"

"Now?" She made a face and reached into one of the totes for a gallon of ice cream.

"Yes, or when you're ready. The pot roast is almost done. I'm just letting it stand. Who knew you had to let beef stand?" He'd been reading up, learning to cook. Poor Holly had to survive on his fried chicken and spaghetti until she took on food chores in high school. "Is fifteen minutes enough time?"

"You're serious?"

"Yes, ma'am, I am."

She glanced down at her wrinkled top and jeans. "I'll need to change."

"I'll leave my door open."

"You're wearing a suit."

"I like to dress up for the women in my life."

She blushed and giggled, and Ed felt a bit dizzy. "What's gotten into you?"

"Truth. And it's set me free."

He helped her unpack her groceries, laughing at her stories of what the two-year-old learned to say last week, then left her to change. He did a jig back to his place and clicked his heels.

Oomph. He fell against the wall. Too old for heel clicks. Maybe he wasn't as young as he used to be, but his heart was going zing, zing, zing.

He set the table with a cloth and china plates. Yes, the ones he and Esmerelda got for their wedding. She scorned them. They were too much like her parents'. He planned to give them to Holly one day. Or his grandchildren. Whichever one wanted them.

Or maybe he'd throw them out and start over. They represented nothing but heartache. But tonight, he decided they represented redemption.

Lighting a few candles, he surveyed the romantic scene. With a nervous twitch, he doused the flames. Too much. *You'll scare her, Ed.*

In his den sat a stack of papers. Typewritten with a fury this week. His story. The real story of raising his daughter alone while trying to hold on to the dream of Esmerelda.

This version had emotion and lots of it. And all the dark, ugly truths.

When he'd written a bit more, he was going to show Jett. He hoped the professor hadn't abandoned their little society. It was just getting good.

He'd just set the pot roast on a serving platter when his phone rang.

"Hey, Dad, just calling to see how you're doing?" She'd called almost every night since the big confession. Since he cried against her.

"Great. Fixing a pot roast."

"A pot roast? That's a pretty big meal for one man."

"Holly," Ed said, "I have a date. At least I think I do."

"A date? Wow, Papa, with who? Don't tell me. Mabel?"

"Yes, but shhh, it's just dinner. There she is at the door."

"Call me later. Tell me everything." Her laugh took him back to when she went out the door on a date.

"*Wake me up when you get home. Tell me everything.*"

"Smells wonderful," Mabel said, holding up a foil-wrapped dish. "I hope you don't mind but I brought a contribution of my own."

Ed slid off the covering. "Brownies."

"I know you shoved them away before but—"

He kissed her without hesitation and prejudice, one hand trembling against her back, the other slipping around her waist.

He was gentle, if not tentative. It'd been a long time since he tasted a woman. Mabel gasped at first, then laid her arm about his neck.

"What's all this?" she said when he finally raised his head. Her eyes beamed with approval.

"About getting on track. Joining the land of the living." He set the brownies on the counter, then took out a knife. "Let's start with dessert. I've been waiting a long, long time to eat a brownie again."

∽

CORAL

The first week since the FBI cuffed and carried out her chief officers was in the history books. She was exhausted yet invigorated.

And she was in love. She felt Chuck's presence everywhere she went. They texted each other all day. Met for lunch whenever possible, and last night, they dined on her terrace overlooking the city.

Next week she would head out on the goodwill tour to regional reps and distributors. And it looked like visits to the London and Paris offices would be needed before the end of the year.

In more good news, Pink Coral was continuing to sell, and Crimson Coral was on the fast track for a holiday release.

She'd given the design team carte blanche, and the mock-ups and product tests were spot-on.

But it was five o'clock on Friday. She was heading home. Tonight was her first party with church friends. She'd invited Jett, but he declined. This time. She'd get him over sooner or later. And she still struggled to think of Lexa moving across the country.

Ed also declined but promised to come to her next movie night.

She must've called her housekeeper and chef five times each today to make sure the food and house were ready.

Around three when she was tempted to call again, she felt the peace in the air. *Leave it alone. It'll be fine.*

She was even more nervous to see Chuck. Not nervous, excited. He loved church. Sang the songs so loud she was forced to sing louder herself. He met with the pastor and even volunteered for an early morning prayer meeting.

She hadn't even done that yet.

She was falling in love, but he seemed stuck on her former life as an almost princess. But she was *so* Julia Roberts in *Notting Hill.* Just a girl asking a boy to love her.

"Matt, is the car here?" She stuck her head around the door between her office and her assistant's.

"On his way. And you have a message from Holly Cook, one of the producers from *Good Morning, New York.* She wants to know if you'll do an interview with them about the prince. She said no pressure. She's willing to just talk. I thanked her and told her no. I can't believe the media is still hounding you—"

"Tell her yes." Her response settled. Was she really willing to tell her story to the world? "I'll do it."

Matt's wide eyes said a million words. She'd turned down every media outlet and millions of dollars to keep her story private.

"Are you sure?"

Coral thought for a moment. "Yes, I'm sure. I've met her. She's the daughter of a very good friend. I trust her."

"Any particular time?" Matt launched her calendar and scrolled through the blocked-out, busy weeks.

"You coordinate. Just let me know. See you Monday, Matt."

She was ready to be bold and tell the whole truth of why she left

Gus. Including her run-in with God. And maybe hint she'd found love once again.

⌒

CHUCK

He had a date. Tonight. With Coral. Nothing fancy. A movie at her place with new friends from church. So yeah, it wasn't really a date. It was a get-together he was invited to attend.

But he jumped at the chance to be with her, to get to know her more as well as her church friends.

His impression of churchgoers had never been too favorable, but the past two Sundays at Grace Church had started to redraw his picture.

He hoped they were as cool tonight as they were in the church foyer, because last week he'd signed up for this God journey. Handed over control of his life to a man named Jesus. Who was also God.

Yeah, sure, he made the decision quick, but he knew it was right. In his gut. With or without Coral, he was going for it. She just made the ride so much sweeter.

In the meantime, he had a fare to pick up in midtown. He slowed as he made his way down Broadway looking for a woman in a red coat and black boots.

He pulled to an open spot along the curb when his phone pinged. She was on her way.

While waiting, he thumbed through his messages, rereading a text sent last night from Trudy's Mom, Wanda.

> I talked to her. She's not as riled about Coral as she was or the fact Jakey said he saw you. Lay low and hang in there.

Chuck nearly wept when he read her words. There was hope. The backseat passenger door opened. "Sorry I'm late."

"I almost left." He glanced at the woman via the mirror. "JFK? Hey, you're the agent."

"What do you know? The magic-book man. Yes, JFK."

"Right, the magic book."

"I had lunch with a children's publisher a few weeks ago and in the course of conversation, told her your idea. She loved it. I said too bad because he was my Uber driver and I couldn't remember his name."

"Chuck Mays." He pulled into traffic. "And my idea is just that, an idea."

"But a great one. I'm putting your name in my contacts. What's your phone number?"

He rattled it off, wedging through midtown traffic, the conversation jerking him a bit sideways. He wasn't a writer.

"Did you give my card to Jett Wilder?"

"I did."

"And?"

"If he hasn't called you, there's your answer."

"Remind him I'm available if he wants to talk. Now tell me what's happened in your life since you last drove me around town."

He told her the simple version of the kids' party, of his friends at the society, and the movie he was taking in tonight with new church friends.

She told him how her high-maintenance author was driving her nuts, but since her book sold at auction for five hundred grand, she was putting up with her. For now.

When Chuck arrived at the airport, Lucy dropped her card into the passenger seat again along with a twenty. "Put my number in your phone. See you again, magic-book man."

For the rest of the day, he thought a lot about his magic book. More stories came to mind. Different adventures his young characters could take.

When he was done for the day, he headed to Ed's, where he added Lucy's number to his contacts and jotted down his ideas on a sheet of paper from the stack Ed kept by his typewriter.

Then he shot the breeze with his friend until it was time to shower and head to Coral's Park Avenue penthouse.

Mysterious invitations. Agents requesting his book idea. Gorgeous heiresses wanting to hang out with him. His ex-mother-in-law texting him to hang in there.

Maybe there was a God looking out for him. Despite his mistakes.

At Coral's, she knocked his socks off when she answered the door. She wore a white T-shirt and snug jeans, and her long blonde hair flowed loose down her back.

"I'm glad you're here." She reached for his hand. "Kirk and Mari just arrived. They have the cutest baby—"

He caught her in his arms and lowered his lips to hers as he ran his hand down her back. She was curvy and warm beneath his palm, and the press of her body made him feel a little bit more whole.

Her lips surrendered to his and when he pulled her closer, he could almost taste the goodness of her heart.

When he broke away, she smiled up at him. "I knew you'd be a good kisser, Chuck Mays."

"Well, if you think I'm a good kisser you should—"

"Hey, don't rev the engine too loud." She tugged on his plaid shirt. "We're not married yet." She gave him a deep, lush kiss. "Come on. I think I smell popcorn. Kirk, Mari, you remember Chuck. My boyfriend."

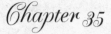

Chapter 35

LEXA

Schlepping through her tiny living room in her comfy sweats with her hair pulled back in a ponytail, she carried her ZB Burger past the open door, the sound of life beyond her walls echoing.

Only tonight wasn't Friday but Sunday. And she'd just arrived home from five days in Seattle. She'd found a penthouse overlooking the bay.

She'd move in on the twenty-fifth.

Dropping into her red chair, she bit into the juicy burger. She was going to miss her favorite gourmet burger. Zane had yet to open a store in the Pacific Northwest.

Wiping her chin with her napkin, she dusted off a bit of her CCW charcoal mask. She'd considered changing her routine once she got settled in Seattle, take advantage of a fresh start and not spend her weekends holed up with goop on her face.

Seattle had a lot of unique culture to explore.

She stuffed a truffle fry in her mouth, washed it down with a swig of Diet Coke, then scanned email on her phone.

Jenn and Ki weren't waiting for her to be boots on the ground. Lexa had officially started work November 11 when Ki and Jenn shifted the day-to-day operations to her.

Human resources, accounting, admin, marketing and promotion, community initiatives, production, and sales were under her command.

Everything she'd handled with Zane. The key word being *with*. She felt a bit alone and adrift at The Glass Fork.

Ki wasn't one for details. He liked to dump things over the wall and move on. He also traveled and worked with large retail outlets and celebrity endorsements. Jenn was eyeball-deep in recipe development and had suddenly become unreachable.

Another truffle fry eased her growing anxiety. Was she in over her head? Zane's lack of confidence in promoting her shouted from the rooftops of her mind.

You're not ready!

Shaking off the thought, she distracted herself with a Netflix rerun. When her phone buzzed, she was happy to see Coral's name and number.

"I loved the picture of your place. How's it being back in New York?"

"Good. Sad. But I love my new apartment. The bay is beautiful at night."

They talked for a long time about Seattle and how to jump into the job with both feet. Coral had a lot of wisdom and advice.

Then she shifted the conversation.

"Since you're not going out until the twenty-fifth, won't you come to Jett's reception? Let it be our final night together as a society before you leave."

"I don't think he's talking to me. I sent him a picture of my apartment and he just said, 'Cool.' I'm not sure he'd want me there."

"He's hiding because you're leaving and he's in love with you."

"Coral, you're the one who's in love."

"I know." She laughed. "He kissed me."

"Chuck? Kissed you? Spill, girl. Spill."

And so the conversation flowed. Chuck was a gentle giant, a great kisser, and Coral was pretty sure, "the one."

"Which brings me back to Jett. Please come."

Lexa set her takeout container on the floor. "I think it will make leaving too hard, Coral. I'd rather have a clean break. No formal goodbye. Just an expectation I'll see him one day. Run into him on the street. Never mind our streets are three thousand miles apart."

"Are you sure you want to move across the country?"

"Weren't you the one who told me I couldn't fix Jett?"

"Don't bite me with my own advice."

"It's a great job, exactly what I want. It feels like . . . kismet." Jett used to love that word.

"Well, if you're sure . . ." Coral's voice dropped low. "I'll text you from the reception. And we're having lunch before you go. I insist."

Lexa laughed through a rise of tears. "Fine. Tuesday? At Virgil's? And no surprises. Just you and me."

Coral updated Lexa on CCW and the holiday launch of Crimson Coral. When they got to talking of marketing, Lexa brainstormed several ideas with the cosmetic heiress.

By the time they hung up, Coral had a list of ten ideas.

"No charge," Lexa said. "My parting gift to you."

They'd just hung up when a knock rattled her door.

"Abby? Come on in. It's open." Lexa dumped the burger and fry wrappers in the trash. "What do you have going on tonight? Oh, do you want my water purifier? I'm not going to take it."

When she came out of the kitchen, the diminutive, lovely Gilda from the library stood in the living room.

"Gilda, what are you doing here?"

"Take this to Jett." She handed over a leather satchel. Lexa recognized it as his much-used and favorite bag from college. "Tonight."

"The reception? I'm not going. Can't you give this to him at the next society meeting? And how do you know about tonight?"

"The unpublished manuscript is inside. It's time. He won't have the courage without you." When Gilda touched Lexa's arm, an electric surge charged through her. "It's time. And Lexa, no more running."

"Running? I'm not running. I'm, I'm *advancing*."

The woman left without another word as the worn and scuffed satchel swung from Lexa's hand. A drop of her crusty charcoal mask drifted toward the floor.

༄

JETT

The cocktail party was hosted by the college president at his Riverside residence, a grand penthouse with a view of the park and river.

Decked in a rented tux and his trademark high-tops, Jett circulated, chatting in circles of threes and fours with his colleagues and members of the literati.

Across the room, he made eye contact with the most recent person to enter—Tenley Roth—on the arm of her husband, a tanned man in khakis and a button-down.

For all the times he wanted to meet her and she refused, he had nothing to say to her now.

What could he say? "Hey, was your great-great-grandfather a fraud?" Or, "Did Birdie Ainsworth write his books?"

In truth, he was the bigger hypocrite. Because even after all the Monday night story society meetings, where the deepest secrets flooded out of his fellow members, he still wasn't honest with himself.

Ed's story of watching Esmerelda fly from the bridge shook him. Plagued his sleep. Even now, the similarities between their stories haunted him.

"Greg, nice to see you." He stepped toward a colleague and away from his discomfort.

Dealing with the truth about that day on the mountain was one thing. It was another to be faced with a professional crisis. All the world seemed to want from him was truth, and he couldn't give it. He was still that kid hiding in the loft, weeping into the hay.

It didn't help that for the past three weeks, every faculty meeting, every hallway conversation, every staff email was about how they'd allocate the ten million.

Continuing his motion around the large open room, Jett smiled, relieved, to see Coral and Chuck enter with Ed and a very lovely, refined woman.

"Jett, this is posh." Coral gave him a friendly kiss on the cheek. "And I've been to a lot of these things."

"Welcome to the academic world, where we look like we have money but we don't."

"Except a ten-million-dollar windfall." Chuck, also in a tux, slapped his big paw into Jett's. "Nice digs." He scanned the ornate reception room with the crystal globe chandelier. "Is this your future? University president?"

"Too much politicking for me."

"Where's the hors d'oeuvres?" Ed poked his head into the gathering. "Everyone, this is Mabel Cochran, my neighbor and lady friend."

He'd overlooked the black-tie requirement but looked dapper in his blue suit. Even better, the old man looked happy. Really happy. Deep-down-in-his-bones happy. Jett wondered what that felt like. He wasn't sure he'd ever known.

"Congratulations, Jett," Mabel said. "Ed tells me this is a big deal for you and the college. You've published a book or something."

"Yes, about Gordon Phipps Roth."

"Really? I loved his books," Mabel said. "Read them all in my twenties. He was a very inspiring storyteller."

"Mabel." Ed tugged on her arm. "Let's check out the food table. Jett, we'll be back."

"Whoa, wait a minute." Jett pulled him back, letting Mabel go on ahead. "Ed, buddy, what's going on?" Coral and Chuck joined the huddle.

"She's my neighbor. Been friends for a while. But once I broke free of how I saw Esmerelda, I invited the lovely creature who lived down the hall to dinner."

Ed peeled away, and Chuck murmured, "Something tells me he's not long for the single life."

"Something tells me you two aren't either," Jett said. He'd noticed how cozy they'd been at the story society last Monday.

Lexa's missing presence suddenly felt enormous.

"I texted and called her," Coral said, as if reading Jett's thoughts. "But she said she thought it best to bow out quietly."

"This is typical Lex," Jett said. "She won't be here."

"Jett, you have to figure out a way to talk to her before she leaves."

"And say what, Coral? 'Stay'? I can't offer her what she wants."

"She wants you."

"Does she know that?"

"Jett." Renée approached. "We need you. Wealthy alumni wanting to talk to the man of the hour. Coral Winthrop, hello, so glad you're here."

As he talked with the former New York College students, his thoughts were on Lexa. Coral said she wanted him. How did she know? Did Lexa say so?

After his speech, he would call her. Saying goodbye would be the hardest thing, but he couldn't let her go without telling her how he felt. All the way. No holding back.

Storm, Gordon, his mother . . . All paled in comparison. They were the past. Lexa was his right-now, his future.

"May I have your attention? Please, everyone . . ." President Gee dinged the side of his wine glass with his big university ring and stood behind the podium. "We are honored to have with us Elijah Roth, from the Roth Foundation, established to support and expand the world of literature." He paused for applause. "We are joined by other members of the Roth family. Elijah's father, Richard, and also Gordon's great-great-granddaughter and Conrad Roth's daughter, Tenley Roth." Elijah, Richard, and Tenley stood to a hearty welcome. "Tenley is here with her husband, Jonas Sullivan, and has just released her fifth novel."

The president waxed on about the Gordon Phipps Roth School of American Literature and hailed the Roth Foundation as a cornerstone to the preservation of the written word in print and electronic forms.

Then he introduced Elijah. Nerves spiked in Jett, the kind that made him want to run. The room was so hot. Crowded. He tugged at his collar, loosening his tie.

"The board of directors at the Roth Foundation have been

looking for a college or university to partner with for some time. The continued success of Gordon's work has allowed us to amass a sizeable endowment for a partnership with a learning institution. After meeting with President Gee, Dean Hanover of the College of English, and his incredible staff, we are pleased to announce an endowment of ten million dollars to establish the Gordon Phipps Roth School of American Literature at the New York College."

The news was old. Everyone knew. But the faculty and guests cheered and applauded with polite dignity.

"We are also pleased that one of your own has just published an in-depth, well-researched, scholarly work on Gordon. As you know, there have been rumors that GPR employed a ghostwriter. While unfounded, the lies and whispers continued. But through Jett Wilder's work, Gordon's name, reputation, and standing among American literary giants will endure." All eyes turned to Jett. "Ladies and gentlemen, I give you Jett Wilder."

The applause pushed him forward along with Chuck's hearty back slap. Pulling his notes from his inside pocket, he stood at the podium waiting for the applause of nearly a hundred guests to die down.

He tugged at his collar again. Could someone open a window? The room was a sauna.

Clearing his throat, he gulped from the water glass and retrieved his notes.

"I first encountered Gordon's books as a boy, a twelve-year-old hurting from his parents' divorce. While I was not GPR's intended reader, I lived the magic of Gordon's stories. Elizabeth, the heroine of *The Girl in the Carriage*, was my pin-up girl." The laugh eased his tension. "When I felt lonely or afraid, I turned to stories. Mostly Gordon's. I imagined growing up into the life he wrote about in his books. Even the *House in Murray Hill*, with its threat of death and heartache, inspired me. He wrote with a beautiful, specific clarion voice. One of purity and sincerity, one without guile." When he looked up, he saw his friends—the story society. Ed, Chuck, Coral and—

Lexa. Wearing the dress from the wedding. She squeezed past the startled guests, a satchel in her hand. His old FSU bag.

He gripped the side of the podium and stumbled on with his speech. "But, um, it was *The Girl in the Carriage* that changed my life." Lexa whispered something to Coral, then caught his eye and patted the side of the satchel. What was she doing?

"And we all know how it changed Gordon's. In grad school, when my marriage was failing, I read *Love on the Thames*, and *Winter in New York*, over and over. After my brother's tragic death, *The House in Murray Hill* once again gave me hope. It was one of the first books in which Gordon wrote freely of his faith. While writing my own space-navy novel, I read GPR over and over. Gordon inspired not only me but more than five hundred million readers and writers around the globe and down the corridors of time.

"The Roth Foundation's generous endowment will make it possible for—" Lexa raised the satchel again. People were turning to stare. A hot perspiration flashed across his forehead and down his ears. "Make it possible for—" A cough. A deep one from among the guests. Jett gazed back to see Ed with his fist over his lips and his date nudging him. "—Students from all walks of life to experience the worlds that live on the pages of timeless stories like Gordon's. And to aspire to do the same for their own generation."

Now Lexa was shaking the satchel, pointing to the clasp. What already?

"If you all will pardon me for just a moment." He left the dais to murmurs and whispers, tucking away his notes in his chest pocket, and cut through the standing guests to where Lexa stood.

"What? I don't understand." Jett took her by the arm and steered her toward the patio double doors. The cold air felt good.

"Gilda came to my place tonight. She said it was time. I had no idea what she was talking about until I looked inside your bag. Jett, the manuscript from the Bower is in here." She shoved it into his chest. "Tell the truth. It's time."

"It's too late." The satchel slipped into his hands. "Lexa, please, don't move. Stay. Or I'll move. I can teach and write in Seattle. They have universities there."

"Jett?" Ed poked his head through the door. "People are waiting."

"Ed, tell him to tell the truth about Gordon. He has the unpublished manuscript and the evidence right here." Lexa knocked the bag with her hand.

"Lexa, please, I can't." He paced toward the low stone wall along the back of the slate patio, wishing he could vanish into the city lights.

"Jett, you will never be free unless you tell the truth," Ed said. "Trust me, I know. Start here, right now, with this one."

"Ed, ten million dollars is on the line. Money that will go to equipment and materials, to writing and reading programs, to education. Never mind my reputation. My career."

"Is it worth your integrity? Your soul?" Lexa said. "This will haunt you, Jett. Someone else will find this manuscript and tell the truth. You'll just be the fool who kept his mouth shut." She opened the patio door. "Come on, leap. Be your own hero."

He glared at her, then tucked the satchel under his arm. "I love you." He angled down to kiss her cold, trembling lips.

Stumbling back to the stage, a fire in his chest, Jett collected his thoughts. *Here goes nothing.*

"Forgive the interruption." He set the satchel on the podium and retrieved the manuscript. "I have a pesky but good friend who reminded me to be courageous and find strength in the truth.

"Two months ago, I walked into the Fifth Avenue Literary Society Library to find I'd been invited, along with four other misfits, to a story society. By whom, we don't know. But in the weeks that followed, I became reacquainted with my ex-wife, with an heiress also known as the Panicked Princess, with a wounded father, and with a grieving widower who wanted to write the love story of a lifetime. Me? I was the semi-ambitious associate professor lost in the grief of losing his brother and his wife." Across the distance, he saw the watery sheen in Lexa's eyes.

"After one of our society meetings where we did more eating

than anything else, I found this." He held up the manuscript. "A rejected GPR book. Not so unusual. Every writer has them. But then I read this letter dated December nineteen-o-two."

He read Daniel Barclay's rejection aloud. Described the margin notes. Even offered his own critique.

"It was not the Gordon work we've come to love."

Then he pulled out the second letter. The one where Barclay conspires to steal a manuscript from a young heiress.

"That book became *The Girl in the Carriage*. Gordon did not write it." The gasp in the room elevated the already warm temperature. Jett tugged off his tie. He saw Elijah Roth rise from his seat. "And if Tenley cares to confirm, I believe Birdie Ainsworth, an heiress and marchioness, was the true author. In fact, she most likely became Gordon's ghost."

"This is an outrage." Elijah stormed the podium, but from somewhere in the crowd, a voice rose above the murmuring crowd.

"He's right." Tenley cut through the guests with their flutes of champagne toward the dais. "My great-great-grandfather employed Birdie to write all his books from *Girl* on. She is the genius we love. Not Gordon."

Silence weighted the guests for a moment, then they exploded, everyone talking at once.

Jett passed the manuscript off to Tenley with a nod and left the argument to the family and the Roth Foundation.

Catching Lexa by the hand, he ran with her and with rest of the story society into the cold, clear night. He'd taken the leap and was flying high.

~

LEXA

It was late. She should go to bed, but she wasn't sleepy. She was still jacked up on the events of the night.

Her rush to the reception with the satchel. Jett's bold declaration. Laughing and talking with her friends at an Upper West Side café, drinking coffee and eating scones and chocolate croissants.

Around ten they said good night. But she wasn't ready to say goodbye. She wanted the night to go on.

Jett rode the subway to Greenwich Village with her and got off at her stop, going his way as she went hers.

"See you tomorrow night?" he said.

"I'll be there."

"I'm glad you came."

"Yeah, me too."

Now, sorting through her clothes, it seemed like a dream.

Lexa held up a pair of shorts and tossed them into a box. She wouldn't need those until spring. Only clothes for the immediate future went in her suitcase. The rest would go in moving boxes.

The movers would be here on Friday. Friday. Five days away. It was happening. And happening fast.

Pausing at the window, she took in the familiar view. Music rose from the village streets. Lexa leaned to see who was playing tonight. Mickey, the Irish singer, usually claimed her corner on Sunday nights.

Sure enough, it was Mickey, gathering a small crowd even though a light snow had started to fall.

Lexa cracked open the window. After next week, the sounds of her life would change.

She'd have the call of the ocean, the screech of seagulls, and a spectacular view of water.

Her phone pinged with a text. Lexa pulled it free to see a note from Coral.

"It's live already. Thank you, social media."

Lexa clicked on a link to the *New York Post* showing a picture of "the gang." From left to right it was Chuck, Coral, Jett, Lexa, Ed and Mabel—whom they all loved already.

Their faces, their pose, was a replica of the famous *Friends* cast shot.

When they'd exited the café, a photographer recognized Coral and snapped a photo as they were saying their goodbyes.

It was a special image. A fitting goodbye to the last two months.

She peered outside again. It had started to snow. Lexa leaned out the window to *hear* the hush of the soft, white flakes.

Mickey waved up at her and started another song.

"I'll miss you, MacDougal Street."

Her phone beckoned again. Skipper this time.

Are you getting nervous?

Yes, I'm thinking of backing out.

Noooo. I booked a ticket to see you. Surprise!

When?

Next weekend.

Really? Lexa batted back tears. Yay! And I'm kidding. I'm going to Seattle!

A crack against the window pane startled her. She went over to see a lump of snow slide down the glass.

Leaning out again, she saw Jett next to Mickey.

"What's the big idea, Wilder?" He still wore his tux from the reception beneath his open coat, his collar loose, the tie dangling.

"Stay there." He motioned to the singer, who began a lilting song. Jett tipped back his head and raised one arm.

"Oh, my love . . ." Cough, cough. "Me, me, me."

"What are you doing?" Lexa waited for an answer as Jett conferred with Mickey again. When the song started over, it was in a lower key.

"Oh, my love, my darling, I hunger for your touch."

Lexa snapped upright, banging her head on the windowframe, her cold fingers covering her lips.

Their wedding song. Three stories below, her ex-husband stood in the angled gold light, snow dotting his dark hair, and sang "Unchained Melody."

When he finished, he began again.

"Jett, what are you doing?" How did he remember?

The song ended and started again.

Trembling, she yanked on her coat and stuffed her feet into a pair of wool-lined Uggs. Out of her apartment and down the steps, Lexa ran across the street and without stopping, without thinking, flew into Jett's strong, firm arms just as he belted, "Are you still mine?"

Lifting her up, he swung around, his lovely baritone resonating in her ear. "I need your love."

He set her down and held her face in his hands. "Don't go. Please."

"Jett, please, don't. I gave the Lees my word." How could she get him to *hear*? To understand? "I can't back out now. Why are you singing to me in the snow?"

"Fulfilling one of your dreams. Long overdue, I might add." He wound his fingers through her hair. "I love you, Lexa Wilder."

He swaddled her in his arms and lowered his lips to hers. His kiss was soft, tentative, and altogether marvelous, engulfing her in tingling warmth.

"I love you too." Shivering, Lexa inhaled the familiar scent of his skin, igniting the cold embers of her passion. She recognized the flame she saw in his eyes. Not just for a physical encounter but for a soul-to-soul, heart-to-heart.

He moved toward her again. His kiss this time was smooth and elegant, and she lost the sense of herself. He electrified her heart and her love for him and resurrected every reason she said yes to his bended-knee proposal.

Gripping his jacket with her chilled fingers, she clung to the hope of his presence, and when he broke away she fell against him, the reality of her love for him now at odds with the course she'd charted for herself.

As the snow continued to cover them, Mickey started another song and Jett began a gentle, steady sway, dancing under the streetlamp to the rhythm of their own hearts.

~

JETT

Now that she was in his arms, he couldn't let her go. He whispered in her ear. "I could come with you."

She raised her face. "To Seattle? What about your job, your career?"

"How sweet, you think I have a job after tonight." He kissed her forehead and continued the dance. He'd given Mickey a crisp Ben Franklin to keep the music flowing. He'd moved from "Unchained Melody" to "Unforgettable" and now "Star Dust."

"Can I tell you something?" he said between songs when Mickey stopped to warm his fingers.

"You can tell me anything."

"He told me he was in love with you."

"Who?"

"Storm. That's what happened on Eiger Mountain the day he died." The plain, simple confession washed away so much tension.

"What?" Lexa gaped at him. "No, no, he was joking, right? Your brother told you he loved your wife? That makes no sense. Storm could have anyone he wanted. Gorgeous athletes, models, actresses." She paced away again, hands pressed to the sides of her head. "He said those exact words? But he loved *you*, Jett. He adored you."

"Two brothers who couldn't be any more different fell for the same girl."

"When did he fall for me? You and I were dating when I met him."

"Actually, we were still just friends. Remember when he came for the Florida State game?"

"Which one?"

"The year we met. Nine years ago. You knocked his socks off. Guess the Wilder boys have good taste in women."

"He never said a word."

Jett was grateful Mickey began playing again, his melodies softening this revelatory, honest conversation.

"He was going to, but if you recall—"

"You kissed me for the first time. And I told you I loved you."

Jett dug his hands into his coat pockets. The temperature had dropped, and the snowfall had become a white wall.

But this was finally happening. Jett didn't want to interrupt the momentum, and as long as Mickey played . . .

"Storm kept his feelings to himself. When we got married he was dating one of the show's producers," Jett explained.

"Right, and he was crazy about her."

"Fast-forward to you and I falling apart. When I was in Switzerland, I went to him for advice. Told him we were not getting along, that I was afraid the marriage might end. He blew up. Called me a half dozen choice names. Instead of helping me he threatened me. Said if I let you go, he'd go after you."

"You're joking. Jett, he was like a brother to me. I never, ever—"

"I know. You didn't encourage him. But he was in deep. Convinced himself he wanted you."

"He told you all of this?"

"Not directly. Things were pretty tense between us. Any attempt to talk ended in a fight." Jett ran his hand over his face, over the icy needles sticking to his skin. "It was the last day, and he was suited up to fly but had forgotten his phone in his room. Dad sent me back to get it. Storm liked for someone to shoot video with his phone for his personal media sites. That's when I found the letter. I thought it was just one of his goofy cartoons—"

"I still have the one he drew of me."

"But it was a letter to you." He could still see Storm's angled handwriting. "'Dear Lexa, I never thought I'd have the chance to say this to you but I'm in love with you. Jett's informed me things aren't going well between you and I won't make a move unless you say so, but I am here for you as a friend if you need to talk.' The letter stopped there," Jett said. "I didn't even need to read between the lines. Storm just put it out there. By the time I got back out to the jump site, I was fuming. We argued in front of everyone. He said if I was stupid enough to let you go, then you were fair game. 'Not for my brother,' I said. To which he replied, 'That's for Lexa to decide.'"

"You told Storm you thought our marriage might end but never said a word to me."

"I wanted his advice. I didn't want to say anything to you when I had no idea what you were thinking or feeling. I half thought you were in love with Zane."

"I was never in love with Zane."

"I know that now, but we were in a pretty good slump between school and work, stepping on each other's wounds when we didn't know it."

"You should've talked to me."

"Of course I should have, but I thought I'd sound it out with my big brother first. Instead he stabbed me in the back."

"So you argued? Then what?"

"You know some of it. The weather was bad and the wind was ripping up from the valley. The conditions were dangerous. Dad and the crew tried to talk him out of flying. Then I showed up with his phone and had a run at him, waving the letter under his nose. And I taunted him."

"Taunted him how?"

"Said if he was brave enough to go after his brother's wife he was brave enough to jump into those winds. You know, it was the only time I ever saw fear in his eyes. And it had nothing to do with flying. It had everything to do with his confession. I think he feared we'd never be right again."

"Oh, Jett." She covered her mouth with her fingers.

"I never thought he'd actually do it. That sort of harassing worked when we were kids, but not adults. Next thing we all knew, he was leaping, piloting his suit. But the current dropped out from under him and he plummeted. He tried to correct his course and ran smack into a rock the size of your apartment building."

Lexa sank down to the snowy curb. Mickey tapped Jett's shoulder.

"Calling it a night."

"Thanks, man."

Jett joined Lexa on the curb. "You know the rest."

She snapped her hazel gaze to him. "It's not your fault."

"That's what Dad said. Even the crew assured me no one was stopping Storm that morning." Jett's warm tears clung to the cold corners of his eyes. "But my final words were hateful. Makes me sick."

He'd scrubbed the image of Storm's body draped over the jutted rocks on the mountainside. But bits and pieces floated across his mind's eye.

"Why didn't you tell me?"

"After our divorce I spent some time with a therapist. He asked the same thing." Jett grabbed a handful of the powdery snow and let it slip through his fingers. "I don't know. I just couldn't give life to the very thing that tore us apart. Maybe the thing that killed my brother."

"It was an accident." Lexa looped her arm through his, resting her head on his shoulder. "I'm so sorry, Jett. So very sorry."

"Deep down I didn't want to tell you about Storm, his feelings, because then I'd have to confess my worst fear. I was losing you. Wh-what would you have done? If he told you how he felt?"

She was quiet for a long moment. "Told him the truth. His brother was the only one for me."

His heart bumped against his chest. "That was true then. What about now?"

Her eyes brimmed and glistened. "Now and always, Jett Wilder."

Reaching into his pocket, he took out the note he'd carried with him since she broke her arm.

"I never gave you this."

"What is it?" She held the folded piece up to the light. "'I'll never tire of taking care of you.' When did you write this?"

"After you broke your arm. When the society wrote you notes."

"Jett—" She brushed her hand over his snow-covered head. "I don't need you to take care."

"Read between the lines, Lexa."

She climbed into his lap and roped her arms around his neck, then breathed new life in him by the force and power of her affection.

He kissed her again and again, tumbling back on a bed of snow, laughing, and held her for a long, long time.

Epilogue

JETT

MARCH IN MANHATTAN

Well this was a fine mess. Love spilled all over the Bower.

Chuck, his former cell mate in Central Booking, had just dropped to one knee and proposed to Coral Winthrop.

She cried out with a vibrant *yes*.

Spring had come to all their lives and kissed them, as well as the cherry-blossom trees outside the library window, with a vibrant pink and filled Jett's bones and muscles with delight.

In the corner, flames crackled in the fireplace, which had not gone dark since their first Monday-night meeting in September.

An old LP played "I'll Be Seeing You" on the vintage record player Ed carted all the way from his uptown apartment.

The glow of the sconces seemed to ebb and flow with the golden light of the fire.

Jett shifted in his seat, balancing his new wife on his knee.

"I'm so excited for them," she said. "Coral, come on. Let's see."

But the cosmetic heiress and former Panicked Princess was lost in private whispers with her man, the indomitable Chuck Mays.

Across the circle, Ed beamed from his chair, a snappy gold band on his ring finger. He and Mabel hit it off and married on New Year's Eve at his daughter's place on Long Island.

The entire society had gone to their wedding, Jett and Chuck boo-hooing more than the ladies as Ed recited his vows.

Mabel declined their invitation to join the society. "I think this is something just for Eddie."

But she sent brownies every week, and once a month they gathered on Sunday evening at Coral's penthouse for dinner.

Jett's wife left his lap as Chuck came over and slapped him a sturdy high five. "Is this real?" He gazed toward the women. "How'd we end up with those two beauties?"

"Luck?"

Chuck shot Jett one of his hooked, easy grins. "Naw, I'd say divine mercy."

Chuck initially followed Coral to church because he was falling in love, but according to him, God spoke and he couldn't go on the way he was before.

Jett remained dubious but watched. Listened. Saw a change in Chuck. So he examined his own life with an eye toward God. Did He care about Jett? If so, he was grateful.

Carrying his plate back to the food table, he picked up a slice of the foot-long hoagie and dropped a few more chips on his plate, mindful he was still on his honeymoon. Too soon for lazy-man love handles.

He winked at his wife—he'd never tire of that word—as he returned to his seat. She held up Coral's hand, pointing to the ring as it caught all the light.

But it wasn't the ring that impressed him, or the fact that an Uber driver could afford such a rock, but the joy on everyone's faces.

The change really started when Ed confessed the truth about Esmerelda. His healing was the lynchpin to everyone's healing.

Since the arrest of Coral's senior executives, she had wrestled CCW from the mud, washed it off, and worked to put it back on top of the cosmetics world. She replaced nearly all of her vice presidents and directors, streamlined the company, and, according to the *Wall Street Journal*, was a business genius.

Her value was up all over the world. She sat down with the hosts of *Good Morning New York* on a Holly Cook–produced segment to tell her story. While the hosts wanted to know every detail of Prince Augustus, Coral steered them back to the real "prince" of her story, Jesus. Long gone was the Panicked Princess.

"Once I met Him, I couldn't let go."

Jett admired her courage.

With his own round of seconds, Chuck dropped into Coral's chair and angled toward Jett.

"Lucy said it went well with your publisher."

"She's a pit bull." In January, Jett left his agent and signed on with Lucy Hughes, who immediately went to his publisher and demanded a repackaging and rerelease of *Rites of Mars*.

"With a healthy promotional budget."

"I told you." Chuck shoved the corner of his turkey and roast beef into his mouth.

With Coral's help, Chuck penned his magic-book story. Lucy sold the rights in a bidding war among three publishers.

The Magic Book was scheduled to release next year with an accompanying board game and mobile app. The film rights sold last month.

Yet he still drove for Uber.

"I'd be bored sitting at home. My best ideas come while driving."

"Any news about the kids?" Jett said.

Chuck shook his head, chewing yet another bite of sandwich. "I finally got my advance and retained a lawyer recommended by Coral's father. He wants to work on getting the judge to remove the TRO, then push for shared custody. One step at a time."

When he sold his children's book, the news broke of his arrest and restraining order. He was almost finished before he started, but Ed's darling daughter stepped in. She had him on the show and let him tell the raw, real truth of what happened that night.

He'd been so afraid to tell the story society, but five months later, he had the courage to tell the whole city.

"I owe it all to you," he said to his friends after the show.

Jett got up for one of Mabel's delicious brownies. The sheen of his pristine platinum ring caught the light and he flexed his hand.

Six months ago a wedding landed him in jail with bruises on his face and knuckles. Now he wore a ring that stood for more than his wedding vows. More than in sickness and in health. More than love and surrender.

It stood for hope. For second chances. For life after the storm.

He didn't deserve all this goodness, the opportunity to start over, to put his past behind him. But he was grateful.

"When's the big day, Coral?" The first bite of brownie made his taste buds dance. He had to ask Mabel for the recipe.

She'd probably say the secret ingredient was love. That's what she told him when he asked about Ed's pot roast.

Coral gripped her fiancé's hand. "Not sure. My mother will want a big to-do." She perched on Chuck's knee. "I owe her one since I dashed out of the royal wedding. Be prepared, darling, to be treated like a prince."

"Well, if I must."

"And I'd like Jakey and Riley to be there." Coral's eyes glistened as she cupped Chuck's cheek. "Let's pray, okay?"

He dropped his head, clearing his throat. "Just another reason why I love you."

As for Jett, after he outed Gordon Phipps Roth, the university conveniently downsized the English department, and he was released from his contract.

The president cited the loss of the Roth endowment, but Jett knew it was for Extreme Humiliation to the Esteemed New York College.

Out of a job, he was free to take the three dozen or so TV and radio interviews as well as the nationwide lecture series.

Now that the truth was out, Tenley was eager to talk to him, even invited him down to Cocoa Beach to see the house where she'd found the hidden room and the hidden truth.

I kept quiet for the family's sake. But when you finally spoke up, I knew I could no longer be silent.

Reworking his dissertation, he took his and Gordon's manuscript to a major publishing house last month and made a nice sale. Being as it was more of a scholarly work, they had room on their schedule.

Behind the Lie: The Partnership of Gordon Phipps Roth and Birdie Ainsworth would ship to bookstores in September.

Funny thing about the truth: it opened as many doors as it closed. For a woman dead almost fifty years, recompense.

In the meantime, he was supposed to work on a sequel to *Rites of Mars* while Lucy knocked on a few Hollywood doors. In her last text, she'd hinted super director and producer Jeremiah Gonda was interested.

He'd just directed the blockbuster and Comic-Con fan favorite, *Sea Dragon*.

After the night on MacDougal Street with Lexa, kissing in the snow—just remembering made him shiver, and not from the cold—he set out on a mission to mend his relationship with his parents.

This summer he was joining them in Scandinavia and the UK for a series of shoots.

The night they agreed, Dad patted Jett's belly. "Better get in shape, son."

He thought he was in shape. Since then, it was up at 6:00 a.m. for a long run, and lean protein and veggies for dinner.

Despite his very cool romantic gesture and the hot kissing in the snow, Lexa kept to her word to The Glass Fork.

It was probably the best thing that ever happened to Jett. Because once Lexa was gone, he found love again.

Through emails, texts, phone calls, and visits. He joined her in Florida for Christmas with Skipper, and Mom and Dad Prescott.

Being a professor had been a ruse for his fears. Was he good enough to be an author? Could he support a family with his pen? Look at GPR, who had to lie to sustain his career.

Around February he'd had enough. While he'd imagined a *Sleepless in Seattle* reunion in either city, he proposed to Lexa one night over FaceTime.

"Marry me. I'll move to be with you."

"Of course I'll marry you."

While he was thrilled, it was pretty anticlimactic since he couldn't hold her or kiss her, or slip a ring on her finger.

Just as the logistics began for his migration west, Jenn and Ki declared bankruptcy. The Glass Fork was up to its eyeballs in debt. A little tidbit they left out of the interview process.

Lexa gave 110 percent to fixing the mess and bailing them out, but it was too late. And Ki refused any of her ideas to streamline and cut back. They closed their doors the first of March.

Jett proposed again when he picked her up at JFK five days later, a classic yet romantic cliché.

On the second Saturday in March, he married his wife in the Chappaqua family barn under the same lights that had twinkled down on Mom and Oz.

He wept when Lexa glided down the aisle alone, a bouquet of spring flowers in her hand. Her parents couldn't make the trip so soon after Christmas, but the maid of honor, Skipper, held up her phone for them to watch from the other side of the world.

That's when he decided. Forever after, Jett Wilder would say yes to all the good invitations in life.

Even after he vowed to love Lexa for the rest of his days, in sickness and in health, and tasted her sweet lips, there was a part of that old barn that echoed, "You're no hero."

Even after outing Gordon, he didn't see himself as a brave, bold man.

But when they got to the part of the ceremony where he painted a big red heart over his "I hate Mom" carving, a bomb exploded in his chest.

Now, he was a hero.

The entire story society made a weekend of it, and Jett never laughed so hard or sang so much or, when he was alone with his bride, made love so passionately.

It snowed at midnight on their wedding night, so Zane—yes, Zane invited himself and his new Nebraska girlfriend—staged a shivaree at the B and B where Jett was about to take his bride in his arms.

There was something poignant and romantic about starting off their second married life in a snowball fight with family and friends, laughing until their sides ached, then drinking hot chocolate in front of a fire until dawn's first light.

Neither one of them had a job, but the future was coming whether they liked it or not. They talked about a puppy. And a baby. They'd lost too much time already.

"Okay, everyone, I have an announcement." Coral shooed her husband-to-be back into his chair and told Ed to stop texting his wife. Jett had a feeling Ed was going to finish his race writing the love story he'd imagined all along. Mabel was a lucky woman.

"CCW is doing so well, thank the good Lord, that I want to celebrate." She pulled a bottle of champagne from the vinyl bag beside her chair. "Next week I'm off to Paris to see a site for our new offices there. Lexa, would you please do me the honor of going with me?"

"To Paris? I'd love to go, but why? I'm not sure I'll be much help. More in the way."

"I guess I left out the important part. Would you go with me as my new CEO?" Coral's semi-formal, semi-businesslike posture broke. "Please, please, please? I've been dying to ask you, but I had to get CCW square first. I didn't want to hand you a mess. Especially when I saw what happened with The Glass Fork. But I'm ready now, we're ready. Please, I need you—"

"Yes!" Lexa flew from her chair, arms wide, embracing her friend and new boss. "Yes! I don't know squat about cosmetics but yes, yes. Coral, I'll work hard, you won't regret this."

"Lexa, please, you don't have to convince me. I only hope we can live up to your standards. I cannot wait."

Lexa covered her tears with the widest smile.

"Here, one of you take this." Coral passed the champagne to Jett and rocked Lexa in a side-to-side hug. "We're going to kick butt and take names."

Ed had just popped the cork when Gilda peeked around the Bower door. "I heard a cheer."

"Lexa's joining CCW," Coral said, moving toward the miniscule woman, holding up her hand. "And I'm engaged."

"To me." Chuck puffed out his chest.

"How lovely. Why don't I let you all celebrate a bit longer tonight?"

While the guys set up plastic cups for the expensive bubbly, Jett went after Gilda.

"Why don't you join us? You've played a rather understated part in our lives the past six months."

"Thank you, but no." She patted his arm. "You young people have a good time."

"Young people? Have you seen Ed? He's older than dirt."

She grinned, shaking her finger. "Don't you believe it, Jett. I was there when He formed the dirt."

"What?" He stepped around to block her departure once more and looked deep into her eyes. "I don't know what you're about, Gilda, but you give me chills. You're the one who sent the invitations, aren't you?"

"Kindly step aside, young man."

"Gilda?"

Her intense gaze forced him back. "Let me get to my work."

"Just exactly what do you do?"

"I am the librarian." She aimed for the door marked Private.

"Gilda, one more question." Jett's gentle plea invited her to pause. "Why?"

"Do I have to explain, professor?"

"It'd be nice. I'm not as clever as I look."

She held out her slender, smooth palm. "The invitation is always waiting. All you have to do is say yes."

"Why the five of us? Did you know all this would happen?"

"Jett, it's a gift. Take it. Exercise a little faith. Be free and don't choose chains again. Let your story inspire others." With that, Gilda disappeared behind her Private door.

With a skip in his step, Jett returned to the party where Ed played DJ with a Glenn Miller record as Chuck held Coral in a close dance.

"Hey, beautiful," Jett said, scooping his wife into his arms and kissing her.

As the music played, Jett rested his cheek against Lexa's soft hair, his gaze momentarily fixed on the rows and rows of books. Precious. Timeless. Capsules of life and history.

But the Fifth Avenue Literary Society Library was not about closed books. It was about open lives.

Joseph Winthrop hadn't just read in this room. He conversed, debated, prayed. He lived in this room.

Jett's life story was not in a book or dictated by the actions of his mother, his brother, or a dead author. His story was right here, with the woman in his arms, and the friends who made his life richer.

His story was written in the days and years to come. And he was going to live each one well.

"Hey, Coral," he said, inching Lexa a bit closer. "What time does your church service start?"

"Really? Ten thirty." She smiled up at Chuck. "I told you he'd accept my invitation sooner or later." To Jett she said, "I'll send you the details."

"We're going to church?" Lexa said. "I'd love it."

He twirled her around and swayed to the music, to saying yes to one more good invitation and yes to the rest of his story. Oh, what a sweet, fine mess. And he loved it.

The End

A NOTE FROM THE AUTHOR

Dear Reader,

Every time I finish a book, I hope and pray it will delight your hearts. This book is no exception.

The story idea came to me while speaking at a local writers group. A casual statement by the leader sparked an idea that became *The Fifth Avenue Story Society*.

As you journey with Jett, Lexa, Coral, Chuck, and Ed, you'll also see characters from *The Writing Desk*: Gordon Phipps Roth, Elijah Roth, Tenley Roth, and Birdie Shehorn Ainsworth.

The more I developed Jett's story problem, the more I realized I could bring in a thread of the Roth story line. I hope readers familiar with *The Writing Desk* will enjoy seeing references to "old friends."

Coral's spiritual journey is the most pronounced in this book. I prayed and thought on how to bring all five characters to some light of truth. Yet as I wrote each day, the story became clunky with too many spiritual epiphanies. They didn't feel real.

One morning while in the prayer room at our church, the Lord whispered to me, "Coral's spiritual journey is all I want."

Friends, I've never had the Lord speak to me so directly about a story before. He asked for one simple revelation from one character.

I thought, *No, surely You want more than that, Lord.*

Yet His voice resonated, and I came to the same conclusion. However, if you read between the lines, you'll find a bit of God-reality in the journey of each character.

I pray God speaks to your heart through this story. I always pray, "Holy Spirit, fill the cracks." I believe He does.

Blessings,
Rachel

ACKNOWLEDGMENTS

I'm starting this portion with some regrets. There are people I promised to give a shout out, people who helped me along the way, and I have forgotten their names. And I lost the piece of paper where I scribbled his or her name. For that, I am full of regret.

The one who answered a post on a public forum, thank you. The New York lawyer who texted with me with answers I needed. The clerk at the Greenwich Village book store Three Lives & Company who answered book signing questions. (I don't think that scene made it in the end.)

To all the folks on Facebook who answered posts about various things, including details about Seattle and what to name Holly's dog, thank you.

I am so very grateful.

Big appreciation to Professor Julie Drew at the University of Akron who not only gave me over an hour of her time on the phone and a dozen great ideas for Jett's character but answered my flurry of emails about dissertations and university life. All mistakes are mine.

I randomly found Julie on the internet and messaged her. She was kind enough to write back. Turns out we were both in Tallahassee at the same time and had I gone to public high school we'd have been in the same graduating class. So it was meant to be that we'd finally meet.

Also thank you to friend, reader, professor Dr. Susan Wegmann for being the first to shed light on the life of a professor.

Thanks to my friend Casey Miller for the advice and information on financial fraud. You gave me confidence with Coral's story line.

As always to Susan May Warren for giving so much of herself to get this book right. After my first revision letter, we launched Facebook video and replotted, rethought the story for over four hours. What a gift from God you are to me, my friend. I'm so grateful. Thank you!

Beth Vogt, Melissa Tag, Lisa Jordan, Tari Faris, Alena Tauriainen, and Susie for all the daily texts, laughs, and prayers. You're all rock stars.

My editor Kimberly Carlton for wrestling this beast to the ground with and for me. I know it wasn't easy. Your many insights were invaluable. Thank you so much.

My second editor Erin Healy for more help and insight. For helping me fine tune Holly's character. You saw an angle I didn't and were right to call it out.

My agent Chip MacGregor. Thanks for your friendship and advice. For always being in my corner. I really appreciate you.

Shout out to my assistant Renee Smith for keeping my social media sites going while I'm working. It's like you live in my brain, which scares me a little. What a gift and blessing you are to me!

Love and adoration to my husband who lives with a novelist. He never complains when dinner is at 10:00 p.m. He keeps the rest of our lives going while I'm working and on deadline. Mostly he keeps me going. Having a man who prays for me is the absolute bomb.

The spiritual thread in this story is different from what I've done in the past. It started when I was in the prayer room at church one Tuesday morning. As I was meditating on Him, as well as the story, the Lord whispered to me, "All I want is Coral's epiphany." What? Surely not. But as I considered His wisdom, I knew He was right. Creating a spiritual journey for five characters put a huge weight on the story. But showing God's heart through one allowed Him to shine and allowed the story to breathe. Isn't God so good? Not just because He helped me with my story—more than once—but because He just is good.

Appreciation to the team at HarperCollins Christian Publishing. It's been fifteen years since we partnered together for *Lost In NashVegas*, now *Nashville Dreams*. I am beyond grateful for all you've done for me. Thanks for helping make my dreams reality.

DISCUSSION QUESTIONS

1. How would you respond if you received a mysterious invitation to a story society? Would you go? Would you have had a similar reaction to our five friends?

2. Since this book is an ensemble cast, which character was your favorite? Why?

3. Jett and Lexa divorced without much discussion. They made assumptions about one another based on their wounds. Was there a time in your life where you made a judgment about a person or situation based on your past experiences?

4. Chuck's response to his wife's affair cost him more than he imagined. Did you think Trudy was justified in her response? What about Chuck's efforts to prove he'd changed? Have you ever been in a situation where your response did not necessarily reflect who you are or want to be?

5. While some of us would love to have Coral's heritage and wealth, the family history became a burden to her. Have you ever faced failure that impacted more than just you? Perhaps your family or family's reputation? Was your response similar to Coral's?

6. Coral is the only character with an overt spiritual journey. What did you think of her choosing Jesus over Prince Augustus? Do you carry the fear of the Lord with you when making decisions?

7. Ed imagined a different life with his wife than the one he lived. How did this impact you? Do you understand why he created his own fantasy? Was he loving well?

8. Jett carried the pain of his last conversation with his brother. What was your response to "what happened on the mountain"?

9. Lexa's high school experience sowed a deep seed of rejection. It wasn't until she attended the story society that she realized her wound. How can we learn to heal from others? Do you have people in your life with whom you can be real?

10. What did you think of Gilda? Who or what did she represent? Do you see the "Gildas" in your life?

DISCOVER MORE ENCHANTING STORIES FROM BELOVED AUTHOR RACHEL HAUCK!

Be sure to check out these stand-alone wedding-themed novels from Rachel Hauck!

ABOUT THE AUTHOR

Rachel Hauck is the *New York Times, Wall Street Journal,* and *USA TODAY* bestselling author of *The Wedding Dress,* which was also named Inspirational Novel of the Year by *Romantic Times* and was a RITA finalist. Rachel lives in central Florida with her husband and pet and writes from her ivory tower.

Visit her online at RachelHauck.com
Facebook: RachelHauck
Twitter: @RachelHauck
Instagram: @rachelhauck